TASTING NOTES

ANNE BURCHETT

ISBN 978-1-914076-02-2 (paperback)

ISBN 978-1-914076-03-9 (ebook)

Formatting by www.preparetopublish.com

'Writing is making sense of life'
Nadine Gordimer

PROLOGUE

Papa opens the 1961 Château Smith Haut Lafitte Marguerite Villa has given him for his birthday.

'It's a stunning wine,' he says, nose deep in his glass.

'Must have cost her a fair bit,' Maman says. She brushes invisible crumbs from the tablecloth and returns to the kitchen. The smell of roast beef wafts into the dining room. 'I suppose she can afford it.' The door closes behind her.

Papa slams his notebook shut. The words "Tasting Notes" stand out in gold letters on the black leather cover. He gets up, empties my water in the potted azaleas on the sideboard and pours a little wine in my tumbler.

Maman comes back with a dish of eggs in aspic. 'Don't lean back in that chair, Christine. It will break.'

I wish it would. The tapestry seat she's so proud of makes my thighs itch.

'This is an exceptional bottle,' Papa says.

The wine is such a deep ruby red it hides the Duralex motif at the bottom of my glass. I take a mouthful. Till now I've only had red wine diluted in lemonade or a sip of Champagne on special occasions.

The taste of ripe blackcurrants explodes in my mouth. It's stronger than fruit though, more complicated. I close my eyes and swallow.

When I look at Papa again, he is smiling at me.

1

A WINE SALESWOMAN

The alarm rings. I'm exhausted and I haven't even woken up yet. Outside my bedroom, a door slams and a suitcase rolls past. A man is talking in the loud voice people use on mobiles. I turn over. The pillow is square, French. I open one eye. The light is Mediterranean bright.

I had the same nightmare again last night, like every night for the past six months: I was climbing stairs, lost my balance and tried to grab the banister but it had vanished and I fell backwards, screaming. I woke up, my heart beating like mad.

I sit up and rub the back of my head; it's throbbing. I look at the air conditioning unit and sure, the green light is on. I turned it off when I left this morning but the maid turns it on when she cleans the room. I swear under my breath and take a sip of water from the complimentary bottle on my bedside table.

The crumpled receipt from last night's dinner says three covers and four bottles of wine. I drink the rest of the water and scribble a note for the maid: 'Please do not turn the air conditioning on. It gives me a headache.'

My index finger is stained purple from the red wines I tasted yesterday: I should have used wine pourers. I try to lick it clean but the stain won't go.

My knees creak when I get up.

The small room is strewn with discarded clothes. My grey suit lies on the floor where I dropped it, the fabric stretched out of shape around the waistband of the trousers. I pick up the jacket and give it a sniff. It still smells of the Chanel No 19 I doused it with in the five minutes I had to freshen up before going out. The lingering perfume competes with the hotel smell of clean laundry, industrial cleaning products and artificial air freshener.

I shower, put the suit on and look at myself in the mirror. I pull my stomach in and look again, sideways this time. I need to lose weight. Being tall is no excuse now I am on the wrong side of forty.

My laptop yawns on the desk, surrounded by a mess of paper. I have been here too long. I arrived in Narbonne late on Monday; Tuesday morning was spent at Villa's local winery with Serge, preparing for Tesco's visit. Serge is Villa's chief winemaker, a title borrowed from New World wineries and easier on foreign ears than oenologist, the French equivalent. After two days in the tasting room, we ended up in a tapas bar last night with Tesco's buyer. A debate on the merit of Rioja versus Ribera del Duero ensued, the finer points of which are unclear to me this morning. Serge's English became more fluent the more he drank; at one point he even dared contradict our guest. The Muga Reserva 2003 was the real star of the evening though, with its powerful fruit flavours, displaying the same grace and balance as an athletic male dancer.

Back at the hotel, I checked my emails, feeling terrific after my copious intake of Rioja. I didn't tear myself away until well after two. Thank God I'm going home tomorrow.

I glance at the clock: eight thirty.

'Merde!' After almost twenty years in England, I still swear in French.

I grab my mobile. 'Serge? It's Chris. I messed up. I set my alarm for seven but my phone is on British time. Could you please look after Andy if he arrives before me? It's Tripp with pp at the end. He gets annoyed if you spell it with one p. He's the buyer for Direct Wines. We can't mess up: one million customers and it's his first visit to Villa. My probation period ends in a month's time, remember?'

I slip lipstick, eyeliner and mascara in my pocket, put my laptop in my bag and run to the lift. I swing by the restaurant to pick up a chunk of baguette and a pain au chocolat and I'm on my way.

Radio Nostalgie is playing George Moustaki's "Ma liberté" in my rental car.

'A 1970 classic,' says the DJ.

It was Papa's favourite song.

The ten-minute drive to the winery takes me through hills covered in black twisted vines. The leaves have turned from green to yellow and red. Olive trees and oaks adorn a view Cezanne could have painted, pure blobs of colours thrown together within dark outlines.

I pass the sign to Vinassan where Papa lived when he left home. I put my sunglasses on. My eyes hurt.

The smell of the pain au chocolat fills the car. I bite into it, turning to the passenger's seat, which is soon covered in greasy crumbs.

I reach the gates of the winery at ten to nine. Large pieces of broken glass are embedded on top of the perimeter wall. I hum along to the lyrics of "Hotel California".

I stop by the side of the security guard's shed, safe from the trucks that trundle in and out. I roll down my car window. The place smells of hot dust and rank wine. The guard walks towards me, hands on hips.

'The English woman. You're still here?'

'I've told you before, I'm French,' I say. 'Does Legerot sound like an English name to you?'

He shrugs. 'You live in England.'

'I'm expecting a visitor this morning: a man in his thirties, tall, blond, English. His name is Andy Tripp. Has he arrived?'

He shakes his head.

'Please don't take his passport. You can ask to see it but that's all.'

His face clouds over. 'The boss told me to keep the identity cards of visitors while they are on site. No exceptions.'

'British people don't have identity cards and they dislike being parted from their passports. Remember what happened on Tuesday with the guy from Tesco?'

'Does the boss know?'

'I told Monsieur Lange.' I cross my fingers behind my back.

The guard walks away, muttering to himself.

I scribble "PASSPORT" on my left hand as a reminder to tell Andre Lange I pre-empted his authorisation to bend the rules.

'Hello, sorry, I have another question.'

The guard turns around.

'How long have you worked here?'

'Ten years,' he says.

'Did you know Pierre Legerot?'

'No. Why do you ask?'

'Never mind.'

He returns to his shed and picks up the phone. He is looking at me but I can't hear what he's saying. I wait but he waves me on and shouts, 'Go. You're blocking the entrance.' I drive on.

The large pale pink building that houses Villa's bottling plant in the Languedoc squats in the bright sunlight, surrounded by an impeccable lawn, far too lustrous for the Mediterranean climate. I turn left into the main car park.

'Merde!'

Three out of the four visitors' parking bays are taken. I stop the car, leave the engine running, and run inside.

'Hello, sorry to bother you but could you please try and keep the last visitors' parking space free for my guest?'

The girl at reception looks up from her crossword. 'I'm not in charge of parking,' she says.

'Come on, there's never a free space in that car park. We may as well put a sign up saying "Visitors Not Welcome".'

She looks at me blankly.

'Please,' I say.

She sighs. 'When is he due to arrive?'

I check my watch. 'Anytime now.'

'I'll see what I can do,' she says and returns to her crossword.

All the other parking spaces at the front of the winery are allocated, the names of the beneficiaries painted in white letters on the asphalt. I park in the one marked Andre Lange and pick up my bag from the boot.

'You can't park here.'

The receptionist is standing behind me, her arms crossed.

'You almost gave me a heart attack,' I say. 'I thought you were not in charge of parking.'

She shakes her head. 'You can't park in Monsieur Lange's space.'

'He's in Paris this week.'

She shrugs. 'So what? Move your car.'

She walks back inside the building without waiting for my answer.

I drive round the building to the shift workers' parking lot. No names there, it's a free-for-all. Dusty, scratched and dented Renaults, Citroens and Peugeots are packed like an angry mob around the building's back entrance. Stickers and dangly gadgets adorn the exhausted vehicles, and towing hooks hint at long summer escapes to Spain or North Africa. I glimpse a Renault 18. I haven't seen one of those in years. My shiny rented Megane looks quite out of place.

The clanking of the bottling line deafens me as I walk through the back door. The dim corridor stinks of vinegar. In my haste, I almost trip on a bucket full of a foamy red liquid. I move it aside, trying not to drench myself in the process.

I almost jump out of my skin when I look up. Jean Jacques, one of Villa's wine buyers, is standing right in front of me.

'Why are you coming in this way?' he says.

'Good morning, Jean Jacques. How are you?'

He doesn't smile. 'I asked you a question. What took you so long anyway?'

'You've asked me two now. I'll answer one. I came in this way because there was nowhere to park at the front. How do you know what time I arrived?'

He blushes.

'Did the security guard call you?'

I point at the bucket. 'It's a bit of a trap in here. Not sure Monsieur Lange would be impressed. Now if you don't mind, I'm in a bit of a rush.'

He looks at the bucket, at me, and at the bucket again. He swears under his breath and picks the bucket up.

I walk past him, my head high. He follows me, slopping bucket in hand. I turn around when I arrive at the tasting room but he has vanished. I close the door behind me and blink in the bright sunlight reflected on the white tasting benches.

Hints of lemon peel and oxidised alcohol linger in the air. The wines we tried yesterday have been cleared away and packed into crates, which wait on trolleys to be carted off to the lab and disposed of. Six dozen freshly washed glasses hang upside down by the sink and two large self-standing spittoons have been positioned in the middle of the room to allow several people to taste together in comfort. A few biros lie on the table, soldiers ready for battle.

I give Serge a peck on each cheek, French style.

'Timotei?'

'Spot on,' he says. 'You've made good time.'

I check my watch. 'I have, even though everybody I've met so far seemed intent on slowing me down.'

He raises his eyebrows.

'The security guard was his usual obnoxious self, the girl at reception wouldn't let me park in Andre Lange's space and Jean Jacques ambushed me as soon as I set foot in the building.'

He laughs. 'You parked in Andre's parking space?'

'What's the big deal?'

He pats me on the shoulder. 'Let's get down to work.'

The young laboratory assistant has sleep in her eyes. The other one's hair shows the indentations from his comb. In honour of today's visit, both have put on clean white coats which hang askew, the folds still marked in the fabric.

As I've kissed Serge, I have to kiss the other two as well. I draw in bad breath and coffee smells.

I turn back to Serge and whisper, 'We've agreed to ban daily kissing in the English office.'

'You're in France today,' he says.

He is wearing a crisp Villa-branded polo but he hasn't shaved.

'Did you come back here straight after dinner?'

'I had samples to prepare for Auchan. How did you guess?'

I point at his top. 'You use the marketing department's cupboard as an emergency wardrobe when you haven't got time to go home.'

'I had a wash,' he says.

'In that bottom-of-the-range Portaloo Andre calls a staff shower? Well done. Did you sleep at all? I need you on top form.'

'There's a couch in one of the meeting rooms.'

'You'll make yourself ill.'

'This time of year is tricky.' He points at the scribble on my hand. 'But at least I'm not going mad. Can't you use Post-it Notes instead of tattooing yourself with your to-do lists?'

'Post-it Notes get lost. My hands don't,' I say.

I crouch in front of the tasting table.

Serge has lined up fifty samples for Andy to try. Only nine weeks after the harvest, their colour varies from pale lemon to light gold. Some show hints of green.

'I've had to be selective,' says Serge. 'The summer was even hotter than usual in the Languedoc and the alcohol in some of the wines went stratospheric as a result.'

'What about the reds?'

Serge nods. 'The new vintage won't be ready to taste till early January but it's likely to be the same. Should we have a quick taste before Andy arrives?'

I pick up a glass. I love these sneak previews. I've come a long way since I tasted my first wine with Papa, but I am still learning.

On the nose, the wines display the exuberant primary aromas characteristic of their extreme youth. On the palate, they vary from grassy-green asparagus flavours for the Sauvignons to tropical mango and pineapple notes for the Chardonnays. One of the Viogniers tastes like ripe apricot.

'This one's fabulous,' I say.

'It's got sex appeal but it lacks acidity. It won't last. If we keep it, we'll need to blend it with something sharper. What about the third Chardonnay?'

'Not my favourite, not enough expression.'

'It'll develop though. Give it three months and it'll be a bomb. I wonder how it'd go with your Viognier.'

Serge picks up a pipette.

'Haven't you forgotten something?' I ask.

He turns around, pipette aloft.

'Shouldn't we wait for Andy?'

He bursts out laughing. The morning's exhaustion has evaporated.

Reception calls to let me know my visitor has arrived.

'Andy, good to see you! Found us all right?' I plant kisses on both his cheeks. It's part of the commercial package.

In my efforts to entice him here, I've forgotten how unpleasant he looks: his suit hangs awkwardly on his tall gangly frame and his lank hair is combed back in a style last seen in the nineteen-twenties. His collar is too tight; angry spots cover his neck and merge with the freckles on the pale skin of his face. Hours in the tasting room have stained his teeth to the point of no return and his sharp nose is the colour of a mature Margaux. He passed his Master of Wine exam at the first attempt though, and he's a brilliant taster. That's all Serge and I need to concern ourselves with.

'Another supplier dropped me off, thanks.'

'We have great wines for you,' I say.

'Haven't you sold the lot to Tesco?'

'Who's been talking?'

'They're going to Val d'Orbieu tomorrow, at the time I'd planned to go.'

We walk back to the tasting room and I spare a fleeting thought for the poor sod who had to tell Andy that Tesco's visit takes priority over his.

'Hi Serge, good to meet you.' Andy and Serge exchange a formal handshake.

'Would you like a tour of the winery or would you prefer to look at the wines first?' I ask. Showing visitors round the Narbonne premises is one of my secret pleasures since I joined Villa. This place meant so much to Papa.

'Let's see what you have to offer. I'll do the visit later if it's worth my while.'

I hand Andy a tasting sheet. He looks at the scribble on my hand and frowns.

'Here's a list of the samples we've prepared.' I hide my hands behind my back to rub the ink off. We've put the Sauvignons together, then the Grenaches and the Chardonnays.'

'I don't want to taste the Grenache Blancs,' he says. 'They're not great wines and the name means nothing to consumers.'

'I was thinking of a £3.99 Vin de Pays blend.' I now have a black smudge on my hand. I try to lick it clean.

'Can you do £3.49?' Andy attacks.

I parry. 'Not with the latest duty increase.'

He lunges, displaying both his secret weapon and his awful teeth. 'You do a £2.99 for Tesco,'

I riposte. 'Their margin requirements are lower than yours.'

'Chris, I'll only consider buying from you if you offer me value for money. Otherwise, I'll stick with my current suppliers.' At this point I expect him to throw his virtual sabre on the floor and go sulk in a corner.

He turns to Serge instead. 'When did you start picking?'

'Around the 20th of August for the Chardonnays in the plain. The Merlots kicked in early September. We had a healthy crop but volumes are down.'

'You list two Chardonnays, don't you?' I say. 'One at £4.99 and one at £6.99? Do you want two Sauvignons as well?'

'No, over £6 people either go for New Zealand, Touraine or Sancerre. It's too hot for premium Sauvignon down here. You don't get enough acidity.'

Andy knows what he wants.

We sip, swirl and spit the first wines in complete silence. Andy writes copious notes on the crib sheet I gave him. We've been at it for almost an hour when my mobile rings. I feel my face turning red. As a joke my friend Sam changed my ringtone to "Mambo Number Five" on Sunday, and I forgot to change it back. I should have turned my phone off anyway, and Andy looks up from his glass with a frown. I mouth a silent apology.

I'm just about to press the off button when I see the call is from Rachel, The Super-Market's wine buyer. She's one of our largest customers and she's in the middle of reviewing her Bordeaux range. It's a huge chunk of business. I sent my quote ten days ago and, last time we spoke, she hinted she was keen to consolidate her French supply. I must take her call.

I don't want Andy to feel slighted though. Like most buyers, he's easily upset. My finger hovers in mid-air.

What if Rachel is calling to say we've won the tender? Will she change her mind if I don't pick up? Maybe she only needs to ask me a quick question? I need this new business. To pull such a coup, two months after joining Villa, would be fantastic.

Andy is watching me. I can see he expects me not to take the call. I clear my throat.

'Sorry Andy, it's my neighbour. It must be an emergency. Do you mind?' It's my second lie today or maybe my third. I've lost count.

Andy grimaces the approximation of a smile.

It's ten o'clock French time, nine in the UK. I retreat to a corner of the room and put on my hello-dear-buyer-this-is-the-call-I-have-been-waiting-for-all-my-life voice.

'Rachel, how are you?'

Silence. She must have dialled the number on hands-free. I wait for the click that will indicate she has picked up. I feel alert, on top of my game.

Success is only seconds away.

2

BACK TO BORDEAUX

Until last summer, I worked for Terrazas de los Andes, an upmarket Argentinean producer from Mendoza. They're owned by Louis Vuitton Moët Hennessy. I spent eight years developing their UK business and sales were booming. I was spending a lot of time in Argentina with clients, prospects and the odd wine writer. Over there I was Dona Cristina, la Francesa, even though I spoke Spanish with an English accent.

I tried to call my parents once a week as I was not able to visit much. Papa's mood swings were worsening as he approached his seventy-fifth birthday. Some days he would go on at length about the seventeen years he'd spent at Villa growing the company into a major player. That company may not have been his, but it was his life's work. He'd talk about Marguerite Villa, his former boss, as if they were still working together. To my knowledge, they had not spoken since he'd left.

He never mentioned the six months he spent holed up in a rented studio in Vinassan after leaving Villa, refusing to talk to friends or family. Maman didn't either and I didn't dare ask.

He'd come back home one day without any warning, looking gaunt and exhausted. After mumbling some apologies to Maman, he'd gone straight to bed. She nursed him back to physical health but he was a changed man – and not for the better.

He'd become intense and argumentative, always preaching about right and wrong and getting into terrible rages if he felt my brother or I didn't measure up to his exacting standards, especially when it came to telling the truth. Despite Maman's attempts to act as go-between, his uncompromising attitude caused many fights during my teenage years as lying and evasion became my way to cope with his intransigence. As much as I loved him, I couldn't wait to leave home. After business school in Nantes, I moved to London and never looked back.

He seemed pleased I'd followed in his footsteps and chosen the wine business but disapproved of my involvement in Argentinean wines. I couldn't tell him there was no way I'd work for a Bordeaux company and have to visit him and Maman in Arcachon – where they had retired – every few weeks. Reminding him my employer was French only caused him to rant about globalisation and its evils. His once brilliant mind ran around in increasingly small circles.

He missed me though. That much I knew.

My own professional life rose to unprecedented heights when Oz Clarke's agent approached Terrazas with a request to feature our Cafayate winery in the "Anything But Chardonnay" BBC series. Cafayate is the best area in Argentina to grow Torrontes, an indigenous white grape variety. Six months later, on a grey April day, I was in Heathrow, about to fly to Buenos Aires with a film crew.

I phoned my parents from the departure lounge.

'Bonsoir Papa. Sorry I didn't call last week.'

'Ah Christine, let me fetch Maman.'

'I only have five minutes.' Too late, I could hear him walking away and calling my mother.

I found his need to involve her in everything infuriating. I paced the length of the lounge until he returned.

'Maman is here. I've put the loudspeaker on.'

'She's a big girl now. You can refer to me as her mother,' Maman said. 'Hello Christine, where are you calling from this time?'

'Do you remember the BBC documentary I told you about?' I said.

'Is it the one with Robert Joseph?' Papa asked.

A Tannoy announcement forced me to raise my voice.

'No, Papa. That was the conference in Cahors about Malbec. This one is in Argentina.'

'Don't shout, Christine!' Maman said. 'Who's Malbec?'

'It's a grape variety,' Papa said.

'How am I supposed to know?' she said.

I covered my ear with my free hand to block out the background noise. 'Can you have this argument some other time? My flight is about to board.'

'We're not arguing,' Maman said.

'You're off to Argentina again?' Papa asked.

I could hear Maman grumbling in the background, and her receding footsteps.

Papa cried out, 'Don't go, darling.'

'What's the matter?' I asked. A door slammed far away in Arcachon.

'I've started writing a journal,' Papa whispered, 'but Maman says it would more useful if I helped her with the garden.'

'Are you sleeping well?'

'I went for a long walk yesterday. Gardening isn't my thing.'

'Papa, I'm all for you writing your memoirs but not if it makes you unhappy.'

He sighed. 'You know the quote: "One of the keys to happiness is a bad memory." My memory is far too good.'

I checked my watch. My flight would be boarding soon.

'I'm sorry Papa, I haven't got time to talk now.'

'You never do,' he said.

British Airways Flight 0247 to Buenos Aires is now ready for boarding.

'Papa, I have to go. What if I promise to come down for the second May bank holiday?'

'Why not the first one? We haven't seen you-'

'Bye Papa.' There was no way I could take time off two weeks before the London International Wine Fair in mid-May.

We were relaxing over an asado at the end of the first day of filming when Maman called. She was crying.

'Your father has been taken to hospital. The doctor says it's his heart.'

'Is it bad?' I asked.

'How soon can you be in Arcachon?'

I closed my eyes. The smell of barbecued meat was making me gag. Everybody around me was joking and laughing in a mixture of English and Spanish. Whichever way I went, it would take me at least two days to travel to the south of France.

I left an hour later. The winery's accountant drove me to Salta. I remember little of those two hours. He booked me in the hotel closest to the airport and told me to try and sleep. I called Maman at six in the morning. It was ten in France. Papa was under sedation. Roland, my younger brother, had come down from Paris the night before, and was at his bedside. The doctors were noncommittal.

The first flight of the day from Salta was at quarter to three, landing an hour and a half later in Buenos Aires. I spent the morning pacing the hall of the small airport, praying Papa would recover.

Once in Buenos Aires, it took me an hour to retrieve my luggage and another one to travel from the domestic to the international airport. The United flight left just after nine o'clock and I made it to Heathrow at seven the following morning.

Papa died an hour later. I was on the bus to Gatwick.

I resigned on my first day back at work. My boss told me the group may be able to offer me a job in France. My friends in the trade said I was insane. Maman was too upset to have an opinion but my brother pleaded with me to give myself time. Everybody agreed I shouldn't blame myself for not being at Papa's bedside when he passed away.

My desperate rush from Salta to Arcachon had become symbolic of the distance I had put between my family, my country and myself. I replayed nonstop my last telephone conversation with Papa, wishing I'd been less flippant.

I worked two months of my notice, and on a sunny July morning, ten days into my self-imposed sabbatical, my phone rang at home in London.

'Mademoiselle Legerot, my name is Jean Tenin. I'm a recruitment consultant based in Bordeaux and specialising in international placements. Are you OK to talk?'

I resisted the temptation to tell him the neighbour's cat may be eavesdropping on me.

'Have you heard of Villa?' he asked.

I opened my mouth but nothing came out.

'Can you hear me?'

'Sorry, sore throat,' I said.

'Villa took over The Wine Shop, the British high street wine retailer, two years ago. They opened a UK office at the same time.'

'I've heard, yes.'

'It's a small office, with two local employees. The current commercial manager lives in Bordeaux but he's leaving at the end of the month. The European export director now wishes to recruit somebody based in London.'

'Why not Bordeaux?'

'The company is committed to growing its UK business with people who have an insider's knowledge of the market. Did you want to return to France?'

'I was thinking about it.'

'Between you and me, it's something you may be able to negotiate a few years down the line. In the meantime, you would have regular trips to the group's wineries, in Burgundy and the Languedoc, and to the Bordeaux head office. Do you have a CV you could send me?'

'Could you spell your email address, please?' I asked.

'jtenin@ jtenin.co.fr. I'll be in touch soon. Hope your throat gets better.'

'My throat?'

'Didn't you say?'

'Yes, my throat! Thank you.'

My hand was trembling when I put the phone down. I'd been thinking of applying for a job with a French company, maybe even a Bordeaux producer but not Villa. Marguerite was still at the helm as far as I knew, even though she must be in her late sixties or early seventies.

I'd always blamed her for Papa's collapse. She'd been more than his boss. Together they had built Villa into the formidable company it is today. He had huge admiration for her, which used to exasperate Maman. He wouldn't have left if Marguerite hadn't wanted him to.

The recruiter called me back the following week. He'd be meeting candidates in London within the next ten days. The recruitment process was to be conducted at a swift pace at the request of the client. I felt a pleasant excitement at the prospect of working for an efficient and decisive organisation.

He phoned again the day after.

'Mademoiselle Legerot, I won't be coming to London after all. There's been a change of plan. Could you fly to Bordeaux the day after tomorrow?'

I picked up a notepad and sat down. 'Who will I meet?'

'The recruitment is managed by Ed de Waast, Villa's European export director but Marcel Villa may also want to meet you.'

'Is he Madame Villa's son?'

He paused.

'Her son and heir,' he said.

Marcel's adoption by Marguerite at the beginning of the eighties had created a scandal in Bordeaux's polite society. Despite being single and never having shown any interest in having a family, she'd flown to South America one day and returned a few weeks later with a good looking seven-year old boy.

Marcel had been scrutinised for any physical resemblance to his adoptive mother and some excitable biddies had commented on a long holiday Marguerite had taken at the approximate time of his birth.

I was fourteen and gloriously selfish at the time but I was intrigued. Even though Papa had left Villa two years earlier, I had asked him what he thought. In doing so, I was breaking the unspoken family understanding that Villa's name should never be mentioned in our home.

'She must be lonely,' he had said.

Maman had gone berserk.

As usual at the end of July, the plane was full of holidaymakers accompanied by hordes of unruly children. The smell of fried bacon and omelette, which dominates early morning BA flights, was soon superseded with a pungent mix of duty free perfumes and children's vomit.

We landed under a perfect blue sky to the delight of my fellow travellers. Their excitement was contagious and I smiled at the customs officer who checked my passport, and at the machine-gun wielding soldiers who've become a feature of French airports.

The sun was shining and I was coming home. I was happy, even though it was my first time back in Merignac, Bordeaux's airport, since Papa's death.

The elegant young woman behind the Avis counter could have starred in an advertisement for the region. She sported the exquisite light suntan only locals have a chance of perfecting and which looks so much better than the bright red or mahogany complexion some Brits see as evidence of a successful holiday. I found myself almost closing my eyes in delight when she also turned out to have the perfect local accent, an elegant version of the Southern vernacular.

Outside the terminal, advertising boards praised the merit of several Bordeaux brands: Calvet, Blaissac, Dourthe, Malesan and Villa. Under the odour of kerosene, petrol and the hot metal of hundreds of cars, I smelled the salty sea breeze and the distinctive scent of the Landes pine forest, reminiscent of my childhood.

My interview was scheduled for eleven thirty. I drove around the Rocade, Bordeaux's very own M25, taking in the landmarks, an endless succession of cheap hotels and furniture stores, and singing at the top of my voice.

I arrived ten minutes early at Villa's head office in the centre of town and asked for Ed de Waast.

The prim lady in reception told me Monsieur de Waast was sorry but would I mind if our meeting was postponed by half an hour. I took one look at the sparsely furnished waiting room and went back outside.

I took a few steps in the midday heat, looking at the white buildings around me. This was a much more impressive setup than the modest office on the Quais des Chartrons which Marguerite inherited from her family, and where she and Papa had worked all those years ago. I somehow ended up in the designated smoking area next to the bike shed. I was feeling rather stupid standing there without the excuse of a cigarette, when I noticed a group of people walking to the car park. They stopped and started every few minutes, talking and gesticulating aplenty. Two women split from the main party and came towards me. They nodded a greeting as they reached the shelter and lit up.

'I can't believe we're going to let a bunch of Krauts teach us how to do our jobs,' the older one said, blowing smoke through her nose. I turned my head to remain out of reach of the noxious cloud.

'Why do we need foreign audits on top of French ones?' her colleague asked.

'To keep foreign auditors busy, I suppose. When I think of the extra work, I feel sick.' She punctuated her comment with a phlegmy cough. 'This new German business is less than a third of what we do with Carrefour and I bet you they'll be three times as much trouble.'

They took a few drags in silence.

'I've heard Japanese customers are the worst,' said the young one.

'All export customers are a nightmare,' said her friend.

Another polite nod in my direction and they were gone, leaving me to mull over this insight into the mentality of my future colleagues.

I had been waiting for forty minutes when a call on my mobile summoned me back inside.

Ed de Waast looked like a giant pistachio. Short, with a prominent belly, he was wearing a pale green suit and matching tie. His head was too big for his body and he was almost bald, except for one thick lock of red hair at the nape of his neck, the lone survivor of the full head of curls he must have sported as a young man. He had the enormous blue eyes of a toddler, now incongruous in his middle-aged face. A strong whiff of Intimately Beckham for Him emanated from his unimpressive physique. He looked very different from the confident manager I'd expected to meet.

He started apologising the minute I shook his cold, flaccid hand. 'My meeting overran, and now Marcel Villa is nowhere to be found. I've left a message with his assistant. Let's go to the meeting room.'

Over Ed's shoulder, I saw a tall handsome man with deep brown eyes and dark wavy hair. He was walking towards us. He came as close as he could without being seen by Ed and cleared his throat in a theatrical manner.

Ed jumped on the spot. 'Monsieur Villa!'

If Marguerite Villa had chosen her son for his good looks, she had done well.

'Monsieur de Waast,' he answered with a little bow. He turned to me with a wide smile, 'Madame Legerot?'

I looked him in the eye but there was nothing there apart from the polite boredom of a powerful man meeting yet another potential subordinate. We shook hands.

Marcel turned to Ed, 'Where are you taking us for lunch?'

The combination of the casual question and the formal *vous*, instead of the *tu* now in use in most French companies, made Ed sound like a bell boy in an upmarket hotel rather than a senior executive.

'I was thinking we could have a chat in the meeting room first,' said Ed.

'You think far too much, monsieur de Waast. I'm hungry.' Marcel threw a bunch of keys at Ed and marched towards the exit.

Once in the car, a top of the range Porsche Cayenne, Marcel turned to me.

'So. . . Madame . . . Chris, isn't it? Or would you rather be called . . . well, never mind. . . did you, did you have a good flight, or maybe you took the train?' He tapped Ed on the shoulder. 'How did she get here, Monsieur de Waast?'

I bit my tongue and let Ed answer.

The restaurant was close by. Once out of the car, we kick-started a proper if superficial conversation. I kept on reminding myself I was there for an interview and not just for lunch. We ordered three entrecotes with fries and a bottle of Villa wine to wash them down. Ed picked up a notepad from his pocket and put it next to his plate with my CV. The page was covered in tiny scribbles. I braced myself for a long list of questions.

'Chris, thank you for visiting us in Bordeaux,' he said. 'Monsieur Tenin tells me you're interested in joining us as UK commercial manager.'

Marcel cut in before I had time to answer, 'Why are you not working?'

'I used to work for Terrazas, LVMH's Argentinean subsidiary,' I said. 'My father was taken ill while I was out there. I couldn't make it back before he died and decided I needed a job with less long-haul travelling.'

'I never knew my father,' Marcel said.

I looked at Ed but he appeared to be engrossed in my CV.

'I am sorry to hear that,' I said.

'Nor my real mother. I'm lucky Madame Villa adopted me.' He sounded as if he were challenging me to contradict him.

'I've heard your mother is a remarkable woman,' I said.

'Indeed.' He fell silent, rolling the breadcrumbs on the tablecloth into a little sticky ball. Ed and I were watching him and waiting.

He squeezed his creation flat with his thumb, sighed and looked at me. 'Are you a remarkable woman, Madame Legerot?

'This is an unfair question, Monsieur Villa,' Ed said.

Marcel ignored him. 'Do you want to join Villa?'

I nodded.

'You speak English?'

'I've been living in England for eighteen years,' I said.

'How much do you want?' He rubbed the fingers of his left hand together in the universal sign for money, his upper lip curled up as if he'd detected a bad smell.

'Sixty thousand pounds.'

'Write that down, Monsieur de Waast,' said Marcel. 'When can you start?'

'If I may -' Ed's eyes were blue mirrors of incredulity.

Marcel turned to him. 'What now?'

'Monsieur Villa, this is something, maybe, we could explore a bit further and discuss together, before-'

Marcel shut him up with a wave of his hand.

'We need someone in London by September, Monsieur de Waast. Madame Legerot seems keen and I'm going on holiday next week.'

Any illusion I'd entertained that Marcel's decisiveness was due to my professional abilities crumbled on the spot.

. . .

I spent the weekend with Maman in Arcachon. We shared a bottle of Bouvet Ladubay Crémant de Loire to celebrate my new job. She had a small glass and I drank the rest. She kept on shaking her head, saying life was bizarre and was I sure about joining Villa.

We tried a new restaurant that had opened for the summer season and went for long morning walks on Pereire beach, enjoying the sunshine and the smell of the pine trees. We talked. I wanted to ask her if I could have a look at what Papa had been writing before he died but I didn't find the right moment.

I returned to London with the feeling we'd turned a corner.

An email from Ed de Waast arrived the day after my return.

Dear Chris,

On behalf of Monsieur Villa and myself, I'd like to thank you for your visit to Bordeaux last week. We have now met all the candidates shortlisted for the position of Villa UK commercial manager and I am pleased to let you know we would like to invite you for a second interview.

Monsieur Villa, being otherwise engaged for the next few weeks, has asked me to finalise an appointment. May I suggest we meet again next Thursday at two at the Hammersmith Novotel?

Marcel Villa wasn't copied in.

3

NOT SMELLING OF ROSES

I got the job – again – the following Thursday, after two long hours of what felt like a police interrogation about every single detail of my work history to date, and at a lesser salary than the one agreed in Bordeaux. My trust in my new boss decreased in proportion to the cut he'd imposed on me.

Rachel's voice brings me back to reality. Four months after my interview with Ed, her good news will reassure him I'm the right person for the job. It may even be a fresh start for the two of us.

'Could you check something for me?' she asks.

'I'd be delighted.' I press the palm of my hand against the cool wall in front of me, trying to keep my voice level and my excitement down.

'Ninety-five customers have complained about your Red Vin de Pays over the last two days. Eight weeks before Christmas, this is the last thing I need.'

'Ninety-five!' I lean against the wall, hugging myself with my free arm.

Rachel ignores my interruption. 'Comments range from "taste of rotten fruit" to "smells of tar" and "disgusting".'

My throat tightens. My stellar future has vanished in a puff of foul smoke.

'Chris? Can you hear me?'

I force myself to swallow. 'Do you have a lot number?'

'Two: L07246 and L07248[1].'

I fish a pen from my pocket and scribble the last three digits of each lot number over the smudge on my hand. 'Quite recent,' I say.

'The third and the fifth of September.'

The first batch of the offending wine was bottled on the day I joined Villa.

'They must come from the same tank.'

'Should I care?' asks Rachel.

'Sorry, just thinking aloud.' I rub my forehead. 'I'm in Narbonne right now. I'm going to retrieve samples of these two bottling runs and get them tasted. Then I'll check the analysis-'

'You have one hour,' she says. 'My customers are buying this wine and drinking it as we speak. I won't take the risk of more of them being dissatisfied with our brand.'

I feel a nervous giggle coming up. If Rachel's customers are glugging red wine at nine o'clock in the morning, the quality of their tipple may be the least of their worries.

The laughter catches in my throat as I absorb the magnitude of the disaster. The Super-Market's Red Vin de Pays sells hundreds of thousands of bottles per year. Its loyal followers would recognise it with their eyes closed and earplugs up their noses. Unless we identify and sort out the problem in record time, a quality issue on this line will damage our relationship with The Super-Market beyond repair. I can forget the Bordeaux deal. We may even lose our existing business with them. Everyone will blame me, and Ed will be first in line.

What do I tell Andy? I've invested so much time and effort in his visit. I spent the last two months building up his image of Villa and trying to convince him we are a quality producer despite our size. I'm not keen to undo all my good work by telling him what's going on but The Super-Market takes priority. Our meeting will be disrupted and I need to give him a reason why.

Should I tell him my cat has run away? I don't have a cat. That my car has been broken into? It's at the airport, my neighbour wouldn't know. I need to think of something to do with home, something which will give me an excuse to come and go. A gas leak? An explosion? An earthquake? Too big. Why is it I can't think of anything when I need a good convincing lie? I return to the tasting table, taking very small steps.

'Everything all right?' asks Serge.

I face him, keeping my back to Andy, and I mouth silently 'The Super-Market's Vin de Pays Red.'

He frowns.

I pull a face and point at my nose to indicate a bad smell.

He grimaces and returns to his tasting notes, gnawing what's left of his thumbnail.

I turn towards Andy. He looks up from his pad, his mouth full of wine. He swirls it around and stares at me like a terrier that's got a whiff of carrion. He spits but instead of writing down his tasting note he asks, 'What did you say?'

'There's been a burst pipe at my place. The water came right through my bedroom and into the flat downstairs. Thank God I'd left the keys with my neighbour. She says it's a complete mess: chunks of plaster and soggy paper everywhere.'

I'm warming to my story. It's not even a complete lie: my ceiling fell through because of a burst pipe five years ago. I remember the musty smell that pervaded the flat until the decorators came. I point at the numbers on my hand, 'I need to call my cleaner and the insurance company straight away. I'll be a couple of minutes.'

I scribble "volume" on my hand to remind myself to check how many bottles were produced, how many were shipped and when.

When I come back after reporting the issue to the quality control department, Andy and Serge are debating the wisdom of adding a few grams of residual sugar to a blend of Grenache, Chardonnay and Marsanne. They look as if they've known each other for years.

Serge tells Andy about the comparative tasting of New World Chardonnays we organised two weeks ago. I nod with as much enthusiasm as I can muster.

'The analysis revealed a wide range of sugar contents,' he says.

Ten minutes. I check my mobile is still working.

'Jacob's Creek came in at two point seven grams of sugar per litre and Gallo's Turning Leaf at a whopping eight.'

I force my face into a knowledgeable smile. 'It confirms big wine brands are getting sweeter.'

What can have gone wrong with the damn wine? I look at the clock. Twenty minutes have gone.

We try different sugar levels with our blend. Andy settles on four grams.

Over an hour passes without any news from the quality control department. How long does it take to collect a couple of bottles from the samples library and try them? When my phone vibrates, I pick up without waiting for it to ring.

'Chris?' It's Jean Jacques. 'I've tried the wines The Super-Market is complaining about. They comply with our quality standards.'

People do not complain without reason. If ninety-five people have taken the trouble to return a bottle to their local store, twice as many will have poured theirs down the sink, vowing never to buy the same wine again. Something is wrong with that wine.

Jean Jacques is a trained oenologist though. He tastes every day of the week. His judgement is reliable.

I turn to Andy and Serge. 'May I abandon you for a few minutes?'

The reek of sour wine and the acrid prickle of disinfectant make me wrinkle my nose as I open the door of the lab. The quality charter signed by Marguerite Villa hangs by the door under her framed portrait. This photo was taken at least thirty years ago. I remember seeing it on a visit to the winery with Papa. My eyes fill with tears. Nobody is there to hold my hand today. I take a deep breath and walk in.

On the floor, open polystyrene and cardboard boxes contain samples of wines Villa may purchase from local co-operatives or individual growers. They're waiting for their turn to be undressed, poked, prodded and maybe given the nod. I shiver and look away. I can't stand the noise polystyrene makes.

The roar from the bottling hall invades the room each time the door opens. Operators bring in new bottles at regular intervals: six at the beginning of each bottling, and six every hour. They're logged, tasted and analysed straight away. Should the results not fall within the expected parameters, the bottling line will be stopped and the stock produced since the last analysis quarantined and maybe destroyed.

With all five lines working, churning out seven thousand bottles each per hour, men in dark overalls carrying heavy crates come and go through the laboratory in a scene reminiscent of a Daft Punk video. I skip across in a zigzag, apologising to moving piles of cardboard boxes held by white-knuckled hands, and trying not to collide with anybody or anything.

People in white coats with a Villa logo on the breast pocket sit among the bustle, lifting long pipettes, swirling liquids in test tubes and recording their findings in large heavy tomes or typing them on the wine stained keyboards dotted around the room.

I crane my neck to try and find Jean Jacques among the white coats. I spot him in a corner of the room surrounded by bottles of The Super-Market's Vin de Pays. I join him and nod a silent greeting to his assistant, the older of the two women I met while waiting for my interview in Bordeaux. She nods back but her eyes don't meet mine. She holds a purple-stained glass upside down between her index and her middle finger and she has the vinous red line halfway up her nose, which indicates how far she pushed it into the glass.

Jean Jacques selects a fresh tasting glass from the wooden rack in front of us. He smells it and checks its cleanliness against the light before picking up one of the bottles and pouring. He has large damp patches under his armpits.

I reach for the half full glass with trembling fingers. Papa used to say, 'Wine tasting isn't an exact science.' Not a thought I need to dwell on now.

The dark ruby red colour shines against the stark white background. Purple hints dance on the surface. The contrast makes my mouth water. I turn towards the window and peer through the liquid. It's clear without any deposits.

I swirl the wine around and take a deep sniff. I look up, flare my nostrils and plunge my nose into the glass again to confirm my first impression.

'This wine smells of shit!'

My outburst echoes around the lab. Heads turn in our direction.

I hold my glass out to Jean Jacques. 'What do you call that smell?' My voice sounds loud and angry to my own ears.

He takes a step back and leans against the bench. His hands are pushed as deep as they will go in his white overcoat's pockets.

'Amylic, like Beaujolais: overripe strawberries, blackcurrant with a hint of smoke and some tarry notes. Complex for a Vin de Pays.' He looks me in the eye.

The familiar vocabulary makes me doubt the evidence of my nose. I take another sniff and recoil from the stink. How can Jean Jacques's perception be so different from mine?

'Jean Jacques, promise me one thing.'

He mumbles something.

'Never, ever buy me any perfume. Because if this wine smells of ripe strawberries to you, then I… well, let's leave it at that.'

He doesn't laugh. He doesn't even smile.

The bitter smells of the laboratory catch in my throat. I wait for the wave of nausea to pass.

I need a second opinion.

I turn to Jean Jacques' assistant.

'Could you please run to the tasting room and ask Serge to join us? He's turned his phone off but I need him to taste this wine.'

She glances at Jean Jacques who nods in agreement. She leaves the room and I pick up my mobile. I dial, staring straight at Jean Jacques.

'Mary, Chris here. Sorry to bother you. Yes, the weather's glorious down here. Listen, could you please pop into the nearest The Super-Market and pick up a bottle of the red we do for them? Make sure the lot number reads L07246 or L07248. Actually, get a bottle of each. No, get two of each. Open one of each lot number, in the car park if you can, taste them and call me back. It's urgent.'

'Your assistant isn't a qualified taster,' Jean Jacques says.

'That's why I want her opinion.'

The first bars of Mambo Number Five erupt from my pocket before I have time to pick up.

'Chris, I said one hour.' Rachel's voice shreds my eardrum.

'I'm sorry Rachel. It's taken longer than anticipated to get the samples. We're just about to taste them.'

'Call me when you have.' She hangs up.

I hate lying, but I need time. I look at Jean Jacques. 'We have twenty minutes, half an hour at the most. You say this wine meets our standards, I say it's faulty, probably reduced.[2] What do I tell Rachel?'

'The analysis-'

'Forget the analysis. This wine stinks!

'No need to raise your voice,' he says.

'Sorry.'

My phone vibrates. It can't be Rachel again. I check the display: Serge. Relief floods over me.

'Are you psychic?' I ask. 'I've just sent someone to fetch you.'

'Chris, I can't get involved.'

'Are you worried about leaving Andy alone? You'll be gone for five minutes max.'

'Trust me,' Serge says.

'I need your help.' I sound pathetic.

My throat tightens. I can take anything from Jean Jacques but Serge is an ally, almost a friend. He can't let me down. I try to snort but what comes out sounds more like a whimper.

'What am I to tell Rachel? I'm not allowed to comment on the condition of the wine without an oenologist's or the quality control department's say-so. You know that.'

Jean Jacques saunters away.

'Can you wait until André comes back from Paris?' Serge asks.

'What's this got to do with him?'

'He's the boss.' Serge sounds shocked. I'd forgotten he's very much André's creature, nurtured and bullied by him over the last ten years.

'How does his position qualify him to assess the integrity of a wine?'

'He takes all the important decisions here.'

'This is ridiculous.' I try a more conciliatory tone. 'André will have to agree the damages we'll pay to The Super-Market but that's far down the line. Right now, we have a customer who wants to know how serious her problem is.'

'He'll be back tomorrow lunchtime,' Serge says.

'You must be joking. Rachel hasn't tasted the wine yet because her office is miles away from the nearest store. The minute she does, she'll go ballistic.'

'Call André.'

Serge's suggestion throws me. I don't relish the prospect of interrupting the winery's big boss trip to Paris. He's hardly spoken to me since I joined the company. I have no choice though. Between Rachel's wrath and André's annoyance, I choose the latter.

I retreat to Serge's office. Calling André from Serge's number will ensure he answers the phone.

'Monsieur Lange, Chris Legerot speaking.'

I hear a sudden intake of breath. I must be calling at a bad time.

'Mademoiselle Legerot, what a surprise!' The voice at the other end of the phone is mellifluous. 'Is Serge looking after our visitor on his own?' André likes it to be known that nothing escapes him.

'All is well with Direct Wines but I have a problem with another customer.'

'Nothing to do with my winery?' he asks with the emphasis on the "my".

I explain the issue.

'Is it the one we switched from corks to screw caps?'

I confirm it is.

'Get Jean Jacques to check a library sample. I can't do much from Paris. We'll talk about it tomorrow.'

I grip the armrest of the chair with my free hand and close my eyes. 'Jean Jacques tasted the wine five minutes ago but he says there's nothing wrong with it. I tasted it and I disagree. I need to call Rachel but I don't know what to say.'

'I know you've been working in the industry for a long time Chris, but I didn't know you trained as an oenologist.'

My nose lacks an official piece of paper to have an opinion.

'This wine stinks.'

'Watch your language. How many bottles did we produce?' A note of warning has crept in his voice.

'Fifty-two thousand over two days.'

'Have we shipped the lot?'

'The Super-Market sells eight hundred thousand bottles per year. Fifty-two thousand bottles only represent three to four weeks sales.'

André falls silent.

'Monsieur Lange?'

'I'm here. Let me call Jean Jacques.'

'What do I tell Rachel?'

'I'll try to fly back earlier than planned. In the meantime, keep your Rachel waiting and don't rush to conclusions.'

Up to one in ten natural corks taints the wine it's supposed to protect, more so at the cheap end of the market. One alternative is plastic closures, which can be difficult to squeeze back in the bottle. Many buyers, including Rachel, are moving their entry level lines to screw caps as a more consumer-friendly option.

Screw caps however are more airtight than corks, which means the quantity of sulphur dioxide injected into the wine prior to bottling needs to be adjusted down. If not, the excess will, over a few weeks, combine with the oxygen in the wine to give off the reductive character I picked up earlier.

I am rushing to conclusions.

I pick up the phone again to call "my" Rachel. It weighs a ton.

'Rachel? Chris speaking.'

'That was a long tasting. I've been waiting for you to call for almost an hour.'

I make it thirty minutes but there's no point contradicting her.

'Rachel, we have an issue with your wine. It conforms to our quality standards but we'd like to run further analyses to understand what's prompting the customer complaints. Could you give us until tomorrow?'

'You must be joking. All I'm asking you is to tell me if I can keep your wine on our shelves? You tasted it. You should know.'

'I'm not a qualified taster.' I move the phone away from my ear.

'What do you mean? You've got your Diploma.'

The Wine and Spirit Education Trust runs courses and awards vocational qualifications which are the benchmark of the industry. The highest one, the Diploma, combines academic product knowledge with tasting skills.

'It doesn't make me an oenologist.'

'Don't go all French on me. What about Serge? He's an oenologist.'

'He's in Bordeaux.'

The lie slipped out so easily, it must be a case of practice makes perfect. I need to keep Serge out of this mess for the time being anyway. He can "return from Bordeaux" later to assess the wine and restore the company's image in Rachel's mind.

'Are there no other oenologists in Narbonne?' she asks.

How can I pretend a large winery such as Villa's operates without an oenologist on site? I say nothing.

'Chris, what's going on?'

'I don't know, Rachel' For once, I'm telling the truth. 'I need more time.'

'Do you have any idea what is at stake?' she asks. 'If I go for a full product withdrawal I'll lose margin and turnover but I'll lose customers if I sell them a dodgy wine.'

Now is not the time to quip it's a "lose-lose" situation. Why does my sense of humour always kick in at the worst possible moment?

Rachel continues. 'I'll get some samples and taste them myself. Call me tomorrow if that's the best you can do but I'm very disappointed. I expected better from you.'

I put the phone down. My cheeks are burning.

I look at my watch. I left the Direct Wines tasting over an hour ago. God only knows what Andy's thinking. I want to curl up in a corner of Serge's office with my eyes closed and my hands on my ears. Instead I drag myself out of the chair and return to the tasting room.

4

LIES AND MORE LIES

Andy and Serge are discussing whether a drop of Muscat would enhance the flavour of their Chardonnay when I tiptoe back into the room. It looks like I haven't missed too much. I prepare to apologise for my absence.

'Bet it took you ages to speak to a real person,' Andy says.

I stare at him. What is he talking about?

'Who are you insured with?' he asks.

'The Super-Market. I am with The Super-Market.'

He frowns. 'I didn't know they did insurance.'

'They've just started.'

'Are they any good?'

'Cheap,' I say. 'I'm sorry it took so long.'

My cheeks are burning again. I pick up my glass and raise it in front of my face as if to check it's clean.

'I need to catch up with the tasting,' I say, jotting down brief notes as I go along. Some samples stand forward of the line-up, to indicate Andy and Serge rate them higher than the others. I sit down to decipher the scribbles Serge's left me on a scrap of paper. Blend 1= 30% Chard. nb 5 + 45% Chard. nb 6.

I turn my attention to the cost spreadsheet on my laptop. Juggling numbers soothes me: figures don't lie. I enter the price for bulk wine adding 3% for wastage during bottling. I tot up the dry goods: bottle, label, cork, capsule, case, dividers.

Andy turns around.

'I'm thinking of moving my French entry level range to screw caps. We've done the same with Chile and Australia and sales have shot up.'

I nod, keeping my eyes on the screen.

'We need to get this started sooner rather than later,' he says.

This is as good as telling me we've won his business. His existing suppliers are small producers who only bottle with corks and can't afford to invest in new equipment. But if our handling of screw caps is confirmed to be the cause of the quality problem with The Super-Market, our bottling practices will need to be reviewed before I grab another slice of business and make a hash of it.

Andy's expectant look indicates he's waiting for me to show some enthusiasm. I stretch the requested smile across my face with great difficulty.

Mambo Number Five interrupts us, its jaunty beat in stark contrast with my mood.

'Sorry Andy, I need to take this one.'

He shrugs. My sympathy capital is draining away fast. I take refuge in a corner of the room, cradling the phone for comfort.

'Mary? Do you have the samples?'

'What's wrong with that wine? It smells horrible.'

'Thank God! I'll call you later to explain.'

I go back to my laptop, my head held high. I'm not on my own anymore.

Half an hour later, we break for lunch. We move to the meeting room to ensure food smells don't pollute the air in the tasting room. We demolish a selection of sandwiches bought from the local bakery, from the classic French jambon-beurre to a more exotic tikka chicken served with lush lettuce leaves. The smell of fresh bread hangs in the air.

All I want to talk about is The Super-Market's wine but it's impossible in front of Andy. Serge tries to help me keep the conversation going but we struggle. Andy is watching us and waiting, his red nose twitching with the scent of disaster.

When he asks for half an hour to make a few phone calls, Serge takes him to his office. This gives me a chance to change my ringtone back to a more classical tune and to return Mary's call to explain the situation to her.

Serge brings me back a coffee from the vending machine. I warm my fingers on the plastic cup and breathe in the bitter smell.

'Shouldn't you call Ed?'

'If I tell Ed what's going on, he'll call André to lecture him on the importance of customer service. Do you think it will help?'

He'll also find something to lecture me on and I'm not in the mood.

Serge sits down. 'André doesn't rate him. He is your boss though.'

I take a sip of coffee and pull a face. It tastes disgusting. 'If I call Ed, he'll also want to talk to Rachel himself to tell her in his atrocious English, how much he wants to help. It will cost us more in the long run.'

Serge nods. 'She's a good buyer.'

'And he is a lousy salesman,' I say.

He laughs.

I fidget with my empty plastic cup, squeezing it flat and letting it pop back into shape a few times. 'Why did you refuse to taste The Super-Market's wine?'

'Do you trust me or not?'

'I suppose so.'

'Villa works in peculiar ways. You've only been with the company four months.'

He has let me down but he means well. It makes a difference.

Andy has been back ten minutes when Rachel calls for the third time. I pick up and close my eyes, ready for the onslaught.

'I'm furious,' she says. 'Your muddled comments led me to believe it would take several tasters to reach a verdict on our wine. I asked three other wine buyers and two of our food technicians to taste the samples with me. Do you want to know what happened?

I whimper.

'They laughed, Chris. They laughed at me. This wine stinks. Why didn't you tell me? Now everybody knows.'

'I-'

'Let me finish.' Her voice is ripping my eardrums to shreds. 'This is going to cost you, and Villa, big time. There are many other suppliers who'd kill for the chance to get their hands on the lines you supply us with.'

Andy is swirling the same wine around and around in his glass and staring straight at me. I press the phone against my ear as hard as I can to try and muffle Rachel's voice. It hurts.

'We're withdrawing all stock of your Vin de Pays from our stores,' Rachel says.

'Could we talk about it tomorrow? This is a huge step.'

She sniggers. 'This is a huge problem even though you don't seem to see it. And since that problem is now the talk of the department, thanks to you, my boss has asked to meet you, and the people responsible for this mess, here in the office. I'll send you an email later with a date and a time.'

I text André straightaway to inform him of the product withdrawal but I don't mention Rachel's summons.

'These constant interruptions are frustrating,' Andy says. 'What's going on?'

'Same problem,' I say, staring at my mobile's screen. 'My neighbour is upset because I can't get the mess cleaned up before I return.'

I look at him. He shakes his head.

'It smells,' I say.

'Your neighbour sounds a lot like Rachel from The Super-Market. Don't you know we used to work together?'

I stare at him for a full minute, taking in the spots, the pointy nose and the wispy hair. I am defeated.

Serge is watching us. He's cocked his head to one side as he does when trying to follow a conversation in fast flowing English.

I put my hands behind my back. 'I've lied to you.'

'Tell me something I don't know.'

'It's an awkward situation.'

He nods again. I wish he would say something.

'The Super-Market reported an abnormal level of customer complaints on one of our lines this morning,' I say. I should have told you but I didn't want it to affect your opinion of Villa. That's why I made up the story about the water leak.' I count the floor tiles between my feet and the table: one, two, three and a half.

'So there's no point in me trying to get bargain insurance from The Super-Market?' he asks.

Is that a joke? The famous British sense of humour? I look up but he is scribbling something in his notebook, not even the shadow of a smile on his face.

He asks for a tour of the winery. He bombards Serge with technical questions. We spend two hours auditing every aspect of our operations in greater details than I would have thought possible. We return to the tasting room to taste the wines we've blended one last time. Andy wipes his mouth. He asks me to confirm our prices in writing and to send fresh samples to his office. I feel as if I were watching this happening to somebody else. I've seldom felt so despondent after a visit.

Serge's mobile rings the minute we return to the meeting room after saying goodbye to Andy.

'Monsieur Lange.' He looks at me and puts his finger on his lips. 'I'll be five minutes.'

He snaps his phone shut and puts it back in his pocket.

'It was André,' he says.

'I'm not stupid, thanks. Is he back?'

'He'll call you later.'

'Did he say when?'

Serge pats my shoulder. 'You're not very patient, are you?'

I snort in disgust and settle down to write the minutes of the meeting with Andy.

'Chris?' Serge is holding the door open. 'You'd better go now.'

I rub my forehead. Tiredness is catching up with me. 'I need to write my report.'

'Go back to the hotel.'

I frown. 'What about you?'

'I'll look at it tomorrow and I'll fill in the gaps.'

I get up slowly, collect my papers and my laptop and leave without a word.

In the car, the radio is playing the song by Fabienne Thibeault's that concludes that whatever we do or think, we're always alone in the world.

I treat myself to a little cry.

My mobile rings yet again as soon as I've dropped my bags on the hotel bed. The poor thing must be as exhausted as I am.

'Mademoiselle Legerot, you've disappointed me.' André's voice is icy.

Is there anybody I haven't disappointed today? I let myself slide against the wall and hug my knees.

'You called me to report an emergency and interrupted an important lunch. I trusted your judgement and flew back as soon as I could. I have complete faith in my team but when there's a problem, the ship captain has to take responsibility.'

I hear a faint echo. André must have put me on speakerphone. He sounds like he is playing to an audience, in all likelihood the team he's just referred to in glowing terms. He continues. 'I've tasted your wine. The nose could be neater but it's drinkable, even more so when it's been left to air for a few hours.'

I sigh. 'People who spend £3.49 on a bottle of wine don't use decanters.'

'They would have copper coins in their purse though. Putting one in their glass and giving it a good swirl would do the trick.[1]'

'You and I know that but most wine drinkers don't.'

'Listen Chris, may I call you Chris? I am trying to help but you have to make an effort too. If you reject all my suggestions, we'll never get anywhere.'

I lick my finger and wipe a tiny wine stain from my phone.

André continues. 'I know you mean well but you haven't handled this situation very professionally. Your young buyer overreacted, and instead of reassuring her and calming her down, as is your responsibility, you sided with her and turned a minor incident into a major crisis. Now the damage is done, if we have to pay The Super-Market a little something to soothe the young lady's pride, we'll do it but that's as far as I'll go.'

I scramble to my feet and take a deep breath. 'Monsieur Lange, with all due respect, our wine may be safe to drink but it smells horrible, which means The Super-Market won't sell it.'

He pauses before answering me, a little louder than before. 'Which side are you on, Mademoiselle? Think about it tonight and let's talk again tomorrow. When are you flying back to London?'

'Tomorrow lunchtime, from Toulouse. I can be at the winery at seven if you like.'

'Make it eight. We won't need long.'

I slump on the bed and close my eyes. I feel sick.

5

THE DINNER THAT GOES WRONG

I should phone Maman. We speak every Sunday but I spent last weekend with Sam messing around with her kids and I missed my weekly assignment. I feel guilty but I can't phone her now. She'd know I'm upset, and in trying to make it better she'd make it worse. She refuses to take an interest in my professional life but it doesn't stop her from making well-meant but useless or tactless comments about it. My current predicament is likely to prompt something along the lines of 'If the oenologist says the wine is fine he must be right. You've always had a problem with authority.'

I'll try her tomorrow, once I'm home. If she has a go at me for not being in touch earlier, I'll say I have been busy. I'd feel better if I could discuss today's events with someone with no vested interest in the matter. Sam would be good. She lets me drone on for hours about work, life, men or whatever bugs me and then she pours forth about her ex-husband and her music. But it's pointless trying her before the twins have gone to bed.

I look at my mobile for inspiration. It's still warm from my conversation with André. A greasy film, half make-up, half God knows what, covers the screen and the dialling pad is encrusted with grime. I wipe the display clean with a tissue and pick up a cotton bud from the hotel courtesy pack. I moisten it and run it around the keys, forcing it in the tiny spaces where grey scum has accumulated. Three cotton buds later, my phone looks almost new. I wish I felt the same.

I drag myself to the bathroom. Jen Turner, The Wine Shop's head of buying, is picking me up at eight. She's on holiday as a guest of Gerard Bertrand at Château L'Hospitalet, a gorgeous hotel in a vineyard nearby, and we've arranged to meet for dinner.

Jen and I first met three years ago when I convinced her to list two Argentinean wines from Terrazas. We've shared a few drinks since and have become friends. When I joined Villa's UK office, we became colleagues, as Villa owns The Wine Shop. I have however nothing to do with the day-to-day running of The Wine Shop.

A quick look at my watch confirms I have no time to change or even shower. My hair could do with a wash. I had no time to go to the hairdresser before my trip down South and a band of grey is showing at the roots. I'm the living proof that some French women miss out on that elusive je-ne-sais-quoi which is supposed to be our birth right. I reach for the bottle of Chanel 19 with a sigh.

Jen is as blond as I am dark. Both in our early forties, we stand at five feet eight in our stockinged feet. Tonight, we look like the before and after of a magazine feature. The soft lights of the hotel lobby can't disguise the bags under my bloodshot eyes, my sallow skin or my lank hair whereas she looks healthy and relaxed with shiny hair and no makeup. She smells of fresh lilac.

She takes one look at me and raises her eyebrows. 'Are you alright?'

'I need a drink.'

She laughs. The blue eyes she uses to petrify a supplier into submission crinkle at the corners and her pale freckled face flushes pink.

I am glad she's here.

We set off for the restaurant in companionable silence. The sun has gone in, the evening is chilly and we walk fast. The plane trees in the streets of Narbonne have started shedding their leaves but the air still carries an elusive summer scent of hot dust and warm tarmac. Old men are drinking Pastis at the few tables left outside the town's cafes.

The rich aromas of Mediterranean food greet us when we walk in the restaurant.

'Smell that, Jen: spices, anchovies, roasted peppers, warm goat's cheese!'

'You and your food! Have you ever missed a meal in your life?' Jen has a British approach to sustenance, evidenced in her skinny frame.

A guitar is playing Spanish music in the background. The waitress approaches us with the constipated smirk, which befits the superior standard of the restaurant.

'Good evening ladies. May I take your coats?'

I hand mine over. Jen shakes her head.

'Would you like a table by the window?'

We sit down on elegant brown leather chairs. Jen tries to hang her jacket over the high smooth back but it keeps on sliding down.

'Are you sure you want to keep it?' I ask.

'I had my jacket stolen last year in a restaurant.'

'In France?'

'South Africa.'

What's left of my patriotism floods my veins. 'It's not the same!'

'Still foreign to me,' she says.

Our languid waitress returns. Her well-trained eyes take in Jen's coat, now squashed at the back of her chair. She points at the garment with a manicured finger.

'Are you sure-'

Jen cuts her short. 'I'll be fine.'

The waitress lifts her bony shoulders by half an inch, not quite a shrug.

'Tonight's special is Tielle, a squid pie. Would you like an aperitif?'

I ask for the wine list. She hands over a thick velvet-bound tome and walks away with a twirl of her black skirt,

'I hate it when they order you around,' says Jen.

'Should I risk choosing the wine?' I ask.

'If you tell me what's bothering you.' Jen can't resist doing a deal.

'Why don't we talk about you instead?'

'Not much to say. Your company is making my life as a buyer a tad difficult but it could be worse.'

'Not my company, the company you and I work for,' I say.

With a perfect sense of timing, the waitress returns to our table.

'Could we have a bottle of Domaine Jones Grenache Gris 2006, please?' I ask. 'Hope you don't mind drinking local, Jen. I don't feel like Champagne tonight and this is a rare and delicious wine made by an English woman in Fitou.'

'Seb isn't bad,' she says. 'but he doesn't really care about The Wine Shop. He is Villa through and through.'

'You know he hates being called Seb.'

'He doesn't want to be called Sebastian either and I can't get my tongue around *Sébastien*.' She mimics a French accent. 'There's no way I'm calling him Monsieur Melot.'

'He's had an easy time in Burgundy and he's doing two jobs at the same time, one of which he dislikes. Marguerite Villa put him in charge of The Wine Shop because he's the only member of her board who speaks good English.'

The waitress brings our wine. The chilled pale liquid tumbles into enormous glasses. Jen and I sigh with anticipation.

'Will you try the Tielle?' I ask.

'No, I'll go for the veal. I feel sorry for Seb. Nobody likes him.'

'We'll have the veal in a morel reduction and the scallops, please. No starters,' I say to the waitress. 'I don't know many people who like their boss.'

'You never know for sure what people you work with think of you.' Her face clouds over.

'Is your job rubbing off on your personality or did you become a buyer because you don't trust anybody? Try the bread, it's delicious.'

She takes a tiny bite. 'The aniseed one is gorgeous.'

I lean over the table. 'Do you know that the skin of fishermen turns scaly after a few years and that wine buyers grow a forked tongue all the better to cheat their hapless suppliers?'

Jen smiles. 'Bloody rep!'

'UK commercial manager, if you please.'

'I'm impressed. What's the politically correct term for dustmen? Sanitation workers?'

'Thanks for the comparison.'

I break into song. '*Do you really want to hurt me?*'

'Don't. I take it back. I'll do anything as long as you don't sing!'

'I'll remember that. Why doesn't anybody ever let me sing?'

'I have no choice but to buy my French wines from Villa,' Jen says.

I pour her another large glass of Domaine Jones.

'How long have you been a buyer?'

'Five years. Sometimes I wish I were still on the shop floor.'

'Is it the job you miss or your twenties?'

'I hadn't thought of it that way.'

'I loved my time as an assistant manager. I'd left France behind and I'd landed a job with the most exciting wine company in the world,' I say.

'I always forget you used to work for The Wine Shop. It was great then.'

We observe a minute of silence.

The waitress deposits large square plates in front of us. Jen's looks like an abstract painting, all splotches of vivid colours.

She inspects her food. 'Where are the morels?'

I lean over to get a better look. 'I can't tell you without a magnifying glass. Try the black squiggle in the middle.'

She dips her finger in the thick sauce and licks it. 'Morels,' she says.

I sniff her plate. 'It smells wonderful for a Kandinsky. Can I try a bit? You were seeing somebody a few months ago, weren't you?'

Jen and I are both single and our love life, or lack thereof, always features in our conversations.

'I hate it when people steal my food.'

'I'm your favourite supplier and you can try my scallops. Look at these plump beauties, hissing their last breath on the hot stone.'

'God, the French and their food! Do you always need to have it slaughtered at the table?'

'Don't worry. I am sure my scallops were killed somewhere in the Atlantic Ocean by kind and considerate Scottish fishermen,' I say.

'I am not Scottish, I am Welsh. What's the obsession with fishermen?'

'No idea. Is the new man a fisherman?' It's good to talk nonsense after today's horrors.

She toys with her napkin 'It didn't last. It was complicated.'

'I'm sorry. Who's the good-looking guy I saw leaving your office last Tuesday then?'

'An Aussie winemaker. He's a supplier. You can have him.'

'Does he come in his own box or will you wrap him up for me?'

'I'm a buyer. I don't do deliveries.'

I've managed to cheer her up. 'Talking of buyers behaving badly, have you heard about…?'

I whisper the name of a well-known industry figure.

'I may have. Could we have more wine?' she asks.

I call the waitress over and ask for the wine list again. She lifts the empty Picpoul bottle half way from the ice bucket and raises her eyebrows.

'It was a lovely wine,' I tell her.

She gives me a tight smile.

'We'll have the Domaine of the Bee, Les Genoux 2004, please.'

'Half-bottle?'

'A bottle. Thank you.'

'Now she's got your goat,' says Jen.

I wave her comment away.

'This is another local wine made by a Brit,' I say. 'A big and rich red from the Roussillon. You'll love it. I saw a Montes Carmenère on the list, 'A Chilean wine in the Languedoc! They'll get a visit from the CRAV soon.'

'No idea what you are talking about.'

'The CRAV, short for Comité Régional d'Action Viticole, are the local protectionist terrorists.'

'Are they the guys who've been blowing up wineries?'

I nod. The waitress brings the wine, opens it and places fresh glasses on the table.

Jen grabs the bottle.

'I was about to pour,' says our minder.

'I want to have a look at the label,' Jen says.

She runs her thumb over the thick creamy paper and puts the bottle down on the table with a thud. 'You may pour now.'

I wait for the waitress to leave. 'You're made for each other.'

'What is it with waitresses in posh restaurants?' asks Jen.

I shrug and take a sip of wine.

'Tell me what these CRAV people are about?' Jen asks.

'A lot of people down here live below the poverty line. They get paid a pittance for their grapes or their wine and when they see us driving rented cars, staying in hotels, eating nice food, they think they're being shafted by the big companies.'

'Are they?'

'I am not involved in buying,' I say.

'It doesn't dispense you from having a social conscience.'

'Some of these people ought to get out of wine altogether but they can't think of anything else to do and their vineyards have been in their families for generations.'

'They wouldn't attack a restaurant, would they?' Jen looks around as if she's expecting masked men to leap from behind the potted plants.

'I don't think so. But they'll end up killing someone by accident.'

'Have they had a go at Villa?'

'I don't think so. Which is odd, now you mention it: it's such an obvious target. Maybe they're scared of André Lange.'

'I've heard of him. He is Marguerite Villa's right-hand man, isn't he?' she asks.

I wince. This is how people used to refer to Papa.

'He sounds formidable. I'd love to meet him.'

'He's nothing special.' I remember our telephone conversation and I shudder. 'Where were we?'

'Indiscretions. Is it this Lange guy who upset you earlier on?'

'Going back to the-buyer-who-shall-remain-nameless…'

'You don't want to talk about it?' asks Jen.

I shake my head.

'He was found starkers and ready for action in a colleague's hotel room during a sales conference.'

I've got her attention.

'You're joking. Who was she?'

'She got rid of him.'

'That's what she says!'

'Where's your sisterly solidarity?'

'No idea what you're talking about.'

I pour her another glass of Domaine of the Bee.

'I've got an even juicier one,' I say. 'You'll love it.'

Jen pats my arm. 'I don't know if it's the food, the wine or my company but you've perked up.'

She's right. I raise my glass in acknowledgement.

'You know Philippe, in my team? He went to the pub with your lot last Friday and bets were placed on who was sleeping with whom at head office. Guess whose name came up?'

Jen pulls a face. 'The Queen's Head regulars are a bunch of wankers,' she says.

'Fine, I'm not telling. Cheese, coffee or both?' I lean back in my chair.

'Go on, you win.'

I'm going to make this one last. 'We're talking about somebody senior.'

'I'll have cheese. Not Seb?'

'Cold, very cold.'

'I've no idea.'

I'm disappointed she's not trying harder. 'The super smug Tim Foster.'

She dismisses my revelation with a wave of the hand. 'Tim? No way. These guys are a damn nuisance.'

The waitress approaches our table. 'Was everything alright?'

'Delicious, thank you. Could we have some cheese please?'

'Would you like a selection or should I get the trolley for you?

'The trolley,' Jen says. 'Tim is single.'

'He may be as he may not be,' I say.

'How do they know? CCTV cameras?'

'Better,' I say. 'Steamy emails. The scrawny guy from IT read out the best bits on Friday. Philippe says the whole pub was in stitches. Didn't say who-'

Jen yells, 'Bastards! They can't do that. I'll get them sacked. Oh my God!'

She covers her mouth with both hands.

'Jen-'

'Don't say anything. Can we go now?'

I wave the cheese trolley and the bemused waitress away, throw my credit card at her and run outside to catch up with Jen. She's crying. There's nothing for it but a hug.

'I'm so sorry. I had no idea.'

'I tried to keep it quiet.' She lifts her hands and lets them drop again in an oddly vulnerable gesture. 'I should've known better.'

6

THE FORMIDABLE ANDRÉ LANGE

Back in the safety of my hotel room, a vicious headache kicks in.: the air conditioning is on full blast again, the note I left for the maid nowhere to be seen.

I pick up my phone, start typing an apology to Jen and stop. Best to wait till tomorrow: in my current state of mind, I'd say the wrong thing again. I'll buy her flowers when I'm back in the office. What if people think they're from Tim though? I can't buy her a bottle of wine; as a buyer, she receives more in a day than she could drink in a month. I'll have to think of something.

The improbability of Tim and Jen strikes me afresh. Tim is head of marketing at The Wine Shop. He's Irish with an almost impenetrable accent, which I assume he cultivates as he's lived far too long in England for it to be genuine. Bright, and brash about it, he has retained the insolence of youth despite being in his mid-thirties. Tall and thin, with an almost feminine grace, an abundance of freckles and a full head of curly pale red hair, he wears the kind of casual clothes that take a lot of effort to look good together. He goes through life as if it were a play, declaiming every comment. Ten or fifteen years ago, when The Wine Shop was a trailblazer in wine retailing, his looks and demeanour would have been spot on. His arrogance now jars with the company's lacklustre performance.

How did Jen get fooled by such a bird of paradise? And how did he overcome her formidable reserve? A magnum of Bollinger Grande Année?

Seeing how he sizes up every woman he comes across, I had him down as a womaniser preying on silly pretty young things. Jen is pretty but she's clever and strong. She's also older than him and a colleague. The excitement of the Queen's Head gang now makes perfect sense. If I'd had an iota of intelligence, I would have guessed what they'd stumbled on.

The men in my life have never had anything to do with work. I would congratulate myself on never mixing business and pleasure but I know this owes more to luck than strong morals: charmers abound in the world of wine and the plentiful supply of alcohol at professional functions encourages flirtation and more.

I had a boyfriend in Bordeaux when I first arrived in England. This stopped me, but only just, from falling for the South African manager of The Wine Shop's branch where I worked at the time. He introduced me to New World wines during so-called training evenings, which often lasted well into the night.

By the time the imbalance between outrageous airfares and minuscule salaries put paid to my long-distance relationship, my mentor had returned to Stellenbosch to become an eternal regret and I'd established enough of a local social circle to meet an Englishman with creative leanings at a dinner party. He broke my heart six months later when he left London to go and run a theatre in Edinburgh.

A long flirtation with an intellectual frozen food supermarket buyer followed and came to nothing. My next relationship, by contrast, almost ended up in marriage as my intended happened to have all his limbs, a job, a driving licence and no artistic interest whatsoever. I got bored though and left after eighteen months, a personal record, to hook up with a destitute writer who lasted only eighteen days.

Toothbrush in hand, my thoughts turn back to The Super-Market. I may have overreacted, but how can André discount ninety-five consumer complaints? I need to convey the seriousness of the situation to him. After a longing look at my bed, I sit at the hotel desk and open my laptop.

Over the next hour I try and explain the situation in an email to

André. I often complement in writing conversations with colleagues and friends to fix what didn't work so well in real life.

I should sleep on this email and have a final read tomorrow morning before sending it but I want André to see it as soon as possible. The click of my mouse echoes in the silence of the night. It's two o'clock in the morning but I've done the best I could for The Super-Market and for Villa.

With my visitors gone, I'd planned to spend the morning sorting out odds and sods with local colleagues before flying back to London. This won't happen now. I force myself to smile all the way to the winery and I turn up the volume of the radio as loud as I dare.

I take advantage of a passing lorry to whizz past the security guard, reducing formalities to a cheery wave of the hand.

I dump my car outside the entrance and rush inside. I pop into the laboratory to gauge the general mood before going to see André Lange.

Jean Jacques' assistant greets me without getting up: no kissing today.

'Happy with the mess you've made?' she says. 'I had the Japs as top of the pain-in-the-arse league table but I'm going to promote the Brits to number one instead.'

She swivels round in her chair and points her finger at me. 'I was supposed to be back in Bordeaux today,' she says. 'I had to cancel all my meetings as André wanted everybody in the quality team in his office at seven this morning. It was awful. I have never seen Jean Jacques so upset.'

I take a step back. 'I am sorry.'

'Who do you think you are, accusing us of not doing our jobs properly? You've only been here what? Two weeks?' Her voice is trembling.

'I'm not accusing anybody and I've been here two months. I'm just doing my job.'

'Fuck your job and fuck you!' She returns to her computer screen.

I take a few steps towards her. She fishes a tissue from her bag and blows her nose. I turn around and retreat.

She yells. 'You're not supposed to know about this morning's meeting by the way, but I thought it would make you happy to have got us off to such a great start.'

In the corridor, I stop and lean against the wall for a minute.

I didn't mean to upset anybody but I'm pleased André has realised the seriousness of the situation. I was right to write that email.

I take the stairs to the second floor two steps at a time. I knock on the closed door at the top. This used to be a meeting room in Papa's days. A loud, 'Come in' invites me in.

The vast Persian rugs, the painted landscapes in golden frames and the matching sofas and armchairs suggest a living room more than an office. A slim laptop sits open on a desk the size of a double bed, next to two pictures. One shows André receiving the *Légion d'Honneur*, France's highest distinction, from the last but one Agriculture Minister, and the other, André's third wife, a statuesque blonde, standing next to a palm tree. She's wearing a tiny sarong and I shiver only to look at her. The ambient smell, a blend of leather, expensive aftershave and wood polish, is that of a gentlemen's club.

André Lange is short and slight, with small hairless manicured hands and slim feet shod in immaculate brogues. He is sitting ramrod straight in a massive ergonomic chair that could have been designed for the villain in a James Bond film.

He waves at me without smiling – he's known never to smile-, points his index finger at a low chair across his desk and turns his attention back to the phone.

His hair colour today is solid mahogany. It's the only thing that detracts from his neat appearance. His resolve not to go grey has not quite extended to securing the services of a decent hairdresser, and his mane is said to change from month to month from dirty brown to almost black and every shade in between. It is the talk of the company, behind his back of course.

'I couldn't agree more,' he says with a flourish of the hand.

My spirits sink. I have heard of this tactic of his: he answers calls or makes them while in the company of a subordinate. The length and nature of the conversation depend on the importance of his vis-à-vis and the message he wants to get across. In extreme cases, he ignores the person seated in front of him. More often, he gestures to him or her to emphasize salient points of the story unravelling on the phone.

A quick debrief takes place afterwards to decipher the call and its hidden message.

'My dear boy, I'd be delighted to help,' he says. 'This is an exceptional situation and we need exceptional people to handle it.' André doesn't do conversations; he delivers addresses like a French politician. I wouldn't be surprised if he broke into the dramatic *Françaises, Français* with which General de Gaulle started his Second World War appeal to arms.

He stares at me with expressionless pale blue eyes. 'I know I can rely on you, Xavier. Loyalty is very important to me.'

I take my phone out of my pocket and start typing a random message I have no intention of sending to anyone. André shifts in his chair and raises his well-modulated voice. 'I'll tell Marguerite Villa. Leave it with me.'

I resist the temptation to look at him. I hear the click of the handset being turned off. I keep my eyes on my phone.

'Have you met Xavier?' he asks. 'He'll go far. He has a perfect understanding of the way companies work.'

I look up. 'I don't think I have.'

'Maybe I should introduce you. He's very good looking, and single. You may be a bit old for him though.'

I let the insult pass.

André swivels around in his chair, picks up a notepad from a drawer behind him and returns to face me. 'What did you want to see me about?' he asks.

I flinch. 'Haven't you read my email?'

'Which one? You send me so many, young lady.'

I grip the seat of my chair, 'The one I sent you last night about The Super-Market.'

He throws himself back in his chair so hard I worry he'll topple over.

'The Super-Market! I told my team this morning how furious I am about this ridiculous affair. We need to get the whole thing back under control.'

He leans over the desk. 'I've had to inform Marguerite Villa. You know how important The Super-Market is to us. Not only were they one of our first customers in England, but what happens there could spill over to other clients.'

No mention of Ed or Marcel Villa, André goes straight to the top. My lips pucker to fight the bile that rises in my throat. I swallow.

'It's a pity you weren't here yesterday to handle the crisis yourself,' I say.

He crosses his hands behind his head.

'Do you like coffee?' he asks.

I frown. 'I'm fine, thank you.'

He rolls his eyes. 'I'm not asking you if you want a coffee. I'm asking if you like coffee.'

'I'll have an espresso after a good meal and the odd latte but I prefer tea,' I say.

'We're the same.' He sounds triumphant.

God forbid, I think.

He leans forwards as if he's about to share a secret with me. 'I drink Nescafe. The real stuff is too strong for me.'

He pauses for a few seconds as if embarrassed by the inadequacy of his taste buds. 'Your pretty young buyer, what's her name now?'

'Rachel?' I volunteer, wondering what her looks have to do with the matter in hand.

'That's the one. She asked us to improve the blend for The Super-Market's red a few months back. Before you joined the company. Did you know that?'

I frown. 'I may have seen something in the file.'

He points at me. 'It was a colossal mistake and I should have stopped her. Those people who buy The Super-Market red didn't like it when the taste changed. Do you know why?

I shake my head.

'Because wine to them is what coffee is to you and me: just another drink they don't want to think about.'

'Are you saying people are complaining because The Super-Market red has become too good for them?' I ask.

He straightens his already straight tie knot and nods. 'It shows a complexity that goes far beyond what can be expected of a generic Vin de Pays. Its aromas are actually not unlike those of a young Syrah.'

'You mean, reduced.'

Reduction is the most common fault in Syrah.

André winces. 'Don't be negative.'

'How come complaints started coming in a few days ago if Rachel changed the blend last spring?'

He raises his hands in a helpless gesture. 'I don't have all the answers.'

'I can't see her taking the blame,' I say.

I'm brave enough to tell him the truth but not to meet his eyes and I deliver my verdict to the blonde in the photo instead. She keeps on smiling. I wait for her husband to explode.

He pauses again.

'I'm telling you what I think happened, but if you think the truth isn't acceptable to your client . . .'

I look at him. I've no idea where this is going.

He concludes. 'It's a commercial decision and as such, it's up to you what you do next. As director of a production centre, I can't assume financial liability for a problem which isn't of our making.' He looks at his watch. 'Now I'm sorry but I have another meeting in two minutes.'

I stand up, swaying a little.

'Make sure you keep me posted,' he says. 'Our customers' satisfaction is my top priority.'

I close the door behind me with exaggerate care. I'm not sure if I should laugh or cry. André has foisted on me the responsibility of the whole problem and I've no doubt this is how he explained it to Marguerite Villa.

I've only taken shallow breaths while in the lion's den. I run down one flight of stairs, stop on the landing, and take a few deep breaths.

I sing all the way to Serge's office to cheer myself up, not too loud though.

Serge is in the middle of a tasting.

'How did it go?' he asks, his nose deep inside a glass of white wine.

I recount my exchange with André.

Serge puts his glass down and shakes his head. 'It doesn't make sense.'

'What do you mean?' I ask.

'I expected him to give you a hard time to start with but I don't understand what he's playing at now.'

'Have you tasted the wine?' I ask.

'You have to be careful. While André maintains his position, nobody here will be allowed to give you any information, or to do anything for you without his say-so.'

I collapse on a chair. 'I'm only trying to do what's right. Surely you understand that. If I explain André's stupid coffee theory to Rachel, we're dead. Does he want me to commit commercial suicide?'

Serge picks his glass up again, takes a sip from it and spits. His eyes dart sideways towards me. 'I'm afraid he probably sees you as expendable.'

I have no time to answer. A short beep alerts me to a text from Rachel:

Meeting The Super-Market House Tues 13.11 @ 10. Please confirm by return. R

Damn! I've forgotten to mention Rachel's invitation to André. I can't return to his office now.

'What is it?' Serge asks.

I shake my head and leave the room. I am not sure I can trust him anymore.

I arrive in the reception area just in time to hear, 'Monsieur Lange will see you now, gentlemen.'

Five men with tanned faces and forearms get up and shuffle towards the stairs to André's office. I assume they're suppliers. I wouldn't spare them a glance except one of them is clutching a bottle of The Super-Market red. It's half empty.

7

BACK TO THE OFFICE

I fall into a comatose sleep the minute I sit on the plane and only wake up when we touch down at Gatwick. I reach Kingston upon Thames at five to three. It's raining.

The Wine Shop's offices, and therefore Villa's British headquarters, are located in an industrial estate, three miles from the centre of Kingston, between a recycling plant and a gypsy encampment.

They consist of a decrepit low-rise building, facing a big yard, which serves as a lorry and car park. The lot is enclosed by a fierce-looking fence, topped with barbed wire. The JCBs operating round-the-clock next door provide a constant rumbling background noise and a pervading cloud of fine dust, which, together with the exhaust fumes from the traffic in the front yard, create a nasty-smelling polluting soup. No tree or blade of grass survives here; the place is so built up I have no idea what colour the soil is.

Dave is lounging outside the main entrance of the building when I arrive. He looks like a bald monkey with oversized sunglasses, which emphasise his hairy stick-out ears. His shapeless tee-shirt hangs over his beer belly. His face is even redder and blotchier than usual.

'Hey Chris! What's up?'

I make sure I stay out of reach of his morning-after breath. 'Not much, you?'

'Big night yesterday.' He mimics downing a glass in one. His hands shake a little.

‘Why doesn’t that surprise me?’

Dave is one of the most active members of the Queen’s Head gang Jen loathes.

‘Work is manic at the moment,’ he says.

I raise my eyebrows. ‘Clearly.’

He lights one of the many cigarettes that give him an excuse for spending most of his time outside the office. Dave fulfils the unofficial but important role of office gossip at The Wine Shop, as his observation post by the front door gives him an unparalleled knowledge of the comings and goings of his colleagues and their visitors.

A commotion makes us turn towards the lorry being unloaded in the yard. Three dishevelled men leap out of the trailer and run at top speed towards the exit of the compound. The guys from the warehouse pause to watch them but make no effort to intercept them. A few seconds later, a fourth man follows, clutching a bloodstained arm. Still, nobody moves.

‘What’s going on?’ I ask Dave.

‘Illegal immigrants,’ he says. ‘They arrive with our shipments of Soave.’

‘This man is injured.’

‘Even more reason for doing nothing: think of the paperwork!’

I stare at him but can’t think of anything to say.

Dave brushes ash from his sleeve. ‘His mates will look after him.’

‘I’m glad you’ve got such faith in human nature,’ I say.

‘It’s not easy to escape detection in Calais, and then in Dover.’ He waves in the direction of the abandoned trailer. ‘These guys are tough. As far as I’m concerned, they’ve earned their freedom.’

I am pondering Dave’s Darwinian approach to immigration when he asks, ‘How long have you been away?’

‘A week.’

He chuckles and turns to return inside. ‘Welcome back,’ he says over his shoulder.

I don’t like his tone.

Mary and Philippe are both on the phone when I walk in. I give them a little wave and collapse in my chair without taking my coat off.

Our office consists of a large square room with wide windows on one side and a much smaller glass panelled room at the back. Four large desks face each other in the middle of the room and the walls are lined with a collection of mismatched cupboards and filing cabinets. A yellowing potted plant is dying in a corner despite or maybe because of Mary's tender care. Even though we never open the windows, the office smells of industrial dust.

Mary and Philippe offer an almost comical contrast. Short, plump and blonde, with kind blue eyes, Mary, my assistant, has the pale complexion of a Northern beauty whereas Philippe, the sales manager, is tall and skinny, with jet black hair, dark brown eyes and the sallow skin tone of a Southerner who's spent too long away from the sun. His hooked bony nose gives his face a raffish look softened by brown tortoiseshell glasses. Both are in their late twenties and have worked for Villa for two years.

My desk is piled high with letters, invoices and trade magazines. Multi-coloured Post-it notes cover the rest of the surface. Four bottles of wine stick out of the mess like tall buildings in a flooded village. Two of them are The Super-Market's red and the third is a Château Camplazens, Marselan I bought from Majestic, meaning to send it to Serge. Marselan is a cross of Cabernet and Grenache and I was wondering if we should add one to our range. I never followed through and now use the bottle as a dummy for mock-ups of potential new labels.

I clear just enough space on the desk to park my laptop,

An English translation for the marketing department in Bordeaux sits on top of one of the piles of paper. Marys has had a stab at it and dotted it with question marks, her way of asking for help. The first sentence of the French text runs to five lines and is so longwinded and tortuous I read it twice without understanding it. It's followed by a few suggested food matches, which may be common fare in the South of France but would belong to the rarefied atmosphere of Michelin starred kitchens this side of the Channel.

'Merde,' I say

'Sorry about the translation.' Mary has come off the phone. 'I meant to do it but I don't understand the French version.'

I scan the document a second time. 'I'll have to rewrite the whole thing.'

'And justify every word change to our lovely colleagues,' says Mary.

I sigh. 'I'll deal with it later.'

Under a bundle of Philippe's expense claims, I find a copy of a six-month-old invoice for IT, totalling nine thousand pounds. "Recharge to Villa UK" is written on each of the three pages. The signature is Matt's, The Wine Shop's head of IT and logistics.

I bang my fist on the desk. 'I knew it!'

Philippe looks up from his computer.

'Do you remember the nine thousand pounds in our accounts that didn't make any sense?' I ask him. 'The financial department has finally deigned to send me a copy of the invoice. Unless you've ordered a couple of laptops and printers and sold them on eBay, it has nothing to do with us.'

'How did it end up in our accounts?' Philippe asks.

'It looks like Matt did a bit of creative accounting. No wonder it took four weeks and several phone calls to get a copy of the invoice.'

'I was wondering why he was being so helpful lately,' Philippe says.

I run my finger over the scrawled signature. *They Do It with Mirrors*, the title of an Agatha Christie, comes unbidden into my mind. Nobody gets killed here but deception and dishonesty pervade every layer of the organisation.

'You don't like him much, do you?' I ask Philippe.

'He's an absolute shit,' he says. 'He does the bare minimum for us and makes sure his team follows suit. We only get anything done because some of them fancy Mary and I go to the pub with them. If it was left to Matt, we'd be using a blackboard and chalk, and smoke signals to communicate with the outside world.'

'I've got to try and keep him on side though,' I say. 'If I upset him, he'll make our life even more of a misery. It's not as if he reported to me.'

'He's a bastard and a thief.'

'How do I call him that without turning him against us?'

Philippe smiles. 'You're the boss.'

My phone rings.

'Chris, welcome back. Sébastien Melot here.'

'Are you spying on me, Sébastien? I only walked in five minutes ago.'

My joke falls flat. 'Could you come over to my office, please? There's someone I want you to meet.'

'Now?'

'It's important.'

The sudden sense of urgency surprises me, coming from the very laid-back Sébastien. He is unlike most of my French colleagues who assert their authority by demanding their requests, however trivial, take absolute priority. It makes for a permanent flurry of last minute meetings and disrupted activities

I scribble "AL" on my hand to remind myself to call André Lange about the meeting with Rachel. Tattooing it on my skin makes me feel like the ordeal is partly over.

'What did I tell you about your new perfume?' Philippe asks Mary. 'Chris took one sniff and she's off.'

'It's not my perfume. It's your expense claims. Did you see her face when she looked at them?'

I raise my hands in mock supplication. 'Stop bickering children. Sébastien wants me on urgent business. Mary, when I come back, can we talk about The Super-Market please?'

'Whenever you're ready,' she says, looking as enthusiastic as if we were discussing a tooth extraction.

I walk back across the car park to The Wine Shop offices, singing Telephone's song about dreaming of another world under my breath,

I wave to Dave, who is busy lighting another cigarette. If not of another world, I had dreamt of a simpler life.

'Notre française! Come in quick and shut the door.'

Sébastien welcomes me with wide open arms across a desk strewn with papers. His looks have deteriorated in the two months I have been with Villa. His long face is marked with deep lines and his skin is dull and grey and speaks of long hours spent indoors. His hair's is now long enough for a small ponytail and his clothes are crumpled. I doubt he bothers unpacking during the four days he spends in Kingston every week. He is slumped so low in his chair, I worry he will slide to the floor.

His office smells stuffy.

A big hairy blond man in his early fifties, with the leathery skin of an explorer, sits opposite him, his elbows resting on his thighs, his legs wide apart. The cauliflower ears say former rugby man. He exudes strength and masculinity and makes Sébastien look even more insubstantial.

He stands up and crushes my hand in his. 'Arnaud Vidal,' he says.

I rack my brain but the name doesn't ring a bell.

'Twenty-five years with Villa.'

He's missed Papa by three years.

Sébastien is playing with a lock of his hair. 'I feel like a greenhorn with my seventeen years of service.'

'Chris Legerot. I joined two months ago.'

Arnaud stares me up and down without a word. His eyes stop on the scribble on my hand and his lips curl in a disapproving grimace.

Sébastien bends forwards from his supine position. 'Chris, Marguerite Villa has appointed Arnaud to take over from me. We wanted you to be the first to meet him but as you've been away…'

'I had no idea you were leaving,' I say. 'I'm sure you'll be missed.'

He winces. 'Marguerite wants me to return to running Villa's winery in Burgundy fulltime. It's been tricky to do both jobs and the team here is very weak.'

He points at the mountain of paper on his desk. 'They're good for nothing. They write emails all day long.'

He turns to Arnaud.

'Emails are a big problem over here. By the time my secretary has printed them, typed my answer and sent it back, we often have to start all over again because two or three more people have butted in. It's a nightmare.'

'I have requested that all emails be sent to me from next week,' says Arnaud. 'The IT guy has promised me I'll have my new laptop by then. You won't need to come back on Monday.'

Seb crumples in his chair. His awkward smile reveals teeth which have been estranged from a toothbrush for a long time. 'That is good, very good. Thank you.'

I force a smile on my face. 'That's brilliant, Sébastien. You never liked living over here much anyway.'

He turns to Arnaud, pointing to me. 'She has lived here for almost twenty years.'

Arnaud stares at him, a puzzled look on his face.

'She hasn't lived in France for twenty years,' Sébastien stresses the 'twenty'. 'She likes it here: the weather, the food, everything.'

'I am moving over here,' says Arnaud.

'You don't want to do that!' says Sébastien. 'There are regular flights to Bordeaux and cheap too.'

Arnaud turns to me. 'We need to talk.'

'I'm at your disposal.' I check my watch. 'I won't be able to stay too long as I've been away but-'

'Not now. My secretary will tell you when.'

Sébastien opens his mouth and closes it again.

I pat him on the shoulder and walk out of the office.

Arnaud and Seb yell at the same time, 'The door!'

I close the door on The Wine Shop's French enclave.

I wish Jen were back. I am curious to know what she'll make of Arnaud. She may welcome a change of regime. She doesn't rate Sébastien. Nobody at The Wine Shop does. He won't be missed.

As per usual music is blaring out of the Marketing office's open door. I decide to pay a visit to Tim. His office is the only one which doesn't smell of dust but of a unique blend of printer ink, incense, and pot.

Large lamps dotted around the place change colours with the beat of the music and colourful posters featuring former promotions hang on the walls.

'Is Tim here?' I ask the girl closest to the door.

She nods and points towards the back window.

'Hello Frenchie,' booms an Irish voice from across the vast room.

Tim skips over to me, phone glued to his ear. He is wearing turquoise velvet trousers and an orange shirt, a sedate outfit for him.

'Stop calling me Frenchie.'

I still can't believe he had a thing with Jen but I notice for the first time he has the most startling green eyes I have ever seen.

He covers the phone's mouthpiece with his hand. 'That's what you are.' He turns his attention back to his phone. 'Busy now. I'll call you later.'

I found Tim insufferable to start with. His posturing and constant jokes drove me mad and I avoided him as much as I could. Then we worked together on a small project and I realised how good he is at what he does. He could achieve even more if his creativity was not systematically scuppered by Sébastien. I wonder sometimes why he stays with The Wine Shop.

'What do you make of the big-game hunter?'

'Is it Arnaud Vidal you call the big-game hunter?'

'Who else, darling?'

Tim uses terms of endearment with gleeful abandon.

'What do you think was his first question to Jim?

'Is Jim the black guy in the post-room?'

Tim nods. 'Where are you from?'

'So?'

'Jim told him he was from Peckham. Arnaud waved his hands in the air as if to say wrong answer and asked him which African tribe he was from?'

'Is he deranged?'

'Jim disappointed him by telling him his family came from Barbados in the fifties and that he was born here.'

'Why should he care about Jim's origins? He didn't ask about mine.'

'Good question, pet. You assumed Arnaud Vidal had spent his twenty-five years of service to the group in Bordeaux, didn't you?'

'I suppose so.'

'If he's ever set foot in Bordeaux, it's been to pay homage to Marguerite Villa.'

'Where has he been, then?'

'Africa, working in Villa's coffee business. From what I've heard, he's lived in Madagascar, the Ivory Coast, Gabon, and Kenya, hence his posting here.'

'You've lost me.'

'Kenya is a former British colony. Arnaud was there for two years and learnt a bit of English. Not good English but I suspect he may have been economical with the truth when Marguerite Villa asked him if he fancied having a go at running The Wine Shop. The old biddy doesn't speak English, does she?'

'I suspect not. I haven't been invited to meet her since I joined Villa.'

Tim doesn't need to know I met Marguerite a couple of times when I was a child.

'You're too low in the pecking order, ma chérie.'

'Since you are so well informed, does Arnaud know anything about wine?'

'He's knows all there is to know about coffee and both wine and coffee are hot.'

'That's a crap joke, even by your standards.'

Tim sits down, puts his feet on his desk and crosses his hands behind his head. 'Look, Sébastien knows about wine and he's a waste of space. At least BGH looks like he wants to try new things. He's already got himself a French-English dictionary!'

'Tim, are you going to keep on calling him BGH?'

'Till I think of something better.'

He makes me laugh. I leave his office, whistling "The lion sleeps tonight".

8

QUESTION MARKS

I rush past Dave but not fast enough.

'Good meeting with your new boss?' he asks.

'Sorry, I need to go back.'

'Of course you do.'

Back in the office, Mary is on the phone again.

'How was it?' Philippe asks.

'Seb is leaving. I've met his successor, a guy called Arnaud Vidal.'

'What is he like?'

'Scary. Dave says he's our new boss.'

'How would he know?'

'He seems to know everything that goes on around here.'

'He makes it up most of the time. Call Ed. He'll know.'

'I haven't told him about the problem with The Super-Market.'

'Maybe it's time you did.'

He's right.

I plug the power lead in my laptop and plunge under the desk in search of the nearest power point. I am on all fours with my backside protruding from under the desk when I hear the door squeak open.

'Hi Matt,' Mary says.

I freeze.

'Chris is back,' she says.

'I can see,' Matt says.

I pull out of my hiding place, force a smile on my face and pat my hair back into place. Matt perches on the desk furthest away from me.

'I didn't hear you knock,' I say.

He waves his hands as if brushing away unnecessary complications. 'I'd hate to interrupt when you are in the middle of something important.'

He starts unfolding a paper clip with great care. With his head tilted sideways, he looks like a bird of prey.

'Matt, it's always a pleasure to see you but is there any particular reason for your visit?'

Matt remains quiet for a while, his eyes trained on the paper clip, as if pondering if my question is worthy of an answer. He then turns his head to look at a distant point through the window. 'You've just returned from France, haven't you?'

'I was in Narbonne though, not in Bordeaux.'

He nods.

'Any news?'

'If getting intelligence on your new boss is the reason for your visit, all I can tell you is that I'd never heard of him until five minutes ago.'

He glances at me for the first time since he walked in and then smiles at various objects around the room, a smile which would be more convincing if it was directed at me.

'What do you think?' he asks.

'I don't know. You?'

He shrugs. 'He ordered a laptop. It's an improvement.'

'Who else has he met?'

'All the heads of department except Jen as she's away.'

I resist the temptation to shout 'Off with their heads!'

'He's taking over on Monday. Maybe we should give it time.'

He sighs and slides from his desk with snakelike grace.

I wait until he reaches the door. 'Matt, before you go,' I say.

He stops and turns around.

'Finance sent me a copy of an invoice you signed, recharging nine thousand pounds to Villa UK. Any explanation?'

He smiles. 'Well done you for spotting it. Your predecessor wasn't as thorough.'

'Is that all you can think of as an excuse?'

He shrugs. 'Seb froze my budget and the guys in sales needed new kit. You can't expect them to work without proper equipment.'

'I'll have to reverse the charge. We may share offices and support systems, but Villa UK and The Wine Shop are run as separate businesses.'

'Are they now?'

He closes the door behind him.

'Don't believe him,' Philippe says. 'He's trying to destabilise you.'

'It's working,' I say.

I turn to Mary. 'Have you heard anything from The Super-Market?'

'Rachel sent an email first thing this morning. You're copied in. They're going to destroy the stock they've got in store.'

'Ouch!' I say.

'She's asking if we want the stock in the depots destroyed as well or shipped back to France. If the latter, we need to hurry up as she wants everything sorted before December. Once Christmas gets under way, the warehouse staff won't have time to process returns.'

'Do we know how much stock is in store and how much in depot?'

'She's going to find out.'

I pick up my calculator. 'If they destroy the equivalent of a week's sales, that's fifteen thousand bottles and fifty thousand pounds at full retail price. And there's no way we can check they only trash the faulty stock.'

'Is there any chance they'd agree to charge us at cost price?' asks Mary.

'Rachel won't forego her margin and it would be impossible to reclaim the duty on a store per store basis. Yet at £1.33 a bottle, it accounts for over a third of the cost.'

I put both hands over my mouth.

'Are you alright?' asks Mary.

'Fifty thousand pounds,' I say. 'It's a huge sum and André will make sure it sticks to my name even though it's nothing to do with me.'

'Would you like a cup of tea?' Mary offers TLC the British way.

'That would be great, thank you.'

She stands up but stays rooted on the spot as if she's debating the wisdom of adding something else.

'In her email, Rachel alludes to a meeting in Leeds. Is it something you've discussed with her? I couldn't see it in your diary.'

'I was unaware of it until yesterday. To make things worse, she wants me to take André Lange. I forgot to tell him about it this morning or maybe I chickened out, I'm not sure.'

'You should tell him.'

I show her my hand with the letters "AL" branded on it. 'I won't forget. Just let me look at my emails first.'

I scan my overflowing inbox. An email from my friend Sam cheers me up a bit. She asks when I'm back in the country and if I'm free on Saturday evening for a glass of wine. Then my eye is caught by Marcel Villa's name in the sender's list. Even though he's copied in a phenomenal amount of correspondence, I've never received an email from him in two months. I click on.

Ladies and Gentlemen, bearing in mind our duty of care and the importance of appearances in the current competitive business environment we operate in, I have resolved to appoint a new team to ensure the highest standards are maintained at our head office in Bordeaux, and also in our production centres of Narbonne and Beaune.

I take a breath and dive back in. That was a long sentence.

Jules CHAPARD, a long serving member of staff here in Bordeaux, has therefore been nominated, with immediate effect, to supervise all cleaning rotas. I trust this will boost morale and help us to achieve our results. With my very best wishes, Marcel VILLA.

. . .

I have another read. Should maintenance be the direct responsibility of the company's heir apparent? And why does he write family names in capitals like in old fashioned French school registers?

A few lines below, I find an email from Ed. He's forwarded Marcel's message to the export team within two minutes of receiving it and he's copied Marcel in.

Ladies and Gentlemen, I'd like to draw your attention to Marcel VILLA's recent email, which I'm forwarding to you. Maintenance matters are often overlooked in large organisations and I'm delighted with Marcel VILLA's personal involvement in the matter. I hope that, each in your own capacity, you'll do your very best to help with this new initiative. I'll send a message of congratulations to Monsieur CHAPARD on behalf of the export team and assure him of our support in his future mission. Onwards and upwards, Ed.

PS: Don't forget to update your monthly forecasts by Monday at the latest. There will be a prize draw with six bottles of wine to be won at the next export meeting but only for those who've submitted on time.

I feel vaguely nauseous.

I take a deep breath and press the speed dial for André's mobile. After three rings, I get his answering machine.

'Monsieur Lange, this is Chris Legerot again. I'm afraid there's been a new development with The Super-Market. Rachel has invited us to visit her and her boss in Leeds in two weeks' time. I'm sorry it's such short notice. Could you please call me back?'

I put the phone down as soon as I've finished my sentence as if there was a risk André would come on the line mid-message. I sit back and stretch, luxuriating in my lucky escape when my mobile vibrates.

My heartbeat speeds up and I hunch forward, tensing up.

'Chris Legerot.'

'Arnaud Vidal asked me to confirm your meeting with him next Monday at eight thirty in his office.'

'Monday?'

'He said it should take two hours.'

I repeat. 'Two hours.'

I put the phone down. 'I've been summoned.'

Mary and Philippe nod in unison, keeping their eyes on their screens.

I open a new email from Ed. It's the latest company organisation chart, marked confidential.

It is huge and impossible to read without the magnifying function of my computer. I look straight at the top, which only shows two boxes sitting on top of each other: the upper one names Marguerite Villa as Chairman of the group, as can be expected. The one below is blank. Surely that is where Marcel's name should be.

'Mary, do you have Villa's previous organisation chart? Not the one we received today.'

'Didn't you get it when you joined?'

I shake my head.

'Don't send it to me. Just tell me who is second in command to Marguerite, please.'

Mary squints at her screen.

'I'm not sure. There is a box under hers but without a name.'

I search for Marcel Villa in the rest of the chart and find him on the next level down, together with eight others. His box is the only one without a title. Still no mention of Arnaud. Does that mean he is the mystery man at the very top?

André Lange shows twice, on the same level as Marcel, once as export director (China) yet not reporting to Ed, and once as "director" with no other qualifier but an impressive number of direct reports. This confirms what I understand of his importance within the company.

While I am at it, I look at the rest but even though I double and then triple check the export markets listed I can't find any mention of the States or Canada. I make a mental note to ask Ed if both countries are considered by Villa as former French colonies, the one explanation I can think of.

The chart also shows Ed reporting to both Marcel and André, something I was not aware of. I start mulling over these anomalies when I notice an even bigger one: Villa doesn't have a human resources department. I inspect the document again, unable to believe a company employing thousands of people can do without but I have to accept the evidence of my own eyes.

I shiver.

Philippe stands up.

'Somebody walked over your grave? I am off to M&S. Do you need anything?'

I compose myself. 'Could you get me a Mediterranean salad, a small seeded roll and some oranges, please? While you're there, would you mind grabbing a bottle of milk? And maybe a lasagne for tonight?'

Mary chips in. 'Could you get me a sandwich as well, please? And an apple. A yellow one, not a red one.'

Philippe sits down and picks up a pad and a pen.

'Start again. If both of you want me to do your weekly shop, I'll have to write it down.'

'Do you mind? It means I can wait till tomorrow to do a proper shop,' I say.

'As long as you pay me back.'

'I owe you £3 from last week, I've not forgotten.'

'He won't let you forget,' says Mary. 'I swear he has some Scottish blood.'

Philippe wags his finger at her. 'You may not get any lunch today if you badmouth me.'

I smile at his retreating back and at Mary.

I call Ed to give him an update on The Super-Market and to tell him about my meeting with Seb and Arnaud.

'Have you seen a ghost?' asks Mary after I put the phone down.

'I'm confused. Ed knows nothing of Arnaud Vidal's appointment. He says his name means nothing to him.'

'If he comes from the coffee business, it's not that surprising, is it?' Mary always has an excuse for everything and everybody.

I swivel round in my chair to face her. 'I'm not saying he should know the man but I was expecting him to have heard of his posting here.'

She shrugs. 'Talking of The Wine Shop, will you go to the Edinburgh wine fair?'

'When is it?'

'Last weekend in November, in time for punters to stock up for Christmas.'

'Do I need to go?'

'It's hard work but the party on the Saturday evening makes up for it.'

'What about you?'

'I'd prefer not to go if it's OK. I've got something else planned that weekend. You could go with Philippe.'

'Does everybody from The Wine Shop go?'

She blushes. 'Most people. Sébastien never went.'

I wonder if everybody includes Tim. He must be fun to party with. All of a sudden I'm looking forward to the end of November.

9

DRIP, DRIP, DRIP, STRESS

Arnaud jabs his index finger at me. 'I will fulfil the mission Madame Villa has given me.'

I've been in his office since eight thirty and I'm starting to fidget.

'I won't share my success with anybody,' he says.

I am tempted to ask, 'Which success?' but think better of it. I need to get out of here. Mondays are busy days. God only knows what my inbox will look like when I finally get around to looking at it.

'Is Madame Villa pleased with your work so far?' he asks.

I flinch. 'I have not spoken to her since I joined Villa. I report to the European export director, Ed de Waast, who reports to Marcel Villa.'

I am not keen to share my childhood memories of Marguerite Villa with Arnaud.

Arnaud slaps his desk hard and burst out laughing. 'You'll get nowhere in the group if you haven't got access to Madame Villa.' He pauses. 'Why does André Lange dislike you?'

'Do you know each other?' I ask.

'He called me on Friday to congratulate me. I mentioned your name and he said I should be wary of you.'

He looks me up and down as if searching for evidence of the threat I could represent for somebody like André Lange.

I shrug. 'Monsieur Lange has been working for Villa a long time. I am a newcomer.'

Arnaud leans back in his chair, stroking his chin. 'Your name rings a bell though.'

I open my mouth and close it again. I don't trust Arnaud enough to tell him my father used to be his boss' lieutenant.

'I may be able to help you,' he says.

I remain silent.

He shrugs. 'Go now, I need to do some work.'

I knock at Jen's open door.

'Have you been in the lion's den all this time?' she asks.

'How do you know?'

'Dave,' she says.

'I thought you hated him.'

'Doesn't mean I don't talk to him.' She winks at me. 'Especially when I have been away for a week and he owes me big time.'

'Well, what's the gossip according to Dave then?

'Is Arnaud your new boss?'

I shake my head. 'He spent the last two hours trying to cow me into submission. He wouldn't have bothered if he were.'

'You don't like him, do you?'

'Look, I don't want to put you off him. He means well, and he'll be more effective than Seb.'

'I'm due to see him this morning.'

'I'll leave you to it then. Lovely tan by the way!'

I make it to the door and turn around. 'Are you going to the Edinburgh tasting?'

'We have too many suppliers attending for me not to go. Why do you ask?'

'No particular reason. Mary tells me it is a good party.'

'Not one I am looking forward to this year,' she says.

I escape back to my office.

'Good afternoon,' says Philippe when I walk in.

'Very funny,' I say. 'I've been stuck in Arnaud's office since I arrived.'

'Dave tells me you left twenty minutes ago.'

'Not you as well,' I say.

I pick up the phone. 'Serge?'

A gargle answers me.

'Are you in the middle of a tasting?'

'Give me five. I'll call you back from my office.'

I turn to Mary. 'Could you please send samples of The Super-Market's red to Corkwise please?'

'Corkwise?'

Mary repeats the last word of my sentences when she doesn't know what I'm talking about.

'The independent lab. Look them up in Harpers' directory.'

The phone rings.

'I wasn't on my own,' says Serge.

'Have you seen André since Friday?'

'He's not budging if this is what you're hoping for. Something strange is going on though.'

'I'm all ears.'

'Remember the guys you saw in reception and you asked me about? You were right: they're directors of the co-operative, which supplies the bulk wine for The Super-Market's red to us. I bumped into one of them this weekend.'

'The joys of living in the countryside…'

'Listen to me. He told me André is blaming the co-op for the quality issue.'

'A quality issue he's yet to acknowledge.'

'That's what doesn't make sense. How can he blame a third party for a problem whose existence he denies?'

'Could it be because he is a lying bastard?'

'He's not. I've worked with him for ten years.'

'And?'

'Look, I'm doing my best to help you. But André must have his reasons. You have to be patient.'

I put the phone down wishing I could inspire such loyalty.

. . .

It rings again within a minute.

'Why don't we deal with Sainsbury's?'

'Good morning Arnaud,' I say.

'We saw each other less than an hour ago. Answer my question.'

'I wish I knew.'

'Have you met Justin King?'

I pick up a blue pen and start doodling on the invoice on top of my to-do pile. 'I did, fifteen years ago, when he was at Asda.'

'The Director of the Banque Populaire tells me he's the boss at Sainsbury's.'

I give a hat and a big umbrella to the character I've drawn. 'I doubt he'd take my call if I tried to contact him. I talk to the BWS team.'

'BWS?'

'Beer, Wines and Spirits.' Big clouds are now taking shape on the page in front of me. I change pen to colour them black.

'In Africa, you go to the top.' Arnaud's voice is peevish.

'Here it's more a question of how much you want to spend. The higher you go in the hierarchy, the more it costs you.'

He put the phone down without so much of a thank you or a goodbye.

The rest of the week and the next one pass in a blur.

André still refuses to admit The Super-Market's red is faulty. As I can't accept liability on behalf of the company without his agreement, I remain evasive with Rachel who's becoming increasingly frustrated with me.

Corkwise confirms my assessment of the wine but Serge pleads with me to keep the information to myself for the time being.

Ed tries to help, demanding answers from André and, I quote, "a more proactive attitude, worthy of a collaborative frame of mind". André sends him packing. Marcel Villa, when informed, refuses to get involved, saying his mother is on the case.

Arnaud uses me as an unpaid directory enquiries service as well as a sounding board for his ideas. He calls me up to ten times a day, always on loudspeaker, never introducing himself and dispensing with courtesies such as 'how are you?' or even 'good morning'. He then puts the phone down on me without saying goodbye.

I sometimes try and second guess when he's coming to the end of a conversation to beat him to it. It doesn't always work.

If my landline is busy, he tries my mobile and vice versa. If he can't get through on either, he calls Mary. I overhear him once while on another call.

'Where is she?'

'Hello. Good morning. Is this Mr Vidal?' Mary asked.

'Is she in?'

'I am afraid Chris is in a meeting.'

'Tell her to call me when she's done.'

She's terrified of him as is half of The Wine Shop's staff. He's had the whole team in his office one by one, starting every single interview with the same question.

'What do you do?'

One well-brought-up employee misunderstood him and answered, 'How do you do?'

He paused and pointed at her.

'I ask questions. You answer. What do you do? Your job?'

Jen asks me if Arnaud is only rude in English or also in French. I confirm his manners are poor in both languages.

Yet he's more popular than Seb. He engages with his team albeit in a blunt way and his ambition to turn The Wine Shop's fortunes around echoes with the wishes of everybody in Kingston.

It puts me in an awkward situation. I'd like to share in some of my colleagues' new-found optimism that they have, at last, found the leader who will return the company to its former glory, but I doubt Arnaud's crude tactics will be enough to regain the interest of British wine drinkers. They have moved on and it would take a huge outlay of well-funded marketing genius to entice them back to The Wine Shop, where they started on their road of vinous discovery, back in the eighties.

It's even worse when I talk to other people in the trade as I must toe the company line and pretend all is well at The Wine Shop. It reminds me of the 1935 song "All is very well, Madam the Marchioness", my great aunt used to sing. The marchioness of the title calls her servants during her holiday, to be told all is well except for the death of her grey mare. She then learns it died in the blaze which destroyed her stables. The fire had spread from the main building where it was started by the Marquis who shot himself after finding out he'd lost his entire fortune. The chorus, stating all is well, is repeated between each revelation. The song was written to deride the attitude of most French people towards Germany in the mid 1930's.

Arnaud is no Hitler but I wish I could find it easier to delude myself it will end well for all concerned. Despite the amount of time I devote to answering his questions and foiling his creative outbursts, I am not privy to his rescue plan and sometimes wonder if he has one.

I spend the weekend trying to avoid children intent on ransoming me in the name of Halloween and drive to Gatwick airport on a grey Monday afternoon to pick up André and Jean Jacques for our meeting with Rachel the following morning.

'Do we have far to go? André asks, making himself comfortable in the front seat of my car. His pungent eau de toilette and his coffee induced halitosis force me to breathe through my mouth.

'About four hours, depending on the traffic,' I say.

'Can you turn that off,' he says, pointing at the car radio. 'I can't understand a word.'

'It's BBC4.'

'They speak too fast.'

He makes a pillow of his raincoat and falls asleep. My mobile rings while I'm negotiating the M25 traffic.

'How much does a moped cost?' Arnaud has had a new idea.

I am in the process of admitting my ignorance when the phone goes dead. Twenty minutes later, it rings again. André is still asleep.

'How many corner shops in the UK?'

'Fifty thousand?' I say, keeping an eye on the Mercedes overtaking on my right.

'In London?'

'No idea. Maybe twenty thousand. Why?'

'If they each sell a bottle of wine a day, that's seven million bottles a year.'

'Assuming they're all licensed.'

'What's a licence?'

I explain you need a licence to sell alcohol in the UK.

He grunts 'Are you sure?'

When I refuse to dignify his question with an answer he hangs up. We make it to Leicester before he calls back.

'You're right.'

'Thanks.' I smile at the rear-view mirror.

'Most of them are licensed. They sell a lot of wine. The one, down the road from where I live, tells me he shifts two cases on a Friday evening.'

'Arnaud, you live in South Ken. That's not representative of the UK.'

André is awake. He taps me on the arm, pointing at a lorry in front of us and signalling I should overtake.

'The shops around the office do well too,' Arnaud says.

'Why the sudden interest in corner shops?'

'We should sell them Villa wines.'

'We do through Booker and Bestway.'

'Never heard of them.'

'They're cash and carries. They sell to corner shops.'

'Not seven million bottles. I say we get half a dozen guys on mopeds to call on all corner shops, pay them on commission and if it fails, you get rid of them after six months.'

I grip the steering wheel with both hands. 'Why me?'

'I can't hire them at The Wine Shop, I'd have a riot on my hands. You do it. Where are you now?'

'On my way to see a client.'

'Come and see me when you're back and we'll sort out the details.'

The line goes dead. I grab a pen and scribble "7M btles" on my left hand while trying to keep the car on the road.

Jean Jacques is still snoring in the back seat.

'Who was that?' André asks.

'The Wine Shop's new boss, Arnaud Vidal.'

'The African? Talented guy, isn't he?'

I look at André. He is staring ahead, his face as inscrutable as ever.

'I didn't know you two had met,' I say.

He chuckles. 'You don't know everything.'

He is lying.

'Arnaud is creative,' I say.

'Will he succeed?'

I shrug. 'He only arrived two weeks ago.'

It is the first time André asks for my opinion. I glance at him sideways. There's a deep frown between his eyebrows and he is tapping his lower lip with his index finger.

'Madame Villa likes people who deliver results,' he says. 'I do.'

'I haven't met her yet,' I say.

He pauses and looks at me. 'Yes, you have, Christine.'

I keep my eyes on the road and grip the steering wheel tight. My mother is the only one who calls me Christine now. Even my brother uses Chris.

'You knew my father, then?'

'He hired me.'

A thousand questions swirl through my brain.

'Your father was devoted to Madame Villa and utterly loyal to the company'

I nod. I feel like crying and now isn't the time.

'I saw his obituary in Sud-Ouest. You joined Villa very soon afterwards, didn't you?'

'Does Madame Villa know who I am?' I ask.

He chuckles. 'Madame Villa knows everything. But she's passed on some of the day-to-day responsibilities of the business to her son and she found out too late you'd been hired. Marcel never knew your father.'

'What do you mean, too late?' I ask.

'Are we there yet?' Jean Jacques asks.

The smell of his rancid sweat wafts over me.

André grips my arm and whispers in my ear. 'There's nothing to be gained from stirring up the past.'

He turns around. 'You snored,' he says to Jean Jacques. 'Give me your phone. My battery is dead.'

He stays on the phone for the rest of the journey.

Dinner is torture. I'm desperate to continue my conversation with André but Jean Jacques proves impossible to shake off. All attempts to agree a strategy for tomorrow's meeting with Rachel also fall on deaf ears.

My choice of white wine, a Villa Maria Private Bin Sauvignon Blanc, fails to please my companions. What I call exotic and herbaceous, Jean Jacques describes as the stink of overcooked asparagus. André says that if this is the best Kiwis can do, Sancerre has nothing to fear. The two of them snigger in complacent agreement. Despite having no loyalty to New Zealand, I feel like screaming. I've heard so many similar comments from stick-in-the-mud French people about Australian wines in the days before Jacob's Creek, Penfolds, Wolf Blass, Hardy et al proved them wrong.

Both men send their meat back for being overcooked and complain about their vegetables not being cooked enough. They make loud disparaging comments about the décor, the cutlery and the other guests. I spend the entire meal apologising to the waitress.

Breakfast is worse. I'd hoped to enjoy my cereals in peace by going downstairs as early as possible, but I'd forgotten my colleagues are still on French time. We sit together like prisoners on a virtual chain gang. André spends most of his time barking loud instructions in French into his mobile to the annoyance of people around us. I catch a few British sighs and raised eyebrows but nobody's bold enough to ask him to stop.

Jean Jacques is mute. He eats little, chewing every morsel of food for ages and swallowing as if his throat is on fire. I try not to look at him as his anxiety is so palpable as to be contagious. My resentment towards him is turning into pity.

We're walking towards the entrance to The Super-Market's offices when my mobile rings. It's Ed. 'Chris, where are you?'

'Good morning Ed. We're about to go and see Rachel and her boss.'

'Who's "we"?' he asks in a high-pitched voice.

'Monsieur Lange, Jean Jacques and myself,' I say, turning towards my colleagues.

'Don't you think I should be there? I only found out about your meeting this morning when I called the London office.'

'I'm sorry Ed, I thought you'd discussed it with Monsieur Lange.'

'As if!' he says. 'We'll talk about this when you're next in Bordeaux.'

I am next in Bordeaux for my probation appraisal, which coincides with an export meeting at the end of November. The last thing I need is for another item to be added to the list of my shortcomings.

'Was that your young boss?' asks André. 'He sounded upset.'

He looks very pleased with himself.

'Didn't you tell me you'd discuss today's meeting with him?'

'Did I? You know what, I may have forgotten.'

He saunters towards the revolving doors, dragging Jean Jacques behind him. He pauses as we pile in and turns towards me. 'Don't worry, he'll get over it.'

10

IN THE LION(ESS) DEN

Rachel greets us with a smile as we come out of the lift, enquiring after André and Jean Jacques's flight and pecking me on the cheek. A French supermarket buyer, in similar circumstances, would be much sterner. André's face breaks into a smirk and his shoulders drop. French people often misread British politeness for weakness and confuse good manners with hypocrisy. I bet he thinks he's amongst friends and 'young Rachel', as he calls her, will give us an easy ride. My heart sinks.

We follow Rachel through a maze of open plan offices. She's wearing the same grey check trousers as the last few times we met. I wonder idly if she owns another pair. She explains that because none of the goldfish bowl-like rooms dedicated to suppliers' meetings is available, her boss will meet us, and the director of logistics, in his office. She makes it sound like an honour. I see it as ominous.

Around us, dozens of conversations, whirring computers and the purr of the air conditioning blend into an indistinct hum. The smell of coffee dominates, signalling the beginning of a new working day. Curious faces follow our progress as we walk through various buying departments, easy to identify by the samples occupying every available space. One plump lady is surrounded by chocolate bars in all sizes and colours. I want her job, any job but mine. I wish I could sneak into one of these cubicles and hide there for the rest of the day.

Two tall young men with open faces, bad haircuts and worse suits stand up when we reach our destination. They belong to that unique Northern British type, which combines good looks, if you like your men tall and rugged, with a complete lack of style: a disastrous waste from a French perspective.

The office is spartan with little touches that hint at the seniority of its occupier. The computer screen on the desk is larger than those we passed on the way, the chairs are wider and somehow more inviting and the desk, table and cupboards more Habitat than Ikea.

Rachel and I introduce our respective colleagues and we exchange business cards except for Jean Jacques who hasn't brought any. André beams at his young counterparts.

'Bonjour James,' he says to Rachel's boss. He pumps his hand with manly enthusiasm, sits down and crosses his hands behind his head. I hope Rachel and her colleagues don't know about body language, or don't care. This posture signals self-confidence and a sense of superiority.

Jean Jacques nods in the direction of our hosts, shuffles aside towards a chair and grab the back of it as if he were about to collapse. We position ourselves around the table, Brits on one side and French on the other. Rachel offers us a choice of tea or coffee and disappears to get our orders from the nearest vending machine.

We settle in with steaming Styrofoam cups in front of us.

'The number of customer complaints on The Super-Market's red now stands at three hundred and two,' says Rachel first in English and then in French. 'I have asked for this meeting to establish the cause of the problem.' She doesn't say she's been trying to find out for more than two weeks, but the hint is unmistakeable.

She follows the checklist in front of her with her finger. Her nails are bitten to the quick. 'I also want to run over what you have put in place to get rid of the faulty wine and replace it with fresh supplies,' she continues. She points to the logistics director. 'You have to ensure our logistics team is aware of what you're doing for the whole process to run smoothly.'

'I'd like to know what you're planning to change to ensure the problem doesn't happen again,' says James. Rachel translates for Jean Jacques and André's benefit and waits for our answer.

André sits up tall, placing both hands on the table in front of him.

I cringe, fearing he may stand up to deliver one of his speeches. Thank God, he stays in his seat.

'I, first of all, want to thank you for your warm welcome,' he says and waits for Rachel to translate. He's using his official voice, well-modulated and stretching the endings of every word for several seconds. I look down at the tips of my boots. Unaware of my embarrassment, he continues. 'I know how busy you are, and I am grateful you should be making time today to see representatives from a small wine supplier.'

'Villa is everything but a small wine supplier. You rank amongst The Super-Market's largest and you're the top one when it comes to French wine,' Rachel says. 'Our time is indeed precious, but this is a priority.' She raises her voice a fraction at the end of the sentence and leans over the table, her fingertips gripping the edge. What I hear is, 'Stop wasting our time. Own up and show us the colour of your money.'

I fold my hands in my lap, praying André gets the message. On my right, Jean Jacques is sweating in silence, dark circles forming under his armpits. I glance at James. He's twirling his pen but he looks more bored than angry. André sits back in his chair and lifts his hands in surrender. The politician's gone. He's now the kind and wise older man who's seen it all and genuinely wants to help.

'You're all much younger than me, despite your many achievements, and I have a lot more experience than you.' He bows in the direction of Rachel's colleagues. 'Wine is my passion, my life, but it's a difficult product to assess. Even experts sometimes disagree. What one taster praises, another one dislikes.' He smiles and pats me on the arm. 'Last night, Chris chose a Sauvignon Blanc to accompany our dinner, which left Jean Jacques-'

'We're not discussing *grands crus* here or what you had for dinner,' Rachel interrupts. 'Our Red Vin de Pays is an entry level product, drunk by people who know little about wine and care even less. They want something clean and fruity. The consignments we're rejecting are everything but and we want to know why.'

I am holding my breath, hoping André will not ask Rachel which type of coffee she prefers.

'Rachel, you're right.' He pauses for effect. 'I used the same words as you when discussing your wine with Jean Jacques the other day. You see, Jean Jacques is an artist, a purist. Good is not enough for him, he strives for perfection. And sometimes, he goes too far.'

The artist's face has turned the colour of a mature Burgundy. He looked up when he heard his name and he now stares at André with the pained expression of a dog who's been kicked by his adored master. André reaches across me to give his hand a little squeeze.

'Jean Jacques wanted you and your customers to have the best possible wine at the price. He's used unstable components, which should be reserved for finer wines. He meant well.' He looks at us, one by one and I am amazed to see the glint of a tear in his eye.

James throws his pen on the table and clicks his tongue in an irritated way. 'Sorry, I am no wine expert. Are you telling me the red you have sold us went wrong because you tried to make it too good?'

'It shows a reduced character, which is typical of some of the finer Syrah-based wines of our region,' André says.

Rachel pounces, 'You admit it's reduced.'

'There was never any question of it. I told Chris right from the beginning, reduction was bound to be the problem. Of course, we had to perform a series of analyses before we could be sure.'

I am glad my chair is wide and sturdy. I may have fallen off otherwise.

Rachel looks pointedly at her boss and turns to me. 'Did you send me anything in writing?'

'Chris hasn't had the time,' says André, raising a hand as if granting me absolution. 'She's had a busy time with the change of management at The Wine Shop.'

'I would have expected our issue to take priority over internal matters,' says Rachel. 'Can I now assume you'll email me as soon as you're back in the office?' Her tone is icy and her stare unfriendly. Her mass of curly hair seems to have grown bigger around her tired face.

I open my mouth and close it again without uttering a word. It's pointless to try and defend myself. I am more concerned André has now put me in a position where I'll have to accept liability on behalf of the company without having had anything in writing from him to cover my back.

'Now we're clear as to the cause of the problem, where have we got to with stock replacement?' Rachel says to an approving glance from James.

'We brought two orders forward when you alerted us to a possible quality issue,' I say, trying to sound professional. 'We've been able to replace the defective stock straight away and we only lost sales when the faulty bottles were taken off the shelves and disposed of. From your own tracking system, it looks like the disruption lasted no more than a few days. Do you know how much was destroyed in the end?'

'It will take several weeks to collate the information. A few stragglers always hold up the system. We'll invoice you as soon as we get final figures.'

André fails to react. I wait a little. He's either not understood Rachel or he's not keen to re-enter the fray.

I take the plunge. 'Rachel, any chance you could invoice us at the landed cost plus distribution?' This would save us the excise duty and VAT plus the twenty five percent margin The Super-Market takes on entry level wine.

'Goods are valued at their full retail price in our internal system once they reach the stores. If I do what you're asking for, it will show a loss at store level.'

André is nodding like a rear window shelf toy dog as if he can't believe how unrealistic my request is and as if he didn't care how much the whole problem will cost Villa.

'Where have you got to with picking up the rest of the faulty stock from the depots?' asks the logistics director.

'It's all in hand. We have appointed a haulier who already works for you to ensure minimum disruption. We were given the exact volume per regional depot last week and I expect the collection to happen this week or the next depending on their schedule.'

I fail to mention I am waiting for André to authorise the advance payment to the haulier. Nothing will happen until he does.

'The earlier, the better,' says Rachel. 'We're getting close to Christmas and our staff is getting busy.'

'I see no reason why there should be any delay. Do you Mr Lange?' I ask, thinking of the payment authorisation which has been waiting for his signature for a week.

'I trust you with the details of the operation,' he says, very much the debonair manager.

The logistics director turns towards Rachel and her boss. 'It looks like we're all sorted. If you don't mind, I have another meeting to go to.'

The other two nod their agreement. After gathering an armful of paper and his empty cup, he shakes hands with us and leaves the room.

James looks at his notes. 'Quality problems happen even in the best run organisations. What I need to know is what you have put in place to ensure we don't have a repeat incident in a few months' time.'

I turn to André.

'Our bottling site in Narbonne operates under stringent procedures,' he says. 'I can assure you such an incident is the exception rather than the norm.' He wipes a fleck of dust from his jacket lapel with a satisfied smile.

Rachel is becoming agitated again, but James remains unflustered. He speaks again, slowly, as if he were addressing a child.

'I have every confidence in the professionalism of your people and the excellence of your organisation. But a problem has happened, which will have a detrimental impact on the trust consumers have in The Super-Market's own label products. It will also have financial implications for your company. How will you make sure it doesn't happen again?'

André is on the spot. He squirms in his chair as if it has become too hot for comfort.

'We taste the wines at reception, after the last filtration before bottling and after bottling. Since reduction is an evolutionary process, we'll add a final tasting before shipping.' A tasting is less reliable but cheaper than a full set of analysis.

Rachel asks, 'How can you be sure to pick up an aromatic deviation? When I first reported the problem to Chris, she told me you could not come to a definite conclusion based on tasting alone, and that she needed further analysis.'

Another rope to hang me with has just landed on the table with a slap. Yet I feel a surge of schadenfreude. I want to shout, 'Go girl!' to Rachel.

André turns to Jean Jacques, the fall guy du jour.

'We keep our library samples at low temperatures. When Jean Jacques tasted the wine you complained about, it was too cold for him to pick it up the reductive character. We'll bring the wines to room temperature before tasting them.'

Rachel looks unconvinced.

'Are you telling me temperature impacts on the perception of reduction? I'm not convinced.' She turns to her boss. 'Are you happy with this or should we ask for additional analysis?'

His eyes have been trained for a few minutes on the screen of his Blackberry. He's drumming his fingers on the table. Something must have cropped up, which takes precedence over us. He puts his phone down and looks at us as if he'd never seen us before.

'It will be fine,' he says, sounding unsure of what he's agreeing to. Rachel looks aghast but there's nothing she can do. The deal is sealed. James and André look pleased with the outcome of the meeting. They shake each other's hands and ours with gusto. Rachel turns to me and I give her a tiny shrug. We have both been betrayed.

Jean Jacques looks like a man who's had a double dose of enema but hasn't been told where to find the loo. I feel sorry for him.

'Are you alright?' I ask him when André trots off to go and wash his hands,

'I'm fine. It's cold in here.' He wraps his arms around himself.

'I'm sorry Monsieur Lange blamed the whole thing on you. It's unfair.'

He stares at me.

'I'd do anything for Monsieur Lange,' he says.

I stare back, wondering if there's a psychological condition, maybe related to the Stockholm syndrome, where victims of bullying end up worshiping their abuser.

I turn on my mobile: I have eight missed calls, seven of them from Arnaud.

11

A HELLISH CAR JOURNEY AND CREATIVE WINE MARKETING

It's raining hard when we leave The Super-Market, which allows André to comment on the British weather and the folly of anybody who chooses to live here. I ignore the dig and suggest we get on to the motorway and stop at the first services for a debriefing.

'Will I be able to buy a decent coffee?' he asks. 'The foul beverage your Rachel made me drink has given me stomach cramps.'

I refrain from telling him the coffee dispensed by the vending machine in Narbonne isn't any better.

As soon as we're in the car, he turns to Jean Jacques.

'Have you ever seen anything like the woman in the lift? What can she have been eating to get to such an enormous size?'

'She may be ill,' I say.

'Imagine being married to that!'

Jean Jacques sniggers in the back.

André continues, 'Did you notice the shoes Rachel was wearing? Walking boots! In the office! English women are so masculine. No wonder all English men are gay.'

Since they arrived, we have covered the weather, food and drink, British women's fashion and British men's sexual orientation. André hasn't left any cliché untouched.

I left my mobile in my pocket and it rings as we pull into Woolley Edge Services. I pick up while trying to keep the car on the road. André tuts but keeps his hands in his pockets.

'Arnaud, can I call you back in five minutes? I am about to stop at a petrol station.'

'Did you get my message?'

I drop the phone on my lap milliseconds before I pass the police patrol car posted at the entrance of the car park.

'Arnaud Vidal again?' asks André. 'He must like you a lot.'

I glare at him.

'I must phone him back. Do you mind waiting for me inside?'

Once they're gone, I lower the window to get some fresh air. The smell of exhausts and cold rain on tarmac provides a welcome alternative to André's eau de toilette and Jean Jacques's body odour. I stretch as much as I can, pressing the palms of my hands against the soft ceiling of the car and call my voicemail.

Arnaud's voice, 'We need new wines. What The Wine Shop buys from Villa won't sell in corner shops.'

'Hi Chris, Mary here. Hope The Super-Market went well. Sorry to bother you but Arnaud seems keen to talk to you. I have told him you're away but he's called twice already.'

Arnaud again, 'I am thinking a Pinot Grigio, a Sancerre, a Rosé, maybe a Bordeaux. Call me back.'

The fourth message consists of an indistinct jumble of sounds. I assume he's pressed the redial button by mistake.

'Where the hell are you?' asks the fifth one and after a beep 'Can we do a sparkling Pinot Grigio rosé from Bordeaux?'

Another beep. 'Where are they from, these corner shop people, which countries? We must hire salesmen from the same origin.'

And finally, 'HR tells me we can't specify ethnic origin on job adverts. Is it true?'

A mixture of dread and irritation fills my mind as I dial his number.

'Why doesn't Villa do a Pinot Grigio?' he asks the moment he picks up.

I drum my fingers on the steering wheel. 'It's an Italian variety, mostly grown in Italy, Eastern Europe and some New World countries. Villa only sells French wine.'

'Can you find French growers who'd be willing to give it a try? It sells huge volumes.'

'There's some in Alsace but it's called Pinot Gris and it isn't cheap.'

'What about Sancerre?'

I wonder for an instant if he is proposing to plant Pinot Grigio in Sancerre but realise he's moved on.

'Sancerre comes from the Loire. Villa has wineries in Burgundy, Bordeaux and the Languedoc. It would be difficult for us to source good quality Sancerre in significant quantities. We don't have the contacts.'

'Why are you always so negative?'

I close my eyes. 'You're asking for the impossible. I am trying to explain to you how things work. What do you need these wines for, anyway?'

'I told you, to sell to corner shops. We need strong names.'

'Surely you must have a Pinot Grigio and a Sancerre in your range.' I say.

'I want to source these wines from Villa, brand them The Wine Shop and sell them everywhere in the UK. We could hit ten million bottles in a matter of months.'

I pause to absorb the enormity of his plan.

'This is not what The Wine Shop is about,' I say eventually.

'I don't care,' Arnaud says. 'Whatever The Wine Shop is about isn't working. Our stores are full of wines nobody's heard of and nobody's buying.'

I am still digesting his news. 'What do you mean by everywhere?'

'Tesco, Sainsbury's, pubs up and down the country and our own shops of course.'

'How will you convince Tesco to sell The Wine Shop wines?'

'They sell pizzas from Pizza Express and coffee from Starbucks.'

I get out of the car and pace the narrow walkway between the lines of parked cars. I yell over the noise of the motorway traffic, 'It's completely different!'

A passer-by gives me a sympathetic smile.

'Marguerite Villa has asked me to turn this business around and I'll do it with or without you. Goodbye.' Arnaud's tone is icy.

I return to the car to compose myself before joining André and Jean Jacques. Sourcing wines from new areas is fine and there's enough Pinot Grigio around for Villa to buy at a good price. We haven't got a hope in hell of buying decent Sancerre in bulk though. It's a small appellation, despite its big name, with few growers willing to sell cheap.

The idea of a big range of own label wines scares me. This is what supermarkets do, not specialist wine merchants. The quality would have to be out of this world and the prices dead keen to make an impact. They're not going to be either, not with the margins Arnaud needs to keep the business afloat. And why would Tesco or Sainsbury's want to sell The Wine Shop branded wines? Presenting such a mad project to them would be a waste of time and jeopardise my professional credibility.

But what if I'm wrong? What if I have been so long in this business I have lost all ability to think outside the box?

Papa would know. Even at the end of his career, he retained a great enthusiasm for new ideas. He'd be able to help me stand back from the constant whirlwind that is Arnaud and assess his ideas with the objectivity which eludes me at the moment.

I rest my forehead on the steering wheel. Who else can I turn to? Jen? She'd go straight to Arnaud, asking what he's playing at. Tim? Are my reasons for wanting to involve him entirely business-like? I have found myself thinking about him more than I should these last few days.

I step out of the car again to try and find André and Jean Jacques inside the building. The latter's sitting on his own, his hands between his thighs, at a table inside Costa Coffee. He's looking at two cups of coffee, which look more like salad bowls to me, with a disconsolate frown on his face.

'Did you need that much perking up?' I ask.

Monsieur Lange was unsure about sizes, so he went for large. He's gone to get some more cash.'

I allow myself a little chuckle until I realise André will blame my absence in his hour of need for his overspend. I order a cup of Early Grey and sit down. Ten minutes later, André hasn't come back. Thanks to Jean Jacques' unnerving capacity to stay silent in company, it feels like half an hour.

'Where do you think he's gone?' I ask.

Jean Jacques pulls the corners of his mouth down and shrugs without a word.

I take a sip of my tea and stand up. 'I'll go find him. Text me if he comes back.'

A queue has formed at the cash point but there's no sign of André. I pop into WH Smith but he's not there either. He can't have gone to the loo again. I am beginning to worry something's happened to him when I spot a Marks and Spencer Simply Food. I walk in on a hunch even though I can't think of a reason why he'd need to go shopping now.

André has collared one of the shop assistants. As soon as he spots me, he gestures for me to come over.

'I'm asking this man where I can find the wine department but he doesn't seem to understand me.'

'We're on the motorway,' I say.

The shop assistant looks from André to me and back as if he were watching a tennis match.

'You can buy alcohol in shops and in restaurants on French motorways,' André says.

'It doesn't mean it's a good idea. I don't like seeing somebody having a drink and getting behind the wheel straight afterwards.'

André looks at me as if I'd given off a nasty smell. 'You're so foreign,' he says.

He leaves the shop without so much as a thank you or a goodbye to the bemused shop assistant.

I back out, saying, 'Sorry, sorry, I am so sorry.'

André's right, no self-respecting French woman would apologise in threes.

'What did Arnaud Vidal want?' he asks me as we return to Jean Jacques.

'He has a new project. I'm not sure about it.'

He frowns. 'Marguerite Villa rates him.'

'I am doing my best to help.'

I cross my fingers behind my back.

'He's been handed the opportunity of a lifetime with The Wine Shop. Even though coffee has brought her wealth, Madame Villa's true love has always been wine. She's never transferred anybody from one business to the other before,' André says.

'What if he fails?' I ask.

‘He’ll be sent back to a smaller African country than the one he came from.’

‘If he succeeds?’

‘I don’t know.’ André sounds glum.

‘What will happen when Madame Villa retires?’ I ask.

He shakes his head. ‘She won’t.’

‘I thought she was in her seventies.’

‘She’s in robust health and Villa is her life,’ he says.

‘Still, it’s an age when anything could happen. My father was only a few years older than Madame Villa.’

I avoid looking at him but he ignores my hint.

‘Marcel will take over.’

‘Does he want to?’

André checks his reflection in a shop window. ‘Loyal and experienced people would help him.’

I wonder how Marcel feels about the prospect of moving from his mother’s tutelage to André’s.

We sit down next to Jean Jacques, who looks relieved to see us. I wonder what he would have done if we’d gone without him. He probably would have stayed huddled in his chair until asked to leave at closing time.

‘Monsieur Lange, I’d like to talk about our meeting with The Super-Market,’ I say.

André smiles at Jean Jacques who sniggers back. ‘Do we have to?’

I ignore the aside. ‘I want to ensure you’re happy with what we agreed with Rachel.’

He winks at Jean Jacques.

‘What did we agree, Chris?’

‘We agreed that the two consignments she complained about were reduced.’ I sound petulant even to my own ears.

‘Did I say that?’ he asks Jean Jacques, stroking his chin.

‘Monsieur Lange, you did,’ I say.

He points his index finger at me. ‘I told her I thought straight away, reduction was the problem. I didn’t say it was my final conclusion.’

My throat tightens. 'But this is what Rachel expects me to confirm in writing!'

He shrugs. 'It's your responsibility.'

I pause, too overwhelmed for words.

André continues 'As for the haulier invoice you want me to pay in advance, I'd rather wait until we know how much they're going to charge for the wine they're refusing to return. Also, it's not the company's policy to pay suppliers in advance.' He leans back as if he were sunning himself, an unlikely prospect indoors, in a cafe on the M1 in November.

I grip the table. 'They're not refusing to return it. They're unable to!'

'When there's a will, there's a way. Why can't their delivery vans return a few cases to depot?' he asks.

'They'd have to pack the bottles in leftover cases, which would take a long time. The vans, as you call them, return to depot empty and there's a strong likelihood breakage would occur in transport. Also, The Super-Market's IT system is not designed to allow returns.'

André mumbles, 'When in doubt, blame technology. I do it all the time.'

I feel like I am reeling in a strong combative fish. 'The transfer I have asked you to sign is for the return of the stock, which is in depot. Since we don't deal with transporters in this country, nobody will agree to help us unless they're paid in advance.'

'Let me think about it when I am back in the office.' He stands up. 'We'd better make a move now. I don't want to risk missing our plane.'

I drain my tea, which has long gone cold, and follow them back to my car, walking as slowly as I can.

André shouts at me, his hand on the car door, 'Hurry up! We're getting wet.'

I sigh and unlock the car. I am not looking forward to another four hours of enforced intimacy with André and Jean Jacques. I like my car free of litter and sweet smelling and it now smells of them. I climb in reluctantly. I wish I could leave them behind and drive away, all windows open, until the last olfactory trace of their presence has gone.

André fiddles with the air conditioning control, without asking for permission, and settles for the ride. While he's not paying attention, I turn the car radio on again and switch to my Ipod. A French ballad may restore some harmony between us.

Gregoire's song about saving the world is poetic if a touch naive. A snort from André makes me glance at him. He looks angry. He can't hate pop music that much. I look away.

'Is this what you want to do, Chris?' he asks. 'Save the world?'

'Isn't it a worthwhile ambition?'

'You should know better.' The bitterness in his voice is unmistakeable. I glance at him again but he's turned his head towards the window. Jean Jacques has fallen asleep in the back and is snoring again, with his mouth open. The song continues without any further challenges from André.

I am tempted to go straight home after depositing my cargo at Gatwick but decide against it. I have too much to do in the office.

Matt is taking measurements of the car park as I drive in.

'What are you doing?' I ask.

'Jack's orders,' he replies.

Everybody at The Wine Shop now calls Arnaud, Jack. It started with Tim calling him the big game hunter, BGH for short. Dave, who apes everything Tim does, misheard him and BGH became BFG. There's only one tiny step from one Roald Dahl story too another and The Big Friendly Giant turned into Jack and the Beanstalk and then Jack, a name with a short, sharp sound, which suits Arnaud much better than the urbane moniker he was christened with. I struggle not to call him Jack to his face.

'He's asked you to measure the car park?' I ask.

'He wants to hang an advertising banner for The Wine Shop's wines on the fence which separates us from the cash and carry next door.'

'Does he think people who've driven all the way here will see the sign, do a U-turn and go and buy wine from The Wine Shop?'

'He wants to build a prefab next to the fence to sell wine here.'

'Don't tell me: he's seen it done in Africa.'

'How did you guess?'

I leave him to his new task. Our relationship has improved since we sorted out the small matter of the £9,000 he'd wrongly recharged to Villa. He's been helpful and pleasant since.

Mary jumps up from her chair when I walk in the office.

She exclaims, 'Hi, hi, Chris!' as if my arrival was the highlight of her day. She trots to the filing cabinet behind her, opens it, closes it without taking anything out and returns to her seat.

'Ants in your pants?' I ask.

She doesn't answer.

'Mary, are you alright?' I insist.

'What about you? Did you have a good time?' she asks the photo of her baby niece that sits on her desk.

'I went to see Rachel with André Lange and his partner in crime. In which parallel universe could this constitute a good time?'

She blushes and her eyes mist over. 'Sorry, I wasn't thinking.'

'What's wrong with you?'

Without looking up from his computer screen, Philippe says, 'Marguerite Villa's assistant called ten minutes ago. The old bird wants to see you as soon as possible. Mary had a bit of a job explaining you couldn't go to Bordeaux this week but that you'd be there for the export meeting next week anyway.'

Mary looks at me like it's the last time. 'You're seeing her next Wednesday at five thirty. I didn't have to change your flights.'

12

CREATIVITY UNLEASHED

I slump in my chair and push aside the papers that have accumulated on my desk. Mary has unpacked a wine sample for me and bits of polystyrene cling to the side of the bottle. I pick them off one by one and drop them in the bin until a pointed look from Philippe makes me stop. I open my laptop. Mary keeps on glancing in my direction as if she is expecting me to burst into tears any minute.

I want to meet Marguerite Villa and talk to her about Papa, but now she's asked to see me, I'm scared. Ed, my useless boss, told me he's only met her once and it felt more like a social call than a business meeting. She refused to look at the presentation he'd spent hours preparing, protesting she didn't want to encroach on Marcel's responsibilities. I need to tell Ed about the meeting. He may know what it's about.

Arnaud has sent me a rare email. His pathological liking for secrecy means he normally avoids putting anything in writing. I open it.

He explains that, while visiting one of Villa's wineries, he's come across a new wine concept which could work for Valentine's Day. He asks me to call him to discuss pricing and volume. I click on the attached image.

The phone rings.

'What do you think?'

'Good afternoon, Arnaud. I have only just sat down. Give me half an hour and I'll come and see you.'

The line goes dead, which, I assume, means yes.

A ping announces the arrival of a new text on my mobile.

Hey Froggy, how did it go up North?

It's Tim. I am pleased he cares.

I text back, *The meeting with The Super-Market was the easy bit.*

I wait a little but my phone remains silent. I sigh and let my eyes drift back to the computer screen.

'Merde!'

The picture of a bottle of Saint Amour, a Beaujolais Cru, fills my screen. The flimsy label features a plump Cupid on a bright red background. A Durex branded wrapper is affixed to the neck of the bottle. Arnaud's new concept consists of a bottle of wine with a condom attached to it.

'What's the matter?' Philippe asks.

A man's opinion is exactly what I need.

'Come over here, please. There's something I'd like to show you. Mary, you too.'

'Holy Mother of God!' Mary says.

'Fuck me,' Philippe says. 'Who sent you that?'

I turn around. 'What do you think?'

'If it's a joke, it's in pretty bad taste; if it's a come on, I'd run a mile.'

'It's gross,' Mary says.

'It's the latest bright idea from one of our French colleagues.'

Mary's hand flies to her mouth. She still believes anybody who's more senior than her in the company knows best.

Philippe goes back to his seat with a disgusted look on his face.

I dial Ed's number. I need to compose myself before I report back to Arnaud.

'How did it go with The Super-Market?' he asks. 'You could have called earlier.'

'You're the first person I have called since coming back.' This is technically true: texting doesn't count and Arnaud called me before I had time to think about what I should do next.

I give Ed a detailed account of this morning's meeting, pointing out the awkward situation André has put me in. Ed tries to provide me with solutions, which I reject one by one. We revisit a number of options I have thought of and discarded. It validates my thought process but it also takes half an hour without really helping. If Villa were a harem, Ed would make the perfect chief eunuch: he tries hard but he lacks the necessary equipment to perform.

'Ed, there's something else. I've been invited to meet Marguerite Villa next week, before the export meeting.'

'You, what?'

I repeat, slowly.

'Do you know why?' he asks.

'I was hoping you would.'

'If she wants to see us, she must have her reasons. You can't expect me to betray her confidence. In my position-'

'Us?' I ask.

'Well, I'm sure Madame Villa means to involve me. I'm your boss. I was busy earlier on. Her assistant is bound to have tried me while I was on a call. I'll check my missed calls.'

I put the phone down.

'Does he know anything?' Philippe asks.

'Does he ever?'

'I remember when Marcel Villa announced his appointment. It was the 1st of April. Everybody thought it was an April's fool.'

'You never told me.'

Philippe shrugs. 'His predecessor wasn't much better but at least he knew about wine. Ed only knows about shampoos and conditioners.'

'What was his previous role? All I know is that he used to work for L'Oréal.'

'He was something in marketing.'

'I thought he'd worked in sales before.'

Philippe shakes his head. 'Do you remember the football game?'

I smile.

Ed had organised for a few of us to go and see a big football match in Stade de France in Paris, days after I joined the company. Thanks to the randomness of corporate packages, we were sitting two rows in front of Asda's French wine buyer. I greeted him but kept my distance as he was with a competitor. Ed spent half of the match in a yoga twist, yelling back comments at the poor man. I never took such an interest in the beautiful game as I did that day. To add insult to injury, Ed berated me, as we were leaving the stadium, for failing to exploit such an excellent commercial opportunity. Philippe mimics him to perfection.

Cheered up by the reminiscence, I grab my notepad and announce my intention to go and see Arnaud before something else crops up.

Dave is at his post, fag in hand. 'You didn't bring back the big French cheese, then.'

'He asked me to send his regards. How on earth do you know André Lange was over here?'

He winks. 'I know everything.'

I take the stairs two at a time, and knock on Arnaud's door.

'Come in!'

He pushes a thick book in a drawer as I walk in. It looks very much like a dictionary.

'If you need any help with translations, please ask,' I say.

He pulls up his sleeves slowly and deliberately as if he is about to punch me. His arms are covered in thick blond hairs that curl over his watch. 'You took your time.'

I shrug.

He points at my notebook.

'Why did you bring a pad? You're not a bloody secretary, are you?'

'I take notes whenever I attend a meeting. How do you expect me to remember otherwise?'

'I don't like people who write everything down.'

'I am afraid that's the way I work. Brain of an alcoholic,' I say.

Grumbling something I don't catch, he plants his elbows on the desk and joins the tips of his fingers together.

'How many bottles can we sell?' he asks.

'Of the St Amour?'

He clicks his tongue as if my question were stupid.

'I am afraid-'

'What is it this time? I thought the Brits were famous for their sense of humour.'

I mumble, 'It's not funny.'

'Speak louder, I can't hear you.'

I take a deep breath and look him in the eyes. 'It's not funny. Alcohol and sex, it's tacky.'

He shakes his head. 'I've never worked with somebody as negative as you. I was warned but still...'

'What do you mean?' I ask.

He closes his eyes and waves his hands.

'I don't have time for gossip. I've prepared a presentation on our new range for your customers. Let me show you.'

He frowns and presses a few keys on his laptop, the tip of his tongue poking between his teeth. If I was not perturbed by his earlier comment I'd be tempted to burst out laughing. The contrast between his thick fingers and the dainty keyboard is comical. Rumour has it that Matt, having been shouted at a few times in the early days of Arnaud's tenure, took special care, when selecting the requested top of the range machine, to find one with the smallest possible keyboard.

The PowerPoint runs to forty-five slides, not a good start. The title page is basic and to the point. In black characters on a white background, it says "The Wine Shop's solution for..." I assume the prospect's name is to be added.

The next slide proclaims "The Wine Shop offers choice of the range".

'Somebody walked over your grave?' Arnaud asks without looking at me.

I shake my head.

A few slides further, a line in bold makes me wince again, "You know food, we know wine."

'Who is this targeted at?' I ask.

'Isn't it obvious? Tesco, Sainsbury's, The Super-Market, all that lot.'

I try to imagine Rachel's reaction to this particular slide but the image gets so vivid, I shudder and close my eyes to dispel it.

A few slides on, a new title catches my eye, "Fridges."

I frown and point at the screen.

Arnaud sighs and rolls his eyes skywards, 'In Africa, I launched a successful programme whereas we would supply coffee machines for free in exchange for an exclusive supply agreement. I want to do the same here: supply customers with fridges and fill them with our wines.'

When I open my mouth to intone the familiar 'We're not in Africa,' he throws in his killer argument, 'don't tell me it can't be done in England: Coca Cola does it. I have seen some of their fridges in corner shops and even in your precious Tesco.'

He throws himself back in his chair, hands behind his head.

I remain silent, trying to sort out my objections in some sort of priority order – "we're not Coca Cola," being a strong contender for number one – when he asks, 'When do you think you could make the first appointment?'

I could point out he has no authority over me and that there's no way I'll go and present some half-baked megalomaniac scheme to my customers. The problem if I go down that route is that he'll retaliate in kind and make every single one of my dealings with The Wine Shop as difficult as possible. Also, there's a fair risk he'll go ahead with his crazy project with or without me. By remaining involved, I can try and limit the damages he causes to both The Wine Shop and Villa. It's a classic case of keeping your friends close and your enemies closer.

The obvious flaw in his scheme hits me.

'What about the wine?' I ask.

'What about it?'

'The new range you want to sell; what is it?'

'I told you on the phone, big names, Sancerre, Chateauneuf du Pape, White Zinfandel, Pinot Grigio. Wines people recognise and are comfortable to buy in any environment.'

'These wines don't exist at the moment, do they?'

He dismisses me with a flutter of his hand. 'They soon will. I have told my marketing guy, you know, the artist, to talk to you about labels and all that stuff.'

'Why do you call Tim the artist?'

'The way he dresses, the way he walks; I'm sure he's gay.'

I open my mouth and close it again. There's little to be gained by challenging Arnaud's vision of the world.

'Arnaud, we can't present products that are yet to be created.'

'Why not? It's the concept that matters!'

'British wine buyers are swamped with offers of new products. They'll never commit to listing something they can't taste first.'

'Send them something to taste then.'

'Do you mean something random?'

'Of course not, something good! You're even thicker than usual today. Is it André Lange?'

'How do you know?'

'The guy at the door, Dave.'

If I were not so exhausted I'd burst out laughing.

Arnaud leans forwards and slows down his delivery, 'We want to get listings. I'm sure we have got some decent Sancerre on our shelves. Ask Jen, or if you must, try a few and send the one you think is best.'

'I can't do that, Arnaud. It would be unethical.'

He frowns, pulling down the corners of his mouth. 'I don't see how. It's business.'

'Not as it's practised here.'

'If this offends your principles, just get a move on and make sure my new range is ready as soon as possible. How long do you need? Two weeks? Four?' The finger wagging starts again. 'I tell you what; I insist on it being ready for Christmas. I have looked at last year's figures and that's when we sell the largest volumes.'

It's my turn to speak very slowly now. 'Arnaud, this is impossible. We're in November. A new range takes months, not weeks to develop. Also, wine happens to be made once a year, not when it suits.'

'You and the artist deal with it. I have left Jen out of the loop, by the way. She's turning into a royal pain in the arse. If we involve her, she'll try to persuade us to buy from her usual sources rather than from Villa.'

'She's paid to source the best wines for The Wine Shop. You can't blame her for doing her job.'

'I'm not blaming her but I'm not involving her. Don't go blabbing.'

'I don't blab. I simply can't understand how you can launch a major new range behind your buyer's back.'

I have let my anger show and Arnaud reacts, his sausage index finger pointing at me. 'I'm the one making the decision here and I don't care if you don't like or understand them. Jen has no company loyalty.'

'That's not fair. She's ultra-loyal to The Wine Shop.'

'Precisely! Villa's paying her wages even if it says The Wine Shop on the payslip.' He put his hand on the phone. 'Have you got all you need?'

I stand up. 'Will you send me your presentation? No rush but it needs tidying up.'

'I don't want you to change everything.'

'The English needs improving.'

He shakes his head. 'That's not a priority. Get started on the range.'

I leave Arnaud's office, closing the door with exaggerate care behind me. I rub my temples with the tips of my fingers to try and sort out the jumble of thoughts in my brain. As I turn around, I bump into Tim who's standing in the middle of the corridor, arms folded across his chest.

He smiles and says, 'Try banging your head against the wall, it doesn't solve anything but the pain is different. Have you got a moment?'

I nod and follow him to his office. 'Were you waiting for me?'

'Yes. I tried to call you but Mary told me you'd gone to see his nibs. She asked me to mount a rescue operation if you hadn't come out by six o'clock.'

'I'm ever so grateful.'

'She had to leave early tonight. I can't let you return to your office and spend time on your own with young Philippe at such a late hour. I have no choice but to entice you to my den.'

Jen's image comes into my mind uninvited. 'Are you a safer option than Philippe?'

He turns around. I only just manage to avoid colliding into him again. I am staring at the hollow at the base of his neck. A vein is pulsating there under his skin.

'What do you think?' he asks.

I am too flustered to think of a suitable repartee. The ring of my mobile saves the day.

'Hi Serge'

Tim throws his arms in the air, 'Here's the French lover!'

Serge continues, blissfully oblivious to his new nickname. 'I hear you've had the royal summons.'

'How do you know?'

'André told me.'

'How does he know?'

'Marguerite Villa told him. He speaks to her every day, sometimes several times a day.'

'Did he say why she wants to see me?'

'That's why I am calling. She wants to talk about The Super-Market's red.'

13

MARGUERITE VILLA

Philippe and I leave Kingston together. No point in taking two cars when airport car parks charge such extravagant rates. Between the two and a half days in Bordeaux for my meeting with Marguerite Villa, followed by the export meeting, and The Wine Shop's wine fair in Edinburgh, we'll be away for five days. The fair gives me the perfect excuse not to visit Maman in Arcachon. If I lose my job, it'll be easier to tell her on the phone.

I drive and talk, trying hard to sound cheerful. I turn up the volume of the radio and sing along to James Morrison's "Wonderful World".

Philippe groans.

I ignore him.

He turns the volume right down.

'I've told you already. Singing isn't what you do best and this song isn't going to lift your spirits.'

'I'm absolutely fine.'

'Then you're a much worse driver than I thought. It's the second light you jump and you almost ran over an old lady in Surbiton. I'm not letting you drive when we arrive in France.'

Arnaud calls. 'Where are the labels for my new range?'

'Have you spoken to Tim?'

'He's out of the office.'

I swerve to avoid a cyclist. 'I thought he was in today.'

'The girl in his office tells me he's gone to the bank.'

'He'll be back soon then. Why don't you try him in half an hour?'

There's something pathological about Arnaud's inability to wait for anything. He wastes a phenomenal amount of his time and everybody else's chasing up people. If the person he calls doesn't answer the phone, he tries somebody else, even though they may not be in a position to help.

The flight is uneventful except for the elderly gentleman sitting next to me, who farts silently but at regular intervals throughout the journey. Since I checked myself in the window seat, I can't even ask the air hostess to move me to a more salubrious seat. He'd hear me. The plane is full anyway. Philippe sits a few rows back, earphones plugged in, oblivious to my plight.

He remembers his pledge though. When we land in Bordeaux under a low cloudy sky, he refuses to let me add my name to the rental car contract. For a split second, I wonder if he's been told he'll have to take me back to the airport earlier than planned.

The beautiful tanned young woman who welcomed me at the Avis counter back in July has been replaced by a dour, thin-lipped older version. Her face, crisscrossed by hundreds of fine lines, is a warning against sun exposure.

The car park smells of exhaust fumes and wet everything. The pine trees have gone to sleep for the winter. Since I'm banned from driving, I fiddle with the car radio. Once I have located Cherie FM, I sit back to enjoy the music. Michel Jonasz's "Y'a Rien Qui Dure Toujours"[1] is followed in quick succession by Serge Gainsbourg's "Je Suis Venu Te Dire Que Je M'en Vais"[2] and Alain Souchon's "L'horrible Bye-Bye"[3].

Philippe gives an exasperated sigh and asks, 'Can you try to find something a bit less gloomy?'

'You can't blame me for Cherie FM programming,' I say.

I try to find a jollier soundtrack to our journey. I cut short Simon and Garfunkel's "Sound of Silence", assuming it won't gain Philippe's approval and settle on RFM. After a brief noisy interlude courtesy of The Ting Things' "Shut Up and Let Me Go", Travis' "Why Does It Always Rain On Me?" heralds a return to doom and gloom.

Philippe reaches across and turns the music off.

My mobile vibrates.

'I can't find him.'

'Arnaud, I'm in Bordeaux and I'm not Tim's minder. His trip to the bank may be taking longer than planned.'

'He came back but he's vanished again.'

I turn my phone off. If I get the sack, Arnaud will have to find somebody else to badger anyway.

Villa's head office has had a good clean since my previous visit. If this is the work of the new maintenance manager, his efficiency verges on the superhuman. The classic eighteenth-century facade, which rises three floors above the Quai des Chartrons, has been returned to its original pale golden colour. We drive through the entrance gate and I point at a parking space in front of the main building.

'Are you serious?' Philippe asks.

'This is where I parked last time I was here.'

'Nobody parks here but Marguerite, the members of her board and André Lange.'

Something else I got wrong without even knowing about it.

'How are you supposed to know?' I ask.

He shrugs. 'You find out, one way or the other.'

Despite our musical differences, he offers to accompany me to my meeting with Marguerite but I turn him down. If I'm about to get the sack, there's no point in compromising him by association.

I try to do some work but I can't sit still. I embark on a tour of the building, calling on my Bordeaux colleagues, searching their faces for clues about my fate. Rumours circulate fast. If I am for the chop, somebody here will have prepared my exit paperwork and he or she is bound to have told someone else in confidence. The classified nature of the information will have ensured its rapid spread.

Ed didn't phone me back after our last conversation and hasn't returned my calls. He sent me a short email the day before yesterday, saying he and Marcel Villa would be out of the office today. He didn't explain why and I see it as a bad omen.

I run out of people to distract and make my way to the small lobby outside Marguerite Villa's office at quarter past five. I choose the more stable of two old-fashioned revolving leather armchairs, resisting the temptation to scratch at the frayed armrests or to spin around like a bored child. The carpet at my feet is threadbare in places, worn out by the feet of many other anxious visitors before me.

Serge could not shed much light on what I should expect from my meeting with our chairwoman. He's convinced André has either engineered or sanctioned it, which doesn't bode well. He reckons however Marguerite Villa would not take it upon herself to fire somebody her son appointed.

I almost told Serge about my family connection with Villa, as I think it explains why Marguerite would want to wield the axe herself. Something held me back though. I have not discussed my father with anybody within the company, apart from André. He seems to be the only one who knew Papa, except for Marguerite Villa.

Arnaud views my impending summit with equanimity. Desperate for any kind of information, I paid him a visit yesterday, hoping he may have heard something. He had not but failed to understand my anxiety. When I tried to explain a meeting with Marguerite Villa could only herald disaster for me, he shrugged, saying he'd met her often and had never found her as difficult as reported outside the company. He said she could be cutting, but only with good reasons. I tried to explain The Super-Market's red saga to him but realised I'd lost him after five minutes.

My phone pings. 'Be strong Frenchie, you're our last hope.' Tim seems to think I can help The Wine Shop's cause and his, by ingratiating myself to our chairwoman. He sees my meeting as an opportunity to get straight to the top and pass on crucial messages about what's needed at The Wine Shop.

I am flattered by the faith he has in me but his lack of concern for my unhappiness disappoints me. I've stopped counting the texts, emails and messages he's bombarded me with, about measures he recommends to save The Wine Shop from sinking into retail ignominy and financial disaster. It's got to the point where he forgets to flirt with me.

The office door opens suddenly, making me topple sideways.

'Did I scare you?' asks a deep gravelly voice.

I jump onto my feet.

She's tiny. I'd forgotten or maybe I didn't see it when I was a child. She's thin rather than skinny, with strong muscular legs. Her face retains the remnants of an earthy, sensuous beauty: her full lips, wide nose and searching dark brown eyes with thick eyebrows exude an intelligence and a lust for life, which make her look younger than her seventy years. Her thick white hair is cut in a flattering loose bob. She's dressed conservatively in a dark grey knee length skirt, a white blouse and a black cashmere cardigan.

She grabs my hand with both hers. 'God, you're tall.'

Her skin is dry and papery but her grasp is firm. I take a deep breath and my eyes close for a split second. She wears Chanel 5, my great aunt's signature smell. I feel like a child again.

'I ought to change perfume,' she says. 'Chanel 5 has become common, now they advertise it on television. But I have worn it for so long, I'd feel naked without it.'

She walks to her desk. With her back turned to me, she adds, 'You'll have to hide your emotions better if you want to survive in business. Is it your mother who wears my perfume?'

I decide my long deceased great aunt may be too ancient for Madame Villa's taste and acquiesce.

She frowns. 'That's odd.'

She gestures at the chair facing her desk. 'Sit down. I wanted Marcel to join us but he's disappeared. You can take a horse to water but you can't make it drink.'

She looks wistful for a few seconds, picks up a pair of elegant tortoiseshell glasses on her desk and puts them on.

'How long have you been working for us?'

'It will be three months at the end of November.'

'You have created quite a stir in a short time.' Her direct gaze rests on me over the glasses.

I look up, unsure of what I should say.

She sits back, her hands crossed on her lap. 'Do you know what my biggest professional challenge has been?'

I shake my head.

'People. To find and retain the best. Take André Lange, for example. He's worked for me for thirty years. I trust him absolutely.'

'He'd do anything for Villa.'

'You say that as if you're not sure it's a good thing.'

'I admire his dedication.'

'But?'

'It's important to remain honest, true to yourself.'

She looks at me. 'Are you accusing André of being dishonest?'

'Sorry, dishonest is too strong a word. What I'm trying to say is that you should do what's right rather than what appears to be in the best interests of the company at a given time. It may cost or inconvenience you more initially, but it pays off in the long term.'

She sighs. 'You remind me so much of your father.'

'You remember him?'

'Of course, I do. We built this business together.'

'He died last spring. It's one of the reasons I joined Villa.'

Marguerite tilts her head sideways. 'I shouldn't have let him go. Did he tell you what happened?'

'I never asked.'

Marguerite picks up a pen and twirls it between her fingers. 'Why do you say you joined Villa because of his death?'

'He was always saying I should work for a French company. I was in Argentina when he fell ill and I didn't make it back in time to say good bye. When the opportunity to join Villa came along, it felt like fate.'

She examines her pen as if she'd never seen it before. 'It certainly is an odd coincidence.'

'Why did my father leave?'

She looks at me and then back at the pen in her hands. Her mouth puckers in a sad little grimace. 'It's not a happy story.' She shakes her head and returns her gaze to me. 'I have a favour to ask you.'

'I'd like to know.'

She waves my concern aside. 'Arnaud Vidal. He's my last hope as far as The Wine Shop is concerned.'

'Is it that bad?'

'I'm not in the habit of losing money. Sébastien is a good man but he's let the company sink even further than when we took over. Arnaud is energetic and decisive. I have given him carte blanche and six months to turn the business round.'

'He doesn't know anything about wine,' I say.

Marguerite jabs her index finger on her desk. 'I don't need a wine connoisseur to run The Wine Shop, I need a businessman.'

'There are good business people in the wine trade.'

'Most of them have got jobs and quite a few don't speak much English.'

'I am talking about British people.'

She looks at me in askance. 'Are you suggesting I put a Brit in charge of The Wine Shop?'

I nod, not daring to go further.

She shakes her head. 'I only appoint people I know to directorships, and I don't know any Brits.'

'How long have you lived in London?' she asks after a few seconds.

'Coming up to eighteen years.'

'You like it?'

I nod.

Marguerite inspects her nails. 'What would you do if you were in charge of The Wine Shop?'

Her question stuns me. Tim may have been right. I take a deep breath. 'The Wine Shop is an iconic retail brand. It introduced wine to a whole generation of people whose parents only drank beer or Liebfraumilch. But these people are now buying wine from supermarkets, or Majestic.'

'Why?'

'They've grown more confident. Supermarkets have upped their game in terms of quality and they offer convenience and good deals. Majestic, on the other hand, has been clever with its warehouse concept: by making people buy in bulk, it makes them feel they're on to a bargain.'

'And Majestic don't have to pay extortionate high street rents!' Marguerite says.

I list action points on my fingers 'To restore The Wine Shop to its former glory, you first need to flush out all the duff stock which tarnishes the reputation of the brand: all the four-year-old cheap rosés and any wine that is over the hill.'

'Couldn't you sell them cheap?'

I sit up straight. 'If you promote something, you draw attention to it.

These wines need to go quietly. Then the range must be cut to make room for new exciting and well-priced wines. Jen hasn't had any support in the last two years to do it. She's been treading water while the competition's moved on and it shows. The range has become unimaginative and dull.'

'Who would supply these new wines?'

'It can't be Villa. The Wine Shop needs to thrive as a retailer in its own right not as a Villa outlet centre.'

Marguerite is looking at me. Is she taking it in?

I unfold my middle finger and plough on, 'Next, you need to let consumers know what you've done to get them back in. There are three ways to do it: well-targeted price promotions, advertising and getting the wine press onside.'

'Why do you think the British trade press dislikes us so?

I go for the soft version. 'Villa's an easy target: it's a large company, which is perceived as too industrial and powerful to be exciting.'

Marguerite picks up her pen again. 'Advertising costs a fortune.'

'Not if we are creative: we could do something viral.'

'Have you discussed any of these ideas with Arnaud Vidal?'

'His head of marketing has.'

'How do you know?'

I feel myself blushing. 'We talk.'

'Do you talk to Arnaud?'

I lower my head. 'He talks and I listen.'

Marguerite points at me. 'You need to try harder.

I shake my head. 'He's got his own ideas.'

'What do you think of them?'

'It feels sometimes like he's trying to do my job and sell Villa wines instead of doing what's best for The Wine Shop.'

Marguerite smiles at me. 'Is this why you're so full of ideas on how to do his job?'

We stare at each other for a while. I look away first.

'What do you think of the shop managers?'

'I was an assistant manager at The Wine Shop for a short while when I first arrived in England'

'I didn't know that. But that's part of the problem. We need seasoned retail professionals, not wine enthusiasts who're here today and gone tomorrow. The Wine Shop seems to be a training ground for anybody who wants to make it in the wine business in the UK.'

I shrug. 'Does it matter if they're good at what they do?'

'It does. You can't achieve anything in six months.'

'Isn't it what you've asked Arnaud to do?'

The minute the words are out of my mouth, I regret them. Marguerite looks at me, a deep frown between her eyebrows. I count to three, holding her gaze once more.

She bursts out laughing.

'I can see why André and Arnaud find you a handful.'

I seem to have got away with murder.

She leans over her desk. 'Listen young lady, I have another meeting in five minutes so let's make a deal. The money you need to settle with The Super-Market will be wired today. I'll tell André to leave you alone. In exchange, I'm asking you to give all the help you can to Arnaud. As you pointed out, he knows little about wine. If you don't do it for him, do it for me.'

She smiles and stands up, her hand extended.

I get up. 'Will you tell me what happened to my father?'

She shakes my hand. 'If you succeed in what I'm asking you to do, you'll do him proud. He lived and breathed Villa. Remember that.'

I leave her office, feeling a couple of inches taller than when I walked in.

Ed emerges out of nowhere. 'How did it go?'

'I thought you were out of the office.'

He waves his hands as if I'd made an irrelevant comment. 'Did she mention me?'

'Not that I can recall.'

'What did you talk about then?'

'The Wine Shop, André Lange . . . Marguerite said-'

'Marguerite! May I recommend you stick to "Madame Villa"? Marcel Villa isn't too happy about your cosy one-to-one with his mother by the way. He'll join us for your performance review tomorrow evening.'

He turns on his heels, taking my brief moment of elation with him.

14

THE CIRCUS AKA THE EXPORT MEETING

Serge arrives in Bordeaux just before midnight. After a flurry of phone calls, he joins Philippe and me in the restaurant of the Mercure hotel where we're staying. While he wolfs down the club sandwich the kitchen agreed to prepare for him despite the late hour, I retrace for him my afternoon conversation with Marguerite Villa. As Philippe and I have finished the 2004 Côtes de Castillon Cap de Faugères we treated ourselves to as a celebration of my survival, I order another one for Serge.

'She said the money would be wired straight away?' he asks in between mouthfuls.

I pour myself a large glass of wine.

'Are you happy about the trade off?'

I snort. 'Do I have a choice?'

He fishes a piece of bacon from between his front teeth. 'She's incredible, isn't she?'

'She is. She helped me secure a payment, which should have been authorised weeks ago, in exchange for my support for Arnaud whose ideas and style I dislike. Yet I walk away with a smile on my face and a spring in my step. That's charisma.'

Serge nods his approval, nose deep in his glass. 'For a 2004, this is very concentrated. I bet they did some serious thinning out in the vineyard.'

Philippe and I look at each other, shrug and take a mouthful at the same time. The wine is silky and seductive but it doesn't talk to us of where it's coming from, like it does to Serge. Papa had the same ability to read into a wine as if it were an open book. I wish I'd inherited it.

'Come on guys, we need to go to bed,' I say.

I'm walking towards my bedroom, wondering why Tim hasn't reacted to the text I sent him after Ed left, when he calls.

'Hi Frenchie! Sorry it's late but I wanted to congratulate you in person.'

'I'm not sure I've achieved much.'

His tone hardens. 'Didn't you say the old bird treated you like a long-lost daughter?'

'I may have been overoptimistic. It's all a bit blurred now. She's amazing though.'

His voice turns silky again. 'Have you been drinking, darling?'

'Not drinking, celebrating. Do you realise how scared I was this morning?'

I wish I could take this last sentence back the minute it's out of my mouth.

Tim's reaction is as I expected. 'Don't have a go at me. Didn't your toy boy hold your hand?'

'Stop it, Tim. Philippe isn't my toy boy. Can I call you back tomorrow? I am tired now.'

I do an Arnaud on him and cut him off.

Serge catches up with me in the corridor. 'Are you talking to yourself now?'

'I'm not. I got a call from a guy from The Wine Shop who thinks he can turn me into his puppet.'

'A colleague called you at,' he checks his watch, 'one o'clock in the morning?'

'It's only midnight over there.'

'Nobody from work should phone you that late.'

Embarrassment silences me. My mind is reeling from tiredness, too much wine and too many contrasting emotions for one day.

'You're right,' I say. 'Tim is a bit off but. . .' I can't think of any way to justify his familiarity so I kiss Serge on the cheek and go hide in my bedroom.

I turn off the air conditioning before I go to bed.

We're finishing breakfast the following morning.

'Is Tim still seeing Jen?' Philippe asks, pushing aside his empty hot chocolate bowl.

'Tim, as in Tim Foster?' I say, dipping my croissant in milky tea.

Philippe rolls his eyes. 'How many Tims do we know who've had an affair with somebody called Jen?'

'Sorry, I'm half asleep. Didn't I tell you about the monstrous gaffe I made in Narbonne?'

'They could have got back together since then.'

'I am sure they've not,' I say.

'Are these people from The Wine Shop?' Serge asks.

I nod and take a big bite of my croissant.

Philippe cocks his head to one side and looks at me, sucking his teeth. 'Tim has been all over you lately. Be careful, the guy's has a reputation. Jen was not his first conquest in the trade.'

'You don't like him, do you?' I ask.

'I don't approve of the way he uses people, particularly women.'

'Thanks Philippe. You've nothing to worry about.'

When we arrive in the office, I feel like Andromeda returning to her father's court after her near-miss with the sea monster. Some of my colleagues pat my back without a word and others greet me with the serious faces reserved for convalescents. I suspect them to have thought they'd seen the last of me yesterday.

After a round of air kisses, Philippe and I sit next to each other in the second-floor boardroom, which has been set up for the export meeting. Tables have been disposed in a U-shape facing a white screen, which hangs against one of the walls. Blinds have been drawn to cover the large bay windows and brutal fluorescent lights have taken over from the pale winter sun.

Serge drops his bag next to me. 'I need to go and prepare the tasting. I may be a while. Tell me if I miss anything important.'

'I'll be your eyes and ears,' I say.

Two members of the export marketing team are huddled by the Toshiba overhead projector, ensuring it's in good working order. The third one totters in, carrying a huge cardboard box. Like magicians and con artists, marketeers need lots of props for their presentations.

The four other European sales managers have already taken their seats and are chatting to each other and checking their emails while sipping dilute coffee from plastic cups and eating mini croissants and pains au chocolat.

What Villa calls Europe includes Africa, a peculiarity that's justified by the coffee's interests of the group in that continent. Asia is André Lange's territory, for which he reports directly to Marguerite Villa. He attends the export meetings only in his capacity as industrial director.

The States and Canada used to be handled by a close friend of Marguerite. Since his sudden death, five years ago, his two sisters have become embroiled in a ferocious legal battle with Villa and the business has gone to pot. This explains the absence of these countries in the organisation chart: I've been told any reminder of that unfortunate situation upsets the old lady so much, that it's been deemed more reasonable to ignore the American continent altogether.

One accountant delegated by the finance director and one of the export assistants, a stick thin lady in her late fifties with an impeccable bouffant hairdo, also sit around the table. She belongs to the generation when a woman living in rural France, however bright, could only aspire to a secretarial job. I'm the only woman in the room with managerial responsibilities. I am single whereas my five export colleagues, including Ed, are all married and have children.

It's now five to nine.

'How come none of the bosses have arrived yet?' I ask Philippe. 'I thought we were supposed to start at nine.'

Before he has time to answer, Ed rushes in, sweating profusely. 'Sorry guys, I was with Marcel Villa.'

Bruno, one of the other European sales managers, leans over Serge's empty seat. 'Ed insists meetings should start on time but Marcel does his best to make him late. Then he himself arrives a few minutes later to show he's the boss, which means André Lange turns up even later. If André arrives before Marcel, he leaves at the first opportunity, only to return after Marcel has arrived.'

'Sounds like playgrounds politics,' I say.

Bruno shrugs.

Ed wipes the sweat off his face with a large white handkerchief. 'Could you please all stop whatever you're doing?' His looks have not improved since the summer. The skin of his face is dried up and shows red patches of what looks like eczema peppered with some angry acne spots. His big blue eyes are bloodshot, giving him the look of a demented sick baby.

'Since most of you are here, we'll get started,' he says.

He reads the order of the day, announcing with quiet confidence we'll break at ten thirty, then at twelve for the comparative tasting Serge has organised, which will be followed by lunch. We'll start again promptly at two thirty in order to be done at five thirty.

An anonymous voice pipes up, 'Make it seven thirty if we're lucky.'

Ed folds his arms across his chest. 'I'm going to ignore that childish remark. Will you now please turn off your mobile phones and your laptops unless you're about to present. I'm sure some of you are expecting phone calls but this is what voicemail is for. As I've said on previous occasions, it's rude not to listen to your colleagues' presentations.'

A rumble of discontentment runs through the room, accompanied by the sound of various machines shutting down. I seem to be the only one delighted to go incommunicado for a while.

'Now I have your attention, let's start with an overview of our results to date and how they compare with the department's objectives.'

Bruno leans forward, his elbows resting on his thighs. 'Which objectives are you referring to, Ed? The ones that were agreed in January with your predecessor, or the revised version you sent us in April without any consultation?'

Laughter ripples through the room.

Ed puffs himself up. 'Which ones do you think, Bruno? Is my predecessor chairing this meeting?'

In the silence that follows, the Eastern Europe sales manager picks up the gauntlet. 'Bruno's got a point. Your revised figures do not add up, especially as you've not increased any of the supporting budgets.'

Another one joins the fray. 'April's far too late in the year to get my distributors to up their targets. I told you weeks ago.'

Bruno adds 'Look, whichever route to market you look at, there's no way you can change the rules four months into the year. Can we have a show of hands to see who's happy with the new deal?'

Nobody raises their hand.

'Who's in charge of this meeting?' Ed asks, wiping his hands on his trousers. 'Now isn't the time to discuss your objectives, whether you are happy with them or not.'

Bruno eyeballs him. 'When would be a good time? I've tried to talk to you about this for months.'

Voices rise in support. Ed turns around this way and that on his short bandy legs, trying to keep the mob at bay, hands raised more in supplication than in appeasement. Everybody is talking at the same time and the noise level is deafening.

André's loud voice silences everybody, 'What's going on in here? Monsieur de Waast, is this an export meeting or a cattle auction?'

Ed straightens his tie. 'We're having a discussion, Monsieur Lange.'

'It sounds more like a riot.' He scans the room and his face darkens. 'Where's Marcel?'

'He's on his way,' says Ed. 'I was with him five minutes ago.'

'It doesn't take five minutes to get here from his office. I'll go get him.'

André slams the door on his way out.

Ed stretches his arms open, Christ-like. 'Can I please ask you to calm down? I've taken your comments on board. It's a pity you didn't voice them earlier as it may now be too late to convince Monsieur Villa to revert to the original figures.'

Protests erupt once more around the room. Ed sighs and starts tapping away on his laptop. A huge spreadsheet appears on the screen behind him.

Furious questions ring out.

'What's that?'

'I can't see anything.'

'Where do these figures come from?'

Ed puts his hands together as if in prayer. He bows a little. His neck has turned red and his shirt collar looks far too small. 'I'm going to proceed with my presentation. For the sake of argument, let's assume the figures I've used are correct.'

Amidst the rumble of dissenting voices, I hear the ping of a mobile being turned back on, the modern protest par excellence. Ed flinches. He squares up his shoulders as if he were gathering courage to confront the offender and scans the room.

Two of my colleagues take their laptop out of the bags where they'd dropped them a few minutes ago.

Ed turns back to the screen, defeated.

He is commenting on his first slide when Marcel Villa saunters in, as if on a catwalk, followed by a grim André Lange. Ed stops and waits for them to sit down.

'Good morning everybody. Please don't mind us.' Marcel offers by way of an apology. 'Did I miss anything?'

'I was about to embark on the comparison between actual sales and targets,' says Ed.

Marcel inspects his manicured fingernails. 'Isn't that what you'd planned to start with?'

Ed looks like he's going to cry. 'It is indeed.'

Marcel frowns and looks at his watch with an exaggerated sweep of the arm. 'I thought this meeting had been going on for half an hour?'

Ed massages his forehead as if to repel a budding headache. 'May I carry on?'

He's hardly turned back to the screen when André's mobile goes off.

Ed pauses.

André pushes his chair back with a loud scraping noise, stands up and leaves the room, phone glued to his ear.

Ed manages to talk for forty minutes with no interruptions. Few people appear to be listening. Marcel is fidgeting. His gaze scans the room and he suddenly points at the Eastern Europe sales manager's laptop, demanding in a loud voice, 'Could you turn that thing off?'

'I'm presenting in five minutes, Monsieur Villa.'

Marcel mumbles something indistinct and returns to the inspection of his fingernails.

Ed concludes his monologue with an apology for the fact we're now behind schedule. He suggests we skip the break and move on to the Eastern Europe presentation straight away. He says anybody who's got urgent phone calls to make can do so now. Bruno leaps from his seat and leaves the room.

'I have deducted Siberwines' figures from my total, which is why they're different from Ed's,' the Eastern Europe sales manager says.

'Since when can you pick and choose your customers?' asks Marcel Villa.

'They're not my customers. I have never even been to Siberia.'

Ed lifts his left hand. 'We have discussed this before, Monsieur Villa. Siberwines buys otherwise unsalable wines directly from Narbonne at less than cost price. It's a way for André Lange to eliminate worthless stock from his inventory. The problem is that it shows as loss-making sales in the export department's stats.'

Marcel twists and turns in his seat. 'Where's André when we need him?'

Nobody answers his question. He frowns and bangs on the table, shouting, 'This is not on! I am sick and tired of Monsieur Lange's abuses of the system. He doesn't run the company, you know!'

I keep my head down to avoid looking at Marcel.

He continues venting his fury. 'I'll talk to him. Let's move on.'

He gets a comb out of his pocket and runs it through his hair in little jerky movements.

From the corner of my eye, I notice Philippe's now rubbing his forehead. Under his hand, his eyes are closed and, like me, he's trying hard not to burst out laughing.

Ed signals to my colleague to continue and we embark on a second presentation based on skewed figures. Bruno slides back in his seat twenty minutes later.

'That was a hell of a phone call,' I say, looking straight ahead.

'Ten containers, at least. Are you enjoying the circus so far?' he says in the same deadpan tone.

15

TESTOSTERONE, TEARS AND TASTING

The third presentation of the day is meant to be a short update by Ed of the "transatlantic situation" as he describes it.

'We all know how important the Canadian and American markets are for French wines and how crucial it is that Villa should be able to start selling over there again,' he says.

Two of my colleagues snap out of their pleasant doze and lean forward, paying rapt attention to Ed's every word. Both of them used to look after the plum American market in previous jobs. Soon after I joined the company, they approached me in turn, to assess my interest in the States. Once reassured my aspirations didn't extend further west than Wales, they both told me they'd been promised – one by Ed, one by André – they'd be in charge of North America, as soon as Villa's got its hands free over there. They're aware of their respective ambitions but both think they've got the upper hand.

Ed has returned to the impotent predicator pose: legs apart, elbows close to the body, and feet and hands splayed open in perfect symmetry. 'As much as I'd like to report progress in the case we're embroiled in, I regret to admit we've entered a lull. Our latest offer has been communicated to the other party and they have three months to consider it, three months during which there's nothing we can or should do, according to our lawyers.'

Marcel twitches. All eyes are on him.

'This is not good enough, Monsieur de Waast.' He stresses every syllable. 'We can't wait another three months for the resolution of this… of that…' Words fail him.

Ed purses his lips. 'What do you suggest, Monsieur Villa? I'm only following our lawyers' recommendations.'

Marcel bangs his fist on the table and shouts 'You need to blow up the lawyers' arse!'

A hush descends. Each of us chooses a fixture of the room to stare at, in order to avoid looking at Marcel.

Ed remains silent for a minute, his palms flickering open and close as if operated by a dying battery.

'I would have thought it made sense to listen to our lawyers' advice, considering how much we pay them,' he says.

Marcel's face turns puce. He's jabbing the desk so hard, I'm worried he's going to hurt himself. 'It's because we pay them too much that they do fuck all. If we continue throwing money at them and not demanding results, they'll string us along forever. That's why you need to blow up their arse.'

He throws himself back into his chair and runs both hands through his hair. After a few seconds, he takes a glance at his mobile, snorts in exasperation and picks up his comb to restore order to his mane. He checks his reflection once more in his phone, and after another snort, leaves the room.

Ed looks perplexed, maybe wondering how he's going to carry out Marcel's very specific instructions. 'Right, well, let's move on to our friends from the marketing department and their big box,' he says with a sigh.

Nobody laughs.

André walks back in, followed by Serge. André makes for the seat he occupied earlier on. He sits down, looks up at Serge who's pulling the chair next to me, frowns and signals to him. Serge shrugs and goes to sit next to him, grinning at me in an apologetic way.

Bruno mumbles under his breath, 'Woof, woof!'

The marketing presentation starts. The manager and his sidekick present the results of various consumer tests, which validate Villa wines' recent labels changes and reassure us that, once on shelf, our wines will leap in shoppers' baskets and Villa will swipe the floor with the competition.

'We need to get more listings though,' he says. 'Our numeric distribution is low and this isn't something marketing can do much about. It's the job of the sales team. It's your job, gentlemen.'

He turns to me. 'And lady, sorry.'

A diffuse testosterone fuelled hostility creeps up around the room. Bruno's jaw is jutting forward and he's massaging his left wrist as if he's about to throw a punch.

It's now the turn of Caroline, the youngest marketing team member to present. She joined the company in the summer, fresh out of business school.

She picks up a dozen bottles out of their cardboard case, and lines them with great care on the desk. Her hands shake a little.

'Some of you have commented that the paper we use for the labels of our Collection range doesn't reflect the quality of the wines,' she says. 'We've also had complaints from some clients about labels tearing. I checked the original specifications and it appears we're not using the stock recommended by the designer. I am not sure how this can have happened but we aim to rectify the situation as soon as possible.'

Bruno abandons his menacing pose and crosses his hands in his lap. The tension abates, even though the virtual gauntlet the marketing manager threw is still lying there, not forgotten.

André is whispering in Serge's ear, seemingly oblivious to what's going on.

Caroline continues, 'I thought I'd take this opportunity to explore alternative paper types. I've dressed bottles with different samples to give you a better idea of the finished look. They are numbered one to twelve.' She pats her creations gently, as if encouraging them to face their audience and takes a step back, still looking at her handiwork. 'I'm not sure what's best,' she says. 'Should I circulate them or would you rather come over here and tell me which ones you prefer?'

'Have you considered the technical feasibility of your little project, Mademoiselle…' André leaves the sentence unfinished. Pretending not to remember her name is his way to let her know how unimportant she is.

She steps into the intended trap with a wide smile. 'Call me Caroline.'

André doesn't even look at her. 'I'd rather not,' he says, his lips curled up in disgust.

Caroline's boss stands up. 'Monsieur Lange, we're at the exploratory stage with this project,' he says. 'Feasibility tests will come later.'

He gestures towards the dummy bottles. 'Caroline has come up with very interesting suggestions, which, I think, are worth looking at.'

Caroline turns pink with pleasure.

André picks up a pen. Pointing it at her, he says, louder this time, 'I don't know how much this young lady is paid to play with pretty labels but I hope it isn't much.' His voice slows down to the consistency of poisonous treacle. 'Let me explain to you how it works, Mademoiselle: in order to keep our costs down, we need the bottling line to go as fast as possible. This means we can only use paper up to a certain thickness. When the specifications from your fancy designers exceed it, we ask our printers for a thinner alternative.'

Caroline is rooted to the spot. She's biting her bottom lip and her eyes are welling up. I can tell she's trying not to blink to stop the tears from rolling down her cheeks. Serge's eyes are flickering. He's on production' side but doesn't condone André's brutal methods. The rest of the room is silent. Even though the victim is blameless, she's paying for her boss' earlier provocation.

Realising nobody else will help, the export marketing manager rallies up. 'Monsieur Lange, I'm lost for words. We're only trying to do our job. What do you recommend as the best way forward?'

'I'll get one of my guys to look at the paper stock we're using, and to send you an alternative.' He throws in the air the pen he brandished during his tirade and catches it in mid-air with a satisfied smile.

While Caroline puts her bottles back in their box with trembling hands, Ed coughs in his hand and suggests, 'Shall we repair to the tasting room? We're behind schedule but it may be a good idea to have a change of scenery.'

We all troop next door but for André who's dialling a number on his mobile, legs extended in front of him as if he didn't have a care in the world. When she passes his chair, Caroline gives him a wide berth as if she's scared he may lunge at her. I see the shadow of a smile on his lips. Once we're out of the room, a few people pat her on the back, mumbling words of encouragement.

I ask Philippe to tell Serge I'll be five minutes late and catch up with Caroline.

'Are you alright?' I ask.

Her eyes well up again and she shakes her head without a word.

'Come with me.' I grab her elbow and make for the coffee machine downstairs. 'What do you take normally?'

'Espresso, no sugar.'

I go for a double espresso with sugar.

'André is a bully,' I say, handing her the steaming cup. 'If Villa had a Human Resources department, this wouldn't happen. The way you have been treated is unacceptable. I can't believe your boss didn't say anything.'

'He's a nice guy.'

'That's the problem. You need a mean streak to deal with André.'

She takes a sip of her coffee and pulls a face.

I pat her arm. 'Go on, it tastes disgusting but it will help you survive the tasting. Otherwise, the alcohol will go straight to your head and you'll end up crying in your Cabernet.' I pour her a large glass of water. 'Drink this as well, otherwise the coffee will mess up your taste buds.'

She smiles.

'Let's go back,' I say. 'We don't want to miss the tasting.'

As we return to our colleagues, we almost barge into André who's bounding downstairs two steps at a time, mobile glued to his ear. He ignores my companion but looks me straight in the eyes with such malevolence I shudder.

'He doesn't like you, does he?' asks Caroline.

'Understatement of the day,' I say.

Back in the tasting room, I sit on the stool Philippe has kept for me.

'Is she better?' he asks.

'I can't believe André's behaviour.'

Philippe shrugs. 'Nobody ever stands up to him.'

We're assessing fifteen wines blind, five of each colour. This is the highlight of the day for me but I notice Bruno is nowhere to be seen and another sales manager is yelling in his mobile at the far end of the room, one hand covering his free ear. I ask Serge, 'Are we waiting for the others before we start?'

Ed answers, 'Bruno needs to make some urgent calls. He may not be able to join us.'

Serge mutters, 'Don't know why I bother.'

He hands over tasting sheets for us to write down our comments and our marks. We're starting with the Sauvignons. 'We have a real challenge with this variety,' explains Serge. 'The distinctive profile of New Zealand Sauvignons appeals to most consumers, especially in Anglo-Saxon markets, but is difficult to reproduce with French-grown grapes. In the cooler climate of the Loire, we get acidity and mineral flavours but not enough fruit concentration. In the Languedoc, because of the heat, we sometimes end up with high alcohol flabby wines. I have found growers in Gascony who could supply us with reasonable volumes. I have selected two different styles for this flight, which I have matched with examples from Chile, South Africa and New Zealand.'

I look at the five glasses in front of me and lift the first one. The wine is pale yellow with green hints but so are the other four with only minute variations. I plunge my nose deep in the glass and start jotting down notes as I progress from one wine to the next: grassy aromas, citrus fruit, hint of asparagus, ripe gooseberry. I try to be as specific as possible. I don't taste as often as I'd like to.

A stool is pushed back sharply, distracting me for a moment. That's quick work, I think, until I glance at the tasting sheet abandoned on the bench. Only plus and minus signs have been scrawled next to each wine's number. I look up at Serge. He gives me a resigned shrug.

The rosé flight presents us with a different challenge: Serge asks us to rate the level of residual sugar in various well-known brands and to determine which would be best for our own Syrah rosé. This is as impossible as asking what's the perfect quantity of sugar for a bowl of strawberries but the exercise is meant to start a debate rather than find instant solutions.

Despite the double espresso, Caroline is beginning to look giddy. Her cheeks are bright red and she's chatting in a high pitch voice that makes Serge wince.

He whispers to me, 'The silly cow doesn't spit. In five minutes, she'll either bawl her eyes out or she'll be dancing on the table.'

'Come on, she's had a hard time this morning,' I say.

'If she keeps on behaving like a twelve-year old, I'll give her an even harder one. Do you know how long it's taken me to prepare this tasting? And the flak I've had from André, telling me consultation with the export team was a waste of time?'

He bites on what's left of his thumbnail. He passes over a tasting sheet to me. 'It's Caroline's. Look at this.'

I pick up the piece of paper. The wines are classified from "Yuck" to "Very nice". If Serge was not so upset, it would be comical.

I plead the younger woman's case. 'What do you expect? She's had zero training.' Serge isn't impressed.

We fly through the Cabernet tasting. Serge doesn't care anymore. André comes back halfway through and asks in a loud voice when lunch will be served. Every now and again, he glances at Serge with a mocking smile as if to say, 'I told you not to bother.'

I make a special effort to describe every single wine to the best of my abilities. This is my way of supporting Serge. Eventually, after yet another sardonic look from his boss, he comes up to me and asks me to hurry up. I hand over my unfinished notes while André walks off, shaking his head.

16

A POISONED CHALICE

We return to the boardroom for lunch. Somebody has pulled up the blinds, and the cold unflattering winter light falls flat on every surface, revealing dust and cobwebs in the corners. The three cardboard crates, in which the plastic trays containing our lunch have been delivered, sit half-torn apart, in the middle of the room, exuding an unpleasant smell of raw meat and wet cardboard.

Caroline and the export assistant hand the trays around and bring proper wine glasses from the tasting room to replace the plastic cups supplied by the caterer. Ed passes around a bread basket containing individual rolls. None of the other men volunteer to help, except Serge, who plonks wine bottles on the tables, the cover they wore during the blind tasting cut open.

Wiping floury hands on his trousers, Ed announces we're more than an hour behind schedule and asks us to try and eat as quickly as possible.

Marcel Villa returns. He takes one look at the content of his tray, pulls a face and clicks his fingers at Caroline who's just taken her first mouthful. 'Is there something else to eat?'

She jumps up. 'Sorry Monsieur Villa, is the food not to your taste? We've changed caterers since the last export meeting.'

He waves her away and starts picking at his food.

I move aside my laptop and my notebook and pour Philippe and myself a large glass each from the bottle of Errazuriz Don Maximiano Serge allocated us.

'What did you think of the tasting?' I ask Philippe.

'It's a shocking waste of Serge's time.'

'Look at that colour,' I say.

The ruby red wine in my glass sparkles in the dim ambient light. 'Why do the others care so little?'

Philippe shrugs. 'Maybe because their markets are less demanding than the UK? That wine's a beauty,' he says, his nose deep in his glass. 'I can smell cassis in there and truffles.'

I swirl the wine around. 'You're right. I also get blueberry, a hint of pepper and green olives.' I take a sip. 'Blackcurrant and blackberry on the palate with just a touch of oak. And enough acidity to maintain freshness and elegance.'

Philippe concludes our joint tasting note, 'It goes on forever.'

We savour our treat in silence while I investigate the content of my tray.

In a hollow on the left sits a limp green salad with pine nuts and smoked Bayonne ham, topped with a slice of melting foie gras, the richness of the dish contrasting with the white bobbled plastic holding it. The seasoning is served in a dainty glass tube with a cork stopper. In the middle of the tray, two slices of roast beef, bright red with a thin grey surround, sport dainty swirls of mayonnaise, which match the pale yellow of the sliced potatoes nestling against the meat. In the bottom right hand corner of the tray, a portion of anaemic camembert leans against a sliver of sweaty Roquefort and an individually wrapped helping of butter. Inches away, a dense chocolate fondant swims in gooey custard, decorated with tightly coiled slivers of orange peel.

'These trays are just like Villa,' I say.

'The food looks good though,' says Philippe.

'I mean they can't decide if they want to be fast food or a gastronomic feast. Look at us: marketing is pulling in one direction, Ed in another, André resisting anything that could curtail his power and Marcel… God knows what Marcel wants!'

Philippe pores at his food. 'Who's the foie gras and who's the beef?'

I serve him another glass of wine.

A loud yell makes me look up. Marcel is on his feet, dabbing away with a paper napkin at a widening red stain on his shirt and jacket. An apologetic Caroline returns his wine glass to an upright position, the heavy water jug she was pouring from in her other hand.

He shouts at her, 'You clumsy thing! Do you have any idea how much this suit cost?'

She doesn't answer, her lower lip quivering once more. He turns on his heels and leaves the room, mumbling, 'I don't know why I bother dressing up for that lot.'

I wink at Philippe. 'Now we know what his contribution to meetings is!'

A blissfully unremarkable presentation on the subtleties of the German market follows lunch, only interrupted by André Lange's unfavourable comparisons with the results he's achieved in China. Marcel is still missing.

Three o'clock and it's my turn to take to the stage. I run through my slides in my head while connecting my laptop with the overhead projector. André sits there, staring at me without a smile. Ed introduces me in a few words, reminding everybody that it's my first export meeting, the previous one having taken place two days before I joined the company.

I start with an overview of the sales figures to date, which show a conservative two percent progression versus last year. I explain how this reflects the mix of our accounts, with Tesco growing at a sustained pace and some of our more traditional customers losing ground. After a few more generalities, it's time to move into my forecast for the current calendar year. I turn sideways in order to avoid looking at André whose gaze is drilling into me.

'Some of you may be aware we've recently experienced an unfortunate incident with The Super-Market. We're still in the process of resolving it and I can only, at this stage, estimate its cost. As it's a QC issue, I'd expect most of the damages to be borne by the bottling site but I have lowered my margin forecast to allow for the worst-case scenario.'

'How much are we talking about?' Ed asks, as if we'd never discussed the situation before.

'As I told you on the phone, it could be anything between forty and sixty-thousand pounds,' I say. 'Not taking into account the ill-will factor that may impact negatively on our development prospects with this customer.'

Without looking up from the piece of paper on which he's been scribbling, André comments, louder than necessary, 'Narbonne transferred two-thousand-five-hundred pounds yesterday to pay for the return of some of the allegedly faulty wine. This will be the sum total of the production site's involvement. All other payments will be from the commercial budget, since, as you put it yourself, they will help you secure the customer's continuing good will.'

'I never said that,' I say.

'Have we established the nature of the problem with the wine?' asks Ed.

I lean forwards. 'We have. Monsieur Lange told Rachel, when we went to see her, that the wine is reduced.' I try to control my voice. 'I confirmed it by email the following day.'

'Thus accepting liability,' says André.

I turn to Ed but he's massaging the back of his neck, his eyes half-closed.

Marcel walks back in. He's changed into a clean shirt and suit. He's smiling and stroking the fabric of his jacket with the palm of his hand. 'What's going on in here? My dear André, I could hear you from the end of the corridor.'

'Miss Legerot has refused to follow my advice and put the company in an expensive fix.'

It's only the two of us now, eye to eye, sparring in front of Marcel and Ed. The rest of the room has receded into the background.

I turn to Marcel Villa. 'I'm glad I have the opportunity to discuss this in front of you, Monsieur Villa.'

He raises his hand. 'Does this have anything to do with your conversation with my mother yesterday?'

'I suppose so,' I say.

'Then, I don't want to know. Once she gets involved, things become terribly complicated and I can't deal with the hassle.' He rubs his temples with his index fingers as if dealing with a horrendous headache. 'Can we move on, Monsieur de Waast?'

Ed gets up and thanks me for my contribution. I open my mouth to say I am only halfway through my presentation but he gestures for me to return to my seat. When I fail to move, he gets up and prods me until I walk back to my chair. Philippe hands me a glass of water without a word.

Bruno takes over from me and delivers a textbook presentation. His knowledge of his market is second to none, his sales show excellent growth while remaining profitable and he avoids any contentious subject. He answers competently a few questions and sits back down to applause exactly thirty minutes after he stood up.

The contrast with my disastrous performance makes me sink further in my chair. I open my notebook and start doodling, trying to pretend I am somewhere else. I wish I could leave but I can't give that pleasure to André.

The sound of raised voices makes me look up. The sales manager in charge of Africa is showing mocked-up posters for an advertising campaign. 'Monsieur Lange, this is a reasonable budget. It will pay for a four-week campaign in three different African countries. We'd never get such a good deal in Europe,' he says.

'It's still a lot of money. Your importer must be pocketing half the agency's fee.'

'I have no reason to suspect them of dishonesty.'

'Come on, this is Africa you're talking about. They're all crooked over there.'

My colleague turns to Ed for support. Ed remains silent.

The meeting comes to an end, only an hour later than planned. Ed signals to me. 'Are you going?'

'I was hoping to. What time do you want to do my appraisal tomorrow?'

'I'm not here tomorrow.'

'Do you want to do it now?'

He glances at André and Marcel, who are deep in conversation by the door. 'Go to my office. I won't be long.'

I pop into the tasting room to tell Philippe and Serge I have to stay behind, 'Sorry guys, more shit coming my way.'

'I'll wait for you,' says Philippe.

'Please don't. I can make my own way back to the hotel.'

'That's fine. I'll help Serge clear up. Everybody else has disappeared.'

'He's furious, you know,' Serge says.

'André? What else could I do?' I ask.

Serge empties the leftover wine, holding two bottles at a time upside down over the sink. He does his sideways whisper. 'I'm not talking about your presentation. That was his way of getting his own back.'

I raise my eyebrows. 'Really? I didn't notice.'

'He's furious about you meeting Marguerite Villa.'

'You told me it was his idea.'

'That's what he led me to believe but I was wrong.'

He puts the last two empty bottles in a case on the floor. 'He's told me it's the first time she's interfered in his running of the business in all the years he's worked for her. Why do you think she did that? It's not as if she knew you.'

I turn around to avoid his gaze. 'No idea. It isn't a big deal anyway. The meeting was over in half an hour.'

'It is a big deal to André.'

'And to Marcel, according to Ed. I have antagonised the two most powerful men in the company thanks to a meeting I never requested.'

Philippe and Serge nod in perfect unison.

I drag myself to Ed's office and settle down to wait. A copy of French Elle lies on his desk, a Post- it note marking the page of an advertorial Villa sponsored. I glance at the picturesque vineyard and the benign elderly winegrower brandishing a bottle of Villa's best-known brand. French advertisers always seem to portray growers who look like everybody's ideal grandfather.

I turn to the horoscope page. I don't believe that rubbish but I still read it. If it's good, it cheers me up. If bad, I try to ignore it. '*Cancer: The situation triggered by the recent clash between you ruler and the uncompromising Pluto.*' I chuckle. I thought he was called André, not Pluto. '*Remaining in your sign until June…*' Just what I need. '*Beware of certain individuals who are blaming you for their problems…*' What nonsense!

I check Tim's horoscope. '*Gemini: Recent changes have enabled you to break away from restrictive situations. Venus moves into your sign towards the end of the month.*'

'What do you think of the advertorial?' Ed asks.

I put the magazine down.

'Good, excellent!'

'Really?' He's beaming. 'Do you think it would work in England?'

'I mean, excellent for the French market.'

He sighs.

'Ed, I'm not trying to be difficult on purpose. British people have their own perception of wine, full stop. If we try to force French concepts down their throats, it won't work.'

'Point taken. Look, I don't want to be here all night and we need to get through this appraisal thing. I've had a chat with Marcel and André and we're unsure of the best way forward.'

My heart skips a beat.

'Meaning?'

'You've proven your abilities in some areas. There's no doubt you're hard working and dedicated. But this business with The Super-Market is upsetting everybody.'

'Ed, you can hardly blame me for a quality issue.'

'True, but with Marguerite Villa getting involved…'

'How is that my fault?'

'I'm not sure. I don't understand why she asked to see you, to be honest. However, I'm not comfortable confirming you in your job as things stand. What I'm proposing is to extend your probation period from three to six months. This will either allow things to calm down or-'

'Or you'll be able to get rid of me on the cheap.'

He nods. 'That's pretty much it, I'm afraid.'

I manage not to cry until I've left his office.

'Is it that bad?'

I freeze. Marguerite Villa catches up with me. She puts her index finger under my chin and pushes my face up. 'You must toughen up, girl or they'll eat you alive.'

I nod, tears rolling down my face, incapable of uttering a single word.

'By the way, I want you at the board meeting next Wednesday,' she says. 'Arnaud Vidal will give us his initial impressions on The Wine Shop. I'd like your feedback as you seem to understand the Brits more than you do your fellow countrymen.'

She winks at me and she's gone, leaving me to contemplate yet another poisoned chalice.

As well as the expected missed calls from Arnaud, I have a voicemail from him, which is unusual. The tone of it, however, is in character. 'Marguerite Villa tells me I should rely on you more but you've been impossible to get hold of all day long. I'm off tomorrow but I'll see you on Monday.'

In the tasting room, Philippe is polishing glasses. He explains, 'André asked Serge to drive him back to Narbonne. He couldn't refuse. I promised I'd finish tidying up.'

'You're an absolute gem,' I say.

I slump in the passenger seat of the car. Philippe turns the radio on. I turn my face to the window. I'll tell him about Marguerite's invitation, but not right now. The tune of yet another French pop ditty distracts me from my thoughts.

I burst out laughing.

The car swerves as Philippe takes a concerned look at me. 'Are you alright?' he asks.

'Did you hear that? "When I grow up, I'll be a Bee Gees or a Formula One pilot. In the meantime, I like to dress up. It's true that all suits fit me."'

'What's so funny?'

'It's a song about Marcel Villa! The suits! Listen!' I collapse in heaps of laughter.

'Listen! He'll know who he is once he's grown up!'

Tears are streaming down my face.

'You are very tired,' Philippe says, the shadow of a smile on his face.

'No, seriously, listen! It says he's dressing up in his bathroom. I can see him now, all dressed up and singing in his bathroom, using a toothbrush for a mike.'

Philippe shakes his head. 'You need a stiff drink.'

I'm still having hysterics when we pull into the hotel's car park.

17

DRUNKENNESS AND TEMPTATION

The taxi stinks of unwashed armpits, takeaways and rose air freshener. I'd open the window but I don't want to be rude. Forth One is blaring out. I can't recall being asked if I minded the radio being on so loud.

When we stop in front of the Parliament House hotel, I throw the fare at the driver, grab my receipt and dive into the quiet darkness outside. I take in a big lungful of clean Scottish night air. The dry cold is a relief after Bordeaux's damp, muggy weather.

Despite the late hour, here's Dave, leaning against the pale grey stone front of the hotel, fag in hand. Was he plucked from Kingston and dumped here, together with the equipment for this weekend's wine fair? I recoil at the smell of sour wine he exudes. His eyes are even more bloodshot than usual. He lifts two nicotine-stained fingers in salute.

'Is she coming?' he asks.

'I beg your pardon?'

His speech is so slurred, I'm not sure I heard him correctly.

'Mary. She's not here.'

'She has something on this weekend.'

I pick up my bags from the boot of the car.

He flicks his cigarette butt away and follows me in without offering to help.

About twenty people from The Wine Shop are chilling out in the mock Tudor lobby of the hotel. The lucky ones are sprawled in large armchairs of various shapes and colours which have been rearranged in a circle by the wooden fireplace. The other ones are sitting cross-legged on the floor.

They welcome me with the enthusiasm reserved to a long-lost friend. I stop and sniff the air, pointer-like. It reeks of alcohol. They all are in various states of drunkenness, way ahead of me and my airline sized Oyster Bay Sauvignon Blanc. A wide array of wine bottles stands on a coffee table, and on the floor in the middle of the group. Tim is sitting in a corner, staring at me with that annoying smile, which makes me blush for no particular reason.

Once I've checked in and dropped my bag upstairs, I join the party. One of the marketing guys leaves me his seat and I pour myself a glass of d'Arenberg 'The Footbolt' Shiraz. It's Friday night and what better choice than a wine named after a race horse to get me in a festive mood. It smells of ripe raspberries and plums with notes of spice and liquorice and a hint of eucalyptus. The alcohol warms me up. My body relaxes.

'Have you lost Philippe?' asks Matt.

'He's flying in tomorrow morning. He has a dinner party in London tonight.'

Dave mumbles, 'I don't give a flying fuck about Philippe. It's Mary I want to see.' He's sitting on the floor, almost folded on himself, and he's staring into his glass, which he holds with both hands.

The others chant, 'Boring!'

'It's all her fault,' he says, pointing at me. 'She stopped Mary from coming.'

'What are you on?' I ask. 'She had better things to do, full stop.'

'We had such a great time last year.'

'You and Mary?'

I can't keep the scorn from my voice.

He nods. 'Yessir, me and Mary.'

'And what did you get up to?'

'We snogged.'

'Never! Stop right there.'

'You ask her.'

'I know what her answer will be.'

I turn my back on him to indicate the conversation is at an end.

He's managed to irritate me when all I want is to relax and get a little bit drunk, just enough to forget about the nightmarish last few days in Bordeaux. The girl next to me walks off and Tim slides into her empty armchair.

'How was the rest of your stay?' he asks.

'Not great. The export meeting turned into a freak show and my useless boss extended my probation period by three months. On top of it, Marguerite Villa wants me back in Bordeaux next week for Arnaud's presentation to the board of his plans for The Wine Shop.'

'That's fantastic!'

He squeezes my wrist and leaves his hand there. I dare not move.

'Which part?'

'The board meeting: Arnaud will have to stick to the truth in front of you.'

'How do you think that will make him feel?'

'He'll hate you but he doesn't like you much anyway.'

I wince. Despite not being a huge fan of Arnaud, I resent been told to my face he dislikes me.

Tim continues, 'This calls for celebration. Let me try and find some Champagne.'

He comes back, minutes later, with two bottles of Pol Roger, which, I suspect, were not intended to celebrate my debatable achievements. I hope whoever's in charge of that stand has allowed for enough stock or they will run out before the end of the weekend. I drain my red wine and refill my glass with happy bubbles. The alcohol in my bloodstream is working its magic. Tim toasts me, looking deep into my eyes. I feel my cheeks burning and I take a quick sip to hide my embarrassment.

'What's Marguerite Villa like?' he asks.

I'm about to launch into a detailed description of our chairwoman when a shapely blond human missile lands in Tim's lap.

'My favourite marketing person ever,' says the invader in a strong Scottish accent. She cups his face in her hands and starts rubbing her nose against his.

'Kate, have you met Chris? She runs Villa in the UK.'

'I hate Villa,' she says, 'but I love you. Will you sleep with me tonight?'

'Kate runs the Princes Street branch. She's one of our most promising managers.'

Tim delivers his introduction with as much professionalism as one can muster when smothered in a passionate embrace.

The future star squints at me with unfocussed eyes, her lips pouting and her chin thrust forward. In her late twenties, she's still at an age when she looks good wasted. Her inebriation makes her both childish and sensual, her body language an open invitation to any red-blooded male. I finish my Champagne and wrap my jacket around me, holding the collar tight against my throat.

I'm staring into my empty glass when a fresh tumble of bubbles brings it back to life. I look up. Tim, the young lovely still perched on his knee, is refilling it, whispering, 'You need only ask.' His deeper than usual tone of voice sets fire to my face yet again. Emboldened by the booze flowing through my veins, I hold his gaze a tiny bit longer than necessary. The promise I read in his eyes feels like an embrace.

'Who's for dancing?'

Kate's swirling in the middle of the group, trying not to topple over a rogue bottle. A few enthusiasts stand unsteadily and grab coats and bags before making for the exit. Their female pied piper turns at the door and winks at Tim.

'Good night lover boy, see you tomorrow! Or later if you're in the mood!'

Tiredness hits me all of a sudden. What am I doing, getting drunk and moping around like a lovelorn teenager? I'm too old for these games.

'I'm going to bed,' I say.

Dave sniggers. I attempt to stare him down but my basilisk impression fails to silence him.

'Let me take you to your room,' Tim says, taking my elbow. I stand still for an instant savouring the closeness of his body and the smell of his skin.

'I'll be fine,' I say, conscious that we're providing entertainment to what's left of the group.

The pressure of his hand increases. He tells our public, 'See you in a minute.'

We walk away, giggles and comments about how much misbehaving you can pack in one minute following us into the lift.

It's one of those very small, slow and creaky lift with a see-through door. I lean against the wooden side panel, trying to keep my eyes on the floor. Tim takes a small step towards me and whispers in my ear, 'I am so pleased you flew in tonight.'

I raise my head and his lips are on mine, warm, salty, tasting of Champagne. Our tongues mingle. I pull back, worried I might taste like an old spittoon. He frowns, and when I fail to react, he enfolds me in his arms and kisses me again.

The jolt of the lift, stopping on the second floor, breaks up our embrace. In two big steps, I have reached my bedroom door. With my back to Tim, I fumble in my handbag for my key, trying to regain control of my senses.

He slides his hands under my shirt and I feel them on the bare skin of my waist, riding up towards my breasts as he presses an unmistakable erection against me.

'Feel how much I want you?'

My wits have deserted me. Instead of the cutting remark such a corny question demands, I moan, my forehead resting against the door, my eyes closed. His hands are inside my bra now, caressing and squeezing. He turns me around as if I were a ragdoll and kisses me again, harder, deeper, his hands forcing their way past the waistband of my trousers, grabbing my buttocks. I feel weightless, powerless. All the shit of the previous months evaporates and tears come into my eyes. This is payback time, I think, trying to justify the unjustifiable.

Jen's face comes uninvited into my head. She's arriving tomorrow on the same plane as Philippe. I push Tim away.

'This is madness.'

'I thought you enjoyed a bit of madness,' he says, undoing the top buttons of my shirt and nuzzling my nipples in turn.

'I can't,' I say.

He grabs my hips and pulls me towards him.

'Not tonight,' I add, trying to give myself some thinking space.

He lets go of me so abruptly I stumble. He takes a step back and surveys me with a smile. 'Tomorrow, then?' he asks.

I lean against my bedroom door and nod, desperate for another kiss, but he's gone, bounding downstairs three steps at a time. I totter back to the lift cage, pulling on my clothes, and I stare through the cold metal mesh, trying to follow him with my eyes for as long as I can. A faint chorus of disappointed voices tells me he's back with the group. I stagger into my bedroom, legs wobbling, and throw myself on the bed, crying with frustration.

I wake up the following morning, whispering sweet nothings into my pillow. My whole body is tingling, aching for sex. The memory of yesterday's unfinished business hits me. I behaved like a bitch on heat last night. How did I let my professional relationship with Tim take such a turn? Was it the knowledge of his affair with Jen that gave me licence to follow in her footsteps? Why did I think I could indulge in harmless flirting with him when I knew of his reputation? I think of Marguerite Villa's comment, 'Sentimentality, that's your problem.' If only it was the only one.

Breakfast is a sober affair. Dave has got his extra-large sunglasses on and nurses a salad bowl of black coffee with shaking hands. Matt and his entourage demolish huge helpings of bacon and sausages with grim determination. It's going to be a long tiring day with more drinking at the end of it, not the kind to be tackled on an empty stomach. Tim is nowhere to be seen, a small mercy as far as I am concerned.

The grief over my father's death took my mind off men for a while, that much is true. But I'm lying to myself when I say I'm too busy at work to think about dating. The truth is Tim and I have been gravitating towards each other for a number of weeks now. I've pretended not to notice, even when prompted by Philippe, to avoid facing up to the fact it would be a disaster to fall for him. Last night put an end to my pretence.

The object of my thoughts is standing outside the hotel, mounting guard by the bus that will take the staff from The Wine Shop to Murrayfield where the tasting is taking place. It used to be held at the Balmoral but a few cases of abject drunkenness, blamed on members of the public, put paid to that partnership. Piles of puke outside bedroom doors jarred with the luxury image they are keen to project.

Tim is ticking names off a virtual list as people troop out of the front door and into the bus one by one, or in small groups. The idea is to ensure nobody is left behind, however comatose they may be. Call it morning after's solidarity.

'Are you ok?' he asks as I walk past. I give him a tight smile.

I must talk to him later and explain we can't be anything but friends. We work together and a relationship between us wouldn't work anyway. He needs a trophy girlfriend, a blonde stunner he can parade around. I'd soon tire of his flamboyant style and his need to be the centre of attention.

Once even the worst affected by last night's carousing are on board, we leave behind the cobbles of Carlton Hill, the initial twists and turns of the journey causing some to moan and clutch their stomachs. Tim stands at the front of the bus, chatting to the driver, his body absorbing every bump like a surfer's.

He's so damn sexy. What if I spent just the one night with him? What happens in Edinburgh stays in Edinburgh, goes The Wine Shop's saying. I wouldn't be the first one to make the most of the Scottish wine fair. Nobody would get hurt. We're both single, as far as I know.

The Georgian magnificence of Queen Street gives way to the austerity of Roseburn Street and ten minutes after leaving the hotel, we turn into the stadium's grounds. Murrayfield is huge. From the outside, it looks like a concrete monstrosity dumped by aliens amidst the elegant buildings of Edinburgh. Like a column of ants, we climb the massive staircase and file into the Thistle suite.

Four rows of white plywood cubicles line the huge room: one against the windows, one against the wall and two, back to back, in the middle.

Philippe is putting the finishing touches to our stand.

'Good evening?' he asks.

I flinch but I know his question to be innocent. He hasn't seen any of last night's crowd yet. I plunge into a cardboard box to pick up a poster.

I answer in pure Jesuitical style, 'You?'

He nods. 'Pretty good. We went to Côte, in Wimbledon. Good food and good value.'

'How many spare labels do we have?'

'Mary put in more than a hundred of each. Should we open the bottles now?'

'May as well. The fair opens to the public in ten minutes.'

Philippe uncorks bottle after bottle and I taste each of them to check the wine isn't corked.

If I sleep with Tim tonight and anybody finds out, we'll be prime gossip material for weeks to come. Arnaud wouldn't find out though. He's too distant from his team for any of them to confide in him. The story of our romance may spread to people outside the company however and go back to Villa that way. That would be disastrous. I think of Papa and I shudder.

Jen arrives. She works the room with Tim, moving from stand to stand, greeting and thanking producers and their agents for supporting the event. Not only have they paid two thousand pounds for their stands but they have also donated the wines that will be tasted or drunk over the two days. In addition, they are spending the weekend serving thirsty customers instead of chilling out at home or catching up with their Christmas shopping. This makes Arnaud's absence conspicuous and much commented upon. As Villa's sole representative, with Philippe, I'm ashamed of the lack of respect it shows towards The Wine Shop's suppliers.

Tim reaches our stand. He grasps the bottle I'm opening. 'Let me do that for you.' His hands are warm and caressing as they envelop mine for a split second.

He turns to Philippe. 'Have you got all you need?'

Maybe we could have a discreet affair? It's a long time since I've been so attracted to a man. I gawp at the triangle of pale skin that shows above the neckline of his T-shirt. His hands stroke the bottle with long, sensitive fingers. I know a liaison between us is bound to end up in tears, mine in all likelihood, but I don't care. I want my Carpe Diem moment even if I have to pay for it later. He's the last delicious chocolate in the box and I don't mind getting sick.

'I believe so,' Philippe says. 'What do you think, Chris?'

'What?' I've no idea what he's talking about.

'Do we have all we need?' He gives me a probing look. 'Are you sure you didn't party the night away? You seem a bit distracted this morning.'

Tim pipes up, saving me from having to answer Philippe. 'Somebody will relieve you around lunchtime so that you can grab something to eat and have a break. Have you got the details for tonight's party? It's up at the Castle and they'll be Scottish dancing.'

He must be repeating the same message at every single stand. His parting shot, however, is just for me or so I hope. 'I look forward to seeing you there.'

'Smarmy git,' Philippe says under his breath, bringing me back to earth with a thud.

18

THE CONSUMER WINE FAIR

A flock of visitors spills inside the room as soon as the gates open. They've paid twenty pounds each for their ticket and most of them intend to drink at least forty pounds' worth of booze during the next few hours. The more practised aim for the Champagne stands before they get too crowded or run out of stock. The candidates for quick oblivion target the spirits ones.

A young woman is choosing wine for her wedding. She introduces me to her bridesmaids and we start tasting my offering, checking prices and labels as we go along. I show her how to hold her glass to twirl the wine around before sniffing it. She soon masters the technique but she doesn't like the idea of spitting in public. She ignores my entreaties to at least try it if she wants to finish the day standing up.

Will I ever get married? Some women tie the knot in their fifties. How does Mrs Chris Foster sound? I freeze, wine bottle held in mid-air, shocked such a thought would occur to me.

'This one is too strong for my taste,' the bride-to-be says, putting her glass back on the counter.

She pats my arm. 'Are you alright?'

'Sorry, I was miles away.'

Why is life so easy for some women? This one doesn't even look special. What made a man decide to choose her as his life's companion?

A lad, who looks like he's already had a skinful, stumbles past my hen party and stands right in front of me, legs well apart for balance. He proffers a wavering dark red stained glass right under my nose.

'Give us a big one of your most expensive wine!'

Philippe intervenes. 'May I help you, Sir? My colleague is looking after these ladies.'

'I'm talking to her. I like older birds.'

Anger rises inside me. I need an outlet for my pent-up frustrations. I push Philippe aside and point at the young cretin. 'This is a professional tasting for the benefit of people who happen to be interested in wine, as opposed to little pricks like you.'

I jab him in the chest. 'One more offending comment and I'll get security to throw you out as hard as they can.'

I jab him again. 'Am I making myself clear?'

The lad takes a step back, his eyes dazed and his mouth slack. My legs are trembling behind the counter.

'I couldn't have put it better,' Philippe says.

A friend of my victim pulls him back, muttering an apology. Groups of young males at tastings tend to fit the same template: one obnoxious character, one guardian angel to drag the obnoxious one away before he gets hurt and the rest of the gang performing the function of a Greek choir.

Tim appears out of nowhere. 'What's going on?'

One of the bridesmaids gives him an appreciative glance and steps forwards. 'One of these guys was rude to the lady.'

He doesn't spare her a glance. 'Do you want him kicked out?' he asks me.

'Not right now but it may be a good idea to get the guys from security to keep an eye on him. I'd be surprised if he didn't cause more trouble before the end of the day.'

He squeezes my hand. 'Let me know if he comes back.'

Philippe frowns at his departing back. 'What's with the knight in shining armour act today?'

I pretend not to hear and turn back to my new girlfriends.

From the corner of my eye, I notice two couples in their late sixties approaching. Even though I'm more or less finished with my bridal party, I keep on talking, praying they'll move towards Philippe. They have all the time in the world though. They wait for me to be free and they strike. The men attack first, pouring a random sample and engaging in a bit of competitive tasting to show off their knowledge of wine. I smile to show my appreciation, and come up with the expected, 'You seem to know what you're talking about, gentlemen.'

This opens the floodgates and I'm soon drowning in reminiscences of good, bad and ugly wines. I manage to smile throughout the onslaught. I don't need to say anything: a few nods are all that's needed. Just as I'm hoping for a reprieve, one of the wives sidles up to me. I guess she stopped listening to her husband at least ten years ago, especially on the subject of wine, but she seems determined to get a piece of the action.

'I'm teetotal,' she says, as if it were the most thrilling revelation I'll hear all day.

I resist the temptation to tell her I couldn't care less and keep on smiling.

'He took me to the Hampton Court Palace Flower Show last summer,' she says. 'Today's payback time. He enjoys his wine so much.'

Her contentment with life and its trade-offs is in such stark contrast with my troubled state of mind that I grit my teeth not to say something I might regret. What if I confided in her that I've been thinking of little else but sex today? That my one and only priority for the next hours is to weigh up the pros and the cons of sleeping with one of the most unsuitable men in the wine business?

'I'm driving,' she says before asking, 'Are you French?' followed by the inevitable, 'Where in France are you from?'

I wish she'd leave me alone. I'm here to pour wine and give advice, not entertain bored elderly ladies with my life story. My answer to her question will either lead to a detailed account of her last holidays in or near Bordeaux, or to a lament of how much she wishes she could go there one day. I brace myself for ten minutes of passive listening when I spot Jen striding towards me, a purposeful look in her blue eyes.

'How kind of you to ask!' I say with sudden warmth. 'I was born in Bordeaux like many great wines.'

'And will you grow old with the same elegance?' the lady says, clearly delighted to have found a subject to rouse me.

The trick works. Jen gestures to me she doesn't want to interrupt and she'll come back later. Relief washes over me even though I know it's a temporary reprieve.

My pensioners move off, to be replaced with several very thirsty groups. They take it in turn to refill their glasses and then pull back from the stand to carry out loud conversations. Philippe and I shuffle on the spot and pour almost nonstop, dropping one bottle to pick up another, reaching out into the crowd towards outstretched arms and empty glasses. My right shoulder starts to ache and I kick off my shoes under the table.

One blonde tells her friend, 'The darker the rosé, the sweeter.'

'I'm afraid not,' I say.

'How do you know then?'

'Read the back label. It should give you an idea of what to expect.'

The blonde looks disappointed with my mundane advice.

'Can I have a word with you later?'

I almost drop the bottle I'm holding. Jen is smiling at me over the back partition of the stand.

'No problem. When?' I say.

'What about lunch? I'll send somebody to replace you.'

'Is she going to give you a hard time?' asks the blonde once Jen has moved on.

I frown, unsure of her meaning.

'You don't look like you're looking forward to having lunch with her. Is she your boss?'

I kick myself. When will I learn to hide my emotions better?

Matt comes out of the ladies, looking harassed. He calls for reinforcement and goes back in like a man condemned. I guess the first casualties of the day need waking up, cleaning up and sobering up.

The press in front of the stand is getting worse as is the noise level in the room. The temperature has gone up by several degrees and the smell of alcohol is overpowering. Through a gap in the crowd, I spot the lad I chastised earlier. He's sitting on the floor, fast asleep, back propped up against a pillar and legs akimbo. He won't cause any more trouble for the rest of the day.

Kate, The Wine Shop's most promising manager, is walking towards me. She looks unscathed from her night of clubbing.

'Jen has asked me to relieve you,' she says. 'She's waiting for you in the dining room.'

I don't ask her how much she's looking forward to promoting Villa's wines. She looks grumpy enough as it is.

I greet competitors and former colleagues on my way to lunch: anything to delay my confrontation with Jen. A short and skinny dark-haired man hails me as I pass by his stand. He looks French or Italian. I don't recognise him but I greet him back and keep on walking until I feel a tug on my sleeve.

'Are you Miss Legerot from Villa?' he asks.

I nod.

'Could I talk to you?'

I stop.

'It's about my brother in law.'

'Do I know him?'

He looks anxious. 'He's a director of one of the co-operatives that supplies Villa in Narbonne. Will you have a moment later? At the party maybe?'

How can I tell him that, today of all days, Villa's Narbonne winery is the last thing I want to talk about? I agree to a chat later on and walk off, cursing myself for my inability to say no.

Jen is waiting for me in a corner of the room that's been set aside for lunch. She has a plate of nibbles on her lap. My heart sinks. I've avoided the subject of her affair with Tim since our disastrous dinner in the South of France but I remember her excitement when she first mentioned the new man in her life, last June. I wonder how long they stayed together. Does she still care for him? Has she heard about last night and does she mean to warn me off?

I fill my plate at the buffet. I'm not hungry but the food will give me a countenance if the conversation turns awkward.

Jen pats the chair next to hers. 'Thanks Chris. I don't want to embarrass you but there's something I need to talk to you about.'

She pauses, maybe waiting for a reaction. I remain silent.

'May I ask you a direct question?'

I bring a spring roll to my lips. 'Go on.'

'It's about Tim.'

I put the spring roll back on the plate. I need a large glass of wine, any wine.

'Our relationship hasn't been the same since we… since the summer. I thought we'd managed to put it all behind us but, in the last ten days, something has changed again.'

I pop the spring roll in my mouth. 'In his attitude towards you?'

'He's become secretive. He hides stuff when I get near his desk. The other day, I bumped into him leaving Arnaud's office and he refused to tell me what they'd been talking about.'

I cover my mouth with my hand while I chew.

She slices a prawn fritter with exaggerate care. 'I'm worried about my job. I love what I do and I think I do it well but I don't think Arnaud sees it that way. I'm scared he's planning to get rid of me. I've been meaning to talk to you for a while but, I know it may sound stupid, I've had the feeling you've been avoiding me.'

I feel awful. My infatuation with Tim has blinded me to Jen's unhappiness.

'You've heard something, haven't you?' she asks.

I grab her hand. 'You've got nothing to worry about. Your job is safe or as safe as any job can be in this company.'

Tim strides into the room with a supplier. He's got to the buffet when he sees us. He takes in our entwined hands and our grave faces. I look at him, daring him to come close. He stops in his tracks, taps his forehead as if he'd remembered something important, turns around and leaves the room.

I don't like him very much all of a sudden.

Jen's gestures towards his departing back. 'Do you see what I mean?'

'He's such a coward! Jen, I'm sorry I've kept you in the dark. Arnaud has got a project, which he doesn't want to involve you in. That's all there is to it.'

It's so much easier betraying Arnaud's confidence than admitting to my own weakness.

'Why not?'

'Because it's a crackpot idea and he knows you'd fight him tooth and nail.'

'Won't you?'

'I can't or I'd lose my job. Also, I hope to limit damages by remaining involved.'

'What about Tim?' she asks.

'Same thing, I suppose.'

'Can you tell me what it's about?'

'I'm not supposed to but, if you come to my office on Monday, you may stumble upon some documents that will enlighten you.'

She hugs me. 'You're a mate. I knew I could trust you.'

I'm glad she thinks so. I'm not so sure myself.

I walk back to my stand in a foul mood. My yearning for Tim remains but it's tarnished by my chat with Jen and the inescapable truth that, once I've given in to him, he's likely to revert to form and behave towards me like the cad he is. I feel like a dog whose food bowl has been snatched away.

His hands are on my waist, making me shiver. 'What did Jen want with you?'

I give him the gist of our conversation. He takes his hands off me.

'Do you realise she'll go ballistic when she finds out about the new range? It's contrary to all she believes The Wine Shop to be about.'

'It is,' I say.

'I know but there's no point antagonising Arnaud at this stage and that's what she'll do. There are other ways to influence him.'

'You can't believe he'll backtrack?'

'He did for the outlet shop he wanted to open at head office. Remember the one with the giant banner?'

He tries to take hold of me again. I pull away. 'Stop that. Jen is a big girl. She's quite capable of making her own decisions.'

The stand's heaving when I get back there. Kate's been replaced by one of The Wine Shop's sales managers. I'm relieved I won't have to engage in polite chitchat with her. I apologise to Philippe for having been away so long and step back behind the counter while he goes off to lunch.

The early afternoon lull brings some good people, including a tall guy who stays talking to me a wee bit longer than his limited knowledge and interest in wine can justify. Maybe I should move up to Scotland. Tim is in his element, chatting to groups of pretty girls, and guiding them from stand to stand as if through a human zoo.

Philippe returns from lunch and we brace ourselves for the final onslaught of the afternoon. Considering how little the spittoons are used, I'm amazed by the number of people who still look sober. Voices are getting louder though, accompanied by extravagant body language. Young women screech and hug each other with enthusiasm. Old men get red in the face and talk at each other like angry cockerels.

A couple start kissing with great enthusiasm, right in front of me. I let them be for a while but the abandon with which they paw at each other soon starts getting on my nerves. You don't wave a steaming plate of food in front of someone considering a hunger strike.

'Could you get them to move aside, please?' I ask the girl's friend, who is inspecting her fingernails, waiting for her friend to disentangle herself. She pulls a face, as if unsure of her powers of persuasion.

I insist. 'Look, I'm delighted they're so much in love but they're blocking access to my stand.'

'Don't know about love. They've just met,' she says, chewing her gum.

I manage a tight smile. 'The magic of wine!'

'Nah, she's had whisky. I told her not to go mad, but she never listens.'

The object of my concern is now having her breasts massaged by her new paramour. I look at the bar sized ice bucket at my feet, now full of icy cold water.

'I wouldn't,' says Philippe, a note of warning in his voice.

'You've no sense of fun whatsoever.'

My little bride comes back, all pink-cheeked and excited, and barges past the lovers. 'I didn't want to go without telling you. Your wines are the best we've tasted today.'

She's swaying on her feet. I hope she's planned a quiet day tomorrow. I'm getting a sympathy headache from talking to so many drunk people.

A new surge of thirsty punters tells us it's four o'clock and the spirits stands have closed for the day. This is the twilight zone when jaded and abused palates search for yet more stimulation. Sensible conversations and offers of product information are now surplus to requirements.

'Hey Janet, come over here. Try this one.'

'I don't drink red.'

'Try it, it's bloody good.'

'It's red.'

'But it's bloody good!'

Similar scintillating dialogues are repeated ad nauseam around the room. This is the moment when we, the professionals, are at our most sober and look down our educated noses at the worse for wear crowd in front of us. Very soon, we'll be equally intoxicated but it's different when it's your job.

Matt walks by, his face like thunder. 'Have you seen Tim?'

'Not in the last half an hour.'

'He's not answering his mobile and I have an emergency.'

My imagination starts to conjure scenarios involving local beauties.

'What's the problem?' I ask, trying to ban the explicit images assaulting my brain.

'The young cretin from my team. I've just caught him in a clinch with a member of the public, wearing his staff T-shirt, no less.'

I grimace. 'Ouch!'

'I'm sending him back to London straight away but I need to find somebody to take him to the hotel to pick up his stuff.'

And he's off. Jen and Tim have had their comeuppance after all. The little twerp that made fun of their steamy email exchanges a few months ago has demonstrated his own lack of restraint. Yet everything would have been alright if he'd thrown himself at a willing supplier or colleague a few hours later. The Wine Shop's rulebook has many surprising quirks.

19

THE MYSTERIOUS DOMINIQUE

Five o'clock strikes at long last. My feet are sore from shuffling on the spot and my knees ache from standing for too long. Philippe lines up all the empties on the floor in front of the stand while I move the half-full bottles out of sight at the back. I'm not fast enough though and two stragglers rush to me, glass at the ready. I shake my head with a smile and they drift off, searching for a last free shot.

The "wall", a line of staff from The Wine Shop that sweeps anybody who's not left of their own accord, walks down the room, getting rid of the last civilians. We can now relax amongst professionals. Not unlike this morning's visitors, Philippe and I march first to the Taittinger stand for a little aperitif. Anything that's open can be drunk before we move on but the good stuff will go first. My friend on the stand pours me a generous glass of Comtes de Champagne Blanc de Blanc 1998. I slide down against a pillar to savour the rare treat. The fine bubbles rise fast in the glass, producing a beautiful mousse that I tease with the tip of my tongue. The nose is an intense fresh blend of white blossoms, vanilla and almonds. I breathe it in with my eyes closed.

Tim collapses next to me. 'You sharing?'

His shoulder rests against mine. I feel his hot breath on my neck. I'm almost cross with him for interrupting my tête-à-tête with this fabulous Champagne.

'A tiny little sip,' I say, my eyes closed.

'Come on, be generous. I'll make it up to you later.'

I open my eyes and take a long hard look at him. 'How do you propose to do that?' I ask in my best matter-of-fact voice.

'How much detail do you want?' he says and, just like that, my hard-front crumbles and I close my eyes again, pretending to concentrate on the wine. I feel his hand on mine, prising my fingers one by one off the cold glass. He takes two sips and returns the glass to me. A wet kiss on my cheek and he's gone again.

'Why do you let him get away with it?'

Philippe is back. He should have stayed with me.

'Have you tasted the Matahiwi wines?' I ask.

'I bought some of their Sauvignon a while back. What are they showing?'

'A couple of Sauvignons and a Pinot Noir.'

'Their Pinot Noir is fabulous. It's got plum and raspberry on the nose and the palate is all smoky undertones.'

His hands are crunching imaginary grapes to accompany his description of the wine. Is it my imagination or is my very serious Philippe getting a tiny little bit tipsy?

After exploring some of the other stands' vinous delights, we pile back on the bus to return to the hotel. Tim stands once more at the front, not unlike the sexy captain of a pirate ship. My imagination may be fuelled by my alcohol intake.

It takes me less than ten minutes to shower, apply a minimal amount of war paint and slip into my party outfit, a black trousers and flimsy red top combo. I don't want to be the first of the girls to come back downstairs though and I lie down on my bed with a book.

I manage a couple of pages until I realise I've been reading the same line for five minutes without taking it in. 'Papa, please, protect me from Tim. I feel lost.'

The perfect solution to my woes comes into my head as if in answer to my plea. I'll call Diana, my friend who lives in Edinburgh, and invite myself over for dinner. She's had a baby two months ago, which limits the chances of her being out tonight. Then, I'll pretend exhaustion and crash at her place to avoid any risk of a late-night visit to my bedroom.

I consider my plan for a proud moment. I grab the receiver and put it down.

It would be rude to phone at such short notice. I don't have a bottle to take with me and florists are closed.

Why should I miss the fun of the party just because of Tim anyway? Am I so infatuated that I can't trust myself to resist him? There will be enough people around for me to have a good time even if I have to avoid him. I march out of my bedroom and close the door behind me.

I pause for a few seconds on the landing, a niggling thought at the back of my mind and open the door again. The socks and knickers I discarded on my way to the shower lie in the middle of the floor, where I dropped them. I stare at them and slam the door without picking them up.

Downstairs in the lobby, the air is heavy with women's perfumes: girly Anais Anais competes head to head with blasts of Calvin Klein's Eternity. The fair's standard issue black T-shirts have been discarded in favour of fancy shirts for the men and bosom revealing dresses for the girls. Dave, deep in conversation with Philippe, has opted for a baggy sweatshirt in a fetching aubergine shade that matches his complexion.

We board the bus once more. Nobody seems to care Tim is missing.

'Is everybody here?' I ask Philippe.

He nods, without looking around.

'You didn't check.'

'I don't need to. We're both here. Villa's staff is accounted for and The Wine Shop's isn't my problem.'

I turn my back to him and loose myself in the contemplation of Princes Street's shop windows. We soon reach Edinburgh's Castle where the party is taking place. A small group of stores' staff is waiting for us, Kate amongst them. While her companions greet their head office colleagues with bear hugs and kisses, she stands on tiptoes at the back of the group and scans everybody who comes off the bus. She's biting the tip of her tongue between perfect teeth and twisting a strand of blond hair with nervous fingers. She frowns when she sees me.

Once the bus is empty, she makes a beeline for Matt, grabs his arm and whispers a question in his ear. Philippe is talking to a guy he met during the afternoon and I leave his side to eavesdrop.

'. . . to the airport. We agreed he'd better wait for him to board just in case the silly bugger tried to come back.' Matt checks his watch. 'He should be with us in half an hour at the most.'

He pats Kate on the bum with a benign grin.

She picks up his hand, moves it away as if it were a slug that had landed on her bottom, and walks off without a backwards glance.

I return to Philippe with a little smile on my face. Whatever Tim got up to on his last visit to Scotland could well explode in his face tonight. The lovely Kate strikes me as a very determined lady.

We troop into a low ceiling room. The bar's covered with overflowing platters of tapas style food and ranks of shiny bottles. Small tables and chairs are dotted around, to allow us to rest before moving on to the serious business of Scottish dancing.

A few suppliers have already sat down, recreating a map of the vinous world. You could pin the flag of a single nation on each table if it weren't for the British agents keeping an eye on their principals. How inconvenient would it be if one found out during a wine fuelled exchange with another that he pays 5% commission compared to his own 7%?

'I'm glad you're here.'

My little Frenchman has remembered our assignment.

'Would you like a drink?' I ask.

'Later, please. But feel free to have one. Shall we sit down?'

It sounds serious. After a brief hesitation, I pour myself a large glass of water, with ice to make it look more festive.

'My name is Dominique.'

He shakes my hand. His grip is firm but his palm is sweaty.

'I'm lucky enough to sell most of what my domain produces every year and that's enough for me,' he says. 'My sister's husband – he's called Thierry – is more ambitious. He became a director at the local wine co-operative two years ago.'

I have no idea why he's telling me his life's story.

'The older directors don't trust your colleague, André Lange. They used to sell only to small companies. It was Thierry's idea to work with Villa and, to start with, it worked well.' He wipes his forehead with a vast crumpled white handkerchief.

'How does this concern me?' I ask.

'You look after Villa's British customers, don't you?'

'I do.'

'Since the problem with The Super-Market came to light, Monsieur Lange has stopped buying from the co-op. He'll only start again if they accept liability for the incident but he refuses to say what the cost will be.'

'How much is Villa buying from the co-op?'

'It's grown to half the total production over the years. One large customer is so much easier to service than dozens of small ones. Right now, the vats are brimming with wine that will be sent to distillation if no agreement is reached.'

He pulls his handkerchief out of his pocket again. His hands are shaking.

'Co-operatives can't go bankrupt, can they?' I ask.

'They can't but individual growers can and they will if no solution is found. Thierry and my wife, I mean my sister, will have to leave the area if it happens. He'll lose his job and become a figure of hate in the village. It would be a disaster for them and for the kids.'

He's close to tears.

I feel sorry for him. André Lange is a despicable individual.

'What can I do to help?' I ask. 'André Lange doesn't take his orders from me.'

'If you could give me an idea of how much the damages will come to, it would help. Thierry is in a terrible state right now.'

Jen knocks on the bar, demanding attention. 'Good evening ladies and gentlemen and welcome to Edinburgh Castle. On behalf of everybody at The Wine Shop, I would like to thank you again for joining us this weekend. Our customers are, with our staff and suppliers, our most precious asset and the wine fairs play an invaluable part in allowing them to explore the depth and quality of our range. The party tonight is our way to show our gratitude for the hard work you've put in today and we hope you'll be recovered enough to put in tomorrow.' Polite laughter echoes around the room, accompanied by a few whispered, 'Qu'est-ce qu'elle dit?[1]'from the French corner.

Jen continues, 'For those of you who are visiting Edinburgh for the first time, there's a short guided tour of the Castle starting in five minutes, taking in the Honours of Scotland and the Stone of Destiny.'

Tim walks in as if on cue. He's wearing black jeans and an eye-watering pale yellow and green paisley shirt, wide open at the neck. I pretend not to notice him.

Jen concludes, 'The Ceilidh will start at ten and I expect to see you all on the dance floor. We'll start, in time honoured fashion, with the Gay Gordons.'

She sits back to enthusiastic applause and a few, 'Who's gay?' from the less well-travelled suppliers.

I turn back to Dominique, 'Is the co-op responsible for the quality issue?'

'It's more likely that the problem happened during bottling.'

I frown. 'Why would your brother-in-law take the blame?'

'To retain Villa's business. Lange made it clear he'll find ways to express his gratitude if the co-op assumes responsibility.'

'A la Don Corleone,' I say.

'I beg your pardon?'

'Forget it. Tell your brother-in-law that we may have to pay between forty and fifty thousand pounds to The Super-Market, a bit less if we're lucky. That's as much as I know.'

He gets a little calculator out of his pocket. 'If I put the exchange rate at one forty, that's equivalent, at cost price, to hundred-and-fifty to hundred-and-sixty thousand litres of the red they sell to Villa.'

I do a quick calculation. Once bottled, that would fill thirteen lorry loads. 'That's a lot of wine. I'm sorry'

'It's not your fault. Thierry will have to decide what's best for the co-op in the long run. Do you mind giving me your number?'

I hand him my card. 'Will you have a drink now?'

He looks at his watch and stands up. 'I don't think so. Today has been a long day, quite tiring on the legs. I'd rather go back to my hotel and have a rest. Thank you so much for your help.'

I pat his arm. 'No worries. Your sister is lucky to have a brother who cares so much.'

He blushes and shrugs. Why is it men dislike being praised for their kindness?

I wait until he's left the room before going to the bar. It wouldn't do to appear desperate.

Tim appears out of nowhere, bottle in hand. 'He's far too short for you. Have you tried the Anakena Pinot Noir? The tasting note says it's great with ribs and sticky drumsticks.'

He's massaging his stomach in slow circular movements and

licking his lips as if retrieving the juices of a succulent piece of meat. At least that's how I choose to interpret his mimic.

'I'll have a glass of it without the special effects, please.'

I'm still upset by Dominique's story.

'What did the Corsican dwarf want with you?' Tim asks.

'He's not Corsican.'

'I'm surprised. There's a distinct Napoleonic look about him. I had him as plotting your Waterloo.'

A superstitious shiver runs down my spine. 'Please stop, Tim. You're not funny.'

He takes a step closer. 'How would you like me to be?'

I look straight into his eyes. 'Sober and at the other end of the room.'

He looks wounded for a millisecond but the bravura takes over. He bows low. 'At your royal command, Madam. I'll see you later.'

Sadness, mingled with tiredness, overtakes me.

Philippe is back from the guided tour. 'Have you managed to put him off this time?'

His constant criticism of Tim is getting on my nerves. 'There's something I've been meaning to tell you.'

He looks worried.

'Marguerite Villa has invited me to next Wednesday's board meeting.'

'Phew! For a moment, I thought you were going to tell me you were having a thing with Tim. Why does she want you there?'

'Because I know the British market better than most people in the company. The meeting is about The Wine Shop.'

He pulls a face. 'That's terrible.'

'I wouldn't go that far,' I say. 'It is flattering.'

He shakes his head. 'The closer you get to Marguerite, the more you'll antagonise André and Marcel. Most people in the company are loathed by one or the other but to get both of them against you is a recipe for disaster.'

'Let's talk about something else then. It's Saturday night, after all.'

'You're the boss.'

20

THE FALL

Three hours later, I've relaxed into some kind of party spirit. The Scottish dancing helped as did my gorgeous and very tall Australian partner. Tim has obeyed my injunction and stayed away from me, even though I can spot his shirt at the back of the room in the middle of a group of locals. Kate's blond hair creates another beacon of light nearby. I don't care.

The revellers are now split into three groups: the business-minded, the fun-loving and the seriously drunk. The first ones are discussing big issues. Jen has been collared by one of her Italian suppliers who's trying, with much arm waving, to renegotiate the terms of a recent promotion. She looks harassed but my attempts to disentangle her are rebuffed by her smiling but inflexible gaoler.

At the bar, a Spaniard and a Chilean compare notes in hushed voices. They keep on looking around them in a worried way. The Spaniard has pulled a worn-out document from his pocket. He's ironing the creases out of it with his thumbnail while listening with rapt attention to his new best friend. I can make out the Tesco logo at the top of the page.

Next to them, a wannabe store manager panders to a loser from head office while a lone German drowns his sorrows in a pint of Guinness.

The fun-loving guys are partying hard. I've lost my dancing partner to one of The Wine Shop's pretty sales manager. From the greedy way they're eyeing each other, I think I won't be seeing him again tonight. Matt is siring the brand manager of a Bordeaux brand on the dance floor. He's using every opportunity the Dashing White Sergeant provides, to grope her in the most inappropriate way while keeping a straight face. The poor girl looks desperate for the music to stop.

Crouching near the dance floor, but lost in a world of their own, Dave and his cronies are working their way through countless bottles.

'When are you thinking of leaving?' Philippe asks.

'Are you tired?'

'It was a late night yesterday and I had to get up early to catch my flight. I don't want to be knackered on Monday.'

'Shall we go now?'

'If it's all right with you.'

I look around the room one last time. Tim's got his back to me.

I take a deep breath. 'Let's go.'

We button up our coats to face the cold outside and walk in silence through the inner yard of the Castle. The moon and a million bright stars light the battlements and the towers above us. I walk with my nose up in the air while trying not to stumble on the uneven cobbles.

'This is beautiful,' I say.

'Really?'

Philippe's elbow digs into my ribs, and he points to our left. A young woman I spotted earlier in the crowd is wrapped panda-like around Mons Meg, the most famous cannon of the Castle, her jeans round her ankles. The pale skin of her exposed thighs and buttocks shines against the dark metal. A man whose face is in the shadow is thrusting into her with great vigour, his hairy bottom an insult to the full moon.

I grab Philippe's arm. 'Do you think she's alright?'

'How do you want me to find out? Walk up to them and ask for the time?'

I shake my head. The girl's thin body is lolling on her support. 'I can't believe she's comfortable or a willing partner in this charade of love. She must be blind drunk.'

Philippe crosses his arms. 'Go on, I'm here for backup.'

I take two hesitant steps in the direction of the girl and her partner. A discreet cough fails to attract her attention.

'Are you okay?' I ask.

Still nothing.

I walk closer. 'Is everything fine?'

She turns her head in my direction, her eyes glassy. 'Never better, thanks.'

I hover on the spot, unsure of the best course of action when her partner hails me, 'Hey lady, you waiting your turn or you just enjoy watching my cock?'

I run back to Philippe, the girl's giggles following me.

'Happy now, Mother Theresa?' he asks.

'Never mention that scene again.'

We're almost at the taxi rank when Philippe says, 'You do know I'm not staying at the Parliament House Hotel?'

I stop. 'Did you tell me? I can't remember.'

'They don't take bookings for just the one night.'

My hands fly to my throat. 'Damn, I've left my scarf at the Castle.'

'Do you want me to get it for you?' he asks.

'No, I've used and abused you enough for one day. You grab a cab and I'll go back.'

'Are you sure this is a good idea?' Philippe asks.

'I'll be fine.'

He shrugs and walks towards a waiting taxi.

I retrace my steps, hands deep in my coat pockets. I feel cold and lonely. The cannon girl and her server prey on my mind. What's right? What's wrong?

'I thought you'd gone without saying goodbye.'

Tim's voice contains a hint of reproach.

'I had but I left my scarf behind.'

'What colour is it and where did you leave it?'

'Off-white, on the back of a chair by the dance floor. I'll get it now.'

He raises his hand to stop me and grabs his mobile. 'Matt, sorry to bother you, mate. Chris just texted me. She's back at the hotel and she's left her scarf behind, a white-ish one. Could you pick it up for her?'

He pauses. 'No, I'm on my way to a club. I left ten minutes ago.'

He pauses again and turns away from me. 'If she asks, tell her what I've just told you. Look, I need to go.'

He takes my arm and breaks into a half-run towards the exit.

'Tim, slow down, where are we going?'

'Back to the hotel, where else?' he says.

I fail to think of a reasonable objection and follow him.

He sits very close to me in the taxi but doesn't touch me. He doesn't talk either. I try to keep calm. I'm squeezing my hands between my thighs and I struggle to remain upright when the car turns this or that way. Tim's warm masculine scent envelops me. I close my eyes. He wears Safari. I'd never noticed before or maybe he's just changed scent. The citrus and spicy notes balance the hot, salty smell of his body. I'm taking sharp little breaths to catch more of the intoxicating blend.

I feel him getting closer. His breath is warm on my neck.

'Keep your eyes shut,' he says.

He takes my face between his hands and turns it towards him. The tip of his tongue follows the outline of my lips. I gasp. He follows my eyebrows in turn with his index finger.

'You have the most perfectly defined eyebrows I have ever seen.'

His voice sounds different, deeper and almost devoid of the usual Irish lilt.

His lips are on mine now, soft, his tongue in my mouth. He tastes of wine. I love wine.

The taxi coming to a halt brings us back to reality. Tim peers at the dark street.

'We've beaten the bus. Come on.'

Five minutes later, we're in the lift, kissing again.

'I feel like I could eat you.' The image he conjures makes me forget almost everything but my dirty knickers and socks, lying on the floor of my bedroom.

'Wait,' I say.

I rush inside my room, scoop the lot and chuck it in my travel bag. I run to the bed and back to the bathroom. I mean to wash my hands but I remember I've left Tim outside. I stop and turn around.

He's leaning against the door frame, like a modern version of Richard Gere in American Gigolo. 'Are you warming up for a marathon?'

'I don't know.'

I try not to look at the bulge in his trousers.

He walks in, pulling his shirt over his head. His chest is smooth and pale with a few freckles. He takes my hand and guides me towards the bed.

'Do you intend to keep your clothes on?' he asks.

I shake my head. My brain has gone numb.

'Let me.'

He sits next to me and starts to unbutton my top with great concentration. He stops half-way to slide a hand inside my bra. He kisses me again, harder this time, and I fall back on the bed.

He nuzzles my ear. 'Are you on the pill?'

I nod. It's a lie but my period is due anytime now. There's no way I can get pregnant tonight.

He undresses me and him with great care, kissing and licking as he goes. My yearning for him is so strong, I feel almost nauseous. Soon we're both naked and I pull the duvet over us. He cups my face in his hands and greets me in a soft voice, 'Hello stranger'. He slides into me, and all I can think of is to move with him and against him.

I keep my eyes closed, my body intent on savouring the moment. He moves with great deliberation, slowly at first and then faster and faster until he whispers, 'Sorry, can't hold on any longer,' and comes in a long grunt.

I open my eyes. 'The joy of sex,' I say.

'Indeed,' he says, rolling over with a sigh. 'You didn't come.'

'I couldn't. I was too excited if it makes any sense.'

He leaps out of bed, butt-naked. He walks around without an iota of self-consciousness. After a few minutes trying to pretend I'm not looking, I find myself staring at his still erect penis.

'Do you mind?' he asks, waving a homemade looking cigarette in my direction.

I shake my head and he opens the window just enough to blow the smoke outside.

'I didn't know you smoked,' I say.

'Only in very special circumstances,' he says. 'Shame the bus is back, I have a bottle of Champagne in my room we could have put to good use. It will have to wait for another occasion.'

He leaps back on the bed.

We make love more slowly second time round. We explore each other's bodies with intensity rather than urgency. He tells me he wants me to get to know every bit of his body. Despite the blatant invitation, I refrain from going down on him. I feel oddly shy.

I come this time, racked by waves of pleasure that make me arch my back and almost throw him off.

'Sorry, it's been a while,' I say, wiping my eyes.

'I make it half an hour at the most,' he says, patting my bottom.

I sleep for a while, fitfully, waking up, looking at him and closing my eyes again. At four o'clock, we fuck again, without a word but with as much hunger as if it were the first time.

A shrill beep wakes me up at six. Yet I'm positive I didn't put the alarm on. Tim is sitting on his side of the bed, watch in hand.

'Sorry darling, I need to get back to my room before anybody comes down for breakfast.'

I stroke his back, using my nails to scratch him a little. I shuffle closer and hug him from behind, my naked breasts against his skin. I let my hand slide between his legs. He shivers and turns around, his sex responding to my caress.

'Is it wise?' he asks, checking the time again. I nod with great energy. I'm so excited I could make love all day long.

He pauses mid thrust and says, 'I want you to spend all day today thinking of my hard cock inside you.'

Amazing how the same word can sound different depending on who's using it and when. I'm on the edge of ecstasy when I feel a cramp forming in my left calf. Pain and pleasure compete for my attention. I try relaxing my leg and taking little shallow breaths.

Tim pauses mid-thrust. 'Are you alright?'

I dig my fingers in his buttocks to get him going again. 'Yes, yes, please.' It's now a desperate race. I want to come first. 'Ouch!'

My calf has seized up and I throw Tim off.

'Cramp,' I say, while massaging my leg.

He sits there, looking contrite, both hands on his deflating penis.

Despite the pain, I burst out laughing. 'You look like a little boy who's been punished.'

'That's what it feels like,' he says.

He puts his clothes on, returns to the bed and pushes the hair away from my face.

'You don't look sleep deprived at all, young lady. That's unfair.'

He kisses me on the forehead and adds, 'You're a great fuck when you don't get cramps.'

Then he's gone, leaving me ridiculously pleased with his endorsement of my sexual talents.

I check the clock. I can squeeze in another two hours of sleep. The duvet wound tight around me, I drift off, feeling so happy I'm sure to wake up and find I've been dreaming.

When the alarm goes off, it takes me a while to emerge from the deep sleep I've fallen into. I stretch a little and curl up again in the warm bed. The blue tartan duvet cover still smells of Tim and I bury my face in it. Pity I can't take it home with me. A few dark thoughts about where last night will lead us creep in but I manage to push them away.

I'm relieved to find only a smattering of The Wine Shop staff in the breakfast room. The book I've taken with me gives me an excuse to sit on my own.

Getting on the bus proves more awkward and I wish I could borrow Dave's sunglasses to hide my eyes. Nobody has any reason to suspect my nocturnal activities but I still blush every time somebody looks at me for more than a few seconds. I feel like I have a neon sign on my forehead proclaiming, 'I had sex with Tim.'

The object of my thoughts is at the front of the bus and appears normal and composed, which I find a bit disconcerting. I can't look at him for long though, or I'd give myself away. He squeezed my arm when I boarded the bus, saying 'Hello sweetheart,' in what I think of now as his special voice.

He's gorgeous. I can't believe I used to find him overrated. Everything about him is perfect, especially his taste in women.

Philippe's beaten me to the stand again this morning and has already uncorked a dozen bottles of wine.

'Did you find your scarf?' he asks.

'My scarf?'

'The one you left at the party?'

'Matt has got it.'

'Matt?'

'Yes, Matt. He thought I'd gone and he picked it up. He texted me to let me know.'

'Didn't you go back on the bus together?'

'He went early.'

Philippe frowns.

I hope he doesn't ask Matt for his side of the story.

I turn my back to him and concentrate on tasting the wines he's opened. Out of fifteen, only one is corked. Not bad.

The 2005 Saint Emilion is showing well. The primary red fruit aromas have calmed down a little to give way to hints of truffles. The texture is pure silk. I swirl it around my mouth, eyes closed. Vivid memories of last night bring a rush of blood to my face, together with the memory of Tim's command for today. A wave of pleasure ripples through my body. Punters today are guaranteed to find me in an excellent mood if not quite focused. I allow myself a little giggle.

'You look very pleased with yourself.'

Kate is facing me, hands on hips, face like thunder.

'Shouldn't I?' I say, maybe with a touch more provocation than I should.

'Do you think he cares about you?'

I retreat behind the counter. 'I've no idea what you're talking about.'

'Let me tell you something. Tim fucked you last night because he thinks you've got the ear of the old bitch in Bordeaux. But you won't keep him long.'

I can take her insults but the disgusted look on Philippe's face hurts more than I thought it would.

21

BACK TO BUSINESS

Monday turns out to be a perfect crisp winter day. Despite my exhausting weekend, I wake up early, alert and impatient to go to work. My office is now the most attractive place on earth as the most exciting man in the world is working next door.

I sing all the way there, skipping any song on my Ipod that fails to match my exultant mood. Desiree's "Life", with its upbeat melody, I play three times in a row. Thank God, Philippe isn't in the car.

Tim and I kept our distances yesterday after Kate's outburst. I assume those who missed it were told about it later: prime gossip material. Philippe didn't make any comments and nobody else confronted me. Not that I care about people's opinion. Right now, I wish I could tell the world about my new-found happiness.

Tim texted me last night to suggest we meet for drinks later on today to talk about my trip to Bordeaux. I felt a twinge of unease at the specific character of the agenda. I resisted the temptation to phone him though, resorting to a stratagem I last used to give up smoking. Instead of telling myself I shouldn't call him, I postponed the call from one hour to the next until I went to bed.

A long post mortem of the weekend on the phone with Sam took the edge off my frustration. Talking to her about Tim made the whole thing much more real somehow.

I wonder where he will take me tonight. Not that it matters as long as we don't end up in the Queen's Head.

The Wine Shop's offices look glorious against the cloudless sky. The JVCs next door are uncharacteristically silent and the lorry being unloaded in the yard is a bright festive red that sparkles in the sunshine.

Mary is late, as per usual, and Philippe has taken the day off. As I'm back in Bordeaux tomorrow, I'll only see him on Thursday. I'm in no rush.

I potter around the empty office, make myself a big cup of tea and go through the junk which has piled up in my absence. Mary has sent confirmation of André's payment to The Super-Market's haulier. The faulty wine should now be picked up today or tomorrow from the warehouse, a few days short of the Christmas deadline. I address a quick prayer of thanks to Marguerite Villa for coming to my rescue. Rachel has been informed but has remained silent. I wonder if I should chase her up on her Bordeaux tender. If our samples have shown well in the tasting and our prices add up, she may still consider my offer.

Andy Tripp's name in my inbox speeds up my heart rate. I followed up on his disastrous visit last month without any hope of getting the business. I cross myself before I open his mail. It won't change anything but it won't hurt either.

Dear Chris, thank you for quoting for our new Vin de Pays range. Your samples showed well against the competition but your prices are too high. Let me know by return what you can do to improve them. We need to move fast.

This was sent on Thursday. I should have checked my mails. I'll never forgive myself if I've missed this opportunity.

'Andy?' I was expecting his voicemail, not the man himself. 'It's Chris Legerot. Sorry I failed to come back to you last week. I was in Bordeaux on business.'

'I thought you were having too good a time in Scotland to bother with business.'

Panic sets in. What does he know?

'Scotland?' I ask.

'The Wine Shop's wine fair,' he says.

'Oh yes, of course, yes.'

'How did it go?'

'Very well, thanks! Brilliant, really.'

He laughs. 'Relax, I'm not after your trade secrets. To get back to the point, I need twenty eurocents off your reds' prices and a bit less on the whites as they're in short supply.'

'What kind of volumes are you talking about?'

'Ten thousand cases of each to start with, maybe more.'

British wine professionals measure wine volume in nine litre cases, the equivalent of twelve seventy-five centilitre bottles. The French use bottles or hectolitres for bulk. I sometimes feel like a walking calculator, translating from one to the other. If Andy is telling the truth, we're talking about a contract of more than half a million bottles, which, in addition to what I expect from existing customers, would allow me to beat my volume target for next year.

'When do you need to know?' I ask, trying to keep my voice level.

'Didn't I say last week in my mail?'

I bite my lip. 'Give me two hours.'

A quick peek at my original calculation confirms what I thought. I can't give Andy what he wants with the cost prices I've been quoted. I need to ask André Lange for help. I'd better call Serge first. After their tête-à-tête during the four-hour drive back to Narbonne, he'll have a good idea of what my chances are.

The phone rings before I've had time to dial.

'How was Edinburgh?'

In the same way I got flustered by Andy's allusion to the wine fair, for a surreal moment, I wonder if Arnaud is asking me about my night with Tim.

I lean back in my chair. 'You'd have enjoyed it.'

'I have better things to do with my weekends,' he says.

'As have your staff and suppliers.'

'Spare me the lecture. I know what goes on during these things. It's not all hard work.'

I return to a more business-like position. 'What can I do for you?'

'I need to see you and the artist this morning. I've no idea where you've got to with the new range and I have to know before…'

I'm expecting him to say Wednesday but he lets the end of the sentence trail away.

He adds as if it were an afterthought, 'You must tell me about your meeting with Marguerite Villa.'

'Would you like me to come over now?'

'Let me call the artist first, he's not always at his best on Monday morning. God knows what he got up to in Scotland!'

I do not comment.

He's now going to interrupt Tim and ask him to join him in his office straight away. Then he'll keep him waiting while he gets me to come over. It would have been simpler to check if Tim was in and to drop us a mail to suggest a meeting for eleven o'clock but Arnaud, like André Lange, is partisan of the maximum disruption strategy. It makes him feel busy as he's doing lots, efficient as he gets what he wants and important as he gets it quick. He doesn't care that we're going unprepared into a meeting, at a time that's possibly inconvenient for Tim and for me.

Mary walks in while I'm on the phone to Arnaud.

'How did it go?' she asks. 'I tried to call Philippe last night but his mobile was turned off.'

'You did a great job. The spare labels helped a lot.'

'I mean the party. What's the gossip?'

She takes a look at me and backtracks. 'Sorry, you were probably too busy to notice but there are always shenanigans happening at the Scottish wine fair. Forget about it.'

I'll have to tell her but I can't right now. Dave's allegations come back to me.

'Talking about gossip, Mary, you may want a word with our resident slouch. He had a drunken go at me for keeping you away from Edinburgh this weekend.'

'Did he?'

'I know it sounds ridiculous. He claims the two of you had a bit of a thing going on last year even though he was a bit vague on the details.'

The phone rings. I pick up, muting the handset with my hand. 'I told him what I thought about his attempts to blacken your name in your absence.'

I lift my hand off the handset and turn away from Mary. 'Arnaud?'

'My office. We're waiting for you.'

I turn back to Mary. She looks close to tears.

'Hey, what's the matter?'

She shakes her head.

'Is it Dave?' I ask.

'I was pretty drunk. And he wasn't drinking and smoking that much last year. All we did was kiss,' she says.

I nod, trying not to look too surprised.

'I hate disappointing you.'

She's sitting very straight in her chair, her hands shredding a crumpled tissue in her lap. The tip of her nose has turned bright pink.

How can I tell her I've done much worse?

'Mary, it's alright.'

She looks up at me. 'You sure?'

'I'll tell you something later.'

Who should I bump into outside but Dave? After his three-day bender, he looks like an ad for a temperance movement. He's changed into clean clothes but they are shaped like the radiator I assume they dried on. They make him look like he's been trampled on. He hasn't shaved and the whites of his eyes are the colour of diluted urine. Today of all days, he should wear sunglasses.

'I need to apologise to you,' I say.

He waves his fag in my direction and tries to dissipate the smoke with his other hand.

'S'all right.'

I feel angry with him all of a sudden, for being such a wreck, for not trying harder and for letting Mary down.

'Even though you were telling the truth about Mary, your lack of discretion was far from chivalrous.'

He looks at me and I realise he had no idea what I was talking about earlier.

'What did she say?' he asks.

'She admitted you snogged.' I say, as if reporting facts in a court of justice.

'Did she?'

'She never lies.'

He looks me straight in the eye. 'I know that. I was drunk and upset. I'll apologise to her.'

It's the first time I hear him alluding to drunkenness without boasting about it.

I decide to push my advantage. 'Dave, do you enjoy killing yourself slowly?'

'Who says it's got to be slow?'

His cockiness has returned but, for a brief moment, I glimpsed the man behind the ape, the man who may well be in love with Mary.

I feel myself blushing as I walk into Arnaud's office. I wish I'd had time to see Tim alone before the meeting.

He's sitting in a chair opposite Arnaud's desk and he winks at me. The vivid pink and red stripy shirt he's wearing would look garish on anybody but him.

Luck is on my side as Arnaud has his back to me. He's standing at the window, legs apart and arms crossed, surveying the car park.

'Bloody hell, look at that!'

Tim and I join him at the window. The yard is empty, except for a tall guy unfolding his convertible's top with the utmost care. He looks like a rep.

We exchange a puzzled look.

'What should we look at?' I ask Arnaud.

He points an accusing finger towards the unsuspecting petrol head. 'I bet he's one of our suppliers.'

I shrug. 'Looks like it.'

'Have you seen his car?'

'What about it?'

'BMW, Mercedes, you name it. Bloody agents! They're rolling in it and they're bleeding us dry.'

'That's got nothing to do with us. The Brits love their cars. Mr Average out there may well live in a poky little flat. But when the top comes down on a sunny day, he's king of the jungle for a few hours.'

Arnaud turns towards me. 'Do you have an explanation for everything?'

I raise my hands in self-defence. 'I aim to please.'

He returns to his desk and I sit down next to Tim.

'Where have you got to?' Arnaud asks.

I nod at Tim and he starts unfolding images of wine bottles. 'A few years ago, Threshers developed a range of own label wines called Radcliffe's, which covered most of the better-known appellations.'

'I told you it was the way to go,' Arnaud says.

'All the wines were supplied by respectable companies but, as their names were not mentioned on the labels, Radcliffe's turned out to be another range of classic names, fairly similar to what supermarkets offer.'

Arnaud frowns. 'What's wrong with that?'

'Supermarkets have a lower cost structure. We need a point of difference to justify higher prices. It's not enough to claim our quality is better.'

'What's the big idea, then?'

Tim takes a deep breath. 'We thought we could develop a range called "The Wine Shop in partnership with". We'd seek out one, if not the top producer for a given wine, and develop an exclusive blend with him. He'd gain added exposure for his name and we'd get instant recognition, especially with the trade press.'

Arnaud bangs on the table. 'Is that what you've been plotting for two bloody weeks?'

Tim and I look at each other and nod in unison, like naughty schoolchildren.

'Where did I say I wanted to source the wines from?'

I step in. 'From Villa and that's no problem for Bordeaux or Burgundy. But when it comes to other areas, we don't have the credibility.'

He yells, 'I don't give a flying fuck about credibility. I told Marguerite Villa I'd pull this white elephant out of the red and I'd grow sales of our wines tenfold in this country. Now you're either going to help me do it or you'll find yourself working in partnership with another company. Get it?'

'I don't report to you,' I say.

'No but he does,' Arnaud says, pointing at Tim. 'Now, Madam, I am going to spell it out once more for you and our bird of paradise here. I want a range of ten wines including a Pinot Grigio, a White Zinfandel, a Chardonnay, a Bordeaux and whatever best sellers you can pull out of our sales figures. I want them supplied by Villa and I want them now.'

I grip the desk with both hands. I am trembling with fury. 'What do you want the labels to say? "Kamikaze by The Wine Shop"?'

Arnaud leans forwards. Our faces are six inches apart. 'You will do what I ask or else. Now go!'

Now isn't the best time to tell him I've been invited to Wednesday's board meeting in Bordeaux. I leave the room without a backwards glance, Tim right behind me.

'Thanks,' I say.

'What for?' he asks.

'Giving me the strength to stand up to this bullying bastard.'

'Are you sure it was the right thing to do?'

I stare at him. He looks upset. Yelling at people and calling them names during business meetings may be acceptable to French people but it goes against the grain this side of the Channel.

'Are you annoyed with Arnaud or with me?'

'I'll call you later,' he says.

He walks off towards his office.

22

COMING CLEAN AND COMING DOWN

I make for Jen's office. I may as well get all my awkward meetings over in one go. She's on the phone when I walk in.

'Hold on,' she says to her caller.

'Do you have five minutes?' I ask.

She gestures for me to sit down before turning her attention back to the phone. 'Don't send him up just now,' she says.

She puts the phone down and folds her arms.

'I'm listening.'

'Where do you want me to start?'

'Did you sleep with Tim in Edinburgh?'

I nod.

'You don't mind being the last one in a long line of conquests.'

I sigh. 'As long as I remain the last one.'

We stare at each other for what feels like a very long time.

'Good luck to you,' she says. 'I don't care about him anymore but the whole thing strikes me as a bit incestuous.'

I could tell her she's deceiving herself. I could try to justify myself or even apologise but none of it will help.

'Do you want me to tell you about Arnaud's project?' I ask.

'Go on.'

When I leave her office, twenty minutes later, I feel a bit better. I have told her the truth, all the truth and nothing but the truth.

As I go downstairs, I bump into the guy with the convertible, on his way to see Jen. Away from his snazzy car, he looks even more ordinary and worn out.

Matt's office is at the bottom of the stairs, a perfect vantage point, opposite reception. He signals to me as I pass his door.

'Hello trouble. Come in here a minute and close the door behind you. I'm not sure I want us to be seen together.'

I ignore the slur and sit down.

'What did Jack want with you and Tim? He was shouting so much I thought the ceiling was about to collapse.'

Matt's office is right under Arnaud's.

'To rip us apart in order to do justice to his nickname.'

'Was it because of…?' He trails off and examines his fingernails.

'Because of what?' I ask.

He looks up. 'Kate's allegations?'

'How would he know?'

'Kate is young and impulsive.' He shuffles the papers on his desk as if looking for something. 'You know the saying: "Hell hath no fury like a woman scorned."'

'She wouldn't, would she?' I ask.

Matt picks up a piece of paper and crumples it in a tight ball. 'I hope not, for your sake and Tim's. Hopefully she's learnt her lesson.'

'Which is?'

He swivels his chair around and aims the paper ball at the waste bin.

'That there are men one should never ever fall in love with.'

I wince but he's not looking at me.

'Goal,' he says. 'Anyway, my turn to go into the lion's den. Arnaud has discovered he has to pay tax on his company car and on the flat Villa is renting for him. He's adamant he won't.'

'Don't tell me. He didn't in Africa?'

'How did you guess?'

'I'll come upstairs with you. There's something I forgot.'

I wait until I'm sure Arnaud is busy with Matt and knock at his assistant's door.

'Sorry to bother you. I've a big favour to ask.'

'As long as it's neither illegal nor dangerous,' she says.

'How is Arnaud getting to Bordeaux tomorrow?'

'As The Wine Shop's finances don't allow for a private jet, he'll have to slum it on BA's afternoon flight,' she says.

'You look annoyed.'

'The bastard told me this morning he's cancelling the Christmas party.'

'Why?'

'Too expensive. Yet, everything we buy for him has to be top of the range. Did Matt tell you he had to send somebody from IT to his home to install a whole bunch of brand-new televisions and computers? All of them paid for by the company, of course!'

'Ouch!'

'My PC is falling apart,' she says, warming up to her theme. 'It's coming up to five years old and I need to call IT almost every week to fix it. And his bleeding fifteen-year-old son gets a brand-new Mac just like Daddy's.'

I beat a hasty retreat before the sound of her raised voice attracts Arnaud's attention.

Dave is leaving my office when I get back there and I almost collide into him. Isn't anybody looking where they're going today or is it me?

Mary looks engrossed in her work but her cheeks are bright pink and there's a bunch of roses on her desk.

'Had a visitor?' I ask.

'He was really nice,' she says.

'I don't doubt it for a minute.'

I sit down in front of my computer.

'Dave told me there's a story going around about you and Tim spending the night together in Edinburgh. I hope you don't think that's what I was alluding to earlier on?'

I shake my head.

'I told him I didn't believe a word of it,' Mary says. 'Tim is a nice guy but he's a bit of a joke. You wouldn't fall for him in a million years.'

I raise my hand to interrupt her before she tells me more than I want to hear. 'I'm chuffed you have such high regard for me but it's not justified.'

She stares at me blankly for a while. Her hand flies to her mouth 'Oh my God! I'm such a fool.'

'Mary, calm down. I'm the fool.'

'I'm so, so sorry. I am sure he's…' She struggles to find a suitable word, 'lovely.'

Her feeble endorsement depresses me more than her earlier scathing comments. It's time to call Serge.

A bubbling sound is the first thing I hear when he picks up the phone. In a thriller, he'd be lying in a pool of blood, his life ebbing away from a gaping wound in his throat while trying to give me the name of his killer. As it is, he's probably yet again in the middle of a tasting and what I hear is wine swirling around his mouth. A neat spitting noise and the thud of liquid hitting the spittoon follow.

'Sorry, but Carrefour is arriving in half an hour and nobody's bothered to taste the samples we're showing them,' he says. 'I can't believe how little some of the French sales guys care about wine. I tell you what, one day, I'll leave them to cope on their own.'

'Why should they bother when they know you do the work for them? Do you want me to call you later?' I ask.

'I'm going to be stuck with them till Tuesday evening. Is it a quick one?'

'I need better bulk prices for Direct Wines. The contract is much bigger than I thought. Do you think André will help?'

I hear another gargle and spit.

'I don't know. I can't understand his problem with you. It doesn't make any sense but it's almost as if he's scared of you.'

'André Lange, scared of me? Are you mad?'

'I told you it doesn't make sense but he said something odd during our drive back from Bordeaux last Thursday.'

'What did he say?'

'I can't remember exactly: something about Marguerite's long memory and loyalty to people who've sacrificed everything for her. I don't understand how it applies to you.'

'Neither do I,' I say. 'What about my prices? Should I tell him I'll come and get him if he doesn't give me the cost prices I need?'

'I wouldn't go that far. Let me think.'

More gurgling sounds follow. It's as if Serge needs to keep his taste buds moist in order to think. Maman hits the roof when I drink tea while talking to her on the phone. She'd hate a telephone conversation with Serge.

'Tell him Castel is best placed to get the business,' he says. 'They have just beaten us to a big deal with Albert Hjein in Holland. What he won't do to help you, he'll do to thwart them.'

'You're a star. Have fun with Carrefour!'

I check my watch. Eleven thirty. Time is passing so slowly today, I don't know how I'll get to tonight without going mad with frustration.

I allow myself a little chuckle. André, scared of me? That doesn't make any sense at all.

It's lunchtime in France: too late to call André but the perfect time to catch my mother. I last called her ten days ago.

The conversation starts well. We compare and contrast the weather in Kingston and Arcachon with short and long-term forecasts for both places. I present her with a rose-tinted version of the latest developments at work and manage to soothe her maternal concerns about my workload and the amount of travelling I'm doing, both of which she considers excessive.

Then, she spoils it all. 'Have you decided how long you'll stay at Christmas?' she asks.

'But Maman, Christmas is-'

She finishes my sentence. 'In four weeks.'

Delicious visions of lazy afternoons in bed with Tim silence me for a while. I can almost smell the fat cinnamon candle ablaze in my bedroom, contrasting with the foul, cold weather outside.

'Are you still here?' Maman asks.

'I was thinking.'

'Your brother is coming with his wife and the girls. He suggested you and I come and stay with them but I prefer all of us to be in Arcachon as it's the first Christmas since your father passed away. I said I'd give the blue room to the children. You don't mind sleeping on the sofa bed, do you?'

A cold draught extinguishes the sweet-smelling candle of my fantasy. 'How long are Roland and Bea staying?

'They have to go back on the twenty sixth. He can't take the whole week off. He works so hard, poor boy. Would you like to stay for New Year's Eve? We could book a table "Chez Yvette" and treat ourselves.'

I love Arcachon, but it's glum in the winter and the programme Maman is suggesting fails to excite when compared with an indulgent week in Tim's company.

'When do you need to know?'

'You don't sound very enthusiastic.'

I cross my fingers behind my back. 'I need to check with my team how we're going to manage the holiday period, that's all.'

'Villa can't expect you to work over Christmas. I know it's a long time ago but in your father's time, production sites closed for the whole week. Things can't have changed so much.'

I stop listening to Maman's reminiscences.

The afternoon passes at a snail's pace. Tim suggested we meet at 6 o'clock at a pub close to mine.

He's on his mobile when I get there and I sit down opposite him, not wanting to interrupt. He is complaining to Matt about Arnaud's telling off, and saying how unhappy he is about the new range we have been entrusted to develop. I go to the bar to get drinks.

'I hope this comes up during the board meeting,' Tim is saying when I return. 'Chris will be there.'

I can't hear what Matt is saying but I don't like the way Tim is smiling.

'She's our best chance to get Marguerite Villa to overrule Arnaud,' he says.

He winks at me, reaches out across the table and squeezes my hand.

While he mulls over various options in what begins to feel more like a business briefing than a lovers' rendezvous, I keep on thinking about my telephone conversation with Maman and the Christmas holidays.

After what feels like an eternity, Tim finally bids goodbye to Matt.

What's on your mind?' he asks.

'I am trying to decide whether I should spend my Christmas holidays here or in France,' I say.

'Won't you want to be with your mother now she's on her own?'

'She has lots of friends and my brother will be visiting,' I say.

He frowns. 'Christmas is for families.'

He makes no mention of his own plans and I don't ask.

When I suggest we repair to my place for something to eat, he checks the time and tells me he's meeting a friend in half an hour. Even though he adds it was arranged two weeks ago, I'm disappointed.

He stands up and kisses me lightly on the lips, joking he wants his champion on top form to defend The Wine Shop's best interests in Bordeaux. I put my coat on slowly, trying to delay the time for goodbyes. He grabs me by the waist, looks deep into my eyes and whispers in my ear he's looking forward to a full debrief on my return. Then he kisses me deeply, turns on his heels and runs off.

I go back home, feeling like one of these cold war spies whose minders used sex to manipulate.

A long telephone conversation with Sam reassures me Tim needs to take stock of the situation after our intense night together and it would be unwise to pressurise him to spend too much time with me so early in the relationship. I bow to her superior knowledge of a man she's never met and retreat to my empty freshly-made bed with a large glass of Errazuriz Wild Ferment Chardonnay and Liz Jensen's "The Ninth Life of Louis Drax". I like a book to reassure me there are worse destinies than mine.

The wine does such a good job of soothing my jangled nerves that I finish the bottle.

23

THE BOARD MEETING

In order to avoid bumping into Arnaud, either at Gatwick or on the plane, I fly EasyJet from Luton the following afternoon. I jump into a taxi at Bordeaux airport, and arrive at my hotel shortly before nine o'clock. Dinner on my own doesn't appeal and I go straight to bed after succumbing to the charms of the minibar's overpriced gin and tonic.

I wake up light-headed the following morning, my two restorative nights in a row making the last weekend in Edinburgh feel like it happened a month ago.

Marguerite Villa's assistant told Mary the board meeting would start at nine. I turn up at the last minute to maximise the surprise effect of my arrival on Arnaud and creep in through the half open door.

The boardroom looks completely different from when I was last here, only a week ago. A mobile partition divides the room in two and a long table of dark shiny wood with a small but elaborate flower arrangement in the middle replaces the foldable modern white desks used for the export meeting. Every surface has been dusted and polished and the room smells of wax and fresh flowers.

Instead of the export department's ill-assorted crew, the five men sitting around Marguerite Villa are dressed in dark, almost identical suits. Seb, whose looks have improved since his return to Burgundy, looks like he's swallowed a walking stick and Marcel could be on his way to his first communion, his shiny black hair gelled back. Only the two financial directors, The Wine Shop's and Villa's, have brought laptops.

Arnaud is holding court. 'It's actually an advantage not to speak too good English in that job. It saves me from having to listen to endless objections to anything I decide. You wouldn't believe how argumentative those guys are,' he says.

Villa's finance director guffaws as does Marcel. Neither speaks a word of English.

Arnaud spots me. His jaw drops and he stares at me open-mouthed as if I'd popped fully formed out of one of his nightmares.

Marguerite follows his gaze and beams at me. 'Christine, come in.' She looks back at her companions. 'I expect you all know Christine Legerot? Arnaud?'

He frowns. 'Christine? Yes, we've met,' he says.

'Is that all?' she asks.

He turns to me. 'Good morning, Mademoiselle.'

'Less formality, Arnaud,' Marguerite says. 'The two of you must work together.'

Sébastien pipes up, 'Good morning Chris.'

'That's the spirit,' says Marguerite.

She pats the chair next to her. 'Come and sit here, Christine.'

Villa's finance director leans towards me and points at Arnaud. 'He doesn't seem too happy to see you.'

I smile back in a non-committal way and fish a notepad out of my bag.

Marguerite knocks on the table. 'Now we're all here, let's listen to Monsieur Vidal's plans for The Wine Shop.'

Arnaud walks to the top of the table, followed by his finance director carrying his open laptop. Everybody turns towards them with a discipline that would make Ed weep.

'I'll start with some figures to give you a picture of the current situation,' Arnaud says. 'I've revised downwards Sébastien's original forecast for this calendar year.'

Sébastien interrupts him, 'The team at The Wine Shop is weak. If it wasn't for them, we'd be on track.'

Marguerite ignores him. 'How many million pounds do we stand to lose now?' she asks.

'We're looking at seven million pounds for this year but I plan to break even next year,' Arnaud says.

Sébastien shivers. 'Sales were terrible this summer. Like the weather.'

'Six months ago, you were planning to break even this year, Monsieur Melot,' Marguerite says. 'Now, if you don't mind, I'd like to concentrate on Arnaud's presentation.'

She turns to me. 'Listen carefully and feel free to ask questions.'

Arnaud looks as though he's bitten into an unripe lemon.

'The losses-'

Marguerite interrupts him, 'Forget about this year. I'm interested in how you're proposing to reverse the trend next year.'

Arnaud signals to his finance director to skip a few slides. 'My plan rests on three key elements: disposal of loss-making branches, cost cutting and sales growth.'

'We have already cut-' Sébastien says.

Marguerite turns towards him. 'Monsieur Melot!'

Arnaud continues, 'Thirty stores are haemorrhaging cash. Some of them have been refurbished but it hasn't helped. They suffer from a combination of poor locations, high rents, and high business rates. We need to get rid of them.'

'How long are the leases on these stores?' I ask.

Marguerite gives me an approving look.

Arnaud clenches his jaw. 'Some of them are on long-term leases. We'll have to find new tenants.'

'How will you achieve that if they're in poor locations?' Marguerite asks.

'What's true for wine isn't necessarily true for other goods. I've planned to task one of the sales managers with this project,' Arnaud says.

'Very weak, the sales team at The Wine Shop, very weak,' Sébastien says.

Arnaud's cauliflower ears turn bright red. He runs his hands through his sparse blond hair. 'Madame Villa, may I continue?'

'You may, Arnaud,' Marguerite says, a half-smile on her face.

'Disposals should save us two million pounds a year. Cost-cutting will take care of another two.'

'Could we talk about how you plan to grow sales?' Marguerite asks. 'You can save as much as you want, but unless sales pick up, the business is doomed and I may as well cut my losses.'

'Villa supplies a bit less than two million bottles of wine to The Wine Shop per year,' Arnaud says. He pauses and looks at each of us in turn. 'I plan to improve on this significantly.'

'Very commendable,' Marguerite says, with a hint of irony.

Arnaud leans forward, propping himself up on his knuckles, gorilla-like. 'Within the next year, I intend to source an additional seven million bottles from Villa,' he says, slowing his delivery for emphasis.

I blurt out. 'That's impossible.'

'I don't do impossible.'

Arnaud looks like he's about to headbutt me.

'Why impossible?' Marguerite asks, without looking at me.

'The Wine Shop already stocks far too many wines from Villa. The range is unbalanced at it is,' I say, feeling like I am suggesting vegetarianism to a convention of butchers.

'What do you mean, unbalanced?' Marguerite asks, still staring straight ahead.

'The Wine Shop's reputation rests on its eclectic selection. If we turn it into an outlet for Villa's wines, we'll be slaughtered by the press and we'll lose even more customers. Jen and I review the range every month to avoid such a situation.'

'Very weak, Jen, very weak. She knows nothing about French wines,' Sébastien says.

'Are you telling me British wine writers don't like our wines?' Marguerite asks.

I take a deep breath. 'Not if they are the only French wines on offer from The Wine Shop.'

Marguerite snorts.

I warm up to my theme. 'You also have the managers to think of. Most of them are passionate about wine, and knowledgeable too. We must feed their enthusiasm with diversity and quality if we want them to perform.'

'Very weak, the managers, very weak.'

Sébastien is slouching now. I worry he's going to slip under the table.

Villa's finance director joins in the fray. 'They're dirty too. Do you remember the fat guy in Birmingham, Sébastien?'

'The one with huge sweat stains under his arms?'

I'm getting angry. 'Have you tried moving cases of wine around without getting dirty and sweaty?'

'They're not projecting the right image for the business,' Villa's finance director says. 'What about making them wear branded aprons to give them some sort of corporate look?'

'You can't do that,' I say. 'The Wine Shop and aprons don't go together.'

'Can we go back to Arnaud's seven million bottles, please?' Marguerite asks. 'This additional volume would make a huge difference to our bottom line.'

She turns to Arnaud, 'Which wines are you thinking about?'

Arnaud looks at me with intense dislike. 'My project isn't as advanced as I hoped it would be by now. These volumes are currently unspecified.'

Marguerite slaps both hands on the table. 'Unspecified wines generating an unspecified turnover yet, I suppose, unspecified large margins?'

Arnaud looks down at the floor. A vein is pulsing on his forehead.

Marguerite shakes her head. 'Monsieur Vidal, I am afraid this isn't good enough. How do you expect me to give my blessing to such a vague concept?'

Sébastien mutters under his breath, 'Very weak, very weak…'

Arnaud raises his chin. 'I'll get back to you on the new range.'

Marguerite sighs. 'Please do and call on André Lange if you need any help. He should have been with us today but he had a last minute emergency in Narbonne.'

She turns to me and pats my hand. 'You know what it's like when you run a bottling site.'

Arnaud frowns.

'Now, I hope the third part of your programme is more impressive than what we've heard so far,' Marguerite says, turning back to Arnaud.

'I've finished interviewing everybody at head office, including the HR Director,' Arnaud says.

'Very weak the HR Director, very weak.'

Marguerite snaps, 'Monsieur Melot, will you please keep quiet or I'll have to ask you to leave.'

Marcel, whom I suspect of being able to sleep with his eyes open, almost topples out of his chair, arms flailing. His mother glares at him. 'Marcel, please.'

He straightens up, recomposing himself in the picture of the dutiful executive. 'Yes, mother.'

'We're going to shift stock management from head office to stores,' Arnaud says. 'This will empower shop managers and give them the chance to show us what they can do. It will also enable us to reduce the headcount in Kingston.'

Marguerite nods. 'Sounds reasonable. How will you ensure stores don't order too much?'

'We'll put quotas in place.'

She turns to me. 'Christine?'

'This is difficult for me. I probably know the people Arnaud means to let go.'

'Very weak…'

Taking my lead from Marguerite, I bark at Sébastien, 'Please, not now!' and continue in more measured tones 'I feel for them but I can see the sense in what Arnaud is planning to do.'

'I'm running a business,' Marguerite says, her brown eyes softening for a brief moment. 'Unfortunately, this often means taking difficult decisions when it comes to people. What else, Arnaud?'

'I'll lengthen promotional periods from monthly to quarterly. It will save on posters and displays in stores and it will also allow us to slim down the marketing team. We have six people in there, listening to the radio all day long.'

I butt in again, 'Listening to music doesn't stop them from working hard.'

'Christine, please.' There's a note of warning in Marguerite's voice. 'The Wine Shop's staff report to Arnaud, not to you.'

'You can't let him destroy the marketing department,' I say. 'They're the nerve centre of the business.'

Marguerite looks at me, her head on one side and I feel myself flushing bright red. 'And Arnaud's suggestion seems to have touched a nerve with you.'

I try to regain my composure, 'The Wine Shop needs a clear, strong strategy to pull out. That's the marketing team's job.'

'No, it's mine,' says Arnaud, his arms crossed in defiance. 'That's why I'm getting rid of them.'

'Very weak, the marketing department, very weak.'

Everybody ignores Sébastien.

'But surely, you can't sack them all?' I ask Arnaud.

'Why not?'

'How will you manage the launch of the new range? What about promotions?'

'I'll outsource. We need new blood. The current team is too stuck in their ways, as demonstrated on Monday.'

Tim was right. I shouldn't have antagonised Arnaud. He'll sack Tim in retaliation and it will be my fault. I can't let it happen.

I turn to The Wine Shop's finance director. He shrugs and shakes his head slowly. Another one whose feathers Tim has ruffled.

I try to appeal to Arnaud's common sense. 'You're taking a huge risk. You need people who know The Wine Shop inside out to relay your ideas, people who have the trust of the managers. Otherwise even your best initiatives will fail.'

'Why?' he asks, a victorious smile on his thin lips.

I'm trying to gain time, searching for a solution. My head is spinning.

'Isn't it obvious?'

'Not to me,' he says.

He comes to stand in front of me, hands on hips. I can smell his acrid sweat. 'I'm the boss,' he says, jabbing his chest hard.

Marguerite isn't impressed. 'Why don't you keep one or two people from the current team?'

I hold my breath.

'I could keep the brunette,' he says. 'She's quite amenable. And maybe the quiet guy who sits in the corner.'

'What about Tim Foster?' I ask.

'That arrogant know-it-all? He's the one I'm most looking forward to get rid of,' Arnaud says.

'I don't think you should get rid of him,' I say.

The Wine Shop's finance director is trying to hide his smile. News travel fast. I don't care as long as he remains silent. His opinion hasn't been sought once anyway, even though he speaks French.

'Why?' Marguerite asks.

I'll save Tim's job if it's the only thing I achieve today.

'He's close to influential wine writers,' I say, making it up as I go along. 'There'll be a huge backlash if he goes.'

'How could some obscure pen pushers damage Villa?' Arnaud asks.

'Decanter ran a survey recently about the most influential people in the wine world. With all due respect, Jancis Robinson came in ahead of Marguerite Villa.'

'Jancis who?' Arnaud asks. 'I've never heard of her.'

Fortunately for me, Marguerite has. 'Christine is right. British wine writers command a lot of respect worldwide. We can't risk upsetting them.'

She turns to me. 'Apart from having friends in high places, is this Tim Foster any good?'

'Brilliant,' I say, trying not to look at The Wine Shop's finance director. 'An original thinker, hard-working and committed to The Wine Shop.'

Marguerite pulls a face. 'I am not sure we need original but never mind. Christine, you've played your joker. I'll be interested to find out if you've chosen wisely.'

Sébastien has the last word, 'Very weak, Tim Foster, very weak.'

24

RUNNING ON EMPTY

I hang about at head office after the board meeting, hoping to catch Marguerite Villa and continue our conversation about my father. Two hours go by but she doesn't make an appearance: time to go back to my hotel for another solitary evening. I crouch under the desk to unplug my laptop.

'Why does Marguerite Villa call you Christine? And why does she think you know what it's like to run a bottling site?'

I bump my head against the desk.

'Arnaud, don't creep on me like that. You scared the hell out of me!'

'I asked you a question.'

'Christine is my name.'

'Everybody calls you Chris, and Marguerite Villa only does first names with people she knows well.'

I get up and continue packing my stuff in silence.

'I am not going anywhere,' Arnaud says.

I take a deep breath.

'My father used to work for Villa a long time ago. Marguerite knew me as a child.'

'Is that why you got the job?'

'You do know how to flatter people, don't you?'

He shrugs. 'It's the way she operates. Nothing wrong about that. What did your father do?'

'He was Marguerite's right hand man. They built the company together and he ran the Narbonne site until he left.'

'Did she get rid of him?'

'I don't know, Arnaud. My father died six months ago. I still find it difficult to talk about him.'

He turns on his heels and leaves the room.

'Sorry,' he says from halfway down the corridor.

Arnaud has apologised to me for the first time ever.

I fly back to England the following day and call Sam at work when I land.

'I am a failure.'

'One of those days?' she asks.

'Make it a week, or maybe a month or three. I'm making a mess of things. I joined Villa in the hope of finding out what had happened to Papa and all I've discovered so far, is that it was 'a sad story' according to Marguerite Villa.'

'Give me a minute.'

I hear muffled voices and the sound of a door closing.

'Could your father have been in love with this Marguerite woman?' Sam asks.

'She used to be stunning but Papa would already have been married when they met.'

Her diplomatic silence reminds me my father may have been fallible.

'Leaving Villa did break his heart.'

Sam makes a non-comital noise.

'It doesn't add up though. He wouldn't have spoken so much of Marguerite in front of Maman if there had been something between them. He only stopped mentioning her after he left the company.'

'Fair point,' Sam says. 'May I suggest you try to forget about the past and focus on the present and the positive? Your sales figures are good, aren't they?'

'They are but the crisis with The Super-Market has spoiled everything and made me lots of enemies.'

'That's annoying but surely your professionalism will win them over.'

'I messed up at yesterday's meeting too. I lied to protect Tim's job.'

'How?'

'I claimed he's essential to the business's survival. The truth is, I'll lose him if he leaves the Wine Shop.'

'You don't know that.'

I snort.

'You may be right,' Sam eventually says. 'You can't tell him you saved his job though. He'd feel emasculated.'

I feel worse when I put the phone down than when I picked it up.

I decide not to call Tim, thus postponing the inevitable debriefing of yesterday's meeting. He doesn't call either, which I choose to read as a positive sign that he's not interested in me only because of my position.

When we catch up the day after at six o'clock in his deserted office, the Edinburgh magic has returned. A welcome snog starts the proceedings on a positive note and I sit on his desk as close to him as decency and the risk of somebody barging in permits. He asks me for an account of the meeting but without the urgency I was dreading.

He caresses my knee while I talk about the disposal program.

'That's rich! Did Arnaud present this as a new idea? Matt has been telling anybody who cares to listen for years.'

'Why hasn't it been done before?' I ask.

Tim's hand slides up and down my leg.

'It's expensive and a big hassle. Arnaud will need some of his African accounting talent if he wants to get rid of these stores and break even next year. Would you like a drink?'

I nod. Tim selects an open bottle from the fridge where he keeps what he calls "samples for research purpose".

'I'm sorry this is nothing special: a leftover from the Sancerre tasting we did yesterday,' he says.

He hands me a glass and starts kissing my neck.

I take a large mouthful of wine.

'Tell me more,' he says.

I continue my report.

Tim is unimpressed with Arnaud's project to transfer power from head office to stores. His fingers venture to my bra, which he unhooks with a dexterity that hints at years of practice.

'Wait until Jen finds out,' he says. 'She'll hit the roof. Imagine the managers don't take to a wine she's bought a shedload of. How will we shift it?'

I'm not sure I enjoy the sudden image of an angry Jen while Tim's hands rampage under my shirt.

After a long kiss, the mention of seven more million bottles being sourced from Villa makes him bang his fist on the desk in anger.

'Arnaud never mentioned that figure to me,' he says. 'No disrespect to you but to shift that volume, we'd need superlative wines at knockdown prices, not something Villa is known for.'

I nod wordlessly. Right now I care more about the progress of his hand on the inside of my thigh than my employer's reputation.

'Anything else you need to tell me before we move on to more serious matters?' he asks, pushing me down on his desk.

'Arnaud plans redundancies as part of his cost-cutting programme.'

Tim shrugs. 'I expected as much. Dan has been talking about returning to Australia and I've asked him to hang on a bit longer so I can make him redundant if need be. He'll get cash and I'll get the kudos.'

He doesn't even consider that his name may be on the hit list. I find it a little irritating but my skirt is now around my waist, putting me in a weak position to argue.

'Tim, what if someone comes in?' I ask.

'It depends what state of undress they find us in.' he says.

He unbuttons my top.

'It also depends what I'm doing to you at the time.'

'What if it's Arnaud?' I ask.

'Then we must give him a proper show.'

He unzips his trousers and grins at me.

My mobile vibrates and then rings. I try to turn it off and press the wrong button. I hear Serge's muffled voice, 'Allo? Allo?'

'Merde,' I say.

I grab the phone. 'Hi Serge. Sorry, I was in the middle of something.'

I try to push Tim away.

He grabs me by the hips, pulls my kickers aside and pushes inside me.

I let out a cry.

'Are you alright?' Serge asks. 'It sounds like you bumped into something.'

'Yes,' I say, 'or rather something bumped into me.'

'Poor you! Look, why don't you call me later. I've got a big consignment of samples to prepare.'

I should chastise him for not delegating this kind of job but I can't keep up the conversation much longer.

I drop my mobile and try to concentrate on Tim's ministrations. We're moving in time with the swirls of the screensaver on his PC. I close my eyes, trying to recapture the excitement of a few minutes ago. Papers rustle under my body.

'I hope I am not crushing anything too important,' I say.

'Everything on my desk is a priority but I pushed you to the top of the pile.'

I let my head drop to avoid looking at his computer and I find myself staring at Tim's CV. I let out a little cry.

'Am I hurting you?' he asks.

'I hope you were not thinking of sending that CV,' I say, trying to keep my voice light and cheerful.

'It's only an insurance policy. You never know what's going to happen next in this mad house.'

I like him a little bit more for admitting, even in an indirect way, that he's aware of his own vulnerability.

The three weeks until Christmas race by. December is when clients want their orders on time. Everybody is on red alert to pour as much wine as possible down the nation's thirsty throats during those precious few weeks of incessant partying. Miss it and come January, the media will be enjoining us to survive on half a lettuce leaf and six litres of water a day.

. . .

Arnaud has settled into a routine of four or five phone calls a day plus the occasional emergency meeting. He treats me with a little bit more respect since he's found out my father used to work for Villa.

The revised bulk prices André gave me under duress have enabled me to secure the Direct Wines business, which means Mary and I are working flat out to meet Andy's deadline for the first delivery at the end of February. As a new supplier, we have to deal with a small mountain of paperwork to reassure our new client we are not squeezing wine out of old socks to fill bottles picked up from the local recycling plant.

The general information forms are tedious but easy to fill in. The product specifications are more challenging as we need the input of our production site's colleagues. Serge has a marked allergy to paperwork and I have to chase him up when Mary tires of him ignoring her emails and phone calls.

We also have to contend with the antagonism from Narbonne's quality insurance manager. She blames me for the issue with The Super-Market. Whereas most of the other people involved have now mellowed towards me, she still behaves as if my sole purpose in life is to make her life hell.

She submits me to a half-an-hour telephonic rant when Direct Wines' winemakers send us a long list of measures they want us to implement to ensure we steer clear of reduction. Meddling fools are the bane of her life and why can't she be allowed to get on with her job the way she knows best? I could point out Narbonne's past performance doesn't put her in a strong position to ignore advice but I don't.

It turns out to be a wise decision as I discover another blooper when I check the "ethical form" she's filled in for The Super-Market. With globalisation, retailers have become vigilant about working conditions at their suppliers'. Despite their reliance on cheap goods, they can't be seen to profit from child labour or other abusive working practices.

This means all suppliers, whether or not they operate in third world countries, have to fill in long questionnaires about their production plants. They include reasonable questions such as, 'Do you employ children under the age of sixteen?', probing ones such as 'How do you ensure nobody under the age of sixteen works in your organisation?', and extreme, verging on the absurd ones, such as, 'Should you become aware children under the age of sixteen are working for your organisation, what procedure would you implement to remedy the situation?'. Answering there's no need for such a procedure since no child under the age of sixteen could ever work for a French company, is not an option and will earn the company an amber rating for ethical matters.

Reading my favourite colleague's honest assessment of Narbonne's ethical stance sends shivers down my spine.

To the question 'Are unions allowed to operate freely in your organisation?' she's answered, 'no' and to, 'Are workers discouraged from joining a union?', 'yes'. Whether it's true or not, it's not something we should publicise outside the company.

I pick up the phone without enthusiasm.

'What do you want?' she asks.

'The ethical questionnaire for The Super-Market,' I say.

'What about it?'

'There are a few answers I'd like you to change.'

'It's my name on it, isn't it?'

'Indeed.'

'So why should I change anything?'

'Do you want to lose The Super-Market's business?' I ask.

'That wouldn't look good for you, would it?'

'Neither would it for Villa and that's the risk you're taking by making it sound like East Germany in the fifties.'

'What do you mean?'

'You can't say we discourage people from joining a union. Also you've written that in some cases, employees' identity documents could be retained by management. What does it mean?'

'When André Lange is caught speeding, he claims his car was being driven by one of the warehouse employees. He keeps copies of their driving licenses so he knows which ones are clean.'

'That's illegal.'

'He needs his driving licence.'

'Doesn't the poor sod in the warehouse?'

'That's the way it works here.'

'The Super-Market doesn't need to know. Please change these answers. If you don't do it for me, do it for the company.'

I put the phone down.

'Try banging your head against the wall,' Philippe says. 'The pain is the same but at least you can make it stop.'

Rachel has gone quiet. She hasn't answered any of my emails or returned my phone calls asking for the final cost of the quality problem. I'm not desperate to know but I'd prefer to provision the exact amount in my end of calendar year's accounts. If I put in too much, I penalise the results of the year unnecessarily but if I don't, the unaccounted-for loss will carry over and affect next year's performance.

I catch her on the last Thursday before Christmas.

I hardly have time to introduce myself before she shrieks, 'Today is not a good day, Chris. I can't even hear myself thinking.'

'Should I call you in the New Year?' I ask.

'Do that,' she says.

'Happy Christmas, Rachel.'

'Happy Christmas, Chris.'

I catch a mumbled 'Sorry.' as I put the phone down.

The day after, I'm stocking shelves at my local branch of The Super-Market. I'm not moonlighting for extra cash, I'm volunteering. Over the busy Christmas period suppliers and head office staff at major supermarkets are requested to work at least a day in store. We're told we're helping, even though the welcome I get from the manager of the wines and spirits aisle is less than enthusiastic. But how would I react if I was sent a work experience student on one of the busiest days of the year?

My hope to make the most of the situation by doing some empiric consumer research in the wine aisle goes up in smoke when he assigns me to spirits. I spend six hours standing, crouching and bending over, my fingers sore from fitting security tags on endless bottles. I'm not even able to impress my temporary boss, as my productivity is poor and made worse by punters' questions. I don't mind, 'Do you know where the eggs are?' or, 'As you're tall, would you mind picking up the bottle on the top shelf?' but I get frustrated with, 'I can't see the price for the Smirnoff' or, 'Why isn't the half-bottle on promotion? I don't want to buy a big one.'

Philippe pops in at lunchtime to cheer me up. He insists on taking some snaps to show the world I don't mind getting my hands dirty. On a whim, I pick up a bottle of The Super-Market red from the gondola end and pull my tongue at it.

'I'll send it to you,' Philippe says.

Life isn't too bad when one has a sense of humour.

25

A CHRISTMAS OF TWO HALVES

I go home to change at five. The Circle of Wine Writers Christmas party, a good opportunity to catch up with other wine professionals, is taking place tonight. Tim is a regular at such gatherings, which, I suspect, he sees as ideal hunting grounds.

I call him to suggest we go together. He sounds surprised and, after a minute pause, tells me he's made other arrangements.

'We don't want to get people talking,' he says.

I can't remember him being that bothered in the heady ambiance of Edinburgh.

As I was hoping he'd escort me, I ignored a call from a girlfriend who'd offered to meet for a drink beforehand. When I phone her, she tells me she's changed her plans. She doesn't comment on the fact it's taken me a week to get back to her but doesn't linger on the phone either.

I take a long bath to soak away the grime and the sweat of the day. My legs have turned to lead and I am tempted for a moment to go straight to bed. Only the prospect of seeing Tim pulls me out of the bath and out the door.

A heavy rain is battering Chelsea when I walk out of Bond Street tube station. I run all the way to Brook Street, my raincoat over my head. Our host tonight is the Argentinean ambassador. Like an indulgent parent, he's left us his residence for the evening with the proviso that we leave at eleven. Whether we'll turn into pumpkins if we ignore his deadline isn't clear.

While checking in at the reception desk, I am lucky enough to bump into someone I know, which saves me from having to climb the large staircase on my own.

The noise of conversations grows louder as we reach the landing. I must have spent longer in the bath than I meant to. The two salons are packed with men and women shouting amiably at each other. Most of them hold a glass of wine and nine women out of ten have slipped into little black numbers for the evening. I went for a red dress.

My stomach flips as I spot Tim in the middle of the room, thanks to the striking electric blue shirt he's wearing. He's in party mode, chatting to a group of people while scanning the crowd at regular intervals to check he's not missing out on anyone more exciting. His hand is resting on the shoulder of a young woman with fabulous auburn hair, which she tosses in his face every few seconds. I imagine the crowd's reaction if I ran to them and pulled her away from him by that beautiful hair. At that moment Tim sees me. His gaze rests on me for a millisecond. He fails to acknowledge me but his hand leaves its perch to retreat to the safety of his pocket.

I walk to the bar and pour myself a glass of Zuccardi Q Malbec. When in Argentina… I swirl it in my glass while keeping an eye on the throng. Who do I want to spend time with tonight? The violet and kirsch aromas of the wine distract me for a moment. I take a sip. The silky tannins call for a juicy bit of steak that's sadly missing from the buffet. How can you have an Argentinean do without steak? That thought reminds me of my last fateful trip to Argentina. I bite my bottom lip. Now isn't the time to burst into tears.

Albert Moretti appears in my line of vision.

'Chris, how are you?' he asks, stressing the 'are' in the caring tone of a doctor or a priest, enquiring after the health of a terminally ill patient.

'Good, thanks. You?'

He presses his hands together and looks around as if he were about to reveal the biggest secret ever. Then he leans towards me and whispers, 'Things are going very well.'

I usually try to avoid Albert unless I am in exceptionally robust form. He has the ability to look at the bright side of whatever happens to him while denigrating everything and everybody else with great subtlety. The wines he sells taste better than any others, the wineries he represents offer fantastic value for money while being the hottest in their respective regions, and his colleagues excel at their job. I have never met his wife or children but I assume they are exceptional too.

'I've heard interesting things about the new MD at The Wine Shop,' he says. 'Sounds like he's got lots of original ideas.'

I don't have time to comment before he adds, 'I've always had great admiration for Villa, such an impressive company.'

I nod, waiting for the twist.

'You, my dear, have been an absolute brick,' he says. 'Your job is so very difficult. You really didn't need that problem with The Super-Market on top of everything else.'

'How on earth do you know about The Super-Market?' I ask with a touch more vehemence than I should.

'Rachel was so upset she needed someone to confide in,' he says. 'She really likes you, you know, and it makes the whole thing so much harder for her.'

His warped solicitude is threatening to tip me over the edge. I wave my empty glass at him and flee, hoping to find somebody, anybody I can have a normal conversation with.

Tim's moved further away from me, his Valkyrie still by his side.

One of Off Licence News' regular contributors taps me on the shoulder.

'Chris, just the person I was hoping to see,' he says, which in journalistic language means, 'Here's a story on legs.'

I take a sip of wine. 'You can't have been expecting much of your evening.'

'A French woman with a sense of humour! Who can ask for more?' he laughs.

The compliment warns me of trouble ahead.

I cross my arms. 'What can I do for you?'

'Direct, as ever.' He chuckles. 'I'll be equally frank then. Could you help me secure an interview with The Wine Shop's new MD? I've emailed him but I'm getting nowhere.'

My heart sinks. 'He's busy, that's why he hasn't come back to you.'

'Is it true he hardly speaks any English? If that's the problem, I can bring a translator along.'

'English isn't the main issue,' I say, wondering how to move away from the subject of The Wine Shop. This is supposed to be a party.

'What is it, then? I've heard he's been tasked with selling the business.'

I try to keep it light. 'Are you thinking of making an offer?'

'How much do you think would secure a deal?'

'More than you or I can afford.'

I turn away from him, desperate to escape.

He follows me. 'Villa has been running The Wine Shop at a loss for two years.'

'Quand on aime, on ne compte pas.'

Jen appears out of nowhere.

He turns to her. 'Some French suppliers claim their products are being delisted to make space for wines from Villa.'

Her blue eyes turn cold. 'Disgruntled suppliers will always find ways to justify their poor performance. The Wine Shop's policy on new listings hasn't changed: we choose the best wines at the keenest possible price and our shelves aren't elastic,' she says.

She grabs my elbow and drags me away.

'It looked like you needed rescuing,' she says.

I grin back at my tormentor. I wish I had her ability to cut my losses and run.

'There's somebody I need to introduce you to,' she says. 'He could be the solution for our Pinot Grigio.'

'Are you thinking of squeezing him into a bottle?' I ask, taking a well-deserved gulp from my glass.

'Don't be flippant. I am thinking about Arnaud's new range. We must ensure the wine is as good as can be. This guy has quality bulk Pinot Grigio to sell.'

I try to locate Tim in the crowd but can't see any blue in the surrounding sea of black outfits. If I'd known the evening would turn into a succession of business meetings, I would have stayed in the bath.

Tim is still nowhere to be seen when we all get chucked out at eleven. I am too tired and dispirited to take the tube. I jump into a taxi and finally shed a tear to Razorlight belting out, 'Who needs love?' on Capital Radio.

The following day, Maman picks me up from Bordeaux airport in her brand-new silver Renault Clio. She used to rely on Papa to take her everywhere as she was too nervous to drive the top of the range company Citroen XM he kept after retiring. It's the first thing she sold after his death. I thought at the time she was taking her revenge on the car for making her feel inadequate for so many years.

She boasted of her car-free status for a few months, claiming she preferred walking or taking the train to driving. Summer turned into autumn, the weather got wetter and her daily shopping trips to Monoprix or Leclerc often left her drenched by a sudden downpour.

She never admitted to having changed her mind but a panicky email from my brother Roland informed me in November that she'd bought a car. He was worried she may have forgotten how to drive. Had she said anything to me?

I admitted I had not spoken to Maman for a couple of weeks.

He emailed back a few days later saying she'd been taking driving lessons and everything was fine.

As we leave the airport, Maman keeps on glancing at me while nattering away about her Scrabble group, the long walks she takes every day by the sea front and the problems she's been having with the owner of the house next door and his wayward tenants. Despite the driving lessons, I'm worried she's going to send us into a ditch.

'What's the matter, Maman? Do I have something on the tip of my nose?'

'Have you seen a doctor lately?' she says.

'I am not ill.'

'You look awful. Have you been eating properly?'

'Maman, can you please keep your eyes on the road?'

'Do you sleep well?'

'I suppose.'

She sighs. 'You work too hard.'

'Maman, you've been saying that since I left university. That's what it's like now. If you slouch, you get kicked out.'

'I'm not saying you should slouch, I'm saying you should keep a sense of proportion. At your age, you have to look after your health. Think about Papa!'

'What about Papa?'

'The doctors said he'd worn himself out. He'd still be with us if he'd taken it easier.'

I shrug and turn to the window.

A sharp swerve from the car tells me she's thrown me another withering look. 'Shrug all you like. I lived with him for forty odd years. You're just like him but without a wife to slow you down and look after you.'

'The idea of a woman waiting for me at home with dinner on the table does appeal but I'm sorry, Maman, I'm not that way inclined sexually.'

'That's not what I meant and you know it.' She throws me a concerned look. 'Are you seeing someone at the moment?'

'Nobody you'd approve of.'

'What's the point then?'

'Do you really want to know?'

'If you think that kind of attitude is attractive in a woman, you're deluded.'

I turn towards her. 'Maman, whatever I say, it's always wrong with you. But since you mentioned Papa, may I ask you a question?'

She shakes her head. 'Not now, Christine. You're here for ten days. We have time.'

The arrival of Roland, Bea and their two girls the following day turns Maman's tidy home into a chaotic campsite. I feel like a refugee, my suitcase tucked away in a corner of Maman's bedroom during the day and brought into the living room in the evening when I'm allowed to unfold the sofa bed for the night.

My nieces rule the household. They jump on my bed in the morning after laying waste to their parents' bedroom, they decide on the activities for the day and get into a paroxysm of excitement whenever Christmas is mentioned. Maman packed me off to Monoprix straight after my arrival to buy them toys, pointing out the sensible outfits I got them from Gap didn't constitute proper Christmas presents.

On the third day of the holidays, I find Maman and Charlotte, the older girl, huddled over my laptop and trying to log in.

'What are you doing?' I ask.

'She wants to play a game,' Maman says.

I push them aside and turn the machine off. 'My laptop isn't a toy.'

'I'll be really careful, Auntie Chris. I use Papa's work computer all the time at home,' Charlotte says.

'Then your Papa should have brought his own laptop. I'm sorry but I have all my work in there and I don't want anybody to mess it up.'

'She'll be careful, Christine. Sophie's gone shopping with her parents and she hasn't got anything to do,' Maman says.

I turn on her. 'I said no. My work's more important than a child's entertainment?'

She squares up to me. 'Your work is more important to you than anything else, even your own family. Just like your father.'

She wipes a tear and takes Charlotte's hand. 'Come on, I'll find something you can play with. Auntie Chris doesn't like sharing her toys.'

I make for the door, rattled by her reaction and the unfairness of the situation.

'I'm going for a walk.'

'Don't be too long,' Maman says. 'Your brother will be back soon and the girls need to eat at twelve. Could you bring a baguette back as well?'

This means I have got to go into town rather than towards the beach. In two days, I have been sucked back into the dependence of childhood. My presence is required at set times for meals and any attempt to break free, even for a short time, is immediately curtailed. I have exchanged one type of slavery for another.

I call Mary who's manning the office over the holiday.

'Is everything alright?' I ask.

'It's quiet this morning. It feels like everybody's taken the day off.'

'Please, go at lunchtime. It's Christmas Eve.'

'Thank you. With Arnaud gone to France for the holidays, our friends from The Wine Shop are having an unofficial Christmas drinks party at twelve. Dave has invited me.'

'Wish everybody a happy Christmas from me.'

'Have you heard from Tim?' Mary asks.

'I haven't. I'll give him a call later. Keep an eye on him for me, will you?'

'I'll do my best,' Mary says.

She doesn't sound too sure.

I return home sans baguette. The queue in front of the boulangerie stretched for two blocks and joining it would have made me late for lunch. Something tells me I'll have to go back later anyway to collect the traditional Yule log Maman ordered weeks ago.

Despite my rational explanation, my failure to obey the simple instructions I was given is greeted with irritation.

'I'm asking you to do one thing and you can't even do it,' Maman says. 'Your father was the same. No patience whatsoever. You know how it ended'

'I don't actually,' I say, but she's left the room.

As it turns out, there's enough bread to feed an army. I resist the temptation to point out my baguette was not needed after all. With Christmas Day a few hours away, Maman doesn't need any excuse to blow her top.

She distributes various last-minute jobs between my sister in law, my brother and I, causing me once more to marvel at the remarkable inefficiency that plagues otherwise organised people when on holiday. She then retires to her bedroom for a nap, in anticipation of this evening's midnight mass while Bea, helped by the girls, attempts to set up the table for tomorrow's lunch to Maman's exacting standards.

Roland suggests we go for a walk.

'How's the job going?' he asks.

'Tougher than I thought it would be.'

'You can't have been expecting a bed of roses.'

'Why not?' I ask.

'The French wine industry is a mess and there's no reason why Villa should be an exception.'

'Is that why you decided not to get into wine?'

'And the fact I wanted to make my own way, and not follow in Papa's footsteps.'

'Do you think that's what I do, follow in Papa's footsteps?'

'You're so like him. Much more than me.'

This is received wisdom in the family.

'Do you know why he left Villa?' I ask.

'God, no! I was a child at the time. What about you?'

'He never told me. To be fair, even though I was older than you, I was not interested either.'

'You should ask Maman.'

'I'll wait until you're gone. She'd rather spend time with the girls right now.'

26

A REST AND A BRUTAL RETURN TO REALITY

I try to call Tim at five. It's four in London and the lunchtime drinks party must be finished by now. His mobile is turned off and I leave him a short message, wishing him a happy Christmas.

In the evening we walk down the road to Notre Dame. Altar servers holding lit torches stand by the entrance. Instead of its usual winter contingent of OAP's, the Basilica is full of well-dressed families who have come over from Bordeaux for the holidays. The smell of smoke, incense and the ancient white stone of the building mixes with the expensive perfumes of the congregation. The mass lasts an hour and a half and my nieces fidget throughout. Maman ignores them. Her eyes are moist. I guess she's thinking about Papa and I pat her shoulder. She reaches for my hand and squeezes it.

We rush back home for a light midnight feast of smoked salmon and Champagne. The girls are exhausted and soon go to bed, protesting they want to wait for Father Christmas. When she kisses me goodnight, Charlotte whispers to me she knows he doesn't exist but she has to pretend for her sister's sake. I wish we could spend longer together and get to know each other properly.

Maman shakes me awake at seven the following morning. Still half asleep, I fold up the sofa bed as silently as I can and help her to carry the multicoloured parcels she's hidden in her bedroom and on top of various bits of furniture throughout the house. She ticks each hiding place off a list and soon a respectable pile of presents sits under the tree.

A big sigh alerts us to the presence of the girls behind us. They stand by the door, hand in hand, in matching pink pyjamas.

'Is it all for us?' Sophie asks.

'Wait for Mummy and Daddy to wake up,' Maman says.

They turn around and run down the corridor to their parents' room. Five minutes later my brother and his wife join us by the tree, dragged there by their excited daughters.

'Let me get my camera,' Maman says.

The distribution begins with the biggest boxes, which are for the girls. The brightly coloured cash register with matching caddy and pretend goodies I bought a few days earlier is welcomed with shrieks of delight while the new clothes are tossed aside without a second glance. Maman was right.

I get books, Benabar's new CD and a bottle of Chanel 19, always a safe bet.

Maman jumps up and runs out of the room.

'I almost forgot,' she says.

She returns carrying a grey filing box.

'This isn't really a Christmas present, Christine. It's your father's work papers and mementoes. He would have liked you to have them, especially now you're working for Villa.'

I open the box with mixed feelings. I don't want to think about Villa right now.

Inside there's a jumble of papers, notebooks and old newspapers cuttings. I pick up the yellowing front page of an ancient Sud Ouest, the local daily paper. The caption reads, 'Madame Villa opens new Narbonne bottling site.' In front of the familiar building's entrance stands a much younger Marguerite, my father at her side.

'It may not be terribly exciting,' Maman says, a note of apology in her voice, 'but it was his life.' She wipes her eyes with a corner of her apron.

I take her hand. 'It doesn't matter Maman. It will be really interesting for me.'

Even to my own ears, I sound dubious.

'Roland, you don't mind, do you?' I ask my brother.

He raises his hands as if to push away the box. 'Rather you than me. You know I have no interest in the wine business.'

Once Roland and his family have gone, I move into the spare bedroom and adjust with guilty pleasure to Maman's sedate lifestyle. We get up at nine, have a leisurely breakfast and set out to town, always finding an errand to run. We have lunch at twelve on the dot and spend most afternoons walking on the Pereire beachfront or in the pine forests which made the reputation of Arcachon in Victorian times. In the evening we treat ourselves to dinner at one of the many local restaurants or we cook a little delicacy, a bowl of moules marinières, a filet of sole, or langoustines with fresh bread and butter. Then we play Scrabble or watch television and eat delicious oyster shaped chocolates before going to bed. I sleep like a baby. Whether it's the lifestyle or the sea air, my energy levels are rising by the day although the waistbands of my trousers tell me I have put on a few pounds since I arrived.

When I question her, Maman tells me she doesn't know why Papa left Villa.

'He never told me. He called from the office in Bordeaux one evening. He was in a terrible state. He said he had to go back to Narbonne because of an emergency and wouldn't be home for a while. He stayed away for six months.'

'You told Roland and me he was away on business,' I say.

She nods. 'What else could I say? He didn't want to speak to you or your brother. I tried to protect you both but it was a difficult time.'

'He kept in touch with you though?'

'He called once a week from a phone box, pretty much to say he was alive but that was it. He was renting a studio in Vinassan but made me promise not to try and visit.'

'Why did you agree?' I ask.

She rolls her eyes. 'Women of my generation obeyed their husbands. Something terrible must have happened. Your father loved his job.'

'I remember when he returned home. He used to wake up in the middle of the night and pace around the house for hours,' I say.

'He was a shadow of his former self. I tried to convince him to see a doctor but he wouldn't.'

'You must have a theory about what happened.'

She snorts. 'He was a proud and stubborn man working with a proud and stubborn woman. That's all I know. I'll never forgive her.'

She doesn't need to tell me whom she's talking about.

I manage to speak to Tim twice but he's too busy both times to stay on the phone for more than a few minutes. He tells me he's spent Christmas with mates, which is his way of warding off any questions he may not want to answer, and remains vague about his plans for New Year. My infatuation with him has not abated, it has been put on hold. Here in Arcachon, where he doesn't belong, he feels almost unreal.

New Year's Eve is shockingly tame. Maman and I walk into town at eight. The weather is mild and the night air smells of the sea with wafts of appetising smells coming out of houses and restaurants along the way. 'Chez Yvette' is brightly lit and fills quickly with diners. An army of waiters and waitresses buzz around the place with purposeful energy.

We treat ourselves to a glass of Champagne as an aperitif. A whole bottle would be in bad taste in Maman's eyes since we have no male companion to justify such extravagance. We tuck into a huge "plateau de fruits de mer" and I order a bottle of Château Malartic-Lagravière, while Maman's not looking. She chides me when the sommelier brings it to the table, saying half a bottle would have been enough. She then drinks happily, even commenting I always pick delicious wines. I savour the rare praise, hoping she doesn't find out how much my refined taste encourages me to spend on a single bottle of wine.

I fly back to London on the second, fortified by my New Year's resolutions to take things easy at work and with Tim, and to try and look after myself a bit more. My newly acquired steadfastness is put to the test as soon as I land. Mary's call comes as I am waiting in the luggage reclaim area.

'Hi Chris, did you plan to come to the office today?'

'Happy New Year, Mary! I didn't. What's up? You sound flustered.'

'Arnaud wants to see you. Happy New Year to you too!'

'He'll have to wait until tomorrow,' I say, a note of smugness in my voice.

'He said -'

'Mary, Arnaud will have to learn I am not at his beck and call. He's put me under a lot of pressure since he took over at The Wine Shop but I am determined-'

'Tim's also popped in,' she interrupts. 'He looked upset. There must be something going on next door.'

'Have you asked Dave?'

I can't believe I said that.

A beep tells me I have got another call waiting.

'Sorry Mary, can I phone you back later?

The other call turns out to be four voicemail messages, all received while I was in mid-flight.

Ed wishes me a Happy New Year and reminds me that the next export meeting at the end of January is the annual get together for all of Villa's branch offices. He proposes to come over next Wednesday to help me polish my presentation. He doesn't say it's to avoid a repeat of my dismal performance at the last meeting but I get the message.

My blood pressure rises by one notch as I make a note of calling him later on to try to dissuade him from visiting.

The second message is from Philippe. His car's been broken into and his laptop's gone, together with his briefcase. Could I ask Matt to order him a new one and also check if there's a spare one he could borrow in the meantime? He won't be in the office tomorrow as he needs to get his car fixed. He's sorry and wishes me a Happy New Year.

I fling my suitcase from the carousel straight onto my big toe while keeping the phone glued to my ear. I bite my lip in pain and Arnaud's voice shatters my eardrum. 'Close the door!'

I turn around.

'That was not for you,' he says. 'I have just told my heads of department of the redundancies we need to make. They are kicking up a huge fuss, your protégé more than the others. They are threatening to expose Villa to the press, whatever they mean by that. I don't mind but I expect you do. Call me. Oh and Happy New Year!'

Tim is next.

'The bastard wants me to lose four people in my department. He may as well get rid of Marketing altogether. Not that it surprises me. He's a complete arsehole. Did you know about it? You mentioned redundancies when you came back from Bordeaux. Why didn't you tell me what he had in mind? Call me when you land.'

He doesn't wish me a Happy New Year.

I phone him back while on board the Gatwick Express and we get cut off six times. In exasperation, I tell him I am coming to the office. I text Mary to let her know and ask her to tell Arnaud, knowing that if I do it myself, he'll take it as a green light to call me back straight away.

I get to Kingston at five. I am still technically on holiday.

Dave's at his usual post, wet fag in hand. 'You've heard?'

'I may have.'

He makes a cut-throat gesture. 'Jack's getting rid of half of head office.'

'Half?'

'I told Tim you had no idea.'

I dislike the idea of Dave interceding with Tim on my behalf.

'What about you?' I ask.

He taps his nose with his index finger. 'He can't touch me. I know too much.'

I feel like saying Arnaud may not have realised Dave is actually working for The Wine Shop since he spends most of his time outside the office but I decide not to antagonise him.

'Happy New Year, Dave.'

'Same to you, Chris.'

Arnaud is leaning back in his chair, tanned and relaxed.

'You wanted to see me,' I say.

‘The artist almost gave me a good reason to sack him on the spot earlier,’ he says turning sideways to his computer.

I sit down. ‘What happened?’

‘I told each Head of Department how many people they had to lose. In some cases I suggested whom they should let go. Most reacted professionally but Foster went ballistic.

I shrug, trying to look like I don’t care. ‘Celtic blood. What’s it got to do with me?’

‘He threatened to get the press on side to stop anybody in this country from buying from Villa.’

My throat tightens. ‘That’s not nice,’ I say, unable to find a better answer.

‘You’d be the first to suffer the consequences.’ He swivels round and leans towards me. ‘Does he know you saved his job?’

I recoil. ‘Why should I tell him?’

He stares at me. ‘You don’t fancy him, do you?’

I thank God I have not seen Tim for a while and I am able to deny Arnaud’s claim without blushing.

He grunts and turns back to his screen. ‘As you’re here now, see where he’s got to with the labels for the new range. I meant to ask him earlier but there would have been little point, the state he was in.’

It takes me a few seconds to compose myself outside the door to the Marketing office. I have not seen Tim in ten days and I would have preferred a more intimate setting for our reunion. Also, four people in there are about to lose their jobs. They may not know yet but I do and it makes facing them awkward. I decide to give New Year’s greetings a miss.

A deep breath and I am inside the door. ‘Hi guys, is Tim around?’

‘Happy New Year, Chris,’ says the brunette, ‘Beware, he’s in a foul mood.’

I guess he hasn’t told them. I mumble something back to her and walk up to Tim’s desk, repeating Supertramp’s lyrics about gaining control to myself like a mantra,

He looks up from the notebook on his desk and I am struck by the coldness in his eyes.

‘It’s nothing to do with me,’ I say.

‘You knew, didn’t you? You found out when you went to that meeting in Bordeaux.’

'I didn't know the extent of it, I promise.'

'How do I choose between getting rid of a single mother who badly needs her job and a bright young guy who's getting married next summer.'

'I'm sorry, Tim.'

'So am I. I won't keep you. I only have until tomorrow morning to make a decision.'

I push my hands deep into my pockets, take a few steps away, pause and turn around. 'Where have you got to with the new labels? Can I help?'

'No, I don't want to give Villa more control than necessary on this project.'

I drop my head and make for the door.

His voice softens. 'The file's over there.'

The designer has opted for a neutral black and cream design, as far removed as possible from the usual extravagant aesthetics of The Wine Shop. It looks fine if a bit bland, a fake Chanel straightjacket for the Amy Winehouse of wine.

'Mind if I take a copy?' I ask.

'Do what you want.' His elbows on the desk, he's holding his head with both hands, massaging his skull as if trying to rid himself of a headache.

When I show him the designs, Arnaud's pleased with their classicism. I praise the quality of the marketing team's work but he silences me with a stare.

27

THE BEGINNING OF THE END

Matt hails me as I pass his door. 'I may not be able to get a new laptop for Philippe straight away.'

I slump in the chair opposite him.

'With half of my team gone, it may take me, let me see, three weeks to order it and six to set it up,' he says.

'What do you want me to do?' I ask. 'Grovel?'

He cocks his head sideways. 'Where do you think we're heading? Villa can't expect The Wine Shop to return to its former glory without either cash or people to run the show.'

'You know why these measures are being implemented as well as I do, Matt. Marguerite Villa will sign another big cheque to bail out The Wine Shop this year and she doesn't want it to become a habit.'

'Then she should have hired somebody competent to manage the company. She's had no shortage of applicants since Villa bought The Wine Shop.'

'British candidates will never do for her.'

'What about you?'

'I know nothing about retail.'

'Arnaud doesn't either. At least you worked for The Wine Shop even if it was a long time ago.'

. . .

I mull over Matt's comment on the way back to my office. His idea, flattering as it is, is born out of desperation. I may win against Arnaud in a popularity contest or even be marginally more qualified to do his job but only a proper retail specialist could do what's needed.

Even though business was supposed to grind to a halt over Christmas, I am amazed at how much has piled up on my desk and in my inbox in ten days. I decide to deal with all the bitty jobs now to clear the decks for tomorrow.

I answer five emails from Marketing, clarify a promotional invoice for accounts, log in future outgoings on a Tesco promotion, pass on several letters to Mary with instructions on how to answer them, ask her to order some stationery, sign the purchase order for Philippe's laptop and commit to buying samples of a competitor's Medoc for a tasting Serge is organising in Bordeaux.

Mary's been gone half an hour when Tim barges in, 'Which side are you on?' he yells from the door.

I stare at him, trying to think where I went wrong.

He strides across the room and leans over my desk, his face inches from mine. 'Do you think sleeping with me gives you the right to go behind my back?'

'Stop it, Tim. You're scaring me. What have I done now?'

He mimics me. 'What have I done? "Good job, Tim," he said to me. "I like the labels. Have a good evening." As if nothing had happened!'

'Is that Arnaud you're talking about?'

'I showed you the labels as a favour. I meant to bring them to him later on, to demonstrate the excellent work my team had done. He's my boss, in case you've forgotten.'

I grip the armrests of my chair.

'And I'm just a pain in the neck, who you're happy to use as a go-between when it suits and discard when it doesn't. Yes, I showed your precious labels to Arnaud. He wanted to see them and considering the mood you were in, I thought you would not indulge him.'

I sit back, shocked at my own outburst.

'Why do you have to meddle all the time?' Tim asks.

'You sound just like Arnaud.'

'Whatever. Go on, tell me.'

'To show him you're a good operator despite your impossible temper, and that he should hang on to you.'

He chuckles. 'You think I need protecting?'

There's scorn in his voice.

'Everybody needs protecting every now and again.'

He leans over me, stabbing the desk with his finger. 'What you do is interfering, not protecting. There's a big difference between the two.'

He makes for the door.

'Tim, is that all you came to tell me?' I bite my lip. I don't want to cry now.

He hovers, his hand on the door handle. 'We need to talk but not tonight. I'll call you.'

I go home and head straight for the wine rack, my healthy living resolutions overridden by my nightmarish day. I discard a Macon Lugny from Louis Latour as far too tame for the situation and pick up a Vasse Felix Chardonnay a friend brought round a few months ago. At 13.5% alcohol, it's strong enough to numb the pain and it's from Majestic, The Wine Shop's arch enemy. Drinking it will feel a little like cheating on Tim. I throw it in the freezer to get it to the right temperature fast and pick up the phone to Sam.

'Did he kiss you?' she asks.

'We were in the office.'

'It didn't stop him before.'

'We had people around us.'

'What about when he came to your office?'

'He was mad at me. Kissing was the last thing on his mind.'

'He hadn't seen you for ten days. He should have been all over you.'

'We're not animals.'

She says nothing.

'You think it's over, don't you?' I ask.

'From what you're saying, it doesn't sound too good. Do you want to come over? The boys will cheer you up.'

I decline, citing tiredness and the prospect of a long day in the office tomorrow. The truth is I can't be near kids when contemplating the end of a relationship. Even though I knew I'd never bear Tim's children, having him in my life still brought me close to the accepted template, for a forty year old, of being in a loving partnership, with kids thrown in for good measure.

The rest of the evening is a long descent into self-pity, punctuated by fits of crying and of course, drunken singing.

Mika's "*This is the way you left me*" feels particularly apt, allowing me to run through resignation and cheap philosophy,

I bawl.

I change the last sentence of the song into,

'*And I am wasted every day,*' which seems more fitting especially when I come to the end of the bottle.

I arrive in Kingston the following morning, hungover and miserable. The first mail I read makes me feel even worse,

Dear Chris,

Please find below my flight details for next Wednesday. I fully expected you to call me yesterday to try and dissuade me from coming over. I am pleasantly surprised you haven't. I attach a few spreadsheets I'd like you to fill in before next week. I look forward to a constructive and positive day together.

Onwards and upwards,

Ed

I completely forgot to call him and now I'll have to endure a whole day with him next week. Even worse, he's only planned to return to Bordeaux the following day, which means I'll have to have dinner with him as well.

Mary senses something's wrong and leaves me well alone. Philippe's in a foul mood after the incident with his car and spends most of the morning going backwards and forwards between our office and Matt's.

In the middle of this gloomy atmosphere, a text from Tim arrives.

Sorry about yesterday. Are you free tonight? Tx

I text back with trembling fingers.

Yep

I hope it will look cool and detached.

8 o'clock, your place?

Yep

I mean to stay in character.

Philippe comments, without looking away from the screen of his replacement laptop, 'Lovers' tiff over for now?'

When I open the door to Tim at eight o'clock on the dot, my heart catches in my throat. He's thrown a light cashmere jumper on his shoulders, French style, and he's wearing one of his perfectly ironed multicoloured shirts underneath. His eyes look greener than ever and when he kisses me just at the corner of my mouth, my legs turning to jelly.

He's brought me a bottle of Vavasour Sauvignon Blanc, the connoisseur's Cloudy Bay.

'A belated Christmas present,' he says.

As the bottle is chilled, I assume he intends to partake of it. Not much of a Christmas present then. I decide to keep mine at the top of the wardrobe for the time being. If I don't give it to him, there's always eBay.

When I come back from the kitchen, he's perched on the arm of the sofa as if there was nowhere else to sit.

I hand him a glass.

'You can relax, I'm not expecting anybody else.'

'Not even a gorgeous blonde for later on?' he asks.

'Is that what you wanted for Christmas?'

I sit down in the armchair opposite the sofa. Despite the banter, my sixth sense tells me all's not well. Cold dread seeps into my veins.

He twirls his glass around but doesn't even smell the wine. His lips are twitching as if he's rehearsing what to say.

I wait one, two long minutes and break the silence.

'What's the matter, Tim? You said we needed to talk.'

His hands warm his glass as if it were Cognac.

'I thought this was going to be easier.'

My throat tightens.

'I'm getting hard just looking at you,' he says.

'You mean it's over but you still want to fuck me.'

I am trying to sound dismissive but I hear my voice breaking.

'It's not like that.'

He looks like a boy of twelve with an unwelcome erection.

'What is it like, then?' I ask.

'There's someone else, an ex-girlfriend I caught up with during the holidays. She's a bit like you.'

'I am flattered.'

'She doesn't work for The Wine Shop or for Villa and it makes a big difference. We can have a normal relationship.'

'I didn't know we couldn't.'

'Working together makes it difficult.'

His sudden sense of propriety incenses me.

'Is that why you went from Kate to Jen and then to me?'

He shrugs and gives me a half smile, looking again like an impish little boy.

'You're right. I am a feckless bastard.'

I burst into tears.

He moves over to the armchair and kneels in front of me. 'Hey, sweetheart, don't cry. I don't want to hurt you.'

'A bit late for that.'

I collapse in his arms and he hugs me close. I look at him through my tears. His gaze is earnest. He's convinced himself he's done nothing wrong. His cock is pressing against me, like a creature with a mind of its own, a creature that still wants me.

'There's a connection between us,' he says as if on cue.

'Fuck me.'

We don't even make it to the bedroom. Our lovemaking is brutal and desperate. I cry throughout, from the huge well of misery inside me, which has filled up over the last six months.

Afterwards, I lie in his arms, thinking of the faceless new girlfriend he's already been unfaithful to. He shifts a little but I am a dead weight. I don't say anything, unwilling to help him make an early exit. He pats my hair like he would a dog.

'Was that what you wanted?' he asks.

'The last fuck or being dumped?'

'Don't say that. We'll still see each other all the time in the office. And you can call me when you want.'

'Lovelorn Anonymous, good evening. Please, Tim, you know it's not true. You have already moved on.'

He shuffles away from me, impatience creeping into his voice.

'All I can say is that you'll be in my thoughts.'

'Right at the back, next to the archives.'

He stands up, a kind, aggrieved man dealing with a bitter, unreasonable woman. He pushes his hair out of his eyes and puts his clothes back on. Once dressed, he takes my hands in his, cocking his head to one side, 'I hope you do not regret our time together.'

I close my eyes, incapable of adding another word. I wrap myself in a blanket and push him towards the door. When we get there, I hug him one last time. His arms close around me.

'Maybe . . .' he says.

'Shut up and go.'

I push him away and slam the door behind him.

I return to the living room, walking like an automaton. I pick up our glasses and the half empty bottle of wine and bring them back to the kitchen. I pour the wine in the sink. I want nothing else from him, delicious as it may be. I throw the bottle in the recycling box so hard it shatters a jam jar. Next, I grab the Hoover and I vacuum the carpet, the rug we made love on, the sofa he sat on. I want to rid my flat and my life of him. When I stop, the air is full of the smell of hot swirling dust but I can still detect a whiff of Safari for Men. I curl up around the warm Hoover and sob my heart out.

The following weeks pass as if in a dream or a nightmare. I wish I could return to Arcachon to regain the peace of mind I experienced at Christmas but business has picked up and I can't afford any time off. If I got sick, I'd have an excuse to run away and hide for a while but even though I look awful, I can't claim to suffer from any identifiable illness. I soldier on.

I arrive in the office early to ensure I don't bump into anybody from The Wine Shop and leave late for the same reason. I avoid visiting Arnaud's office as much as possible and correspond with Tim by email. We have to sit in the same meeting twice but Arnaud's presence ensures I keep my cool. Jen's now joined the new range taskforce, which helps to take the pressure off.

. . .

She and I go for a beer at the Queen's Head after work a few days after Tim and I split up. She's heard the news from Dave.

'I never asked before but why did you go for him?' she asks. 'I remember you saying he was not your type at all,'

I draw shapes on the wooden table with my finger.

'Dunno. Maybe because he embodied a certain idea of The Wine Shop?'

She frowns. 'What do you mean?'

'I told you why I joined Villa initially, wanting to follow in my father's footsteps, wanting to do something for French wine. When that went pear-shaped, I thought I could do my bit for The Wine Shop. With Arnaud's arrival that became impossible as well.'

'Was Tim your reward for trying?'

'Or my compensation for failing.'

She takes a sip from her Guinness.

'Do you think it was love?'

'I'd go as far as a bad case of lust.'

'It still hurts, though, doesn't it?'

'I'm a dreamer… Don't worry, I won't sing it to you.'

'I don't mind Supertramp. It's your rendition I worry about. What will you do now?'

'I will have been with Villa for six months at the end of January. I'm trying to convince myself I should give it a year before I move on. But I may be kicked out at the end of my probation period anyway.'

'You'll find something else easily.'

'I am not so sure and money's tight. I bought my flat last year and I'd rather not lose it straight away.'

We pause.

'Are you going to the Australia Day Tasting?' she asks. 'It's a good place to nose around for job opportunities. I can introduce you to a few people there.'

I shake my head. 'I've got an export meeting in France that day. If it's anything like the last one, it'll be a complete waste of time but I still have to go.'

'You have already missed the New Zealand Tasting.'

'I was not in the mood. Anyway my poor father would turn in his grave if I ended up selling Australian or New Zealand wines.'

Jen purses her lips. 'Do you have a stand at France Under One Roof? If you want to stick with a French company, it will be your best bet.'

'I'll be tied to my stand.'

'Can you find an excuse to go to Prowein or Vinitaly?'

I pull a face. 'Not really, even though Prowein sounds interesting. Not sure about Vinitaly: there's something about Verona in April I can't take seriously.'

'You're wrong. It's brilliant for Italian wines.'

'I'll stick to the Definitive Italian Tasting in July. Lords may not be as exciting as Verona but it's easier to get to.'

'You have also got Wines of Spain in April, the Wine Fair in May and Vinexpo in June.'

I burst out laughing. 'You make me think of the "Europe in seven days" trips the Japanese used to go on. Instead of "if it's Tuesday, it's Bruxelles", we have "if it's September, it's Wines of Chile, if it's October, it's Wines of South Africa".'

'Is Claudia still working there?'

'At WOSA? I think so. Thanks Jen, by the way.'

'What for?'

'Not giving up on me.'

'It's alright.' She takes another sip of her Guinness, her blue eyes softer than I have ever seen them.

28

OLD SINS

I get an email from Rachel the following day. She's had all the info back from stores and she's about to invoice Villa for £27,753. Could I confirm this is acceptable?

Her question is purely academic. Supermarkets deduct whatever they want from suppliers' payments and the ensuing disputes are lengthy and fraught with pitfalls. Yet I write back stating that, following her mail and previous correspondence on the subject, Villa will honour the invoice she's about to issue.

Even though the amount is a large one, I am relieved to have a final figure, especially as it's below the £35,000 I provisioned. Once it's paid, I hope we'll all be able to put this unpleasant incident behind us. André may even warm up to me at some distant point in the future. In the meantime, I forward Rachel's email to him.

My French friend from the Scottish Wine Fair phones me a few days later on a busy morning. He starts by wishing me a Happy New Year according to the French tradition which deems it acceptable to do so up until the end of January.

As I assume he's not calling to discuss the weather and as I don't want to spend half an hour on the phone, I tell him The Super-Market has now confirmed they'll be charging us £27,753 to settle their claim. I get a bit annoyed when he makes me repeat the figure three times. He tells me he's pleasantly surprised the figure is less than the one I quoted originally. We part good friends and he makes me promise to give him a call if I ever have spare time during a trip to the south of France.

Three weeks later, Philippe and I are on my favourite motorway. The poetically called "autoroute des deux mers" connects Toulouse, where our flight landed, and Narbonne where we're heading.

'This drive is like a geography lesson,' I tell Philippe. 'We started in the plain and now we're climbing up to the pass between the Black Mountain and the Pyrenees. Then on the other side, it's the Med-'

'-where the weather is often completely different,' he says, finishing the sentence for me.

'Have I told you before?' I ask.

'When we came down here in September. Word for word.'

'Am I going gaga?'

'I'll only speak in the presence of my lawyer.'

I lean sideways to elbow him in the ribs.

He pushes me away.

'Watch the road, crazy woman. I'm too young to die.'

'Maybe you've gone through my entire repertoire of anecdotes and jokes in the last six months and I'm beginning to repeat myself?' I ask.

He lifts his hands in mock protection. 'There are some I'd rather avoid the second time round if you don't mind, especially if they involve singing.'

I open my mouth for a biting repartee but am cut short by Veronique Sanson belting out '*Toute Une Vie Sans Te Voir*' on the car radio. My eyes mist over but I manage not to cry, which represents a vast improvement on past performances.

Philippe looks straight ahead of him, thus avoiding the need to make any comment on the sudden darkening of my mood.

Once the song is finished, he puts on his best tourist guide voice. 'On your left, the gorgeous city of Carcassonne, one of the best preserved medieval cities in Europe, together with Rothenburg ob den Tauber where my boss spent a dirty weekend way back in the eighties.'

I clear my throat to ensure I sound suitably light hearted. 'When did I tell you that?'

'You didn't but you hinted and as I got to know you better, I came to my own conclusion.'

'Do you think one should separate one's private life from business?'

'I do but I am lucky never to have fallen in love with anybody at work.'

I wink at him. 'Not even Mary?'

'Keep your eyes on the road. Mary sits opposite me all day. It would be crazy.'

'Charles Bukovsky wrote "Some people never go crazy. What truly horrible lives they must live."'

We pass Carcassonne, oblivious to its medieval splendour.

'You shouldn't believe everything you read,' Philippe says.

I tighten my grip on the steering wheel and ask, 'Do you despise me for going out with Tim?'

'I don't but you should have known better.'

I shrug. 'Why do I always come to my senses afterwards?'

'Maybe because your senses get in the way beforehand?'

'I've missed Carcassonne now.'

'It'll still be there when we drive back tomorrow.'

The weather changes, just as I'd forecasted, once we cross over into the Languedoc and we arrive in Narbonne under a bright winter sun.

The export committee meeting, to give it its proper name, is an annual event which usually takes place in Bordeaux and brings together the executive staff of Villa's foreign subsidiaries, and the export managers based at head office. It aims to create the feeling of a family reunion.

This year, Ed has decided to hold it in Narbonne to include "our colleagues from production". As the travelling budget for the event is astronomical, Ed's tried to limit accommodation costs by scheduling the meeting from lunchtime on the Thursday to lunchtime on the Friday. It gives those who have travelled from far away the option to treat themselves to a weekend in France. A few years ago, when being away on a Saturday night brought down the price of a flight, it would have been compulsory.

. . .

At the gates of the winery, I recognise the security guard from my last visit. I slow down, wave at him, point to Philippe whom I assume he knows and speed up. The shrill sound of a whistle makes me stand on the brakes. I look back. The security guard is gesturing at me to reverse.

'What does he want?' I ask Philippe.

'No idea but you'd better go back if you don't want him to pursue you into the meeting room.'

I check my watch. 'We haven't got much time to spare.'

Philippe gives a fatalistic shrug.

I turn the car around and drive back to the gates. The guard signals for me to park by his shed and to follow him inside.

'What the hell is going on?' I ask Philippe again.

He ignores my question and I get out of the car leaving the engine running. I march inside the shed. Before I have time to say anything, the guard points at the car, 'Engine off, please'.

I open my hands in a conciliatory gesture. 'We're employees of Villa's and we're due to be in a big meeting in five minutes.'

'Engine off, please,' he repeats, looking away from me.

I return to the car, fuming, and I kill the engine. Once back inside the shed I ask, 'what's all this about?'

He ignores me and picks up his glasses. He wipes the lenses with great care, checks their cleanliness against the light and puts them on slowly.

'Passport, please,' he says.

'This is ridiculous. You know who I am.'

He looks at me with an impassive face. 'Last time, you tell me no passport for English people. I believe you. When boss checks reports, he asks why no passport number for English visitor.'

I remember now I forgot to tell André about my white lie to the security guard. 'I am sorry. Did you get into trouble?'

'Boss gave me warning. He says he's boss, not you and not to believe you. Ever. Passport please.'

I return to the car for the second time.

'So?' asks Philippe.

'Paying for old sins with interest,' I say.

The guard scrutinises my passport with the diligence of an East German border guard from the Honecker days. He copies the number in his register, one digit at a time, his tongue poking between his teeth. I stay silent, aware that the slightest provocation will cost me another five minutes.

Luck's on my side though, as no other vehicle arrives during the proceedings. The security guard eventually runs out of delaying tactics and Philippe and I are free to go.

Ed's welcoming his troops when we file in the meeting room.

'I am disappointed some people have not managed to get here on time when others from further away have.'

He gestures to three Japanese in the corner who bow in unison. I doubt they have understood Ed's comment. He's spoken French as everybody is asked to throughout the meeting to ensure Marcel Villa can understand what's going on.

There's no point in answering, especially as the rebuke isn't specific, and Philippe and I squeeze ourselves between the Dutch and the Polish contingent, smiling and nodding left and right.

All the luxury in Narbonne being reserved for André's office, the meeting room lacks the grandeur of its equivalent in Bordeaux. It's stark and utilitarian and not big enough for such a large gathering. Square windows with blackout blinds occupy one side of the room and the three other walls are rendered white and bare of any decoration. Tables with metal legs and laminated white tops have been arranged in a U-shape and a motley collection of chairs are gathered around. As space is tight, some people sit outside the first circle as if waiting for their turn to come to the table.

In between foreign clusters arranged around the relevant export managers, my other colleagues are placed according to rank, allegiance and global geopolitics. The marketing team provides a buffer between Japan and China, and Sébastien between Poland and Russia. Marcel and André sit next to each other, welded together by their distrust of each other and Serge flanks André on the other side. Philippe and I link up Holland and Germany thus recreating the alliance of two centuries ago against revolutionary France.

I don't anticipate anything revolutionary from this meeting, only a dreary repetition of the last one on a bigger scale. Marguerite Villa's absence surprises me though. Despite her avowed intention to have Marcel replace her at the head of the company, I would have expected her to preside over such a large gathering or at least to join us for part of the proceedings. Maybe she'll turn up later.

We go through the German presentation in a benign mood. Something makes me feel uncomfortable though. The chair's admittedly a bit hard and we're squished around like sardines but there's something else. Only when I meet André's gaze do I realise he's staring at me with barely suppressed hatred. What have I done now? I rack my brain but can't think of anything.

A long expose in halting French on the ordeal our Russian office endured to ensure Villa's compliance with the latest regulation on fiscal strips puts the room to sleep. It fails to distract André despite pointing the finger at the shortcomings of some of the staff in Narbonne, something he doesn't take to lightly in normal circumstances.

When Ed grants us a ten minute break, I stay in my seat, waiting for André to attack. When I look up, he's left the room. This puzzles me. What can be the problem if he's not even willing to confront me about it? Serge has vanished as well, which is even stranger as we have not exchanged a word yet and I would have expected him to come over for a chat. I assume he's been dragged away by his boss, or he's up against it and trying to catch up. He could also be avoiding me if he knows why André's on my case. What I call courage and he, foolhardiness, isn't his strong point as I have found out before.

The young head of the Polish office comes up to me with a beaming smile.

'Hello, we have not met before. I am Zbigniew but call me Zeebee. You're the London office, aren't you?'

'I am indeed. How do you do?'

'There's an idea I want to discuss with you.' He plonks himself next to me, clearly determined to seize the moment. 'A lot of Poles live in England.'

'That's true.'

'We have created a French Table Wine brand. It's bottled here and it sells well in Poland. Why don't you try and introduce it in your country?'

I don't think I have ever met somebody with such a radiant smile. It makes it difficult to remind him that despite the presence of a sizeable contingent of his countrymen and women in my country, as he calls it, the vast majority of the population still happens to be British. And that Brits left French Table wine behind sometimes in the Eighties. I try to play for time.

'Do you have a visual you could show me?'

He jumps on his feet and returns seconds later with an A4 picture of a nice ordinary bottle of red plonk. He's still smiling broadly.

'You should have a chat with Philippe.' I tell him. 'He deals with the Cash and Carries where Polish corner shop owners get their supplies from.'

'You don't mind?'

'No, be my guest.'

He pumps my hand with boyish energy. 'Thank you so much. I think we'll do big business together.'

I am relieved when he leaves me if a bit guilty to have passed on the responsibility to disappoint him to Philippe. I massage my jaw which was beginning to ache from trying to match his Cheshire cat grin.

People are now trickling back in the room. It looks like I missed out on the break.

The next presentation, from the new head of the Chinese office, fascinates me. In what I understand to be the spirit of this get together, he explains the cultural differences between France and China, and how to make the most of them in a nice way to sell our wine. He then proceeds to reveal impressive progressions, cleverly expressed in percentages as he started off from a tiny basis.

André's still glowering at me, uncharacteristically failing to bask in the reflected glory of his pet market. Could I have upset him by asking for the bottling of The Wine Shop's Pinot Grigio to be brought forward? Or is he annoyed I didn't consult him on the date of Marks and Spencer's forthcoming visit? Surely, he knows I was not given any choice in the matter. These are trifles anyway. None of them justifies the icy stares he's been subjecting me to.

It's my Dutch friend's turn to go to the rostrum. He treats us to a slick and well-honed review of last year's business, packed with so many props I am amazed he didn't exceed his luggage limit on the flight down here. His grand finale is a short film taken during Amsterdam's gay pride at which the company sponsored a float.

Possibly enticed by the lively music, André stops staring at me to watch the show. If I was not so worried about his attitude, I'd burst out laughing. His eyebrows rise higher and higher until they almost meet his hairline. When a dancer, clad in a tiny pink swimsuit which leaves little to the imagination, crosses the screen and waves happily at us, he gets a coughing fit and Serge has to slap his back to calm him down.

29

MISUNDERSTANDINGS

Ed joins in the applause which concludes the performance and proudly announces we're only running twenty minutes late, quite a feat by our usual standards. He then gives the mike to the export marketing director who proceeds to tell us about the organisation of the international fairs where Villa's exhibiting this year. We'll be supporting Prowein in Düsseldorf at Bruno's insistence, the London International Wine Fair at mine, and Vinexpo, a must attend for the company as it takes place in our hometown of Bordeaux.

Caroline passes round drawings of the stands and fields various questions ranging from the practical – what's the stand number? – to the controversial – why weren't we shown these earlier? –. Why does the marketing presentation always seem to awake the worst in the sales team? Is it because they get the awkward slot at the end of the day? Or is it because their attitude is all about knowing what's best without getting their hands dirty?

Our placid German colleague raises his hand. He's turned bright red. 'Why does the sign on the stand read "Groupe Villa"?'

'This is the new corporate identity we're going to use from now on.' Caroline says.

'Is it the name which will appear in the catalogue?'

'Of course,' she answers as if talking to a particularly dim child. 'It's our new corporate identity.'

'But our clients and prospects know us as Villa,' he says.

'They'll have to get used to the new name.'

'I understand. In the meantime, they'll look for us under the letter V in the catalogue and they won't find us.'

Caroline looks at her boss for help.

'I think you underestimate your clients, Georg.' He says. 'When they don't find you under Villa, they'll realise you have changed identity and they'll look under Firma Villa or Gruppe Villa.'

'With all due respect, I think you overestimate our own importance.' Georg answers. 'When our clients don't find us, they'll go and pay a visit to one of our competitors. The money we have invested in the stand will be wasted unless they find us by chance. Prowein is a huge exhibition.'

'He's right,' Bruno says. 'What's this new nonsense? Can't you think anything through?'

The discussion threatens to develop into a full blown argument similar to the one we had at the last meeting. Export managers hunt in packs. Now Bruno's taken the first bite, his peers are shifting in their seats, ready to join the fray.

'Excuse me. May I have your attention?' Marcel Villa's woken up from his afternoon nap.

Even though I expect his intervention to silence my team mates' criticisms, I am pleased he's exercising his authority to nip rebellion in the bud. It's one thing for an ordinary export meeting to turn into a bun fight but our undignified squabbling doesn't need to be shared with a public.

'Have you thought about the polo shirts?' he asks. 'They'll have to show the new logo.'

The marketing director takes over as is proper when the future head of the company is talking. 'As the font remains the same and we're only adding the word "Groupe" in front of "Villa", we thought it would not be necessary to buy new polo shirts straight away.'

'We can't have "Groupe Villa" on the stand and "Villa" on the team's polo shirts. It's confusing.' Marcel says.

We avoid looking at each other. The confusion is minimal but nobody wants to risk antagonising Marcel.

'New polo shirts will be ordered for Prowein, Monsieur Villa,' says the marketing director, kowtowing to the absurd. He turns to us, 'You'll all be issued with one shirt per day for your own convenience.

This means you'll be expected to be impeccable even on the last day. Needless to say, it'll then be your responsibility to wash and iron your shirts for the next fair.'

Having thus re-established his authority, he goes back to his seat.

'Before you order anything new, shouldn't we have an open discussion about this new corporate identity?' Bruno asks, like a dog whose bone has been snatched away.

The marketing director turns towards Marcel in a mute appeal. Marcel fails to react. He's frowning at his Blackberry as if he's just found it on the floor and is unsure of how to use it. Then muttering an apology, he stands up and leaves the room.

We look at each other and soon the room has descended into chaos. Everybody is talking at the same time with the kind souls translating the argument for their non-French speaking colleagues adding to the ambient noise.

André gives us five minutes and yells, 'Shut up. This isn't the time or the place for this argument. Monsieur de Waast, please bring this meeting to its conclusion. Some of us have got actual work to do.'

Ed does as he's told and the simultaneous scraping of our chairs' legs on the floor tells of our impatience to leave the room. I have almost made it to the door when I am stopped in my track by André's cold voice.

'Miss Legerot, a word, if you please. Monsieur de Waast, could you join us?'

Philippe takes a step closer to me.

André points at him. 'Your presence won't be needed.'

As we traipse behind André, Ed whispers to me, 'What does he want with you now?'

'I have no idea,' I say. 'He's been glaring at me all afternoon but I can't think of what I could have done to displease him.'

'I don't know why the two of you can't get on,' he says.

I snap back at him. 'I don't either.'

When we walk into André's office, I have the disagreeable surprise to find Marcel Villa sprawled on the sofa. He's still engrossed in his Blackberry but doesn't express any surprise when he sees us. This means he was expecting us and probably knows what André has against me. My crime must be heinous for him to be involved, considering how fraught his relationship with André is.

I fall into a chair more than I sit, my legs failing to support me. Ed indicated when he visited me in Kingston that we'd take five minutes with Marcel during the committee meeting to confirm me in my job. Another crisis with André is bound to jeopardise this plan. And whenever I have thought of leaving Villa, it's always been of my own accord, not pushed off because I haven't made the grade.

'I'll be direct.' André says, looking at Ed. 'I can't work with Mademoiselle Legerot anymore.'

'Direct indeed,' Ed says. 'May I ask why?'

'She has no understanding of the most basic rules of business.'

'You surprise me. Chris came to us highly recommended by her previous boss. He praised her business acumen.'

'She must have left it behind when she joined Villa then.'

'Can you give us an example?'

'I don't have to look far. Look at the mess she's made of the incident with The Super-Market.'

'I understood the matter to have been resolved.'

'It was, until Blabbermouth here compromised everything.'

Ed's adopts his penguin pose: feet and palms of his hands splayed open in perfect symmetry. 'I'm afraid, you've lost me.'

'Once it became clear this young lady would agree to any compensation The Super-Market demanded without even trying to negotiate them down, I arranged for the total cost of the incident to be borne by a third party. What did I find out yesterday?'

'The brother-in-law!' I exclaim. 'Did the co-op refuse to pay?'

Ed looks from André to me and then back as if he were watching a particularly mystifying tennis match. Marcel's cocked his head on one side and is staring at me in what I can only describe as a speculating way.

'They will honour their commitment but they will not pay a penny more than what we have been invoiced. And they insist on seeing a copy of the invoice,' André says, exaggerating every syllable.

'Why is that a problem?' I ask.

André slams his fist on the desk. 'Nobody's ever doubted my word before, apart from your father, as you well know.'

I don't but now isn't the time to ask for clarification.

'This could ruin my reputation and Villa's.'

'You're not Villa, you know,' Marcel says.

André is too overcome to mind the trap.

'Down here, I am. They would have paid us £45,000 without discussion and that stupid cow told them they could get away with £27,753,' he says.

'Why should they pay us more than what's owed?' I ask.

'It's business. You take as much as you can and you leave the rest. And if you don't understand that, you'll never get far, just like your father.'

I am shocked into silence.

Ed looks bewildered by André's angry outburst. It looks like his natural cautiousness is battling with his desire to do the right thing. I am pretty sure he doesn't understand the situation though, and is mystified by the references to my father.

Marcel's looking at me with a sideways smile. I feel as if he's spurring me on.

I turn back to André. 'Thank you for the masterclass Monsieur Lange, but I'd rather not go far than turn into a bully like you. It was wrong in the first place to shift the responsibility of the problem on to our suppliers but it would have been even worse to take advantage of the situation and make a profit off their backs.'

I turn to Ed and Marcel. 'I may have been hopelessly naive in talking freely to the brother-in-law of the co-op's director but I have a clear conscience, something Monsieur Lange hasn't had in a long time.'

André lunges at me but Marcel's bag trips him and sends him sprawling. I can't remember that bag being there five minutes ago.

'André, try to retain some dignity, please,' Marcel says. 'Don't forget you're Villa down here.'

He turns to me. 'Mademoiselle Legerot, I agree with Monsieur de Waast. You have done a good job for us in England these past six months. I am glad to say you've passed your probation. Congratulations.'

He stands up and leaves the room, whistling the first bars of "Le Blues du Businessman".

André gets up slowly.

'Right, I am afraid, Monsieur Lange, you've heard Monsieur Villa,' Ed says. 'I hope you'll join me in wishing Chris many successful years with the company. In time I am positive the two of you will learn to work together.'

He grabs my arm and we half-run, half-tumble out of André's office and down the stairs. I am shaking so much I have to sit on the bottom step when we arrive in the reception hall.

Ed wipes his brow. 'There will be hell to pay.'

I nod.

'Why does it always have to happen to me?' he asks.

I prefer not to comment. I'm relieved he's feeling so sorry for himself that he's forgetting to ask why André should know and refer to my late father.

I can't get André's words out of my head. 'Nobody's ever doubted my word before, apart from your father, as you know.'

Marcel vanishes after saving my skin and texts Ed a few hours later. He's had to return to Bordeaux unexpectedly and won't be able to attend the second day of the export committee. André sends word he won't join us for dinner.

Serge appears out of nowhere as we're sitting down.

'May I?' he asks, pointing at the chair next to mine.

'Are you sure? What if André changes his mind and decides to join us?'

'I'll run to him, of course.'

'Let's hope he doesn't, then.'

I pour him a glass of Villa Pouilly Fuissé, keeping my eyes on the bottle.

'Why didn't you warn me he'd try to get rid of me?'

'He didn't!'

He sounds genuinely shocked.

'He did.'

'He's unbelievable!'

I look up. 'Is this condemnation or praise?'

'He's bloody clever but I still don't understand his problem with you.'

I don't feel like going through the whole story again.

'Don't you know the latest?' I ask.

'I know what he told me, which could be different from what he told you.'

‘He accused me of scuppering his chances of cheating our suppliers out of nearly £20,000.’

Serge’s loyalty to André reasserts itself. ‘You shouldn’t call it cheating. It is money we paid to The Super-Market.’

‘It isn’t. He meant to charge the co-op almost twice as much as we’ve been charged.’

The Japanese delegation looks at us in askance from across the table. I shouldn’t have raised my voice.

Serge answers me in a whisper. ‘You’re kidding me. Bastard . . .’

‘My thoughts entirely but you still haven’t answered my question.’

He pauses for a few minutes. ‘I owe you an apology.’

I sit back and cross my arms. ‘Go on.’

‘André called me to his office, two or three days ago. He wanted to know if I’d discussed the email from The Super-Market you forwarded to us with anybody. When I said I had not, he asked me if you knew anybody at the co-op.’

‘You told him I’d met Dominique in Edinburgh?’

‘He said he’d thought as much. But it gets worse. When you mentioned this guy to me, his name didn’t ring any bells.’

‘Not another liar.’ I say.

‘I am afraid so. The person you met is Thierry, the co-op’s director. He doesn’t have a brother in law. André was delighted you’d been fooled.’

I screw up my face in disgust. ‘Why did Thierry or Dominique or whatever he’s called, tell him?’

‘He didn’t. He would not reveal his sources, which is why André suspected me first. It’s only when I mentioned you’d met someone called Dominique, Thierry’s brother in law, that André told me no such person existed and you were the source of the leak.’

I feel myself welling up. ‘Why did he lie to me? He seemed like such a nice man, so down to earth, so genuine. Is there anybody who can be trusted?’

Sege pats my hand. ‘I don’t think he meant any harm. He only knew you worked for Villa when he approached you. You could have been André’s partner in crime.’

‘I am getting fed up with all this deception. Does anybody ever tell the truth?’

‘What about you?’

I never told Serge about Tim. I don't want to disappoint him.

'What do you mean?' I ask.

'André told me you'd suggested the co-op refuse to pay us anything. He said you'd overstepped your responsibilities and needed to be taught a lesson.'

'And you believed him?'

The Japanese glance at us again, smile and bow. I take it as a polite yet clear warning that I am being too loud.

'I tried to warn you.'

I cross my arms again. 'How kind! What stopped you from not just trying?'

'I called you in the office but you were out. I told Philippe I wanted to ask you exactly what had happened in Edinburgh. He said it had gone pear shaped and you wouldn't want to talk about it.'

'Oh my God.'

Serge stares at me.

'He was referring to something else, wasn't he?' he asks.

'As I'm sure you've figured out.'

'I wondered at the time but didn't want to probe. It's none of my business after all.'

I try to return to the matter in hand. 'I don't approve of André's bullying of the co-op but I would never presume to interfere. All I did was tell Thierry how much The Super-Market had billed us for the QA issue when he called me a few days ago. I had no idea André would try to overcharge them.'

Serge doesn't answer and eats his starter in silence. I push my food around my plate. I've lost my best friend in the company because I've slept with a clever cretin in a moment of weakness and it has complicated an already impossible situation.

'Why didn't you tell me?' Serge asks.

I try not to look at him. 'I didn't realise the importance of that phone call.'

'This is not what I am talking about and you know it. I thought we were friends.' He's patting my hand again. I am sure everybody is watching us.

I give him the short version. 'I knew you'd disapprove so I didn't tell you.'

'You should have. I am not good with people but I really enjoy working with you, more than with anybody else, apart from André of course.'

He winks at me. I shake my head. Kindness always makes me cry and I am trying hard not to right now. Maman would say there's a time and a place for everything.

'If you don't stop right now,' I say, looking at my untouched food, 'I am going to burst into tears and we'll have a hell of a job convincing the others we're only discussing business.

He squeezes my hand one last time. 'Remember what I've said. Don't doubt me ever again.'

'How could I ever?

Marguerite Villa doesn't show up the following day either. When I ask Ed why, he's as puzzled as I am.

30

GOOD BYE TIM

February vanishes in a flurry of client meetings, short visits to France and long telephone calls with Arnaud. He's become so impatient he doesn't wait for me or anybody else to get to his office when he needs to talk. He carries out pretend long-distance meetings where he conducts conversations with up to three different people, one in front of him, one on the mobile and one on the landline. All three may be sitting a few yards from his office. If he needs a fourth, he'll drop the least relevant person and call their replacement. This panders to his liking for secrecy and absolute control as the people he talks to don't know what the others are saying. It also means he wastes record amounts of my time and everybody else's. I never know when he hangs up if he's done or if he'll call again five minutes later. The small room at the back of the office, where we have lunch and our rare formal get-togethers, has turned into my refuge whenever I have something important to work on and don't want to be interrupted. Mary knows to tell Arnaud I am on the other line and can't be disturbed when I have retreated there. She used to say I was out of the office until the day he asked why he could see my car from his window.

We launch The Wine Shop's new own label range on the first Saturday in March. Bearing in mind the initial concept dictated by Arnaud – to generate maximum volume and margin for Villa regardless of the product sold – the result isn't too bad: the labels are neutral and elegant and Serge and Jen have sourced decent if unexceptional wines.

The prices are high though and the range lacks that little spark of genius which would get the press on side. The first reactions are muted, with *Harpers Wine and Spirits*, the industry's weekly, announcing the launch but reserving its comment until the following issue of the magazine when the wines will be in store. Same in *The Drinks Business*. Nothing in *Off Licence News*, which has given The Wine Shop, or what it calls "its elusive management", a tough time of late. We have missed the February issue of *Decanter* and it's too early for March. I can't see them getting excited about such a motley collection though.

Arnaud has imposed selling targets to all stores to try and meet his self-imposed goal of two million bottles sold in the first year. When I ask him how he reconciles this with the seven million figure he aimed for only a few months ago, I am met with a blank stare.

A central London shop manager, who fails to shift enough of the new range over the first days of the launch, receives an official warning. When he says promoting it would lower his average selling price by two pounds a bottle and risk alienating his more discerning customers, he is ignored.

I try to stay away from the debate. Now I have delivered what was required of me, I hope Arnaud will give me some breathing space and allow me to get on with the rest of my work, if only for a few weeks. I have half convinced him we should test the new range before trying to sell it to other retailers and that a success story will be our most compelling argument. I am buying time and hoping the problem will go away on its own.

Tesco are tendering a half-price deal for next September and I may soon get an opening with Marks and Spencer. In the more immediate future, Direct Wines' new range is about to go into production as is Sainsbury's next promotion. Mary tells me bottling dates have been postponed twice already. She's been told our bottle suppliers have failed to deliver either the correct bottle type or the right quantity several times in a row. This sounds to me like a classic cop-out from our production colleagues and I fear another battle with Narbonne is looming.

France Under One Roof, a one day trade fair dedicated exclusively to French Wines takes place on Wednesday, the 14th of March. Ed's coming over. It will give me a perfect opportunity to demonstrate our progress to date to him. I have chosen with care a selection of lesser Bordeaux Châteaux to show on the stand, together with a few of Serge's special Languedoc blends and some Burgundies from Sébastien's extensive range. Villa's handling of The Wine Shop may be open to criticism but it doesn't mean my side of the business needs to suffer any collateral damage.

With two days to go before the fair and Ed arriving tomorrow lunchtime, I get to the office at seven on the Monday, full of enthusiasm and hope for the week ahead. By eight thirty English time, I have made four telephone calls, which have confirmed a serious shortage of wine bottles in Europe. This hasn't occurred in over twenty years but in hindsight, it was a problem waiting to happen.

The four main glass suppliers in Europe operate an unofficial cartel way. The American group Owens, which became the market leader when it took over the French BSN, first put pressure on availability when it closed several ovens and reduced its range in order to increase profitability. St Gobain, the market's number two, promptly followed suit. When it decided to sell its glass business, strikes followed, further lessening the global bottle stock. A major breakdown at a French oven, a similar incident in Spain and a surge in demand in the spring, compounded by customers stockpiling to avoid running out of stock, worsened the situation.

I send a mute apology to my colleagues in Narbonne and set to compose an email to inform our main customers of the situation. When my phone rings, I bury my head between my hands and signal to Mary, who crept in ten minutes earlier, to pick up. What should I write? I don't want to lose any orders but if we do run out of bottles, even for a short time, I need to ensure customers understand the crisis is global. It isn't whether I should tell the truth or lie but how to dress up an unwelcome truth in as acceptable a garb as possible.

Mary coughs to attract my attention.

I turn towards her. 'What now?'

She gives me an apologetic smile. 'It was Arnaud.'

'Can it wait?' I ask.

'He needs to see you now. He says it's important.'

'Bloody hell, I thought he'd grown out of his habit of pulling me in at a whim.'

'Sorry,' says Mary

'Please, don't apologise on his behalf, you're making it worse.'

I walk to Arnaud's office, mulling over the glass shortage issue and feeling cross with myself for snapping at Mary. She's doing her best to help me and she's the last person I should be unpleasant to. I resolve to direct my resentment towards a more deserving target but Dave's not at his usual post. At a stretch, I am sure I can find a way to blame Arnaud for the shortcomings of the glass industry.

I throw myself in the chair facing Arnaud's desk without waiting for an invitation. 'You wanted to see me.'

I cross my arms and my legs for good measure. I am determined to show him I have had enough of his bully boy tactics.

He growls. 'And with good reason.'

I don't take the bait. Instead, I mark the beat with my foot, waiting for a more specific pointer.

'In case you have forgotten, you and I are on the same side. We don't have to be best friends but we must be as honest as possible with each other,' he says.

My jaw almost comes unstuck. How dare he?

He continues before I have time to decide if I should erupt in self-righteous anger or burst out laughing. 'Why didn't you tell me about the artist?'

The laughter dies in my throat. I feel myself turning bright red. I uncross my legs and cross them again on the other side.

Arnaud points at me. 'Ah! Got you there! Your face says it all. Don't try to tell me you didn't know.'

His choice of words gives me a small glimmer of hope. I manage to croak. 'Didn't know what?'

He leans over the desk, supporting himself on his hands like a gorilla, and spits out. 'He's leaving.'

He remains in the same position, staring at me for what feels like a long time, and throws himself back, adding. 'You didn't. And I would have sworn the two of you were thick as thieves.'

I manage to articulate. 'When is he going?'

'This morning or tomorrow, I am not sure. Depends how long it'll take him to clear his desk and sort out the paperwork with bloody HR.'

'Doesn't he have a notice period?' I ask.

Arnaud is looking at his computer screen. 'We agreed it was best if he didn't work it.'

'You had an argument,' I say.

'A big one.'

Arnaud looks back at me. He's smiling the sheepish smile of the little boy who's both relieved to have told the truth and secretly proud of his misdemeanour. 'I have wanted to put this arrogant git in his place for a long time. My English is much better now.'

'Why did you argue if he's the one who asked to leave? You've wanted rid of him as long as you have been here.'

'I make the decisions here. I agreed to keep him when others had to go. I am hardly going to applaud him when he saunters in here two months later to tell me he's found a better job elsewhere.'

'Men's egos! Where's he going?'

'One of our suppliers, of course. Silly name. Michelin something.'

'Bibendum?' I ask.

'That's the one. Why do they call themselves after a tyre company?' Arnaud muses.

'Bibendum means "let's drink" in Latin.'

His jaw juts forward. 'How do you know all that crap?'

'I did Latin at school for a few years.'

'Good for you.'

He pauses. 'So, you didn't know anything about the artist's leaving. Fancy that! You can go now.'

He dismisses me with a little wave of his upturned left hand, his eyes already trained on something more interesting than me.

Why can't I remember to play dumb when I am with him? Any pointless bit of information I provide him with only serves to fuel his resentment of me, as if we were engaged in a real life University Challenge.

I am surprised he hasn't taunted me for my support of Tim when his job was on the line. It would force him to remember his humiliation at the hands of Marguerite Villa though. His pride does have some advantages after all.

. . .

Now is the time to go and have a little chat with Tim, while my anger still gives me the courage to do so and before the realisation of his leaving has fully sunk in.

I bump into the head of human resources in the corridor. He's got a thick folder under his arm and looks hassled.

'Good weekend?' I ask.

'What are you talking about? I am so stressed I feel like it's Friday already.'

'You wish.' I laugh and walk into Tim's office. The music is off and his only remaining colleagues are nowhere to be seen.

He looks up and drawls, 'Long time no see.'

He pushes his hair away from his eyes in a gesture I remember with a little pang of tenderness and continues to pile folders and loose papers in an empty case of Bruichladdich Single Malt Whisky. I hide a little smile behind my hand. I bet this was not the first box which came to hand in the warehouse but Tim's too fastidious to be seen leaving the building with a box of The Wine Shop's Pinot Grigio even if it's full of his belongings.

'I hear you're off?'

I lean on the doorframe with my arms crossed. I don't trust myself to get too close.

He doesn't even look at me.

'Ripper's told you?'

I nod. 'He said you had a flaming row.'

My voice is calm and composed.

'I enjoyed that. It was long overdue.'

He pauses, a file in hand and smiles his cheeky boy smile. 'Don't tell me I shouldn't have. You'd do the same, given the chance.'

The closeness he suggests makes my stomach flip.

'I would not dream of lecturing you.'

I curse myself the minute the sneering remark is out of my mouth.

'Are you sure you can resist the temptation?'

He's now got his back to me. He's picking books off the shelf behind his desk.

I ignore the question and cut to the chase. 'Why didn't you tell me?'

'Should I have?'

He pauses for a moment, cocking his head sideways and lifting his eyebrows and resumes his packing. 'We've not been that close lately.'

I take a long look at him. Never again will I be able to eye him so greedily, to take in his tall lean body, his long elegant hands covered in freckles, his stupid face. My eyes mist over and I could almost pretend he's looking at me as he used to, with warmth and laughter in his eyes instead of barely suppressed boredom. Next time we meet, I will have lost him completely. I wish I could say something witty, something which would make him smile, but I can't trust my voice to remain steady. I shrug my shoulders and slink away before the tears come.

By Tuesday, Tim's gone but it hasn't sunk in. He could be away for the day or locked in his office. I choose to believe the latter. Even if our relationship's dead, his physical proximity dulled the sorrow of never again.

Outside, it's a typical March day, too early to be called spring but not harsh enough for winter. The weather's unhappy, like me, unsure of what to do next. It tries a few sunny spells early on and gives up. Too much hard work. When I drive to the station to pick up Ed, a desultory drizzle is falling, not sustained enough to be called rain but enough for him to grumble, 'bloody English weather'.

Still no sign of Dave when we arrive in the office. A small downpour has never been enough to keep him away. Could Arnaud have got rid of him?

31

A DAMNING ARTICLE

Ed's grumpy and won't say why. He greets Philippe with a mumble and a half-hearted nod from the door instead of his usual politician-on-the-campaign-trail handshake. Mary has to repeat her offer of tea or coffee twice before he shows any sign of having heard her. Once in the meeting room, he slumps in the first chair he bumps into. He places his mobile next to his laptop and keeps one hand on it, tilting it every few seconds to check the blank screen. When I ask if he's expecting a call, he denies it. All my attempts to engage him in conversation fail miserably. I am not even sure he's listening to me.

'Sainsbury's promotion is scheduled to start on the third Monday in April. The wine needs to reach the depots between six and ten days before. This doesn't give us much leeway if the bottle shortage worsens,' I say.

'Have you spoken to André Lange about it?'

His eyes are glued to his phone.

'He's about the only person I have not spoken to. I don't think he could help though.' My serious tone makes him look up.

'Ed, it's a global crisis.'

He throws another glimpse at his mobile. He picks up the silent phone and plays a little rap with it on the table.

'Louis the sixteenth was guillotined first. His wife followed six months later,' I say.

'Sorry, could you repeat?' he asks.

'Right from the start or only the last sentence?'

'The last sentence.'

'His wife followed six months later.'

He frowns. 'What are you talking about?'

'I was trying to find out how much attention you're paying me. The answer is, very little.'

His face turns red. 'Your attitude now and then verges on the disrespectful. I am your boss.'

I lean over the desk. 'We have a major crisis on our hand, a big trade event tomorrow and you couldn't care less.'

'Don't you think you're exaggerating?'

Mary knocks at the door. 'Sorry to interrupt. Chris, I've got Simon Woods on the phone. He says it's important.'

Simon's a well-respected wine writer. What can be so urgent?

'Do you mind?' I ask Ed.

He raises his hands, palms facing me.

I return to my desk and pick up the phone.

'Simon, how are you?'

'Pretty well but I won't return the question. I'm afraid I'm the bearer of bad news.'

'Go on.' I grasp the phone with both hands for comfort.

'I have seen a copy of the latest issue of Off Licence News. It will be distributed at France Under One Roof tomorrow.'

I relax my grip on the phone. 'Are they still going on about The Wine Shop?'

'It's more pointed this time. Most of the front page is taken by an article about Villa's poor handling of The Wine Shop and you're quoted several times.'

'Me? I have not spoken to anybody at OLN about The Wine Shop.'

'Don't shout at me. Somebody else has given them pretty damning information and the whole thing is woven up quite cleverly with your quotes. Do you want me to send it to you?'

'Is there anything I can do about it?' I ask.

'Nope. But you'd better be prepared. It will be the talk of the show tomorrow.

'Thanks.'

'Don't shoot the messenger. I'm only trying to help.'

'Sorry, that didn't come out the way I meant it. I didn't mean to sound petulant and I'm grateful for the advance warning.'

I lean back in my chair, waiting for Simon's email to arrive.

'What's the matter?' asks Mary.

The article is headed 'Villa's way'. It goes on to pan the new range, quoting anonymously several store managers who are said to despair of having to push such uninspiring wines down the throat of their customers. It speculates about the future of The Wine Shop under Villa's direction. Jen and I are mentioned as well as an unnamed source, which is referred to as close to The Wine Shop's top management.

The Circle of Wine Writers' Christmas party comes back to me as does my brief chat with the guy from OLN. My flippant remarks have been massaged into considered business appraisals of The Wine Shop's situation.

'"More" was the answer of Chris Legerot, head of Villa UK, when asked about The Wine Shop's price tag. Not denying the once vibrant retailer could soon be up for sale, Legerot went on to stress how much of Villa's money has been poured into The Wine Shop so far.'

'All I said was, "Quand on aime, on ne compte pas!"'

'Are you alright?' Mary asks.

I turn my laptop towards her. 'Read this.'

'Oh my God!' Her hand flies to her mouth. 'Didn't you say Arnaud's poor English was the reason he refused to give interviews?'

'What do you think? How can you, of all people, believe I could be so stupid?'

She bites her lower lip. 'If it was a day he really annoyed you?'

I stare at her and my eyes mist over. I put my elbows on the table and my head in my hands.

'Do something!' Philippe says to Mary from across the room. She lays a tentative hand on my shoulder.

'I am sorry. Would you like a cup of tea?'

Mary's a firm believer in the restorative properties of milky tea whatever the patient's condition.

'What's going on?'

Ed's standing at the door of the meeting room.

Mary points at my laptop's screen.

'Could Villa wines make up half of The Wine Shop's range?'

Ed's eyes are shining with excitement.

I sniffle. 'It was one of Arnaud's early fantasies. It won't happen.'

'Why? Has he gone native?'

'Ed, French wines account for one bottle in five sold in this country. For The Wine Shop to source every other wine from Villa would be commercial suicide. Even Arnaud understands that now.'

'Villa doesn't have to limit itself to French wines. The Wine Shop could be the opportunity for the company to diversify into other countries of origin.'

I point at the article still displayed on my laptop's screen. 'Look at how positively our foray into Italian wines has been received.'

Ed reads on. 'It's not an encouraging review, is it?'

He frowns. 'You told me the wines were good.'

'They're not bad but they're not exceptional. And as a symbol of the heavy handed way Villa is running The Wine Shop, they have zero chance of being praised by the critics.'

'Does The Wine Shop still choose the best wines at the keenest possible prices, as their head buyer tells me?' Ed reads aloud. 'The hefty price tag on some of the new lines contradicts this statement. A source close to the retailer's French managing director tells me margins have crept up in the last six months by up to twenty points and suppliers who refuse to co-operate are replaced with more accommodating ones.'

'I wonder who the source is,' I say.

'Isn't it you?' Ed asks. 'Look, there's a reference to the QA issue with The Super-Market. How many people at The Wine Shop would know about that?'

I pull the laptop back towards me.

'You're joking.'

Ed points at the screen and continues reading aloud. 'Had it not been for its ownership of The Wine Shop, Villa would have been unlikely to grab such a sizeable chunk of business. One can only hope this new venture doesn't end up in tears. A well-known British supermarket is understood to be reviewing its extensive contract with Villa following a recent quality problem which affected one of their bestselling line.'

He turns to me. 'Is it true?'

'I don't know,' I say.

I am holding on to the table for support.

We read on in silence.

'It doesn't say the information comes from The Wine Shop,' I say.

Ed's eyebrows rise. He looks at me, pressing his fingertips against each other as if testing their elasticity.

'I may have mentioned it to some people next door. It's all I could think about, last autumn,' I say, hanging my head in shame.

Ed straightens up. If he was wearing braces, he'd be hooking his thumbs through them. 'It's not my style to kick someone when they are down but I'd like you to learn from this regrettable incident. You seem to be unable to keep your mouth shut. Didn't André Lange's issue with you revolve around the same problem?'

He gives me a twirl and returns to the meeting room.

'Send this on to Arnaud and Jen, please,' I ask Mary before following Ed.

Lords may be a hallowed site for cricket lovers but it's also developed a serious vinous side-line in the last ten years. The Nursery End Pavilion is a large airy room with plenty of natural light, which offers ideal conditions for tasting wine.

I meet Ed at his swanky Belgravia hotel and we take the tube to St John's Wood. He's still fidgeting with his mobile and I assume the call he was expecting still hasn't come. Philippe's driven to Lords earlier this morning with a box of leaflets and tasting notes and the bottles our marketing colleagues decided we should show to prospective clients at the last minute.

On the way from the tube station, Ed and I catch up with two girls from Enotria, a large wine agency. I strike up conversation with them, trying to find out if they have seen the latest issue of OLN. They have not or else they are remarkably good actresses.

The room's buzzing when we walk in. More than a hundred tables line it, representing over sixty exhibitors. The largest agencies command up to five tables each displaying the wines of several of their principals. Swarms of eager salespeople unpack crates of bottles and arrange them on still immaculate tablecloths, chatting and joking with each other as they do so. A large counter near the entrance is crammed with hundreds of clean glasses. Round the corner, at the back of the cloakroom, a long bench displays the best wines of the show, one or two per exhibitor, as chosen by producers and agents. It will be the first port of call for most journalists and wine writers.

Piles of freshly printed copies of OLN have been arranged around the room and a few exhibitors have picked one up to kill time while waiting for visitors. I blush as I catch the eyes of one of the readers and he lowers his gaze back to the paper, whether by chance or to avoid looking at me, I don't know.

Ed tugs at my elbow. 'Move on. You look like you've seen a ghost.'

He drags me to our stand at the far end of the room. Philippe's straightening a last bottle as we join him. He's done a great job and our table looks great but the damning murmur rising out of all those reading a copy of OLN is all I can hear.

Albert Moretti, my other Circle of Wine Writers nemesis, is my first visitor. He grabs my hands without giving me a chance to escape behind the stand and closes his eyes as if for a blessing. 'Chris, I am so sorry. My heart went out to you when I read that vile article.'

He shakes his head. 'You're so brave to be here today.'

I'd like to tell him I'd rather be anywhere else but honesty isn't an option.

'Albert,' I drop my head sideways in the age-old stance of the grieving relative. 'Thank you so much. Your sympathy means a lot to me.'

His head bobs in time with our double handshake. Onlookers could be mistaken and think we're about to embark on a bout of country dancing.

I drop my clanger. 'I am not worried though.'

A flicker of disappointment crosses his face. 'I have not seen such a direct attack in a trade paper for a long time,' he says.

'I agree. It's incredible how jealous people can get. Mind you, it must be so frustrating for some of our competitors to find Villa's ownership of The Wine Shop barring their route to market.'

I smile one of the most insincere smiles of my whole life.

Albert insists. 'To allude to your problem with The Super-Market was below the belt.' I flinch and he raises a cautionary hand. 'Don't worry. I would not dream of sharing what I know with anybody.'

I study his face for a minute but there's no guilt there. He is convinced all knowledge is power and power is as indispensable to him as the corkscrew he carries in his briefcase.

Andy Tripp's striding towards me, his face set in a grim frown. Albert takes the hint. He mouths 'See you later' and vanishes in the crowd.

I brace myself to welcome Andy when I notice James, Sainsbury's French wine buyer making his way to our stand from the opposite direction. The lack of interest from visitors at trade fairs is the bane of the exhibitor. It's especially embarrassing at open plan events such as this when one's success, or lack thereof, is easy for all to assess. The simultaneous visit of two major buyers however is even worse. Should I accept the offer of one of them to return later, there's a risk he won't, only to comment afterwards, 'You were too busy looking after my competitor when I tried to taste your wines.'

Trying to deal with both at the same time will only lead to two semblances of meeting. Neither party will tell me which of our wines they like best nor will I be able to discuss terms with them.

I turn to Philippe and Ed. 'I'll take Direct Wines, you take Sainsbury's.'

Andy looks like he's just buried his entire family. He's cut himself several times when shaving. His shirt collar shows a long streak of dried blood.

I take a deep breath. 'Andy, how good of you to come and see us.' My smile stretches so far, it lifts the corners of my eyes.

'I don't believe everything I read in the papers but I am not happy with the negative hype around your company. The range we're developing with you is critical for our next financial year and we can't risk a mauling such as the one you're getting with the new wines for The Wine Shop.'

Tim chooses this moment to pass by the stand. He waves at Philippe.

Andy peers at me. 'Chris?'

'Sorry, I have just remembered something. I would not worry about the press, Andy. Because Villa owns The Wine Shop, whatever we do there attracts a lot of unhealthy attention.'

Andy doesn't look convinced. 'I am going to walk around the room and talk to a few people. We may have to scrap the whole project.'

He looks at me and adds more kindly. 'Don't look so shocked. It would only be a last resort. But I can't take the risk of launching a new range if it damages our reputation. I'll let you know before close of play today.'

Once he's gone I take a moment to try and calm down. We have invested a hell of a lot of time and money in this Direct Wines' project. Wines are blended, labels printed, cases ordered. To pull the plug now would be a disaster. To imagine André Lange's reaction makes me want to curl up in one of the empty boxes under the table and fall sleep for a very long time.

32

THE PITS

I hear raised voices coming from the left. Sainsbury's buyer has stepped back from Ed and Philippe. He looks cross. Philippe glances at me and urges me to come over with a nod.

I take the few steps which separate us, trying to reinstate some sort of smile on my face.

'James, sorry I have been detained. Thanks for stopping by.'

Ed's face is bright red.

'I am not sure I should have,' James says. 'This gentleman, who I understand to be your boss, doesn't seem to understand the way we work.'

'I merely suggested,' Ed does his open hands thing, 'that James postpone his promotional period by two weeks. This would give us a bit more time to deal with his order. Ten containers is a lot of wine.'

James turns to me. 'Chris, if Villa can't bottle ten containers in time for the promotion, I'll have to scrap it. But there are lots of people in this room who'll be delighted to pick up the pieces.'

I turn to Ed. 'Sainsbury's promotional periods are not specific to the wine department. James can't move them.'

'Has any other supplier mentioned the bottle supply crisis to you?' I ask James.

His mouth twitches and he looks up to the right. 'What are you talking about?'

I explain all I have discovered and the uncertainties our

production sites are facing. I should have taken the time to finish my email.

'Why don't you import bottles from Spain or Italy?' James asks.

'It's a European issue.'

I am now convinced he knows about the situation and he's only trying to get to the top of the queue. I wish I could give him priority but I can't. Even if my relationship with André was perfect, industrial constraints would stop him and me from favouring one customer over another. My best bet is to shut up and wait for James to come to his own conclusion.

He bites his lip but his face tells me he knows we're facing exceptional circumstances. I hold my breath, waiting for the inevitable acknowledgment.

'James, may I call you James?'

Why is Ed piping up now?

'It sounds like we had a small misunderstanding earlier on.'

James cocks his head to one side and waits for Ed to continue. He's a good buyer. I fear the worst.

Ed puts his hand on his heart and closes his eyes. 'I don't want our first meeting to be marred by a difference of opinion. I am going to make a pledge to you. Your orders will be bottled on time.'

James raises an eyebrow a la Sean Connery. 'Even without bottles?'

'Even without bottles. . .' Ed repeats, good little lamb to the slaughter that he is.

I open my mouth but Philippe kicks me in the shin.

'Thank you so much, Ed,' he says.

He turns to James. 'Problem solved. The boss has spoken. Would you like to taste a few of the wines we're showing today?'

Ed's face bears the smug satisfaction of the man who has bid all his worldly possessions on red the second before the ball settles on black.

I am shocked into silence.

James whispers to me as he leaves, 'I am not sure which is worse, OLN or your boss. But a promise is a promise.'

I manage a feeble grin.

Loud laughter makes me look up. Tim's walking past, arm in arm with a blonde. I always assumed the wine trade not to attract stunners but the bastard always seems to be escorting good looking girls. Do they join for the day or does he have a special talent of sniffing them out? It hurts to see him having so much fun.

Jen pays me a visit and cheers me up a little by promising to knee our friend from OLN in the groin. Sadly he's nowhere to be seen, unlike Tim who crops up everywhere I look like the ferret of the French nursery song.

'*Il court, il court, le furet*
Le furet du bois joli.'

'Hello young lady, are you from Villa?' The tall stooping elderly man in front of me wears a 'Wholesaler' badge.

'I am indeed. How may I help you?'

'I'd like to taste your varietal range, please. I sent my first order last week but I am thinking about adding a Sauvignon. It seems to be all the rage.'

'Your first order?'

He nods.

'To Villa?'

He nods again.

'May I ask, are you UK based?' Despite his posh British accent or maybe because of it, my visitor may work for a foreign company and take advantage of the fair to visit some potential suppliers.

'We're in Worcestershire. Here's my card. May I taste your wines now?' A note of impatience is creeping in his voice.

I stare at his business card, question marks popping in my head like silent fireworks. I know every single one of our prospects and customers and this guy's most definitely not one of them. I may have been wrong to neglect him but I fail to understand how he can have placed an order with us.

'Sorry to be so blunt. Who's your contact at Villa?' I ask.

'A gentleman called André Lange. He's a friend of a friend. Us old codgers like to do business together, you see. I assume you're his assistant, aren't you?'

I mumble something indistinct instead of pointing out that being a woman doesn't necessarily mean I am assisting someone endowed with a penis.

Ed rushes to me as soon as my companion has departed. 'Why

didn't you introduce me? There's no point for me to come over if I don't get to meet our customers.'

I could tell him his handling of James has lost him any such rights but in this instance, I have a less contentious motive.

'I didn't introduce you because the person I was talking to is under the impression I report to André Lange.'

'Why didn't you put him right?'

Ed rocks on the soles of his feet like an impatient toddler as he does every time his position is challenged.

'Because he's about to start doing business directly with Narbonne and I smell another dirty trick from our friend André.'

'Another Siberwines?' Ed asks.

'No, this isn't dumping.' I say, looking once more at the business card in my hand. 'This respectable gentleman may unwittingly be part of yet another cunning plan to strip me of all commercial credibility.'

Ed looks lost.

'Marguerite Villa is a fervent supporter of the go-getting commercial mentality. How do you think she'll react when told a British prospect had to place an order directly with one of our production sites because he had not seen anybody from Villa UK in months?'

Ed puts his fingertips together. 'I have to admit it is disappointing. We may have to sit down at some stage and take a look at your priorities.'

I don't bother answering him. I may have to call Marguerite Villa to beat André to it.

'I'll get a sandwich, then,' Ed says.

I turn round and almost collide into Rachel. 'Sorry, I was not looking where I was going.'

She looks grim.

'Are you alright?'

'I have something serious to discuss with you.'

The article in OLN. She's taking her business away.

'Do you mind if I have some water first?' I ask. 'Would you like any?'

She declines. I pour the water slowly in my glass and I take small sips, trying to compose myself.

'Do you know how important The Super-Market own brand is to me?' she asks.

I relax my grip on the table. This is one of Rachel's favourite hobby horses but I can't think of anything we have done to harm her brand since the autumn.

'And to Villa,' I say. 'Your wines represent a big slice of our business over here and I have not given up on your Bordeaux range yet.'

'I could not give you any more business straight after the latest incident,' she says. 'But as your samples showed well and your prices were the keenest, I took it upon myself to put the project on hold for a few months. Last week I mentioned the contract may go to Villa during the buying meeting.'

'This is great news.'

My sixth sense tells me there's a 'but' somewhere.

'Do you know Vera who buys Spain and Italy?'

'I have heard of her.

'She studied for her Diploma with somebody from The Wine Shop, a guy called Dave. It was either last year or the year before, just before she joined The Super-Market.'

I am getting a bit confused but I keep on listening.

'They became friends on Facebook. Philippe is also a Facebook friend of Dave's and Vera became friend with him.'

I look at Rachel blankly. She's lost me.

'It means she can see Philippe's Facebook photos especially when Dave comments on them,' she says.

The picture with the bottle of The Super-Market red! I remember pulling a disgusted face, maybe even pointing at the label. Philippe sent me the result, mocked up as a Christmas card, wishing me better luck for the year to come. I looked so awful I binned it straight away. Why on earth did he put it on Facebook?

My legs give way. I walk round the table and sit down.

'I am really sorry, Rachel.'

'Do you realise how serious this is?' she asks. 'The caption says, "Chris's least favourite tipple". It makes a complete mockery of The Super-Market.'

'I can try and explain. Philippe came to visit me when I helped out in the Roehampton store at Christmas. I was tired and still upset by the whole episode with the Vin de Pays red. He took a first picture of me filling the shelves that turned out blurry. When he took the second one, I grabbed a bottle and pulled a face.'

'What were you thinking of?'

Sex. I'd spent the morning wallowing in my most intimate memories of Tim.

I opt for a more reasonable answer. 'It was a moment of madness.'

'Ask Philippe to take that photo off Facebook as soon as possible and give me a call next week. I haven't got time to taste anything right now.'

She's off before Ed comes back and just as he does, Tim takes another turn by my stand like a Jane Austen heroine, arm in arm with another blonde. At this rate, he will have covered a half-marathon by tonight.

Philippe gives me a sandwich and I bite into it with all the frustration I have accumulated since the morning. A sharp pain shoots through my lower jaw. I probe my teeth with the tip of my tongue and my suspicions are confirmed. A large filling my dentist warned me about has fallen off. I can't resist having another try and I am rewarded by a second stab of exquisite raw nerve pain.

I am falling to bits. This job is killing me and I have ignored various reminders to visit the optician, the dentist or my GP over the last nine months.

My phone vibrates the minute I step outside the hall to call the surgery. Arnaud must be back from France.

'Didn't you say you were friends with most wine writers?' he asks.

'I may have.'

He laughs. 'If that's what your friends are like, I don't want to meet your enemies.'

'I'm sorry,' I say.

'I don't care about the bastards but what about your customers?'

'I've had better days.'

His sympathy feels like another evidence of my utter failure. I wish I had the strength to ignore it.

'Do you want me to have a word with the artist?'

'What's Tim got to do with it?'

'He's got to be the mysterious source the OLN guy refers to. Jen swears blind this has nothing to do with her and Philippe isn't the type to go behind your back.'

I lean against the wall. He's right. Who else could know so much about The Wine Shop and Villa? I feel sick.

'Leave it,' I say. 'He's gone now.'

'His last month's salary isn't. It's your call. You're around tomorrow?'

'I need to go to the dentist but I'll be in the office later.'

'Rather you than me. Call me when you're in.'

The line goes dead before I have time to answer him. Some habits die hard.

A restless night and an hour in the dentist chair give my resolve to appeal to Marguerite Villa time to strengthen. André's dislike of me continues stronger than ever if his latest meddling is anything to go by. Villa's UK business is at risk of falling apart and I can't rely on Ed to help. I hum the French singer Rose's depressing ditty under my breath: something about the game being over.

I lock myself in the meeting room with a glass of water and my notes and tell Mary only to come in if the building goes up in flames. I grimace a few times to stretch my mouth, still numb from the anaesthetic.

When Marguerite Villa's assistant picks up, I introduce myself and ask to speak to the old lady.

'She's away at the moment. What is it regarding?' she asks.

'When is she coming back?'

A tiny pause. 'I am not sure. Would you like to leave a message?'

'I'll try her on Monday.' Marguerite never leaves the office for more than a few days.

Another pause. 'She may not be back.'

I try to think of a justification for a lengthy absence. 'Has she gone to China?'

'Are you sure you don't want to leave a message? '

'I'll think about it.'

I have underestimated André. His silence of the last few weeks was not a lull in the hostilities but a battening down of the hatches. He's barred my access to Marguerite. I am on my way out.

. . .

I push the door to Arnaud's office without knocking. I am past caring.

'You wanted to see me,' I say, slumping into the chair opposite him.

He frowns. 'Are you ill?'

I shrug.

He examines me, not unkindly. 'You look terrible,' he says. 'Are you sure you don't want me to dock Tim's pay?'

I probe the corner of my mouth with the tips of my fingers. The effect of the anaesthetic is receding and the mangled nerve of my damaged tooth pulses out a dull pain through my jaw.

'Not worth it. It's against the law anyway.'

'The law! If we were in Africa- '

One look is all it takes to silence him.

'Go home,' he says.

I frown.

He points towards the door. 'Go home,' he repeats, separating each syllable. 'Take a couple of painkillers and go to bed.'

My eyes fill with tears. It doesn't take much at the moment and his unexpected kindness is enough to set me off. I stand up and wipe my eyes.

Arnaud shuffles papers on his desk and pretends not to notice.

33

PAPA

At home and loaded with Nurofen I am too restless to lie down. I pace the living room floor, my mind racing, disregarding my tired and aching body. The first anniversary of Papa's death is in two weeks. What have I achieved since that mad race out of Argentina?

My throat tightens and my eyes well up again. Arnaud is right. I'm a complete mess. If only I could talk to Papa. I cross my arms and shiver. I've turned the heating off during the day and the flat feels damp, chilly and empty. I pick up the box file containing Papa's papers from the top shelf of the bookcase where it's been gathering dust for three months and set it down at the kitchen table.

Under the newspaper cutting showing Marguerite Villa and my father in front of the Narbonne winery and a thick file of health and safety procedures for the site I find a bundle of letters tied with a rubber band. The top one is headed *Ministère de l'Agriculture*. It bestows the *Ordre du Mérite Agricole* to my father for services to the French wine industry.

I lean back in my chair and remember the ceremony at Villa's head office. Maman had bought a new red dress for the occasion. Papa had told me the distinction he was about to receive was nicknamed "the leek" and I kept on getting the giggles. I was eight. Marguerite Villa, herself an officer of the *Ordre du Mérite*, pinned the little medal hanging from a green ribbon on my father's chest, like an army general decorating a brave lieutenant after the battle.

Under the letter from the *Ministère*, I find an old fashioned carbon copy of Papa's resignation letter.

Madame,

Following our conversation on Friday, I am writing to you to confirm my resignation. Considering the circumstances, I am sure you'll understand my wish to leave the company as soon as possible.

Short and to the point. What could he have done? It must have been pretty bad. The letter makes it sound as if he had no choice but to fall on his sword. But why did Marguerite tell me she shouldn't have let him go?

All the other letters form part of a correspondence between Papa and André Lange, which covers several months. Most of them are copied to Marguerite Villa. I spread them in a fan shape on the table, catching fragments of text as I do so.

It has come to my attention that you have, on several occasions in the last few weeks, failed to implement the safety measures, which should be the norm in Narbonne whether or not I happen to be present in the building.

This is from Papa. Another one is dated three months later.

The safety of our staff should take priority over productivity increases. The reckless speed to which you pushed the bottling line today would certainly have caused an accident, with a high chance of one or several operatives being injured, if I had not returned earlier than planned from Bordeaux and slowed it down.

And another one.

. . .

I congratulate you on your promotion. As you know it was Madame Villa's decision to promote you, not mine. I urge you however not to neglect the well-being of your employees in your new position. You may see some of the processes I have put in place as old fashioned and unnecessarily cautious but please remember they are the result of twenty years' experience in running production sites.

My heart breaks. How hard it must have been for Papa.

Only two of the letters are from André.

Monsieur Legerot,

Madame Villa has asked me to improve the efficiency of the Narbonne site. I would appreciate your support in this project.

And then,

Monsieur,

Madame Villa has authorised me to dispense with some of the more onerous procedures you implemented in Narbonne. Should you have any objections, I suggest you discuss them with her.

Is this why Papa left? Because Marguerite let André have his own way in Narbonne? Did Papa feel undermined to a point where he could not bear it anymore? He was a proud man but not overly so. Villa was his life. He would not have let go so easily.

A slim volume in a tattered cardboard sleeve lies at the bottom of the box. I pull it out and trace the faded gold letters on the cover with my finger: Tasting Notes.

I have not seen this book in years. I bring it to my nose and close my eyes. The leather has lost its smell but the thick creamy paper gives off the metallic tang of dry ink over dusty vanilla. I stroke the cover and open the book on the table.

I flick through the pages where Papa has recorded the best wines he's tasted. Here's the Smith Haut Lafitte 61 he made me try. He's written down: Christine's first grand cru. I wonder if he realised how important that moment was for me.

Towards the end, the writing is upside down and much more closely packed. I turn the book around.

'*Fear, not to be confused with caution, is a poor advisor as it obscures one's judgement. How many of us avoid taking risks at any cost? But is life worth living without risks? I like to believe I have never gone for the easy option.*'

This looks like a journal. I go back to the beginning.

'*I am in the dog's house again, this time for having a row with Rémi. His obsession with the French Resistance drives me mad. Why have so many of my friends become so dogmatic in their old age?*

Disappointment washes over me. If Papa wrote these lines later in life, they will not tell me about his time at Villa. I read on for the illusion of spending time in his company.

'*The two of us went on an outing to Oradour-sur-Glane at his request. In the car he would not stop talking about the "ordinary heroes who saved our country from German rule". There's no point mentioning the Allies to him, he's forgotten their existence altogether.*

He'd done some research into the massacre beforehand and when I asked him if résistants had been among the six hundred or so people killed by the SS on that fateful day of June 1944 he nodded and said a few freedom fighters had indeed lost their life in Oradour even though the Germans had not been aware of their existence until much later. He added quite forcefully that the resistance could not be blamed for what happened on that day.

We walked the desolate streets of the martyr village for an hour or so and the contrast between the ordinariness of the site and the extreme brutality of its plight moved me deeply. Rémi kept on talking, displaying an encyclopaedic knowledge of the dramatic events of these few days. After visiting the memorial on the other side of the road and examining all the exhibits gathered there, we returned to the car in silence.

I was mulling over his earlier comment and asked him how he could claim the resistance had nothing to do with the massacre. The kidnapping of SS officer/ commander Kampfe may have been necessary to delay his division's progression towards Normandy but it was obvious to me it had been the trigger for the SS reprisals in Oradour.

Rémi stopped walking and turned towards me, looking as shocked as if I'd said I sided with the SS on that one. Although I can't remember every word of the tirade he subsequently launched against what he called my revisionist and neo-pacifist tendencies, I was struck by his inability to entertain any challenge to his own vision of the truth.

It made me realise how much I have changed since the days I tried to impose my own vision to André. Would things have turned out differently if I'd shown more flexibility?

I am about to turn the page when the phone rings. I glance at the display, hoping for a random caller's number but it is Philippe.

'I have deleted your photo from my Facebook page. I'm so sorry, Chris.'

'Don't worry. I know you didn't mean to cause any trouble.'

'Do you want me to apologise to Rachel?'

'She asked me to call her next week. Not much point in bothering her right now.'

The next page looks like a new entry. Merde! I scan it quickly but can't find any mention of André. I turn to another page and my heart skips a beat.

'*I wish Christine would visit more often. There's so much I need to tell her. She has inherited my intransigence and I worry she'll get hurt. She was furious when she called today because she found out a colleague of hers lied to their boss to cover a mistake he'd made. I hope she never has to deal with the likes of André. It would crush her.*'

. . .

The entry stops there. I throw the book on the floor in frustration. Something definitely happened between Papa and André, something which had to do with the truth and not wanting to compromise, something which changed Papa's outlook on life.

The words *Tasting Notes* on the cover of the diary come across as a provocation. The first lines my father wrote in there had to do with the art of putting the essence of great and not so great wines into words. It looks like he moved on to try and decode in those same pages the meaning of events in his life. Could the whole story be in there?

I pick up the book and open it again.

'*Wars are almost always started by lies. The case of the Ems Dispatch is of particular interest. Bismarck altered, in what would now be called a sensational press release, the factual minutes of a tense but courteous meeting between Kaiser Wilhem and the French ambassador. Not only did he emphasize the extravagance of the French demands but he turned the Kaiser's refusal to discuss the matter further into a refusal to meet the ambassador again. The French translation reinforced the inflammatory tone of the message, which was released on Bastille Day. Five days later, France declared war.*'

Truth and lies again. I could scream in frustration.

'*Isn't some kind of deception always necessary to justify military action? How can one otherwise defend sending men to their death even if it is to save others? The plain truth can be too much to handle.*

Is that what happened when Marguerite tore my report about André to pieces? I wish she'd at least waited for me to leave the room.

I read recently that execution squadrons used to be provided with eleven live cartridges and a blank one. Like the blindfold hiding the eyes of the condemned man, it was supposed to make it easier for the soldiers to fire at another human being: little deceptions to make the abominable acceptable.

I suppose my mistake was to tear the blindfold away.'

I leaf through the book in mounting exasperation. There must be more than a hundred pages of closely written text. I must read them all if I am to have a chance of ever piecing together what happened between Papa and André. Despite my dislike of the older man, I don't believe him capable of murder but could it be what Papa is alluding to? I am suddenly scared of what I am going to find out.

My phone rings again.

'Hi Andy,' I say with false jollity. I have just remembered he never returned to our stand yesterday.

'I am sorry to hear you're unwell but this is a genuine emergency. Is there any chance you may be able to come over this afternoon for a chat with my boss? He wants to talk about the new range.'

I stroke the smooth cover of Papa's diary and slide it back in its worn out sleeve with a sigh. 'I'd be delighted, Andy.'

Andy misled me, whether on purpose or by accident, I am not sure. His boss didn't even mention the article in OLN and seemed comfortable with the idea of Villa supplying a new range to Direct Wines. He asked me a lot of questions about the organisation of the company but none which could explain the urgency of his summons. Maybe he's another Arnaud who can't wait for anything.

I get caught in traffic on the way back home and arrive after seven. Papa's diary is on the coffee table where I left it earlier. I dump my bag and my coat in the middle of the room, throw myself on the sofa and grab the book.

Ten minutes later, it's still lying in my lap, unopened. I need a glass of wine.

After much consideration, I open a bottle of Minervois, Chateau Maris. I bought a case for Papa two years ago. When he saw the label, he frowned and mumbled something about Languedoc upstarts. Maman told me afterwards he'd served it to some of his wine buddies, describing it with pride as 'one of Christine's discoveries'.

I pour the wine in one of my prized Zalto glasses, pull the curtains shut, turn my mobile off and sit down again, ready for an ultimate conversation with my father.

I skip the Oradour pages I read earlier. The next entry follows on the theme of lies and selective truth being woven into the very fabric of human life.

'I have rewritten the act of contrition: people lie, as opposed to sin, in their thoughts and in their words, in what they do and in what they fail to do. Aren't most sins based on lying?'

I yawn. Papa could be a touch heavy handed with religion. I hope this won't turn into a theological thesis.

'Look at the original sin. God lied first when he said 'You shall not eat of the fruit of the tree which is in the midst of the garden, neither shall you touch it, lest you die.' The serpent then tempts Eve by introducing an element of doubt in a straight forward situation, a classic premise. He asks, 'Did God say, 'You shall not eat of any tree of the garden'?' When told only one tree is forbidden, he cajoles and reassures, 'You will not die' and comes up with the first instance of selective lying, 'You will be like God, knowing good and evil.''

I am struggling to keep my eyes open. The next entry arouses my interest again.

'Was Marguerite right to think the truth would ruin Villa? A little cover up, she called it. She listed all sorts of cases when lying turned out to be a good thing. Commerce,' she said, 'thrives by lying or at least being economical with the truth. My product is the best and the cheapest' is seldom true.' I must have looked dubious and she went on. 'Spying relies on lying and yet, it is indispensable to protect democracies. Even the

pharmaceutical industry lies when testing new drugs through the placebo method.'

She looked pleased with this last one and handed over the cash with a smile.'

The cash? What is he going on about?

34

THE TRUTH

I continue reading.

'I could have told her that parents lie to their children. I misled Christine about the realities of the wine business. Because it meant so much for me, I made it sound better for her, brushing over the long hours and the poor pay. I was so proud when she chose to follow in my profession. Would she be a wife and a mother now if it had not been for all the travelling? Is it too late to put things right?'

I never knew Papa worried about me so much. It was always Maman who asked me awkward questions.

'Marguerite was right. What's true for one person isn't for another: religion, beauty, everything is relative.

André maintained Manuel died through his own fault. I believe André caused his death as surely as if he'd pushed him into the vat. Marguerite chose to go with André and I didn't have the strength to fight them. I'd invested so much in Villa. Doing what I was told to do and leaving was the easy option.'

. . .

I stand up and pace the room. I have no idea who Manuel was but this doesn't look good.

'I didn't even like Manuel much. He was lazy and undisciplined, argumentative and hot tempered. He didn't deserve to die such a horrible death though. His youngest son has been in and out of prison all his adult life. The shame of it drove his mother, Maria, into an early grave. I grew fond of her through the years. She never blamed Villa, never contested our version of the story. She soldiered on, bringing up her three kids the best she could.

Manuel would never have died if André had not cut down on the security measures I'd implemented at the winery. All to save a few francs and show off in front of Marguerite. What if the company had admitted liability and paid Maria a decent pension? Would it have helped keep the boy on the straight and narrow? The accident would have had to become public knowledge. There would have been questions asked. André would have been held accountable for his decisions.

I'll never forget the day I brought Marguerite's money to Maria. She thanked me. The poor woman had never seen so much cash. She fancied herself rich. A smaller sum, paid over a longer period would have been more beneficial.

But Marguerite was having none of it. She liked big gestures. I remember her instructions. 'You go. It will mean a lot more to her if it comes from you. She probably doesn't even know who André is. You give her the envelope and tell her how sorry I am her husband has run away.' She knew I would do her bidding even if it destroyed me. 'You're my secret agent,' she said and, when I failed to respond, 'and one of my few friends.'

I looked at her but she was shuffling papers on her desk, already thinking about her next task. A man had died in our care but like in primitive societies, she'd paid blood money and moved on. I fled her office, the bulging envelope held at arm's length as if it were contagious. I never saw her again after that day.

I fled Maria's flat in much the same way the day after. She'd opened the envelope and she was passing the banknotes from hand to hand, not even counting them but relishing in their sheer number. 'Gracias, muchos gracias,' she said, reverting to her native Spanish. She tried to kiss my hand but the baby started crying which gave me an excuse to leave. Maybe she was not too upset her good for nothing husband had vanished without trace. I felt sick.'

I do too. This is awful. I can't believe what I am reading.

'The money lasted a year. Maria was a kind and generous woman with many relatives. I tried to help her a little but I had to be mindful of her older son. One day, he must have been fifteen or sixteen, I'd brought some clothes Christine had grown out of for his little sister. His mother was not there. He pushed the bag back into my arms, saying 'We don't need your charity.' When I protested my good intention, he took one step towards me and said 'I can look after my mother. You are not welcome here anymore.' He slammed the door in my face. I never told Maria.

I kept on sending cards for New Year with cash inside, always claiming it came from Villa. I don't know if she believed me or cared. I'd long left the company by then but she may not have known. One year, the card came back with the cash and a note from the son saying his mother had died and he didn't need my money.'

I put the book down and take a big gulp of wine. This explains André's attitude when I joined Villa.

I leap from the sofa and grab another file. A drawing of the layout of the Narbonne site falls out. I turn it around, trying to find my bearings. Here's the extension with the new bag in box line and the warehouse. Hatchings mark a row of small fibreglass vats which were moved during the works. The last one looks like it's been walled in. It's marked with a cross.

Another document has been scribbled all over. It lists rules and regulations for the Narbonne site. Half of them have been crossed out. One such line is underlined twice in red ink. It reads, '*should underground vats need to be kept open at any stage, metal crosses will be positioned over their opening to ensure operatives' safety.*'

Another crossed out and underlined sentence further down reads:

'*no hosepipes are to be left lying around in the vat room at the end of the day.*'

I close my eyes. The large room which is built on top of the underground vats sits at the heart of the winery. I have often heard my colleagues in Narbonne wonder why two of its original entrances have been condemned, making it impossible to use it as a shortcut from one end of the site to the other. It makes sense now.

I can imagine Manuel, an anonymous silhouette in blue overalls, walking across the room, maybe carrying a case of wine or a parcel which would have obscured his vision, tripping over tangled hosepipes and plunging head first into a vat full of wine. If he had not knocked himself unconscious, he would have kept afloat for a few hours, maybe more, shouting himself hoarse, but the alcoholic fumes would have got to him eventually and he would have drowned. There are no ladders inside those vats, only sheer curved walls.

I shiver and wonder who found him. Maybe Papa or André himself or one of his henchmen. Could it have been Jean Jacques? If it was, it would explain why he would not balk at lying over a quality issue. What's a touch of reduction compared to complicity to manslaughter.

Whoever it was would have pulled the body out and moved it to the smaller vat. A year later it would have gone, dissolved in wine. If Papa's jottings are correct, a year later, the small vat marked with a cross was hidden behind a wall anyway. Only the shoes would be left floating in the wine, and maybe some bits of clothing. Not enough to incriminate André.

Slowly I put everything back into Papa's box. What should I do, or rather what can I do more than twenty five years after the events? Exhaustion overtakes me and I decide to postpone any decision making to tomorrow morning.

I turn my mobile back on before going to bed. A minuscule part of me still hopes against reason that Tim may try to call me.

I have a text from Mary. She wants to know if I mind if Dave joins Philippe, her and me for a drink in the pub tomorrow evening. Dave? The world's gone mad. I head for the bathroom and bed.

. . .

The ring of my mobile wakes me up. For a few seconds I can't remember where I am. The massive dose of Nurofen I took yesterday to numb my aching jaw combined with half a bottle of wine and what I discovered in Papa's diary made for a restless night.

I worry I have overslept but a quick glance at the alarm clock tells me it's only quarter to seven. Maybe it's Mary wanting to explain last night's strange text? She would not call so early though. I grab the phone with both hands, toddler like.

'Have you heard?' asks Serge in a whisper.

'Do you know what time it is?' I say.

'Sorry, forgot about the time difference. It's big news though.'

'What is?' I sit up and rub my eyes open.

'I am not sure where to start,' he says.

'Now you woke me up, you'd better make it worth my while.'

I jump from the bed, struck by a mad idea. 'Is it to do with Marguerite and André?'

'You know.'

He sounds disappointed.

'How did you find out?' I ask.

'André called me in last night. He made me promise not to talk to you until this morning though.'

I can't believe his allegiance is as strong as ever now he knows the truth about André.

'It took him over twenty years to come clean and he has the cheek to ask you to wait twenty four hours,' I say.

'Come on, she's only been dead a week.'

'She?'

'Marguerite Villa.'

I slump back on my bed.

'Marguerite Villa is dead?' I ask.

'You just said you knew'

'Don't worry. What happened?'

'She's been ill for a long time but the few people who were aware were sworn to secrecy. Do you remember when Marcel left the export committee? She'd gone into hospital that afternoon.'

'This is why her assistant wouldn't put me through yesterday. It all makes sense now.'

'It would have been difficult.'

'What's going to happen to the company? Will Marcel take over or will André?' I ask.

With Marguerite gone, it will be easier for me to bring André down. It may be more dangerous as well as I won't have anybody to protect me anymore but I can avenge Papa and restore the truth.

'Villa has been sold to an Australian group,' Serge says.

'You're kidding. What does André think about it?'

'He's leaving.'

'What?'

'The Super-Market incident destroyed his credibility with the local coops. Your friend Thierry hinted to our new owners they could have another Aniane on their hands if André was allowed to stay. He had to go.'

'Aniane is the village where Mondavi wanted to plant a vineyard, isn't it?'

'And where they were told to take their dollars and go home. Same here. Thierry told them keeping André would make their ownership of Villa difficult bordering on unmanageable.'

'Who's going to take over?'

'Too early to say but you have forgotten to ask about Marcel.'

'Doesn't everybody forget about Marcel?'

'Hold on. He's bought a fashion house in Paris with his inheritance and he's leaving the wine business altogether.'

I burst out laughing. 'Good for him. I always felt sorry for him, having to follow in Marguerite's footsteps. He may have to learn to speak English now.'

'Why did you say it took André over twenty years to come clean by the way?' asks Serge.

'It's a long story. I'll tell you another day.'

I put the phone back on my bedside table and throw myself back on the bed. Today looks like it will be an interesting day in the office.

Arnaud calls me just as I am stepping into my car.

'Feeling better? Good. Come and see me when you arrive.'

I don't even have time to tell him I know what's happening.

He's standing behind his desk when I walk in, piling paper into a cardboard box. For an instant, I am reminded of Tim on his last day.

'Are you going as well?' I ask.

He looks up. 'Back to Africa. Can't say I'll miss this place.'

'Why so soon?'

'Villa's been split up. The kangaroos bought the wine division. We've been sold to a Brazilian hedge fund.'

'We as in the coffee business?'

He nods.

'Will you do me a favour?' he asks.

He hands me over an envelope without waiting for my answer. 'Will you give this to my assistant on Monday? She's taken today off.'

The envelope is nicely padded. He's got a heart after all.

'Will you miss the wine business?' I ask.

He shakes his head. 'Nutters, all of them.' He points at me and adds, 'you included.'

I could kiss him and I do, a little peck on the cheek before I leave his office, taking with me this last image of a big man, eyebrows raised and a French English dictionary in his hand.

No sign of Dave outside. Maybe he has been let go in the general mayhem and Mary's taken pity on him and invited him to join us tonight. She's a great one for lost dogs without collars.

She and Philippe look up when I walk in. News travel fast.

'What do you know already?' I ask.

Philippe counts on his fingers. 'Villa's been sold to an Australian company, Arnaud is packing and everybody is leaving with a fat cheque except us.'

'I like your ability to summarise,' I say.

'Somebody called John Westfield called for you from Bordeaux ten minutes ago,' says Mary. 'He left a number. Don't they have an office in Guilford?'

I sit down. 'Look, I haven't got a clue what's going to happen but I'll try as hard as I can to protect your best interests.'

I put my hand in my pocket and pull out the envelope Arnaud's given me. I put it on my desk and pat it gently.

'Today my faith in human nature was restored,' I say.

'You always were insanely optimistic,' says Philippe under his breath.

'Have you heard from Ed?' I ask.

Philippe and Mary nod in unison.

'He is on the last transport out of town,' says Philippe. 'He asked me to apologise to you for being a little distracted on Wednesday but he was waiting to hear about the size of his severance payment.'

'Will he call back?' I ask.

Philippe shakes his head. 'I think it's a case of grab the cash and run.'

I shrug. 'Good riddance.'

I can't help being a bit dismayed by the ease and the speed with which everybody is casting off.

'Are we still going to the pub tonight?' asks Mary.

I'd forgotten about our planned outing. 'What's this about Dave joining us?'

Mary blushes crimson.

'You're not-'

She nods. 'You don't really know him. He's given up smoking for me.'

I raise my hands in surrender. She's right. What do I know?

'Sorry Mary, I'll trust your judgement on that one. I'd better call this John Westfield now.'

The phone rings. 'Rachel,' mouths Mary.

'Put her through,' I say. 'I am sure John won't mind.'

'Congratulations,' says Rachel. 'I hear Villa has gone global.'

'You are well informed. I trust this is good news for our trading relationship.'

'We do a lot of business with your new owners and this is the reason for my call. Considering you'll now be operating on a much larger scale, could you have a look at reducing your Bordeaux quote?'

I burst out laughing. 'Rachel, I can't believe you. The news of the takeover isn't even official yet and you're already trying to take advantage.'

'It's my job, isn't it?

She sounds a bit miffed.

'I don't even know if I still have a job,' I say.

'Sorry, I may have been a bit hasty.'

'I'll keep you posted, I promise.'

The phone rings again the moment I put it down,

'Congratulations Chris!'

'Good morning Albert, how on earth do you know what's going on and why do you think it warrants congratulations?'

'Have I ever told you my wife is French and comes from Bordeaux? Her cousin is a nurse and works at the St André hospital.'

I burst out laughing.

'Don't take it the wrong way but I'll call you back later Albert.'

Time to call Mr Westfield.

His voice has that faint trace of transatlantic accent which reeks of an expensive American education. I'd assumed him to be Australian.

'Sorry I didn't call you earlier. The phone's been red hot since the news spread.'

'No worries. How soon can you be in Bordeaux?'

'When would suit you?'

'Could you make it Monday?'

'I'll be on the first flight. How long do you need me for?'

'End of the week? We have lots to talk about. The winemaker, Serge, speaks highly of you. You know how we value those guys in the New World.'

I pause, a bit surprised by his earnest tone. 'May I ask what's going to happen to The Wine Shop?'

He pauses. 'We'll talk about it when we meet. This takeover could be the chance of a lifetime for you, Chris. I'll see you next week.'

He puts the phone down so fast I wonder if he's taken lessons from Arnaud.

The chance of a lifetime indeed. I'll have to tell him about Manuel though. The truth needs out. Arnaud's gesture earlier showed me redemption is always possible even at the eleventh hour. It won't be easy but I have to stop this cycle of duplicity if it costs me my future.

I grab Arnaud's envelope. It's become my talisman, a symbol of what's pure in business. I can't believe he's been so generous. There must be at least a hundred pounds in there.

The envelope has come undone just a little. I would have sealed it with Sellotape but trust a man not to pay attention to details. I pull the flap up and it opens without any resistance. I take a quick peek inside and I collapse on my desk in a fit of nervous giggles.

Arnaud's parting gift to his assistant consists of his last expense claim.

I think of Manuel, of André, of Papa: all dead or out of my life. This is a new start for me. Who do I think I am to want to put old wrongs right? All successful people have skeletons in their closets. Mine will be in a vat. I may have to reconsider my strategy for next week.

'Mary, Philippe, turn off your computers, we're off to the pub,' I say. 'Lunch is on me. And Mary, ask Dave to join us, considering he's a reformed character.'

THE END

NOTES

3. Not Smelling of Roses

1. L stands for 'lot', the next two digits for the year when the wine was bottled, in this case 2007, and the last three for the day of the year when it was bottled.
2. A wine is reduced when it displays above-threshold levels of volatile sulfur compounds (VSCs) such as the foul-smelling hydrogen sulfide (H2S). A reduced wine is harmless but its stench makes it unpleasant to drink.

4. Lies and More Lies

1. Copper reacts with the foul-smelling hydrogen sulphide and turns it into odourless copper sulphide.

13. Marguerite Villa

1. "Nothing Lasts Forever"
2. "I Came To Tell You I am Leaving"
3. "The Horrible Goodbye"

19. The Mysterious Dominique

1. What is she saying? in French.